MEN in BUCKSKIN

BY

HERBERT E. STOVER

CATAMOUNT
PRESS

an imprint of Sunbury Press, Inc.
Mechanicsburg, PA USA

CATAMOUNT
PRESS

an imprint of Sunbury Press, Inc.
Mechanicsburg, PA USA

For information about special discounts for bulk purchases, please contact Sunbury Press Orders Dept. at (855) 338-8359 or orders@sunburypress.com.

To request one of our authors for speaking engagements or book signings, please contact Sunbury Press Publicity Dept. at publicity@sunburypress.com.

FIRST CATAMOUNT PRESS EDITION: December 2022

Set in Adobe Garamond | Interior design by Crystal Devine | Cover by Lawrence Knorr | Edited by Sarah Peachey.

Publisher's Cataloging-in-Publication Data
Names: Stovert, Herbert E., author.
Title: Men in buckskin / Herbert E. Stover.
Description: First trade paperback edition. | Mechanicsburg, PA : Catamount Press, 2022.
Summary: Simon Braide, scout and cartographer living in the Lycoming Valley of Pennsylvania, becomes embroiled in the events of the American Revolution.
Identifiers: ISBN : 979-8-88819-027-2 (softcover) | ISBN : 979-8-88819-028-9 (ePub).
Subjects: FICTION / Historical / Colonial America & Revolution | FICTION / Small Town & Rural.

Product of the United States of America
0 1 1 2 3 5 8 13 21 34 55

Continue the Enlightenment!

To

ANNA JANE and MARJORIE

FOREWORD

MEN IN BUCKSKIN. The story of the forest rivers is theirs. When a desperate English king, stung by the surrender of one of his great armies, turned loose his swarms of Indian soldiers, these men with their rifles checked the tide that might have swept on southward to destroy the desperately needed patriot arsenals and grain fields.

None of us knew exactly why General Knox, the right arm of his great leader Washington, had come to Fort Pitt. Certainly he did not take any of us into his full confidence. Perhaps, even then, he was planning for the road Boone was to cut to the Lake of the Eries; again, it may have been an inspection trip. Anyway, he arrived just when we Lambs had returned with the Spanish powder.

It was then he laid on my shoulders the task that brought so much heartache, so much danger, and so much bewilderment. Yet, I was permitted to work out my struggle along the bright waters of the rivers General Knox felt it so important to hold. There, by my side, were other valiant, buckskin-clad warriors who rode with me and marched with me. Even now, I can close my eyes and hear the drum of the hooves of many horses and, after a little, the whisper of moccasined feet on streamside trails.

These rivers that we defended furnished a way for the pioneers to come into the rich valleys but they also served as a highway for the natives who sought to drive the settlers out. Neither privations nor painted warriors, however, could loose these stubborn woods—country farmers from a land they had found good. Nor would they relinquish their cherished freedom to anything a king across the ocean could send against them.

So—before the new fort was finished and its walls frowned across the flat lands, men in buckskin made the upcountry land safe.

So many things troop through one's mind: treachery I did not understand behind a smiling face, Yonido with his cunning and his knowledge of medicine, valiant soldiers, kindly leaders. But, most of all, my mind and heart are full of the girl who herself wore buckskins and rode with us, her scarf fluttering back in the breeze of her going.

CHAPTER ONE

NOW THAT General Knox had stopped talking after a full hour of explaining his mission to us, the low-ceilinged upper room in Fraser's Tavern was quiet but for the general's heavy breathing and the faint noises that came down to us from the fort. Sitting there at the table in his tight buff and blue uniform coat with its cloth collar soiled a bit by sweat where it touched the back of his thick neck, he looked vastly uncomfortable and not too clean.

Presently, he raised his crippled left hand and studied the maimed fingers for a moment as though he had just become conscious of their condition, a gesture with which I was to become very familiar. Across the table from him, Colonel Kelly mechanically rearranged the three scalps that lay there—two with wrinkled, dried skin and long coarse black hair; the third, a tiny thing with the soft locks of a child—carefully strung on a bit of willow bent in the shape of a lady's embroidery hoop.

Standing with my shoulder pressed against the rough boards of the window frame, I was uncomfortable in town clothes after so long in buckskins and linen. I had not so dressed myself in honor of the sudden visit of these officers, but for the impending celebration from which I was being detained by this call to duty. From here I could watch my companions in the room and still steal an occasional glance backward toward the fort, with my thoughts going that way in the hope that one there would be as eager to meet me again as I was to see her face. After all, for months I had seen only the faces of Indians, river cutthroats, Spanish jailers, and our own hard-bitten crew. I shook off the abstraction and turned my attention to what was being said and done.

John Wigton, his bearded face impassive, sat teetering back and forth in his chair which he had tilted carefully to stand on its back legs. Kelly's worn buckskins gave him an air of comfort. Of us all, he looked the most alert.

General Knox made an impatient gesture as he picked up some papers from the table before him, and his clumsy hand knocked over the ink pot, which Wigton retrieved while Kelly leaned forward and neatly sanded the blot where the ink soaked into the soft board of the tabletop. Knox pointed to the scalps.

"For God's sake, John, bury the damned things. Every time I look at them my appetite's off for days."

"Yes, sir."

Kelly's voice was respectful enough, but he grinned; there was little doubt he enjoyed baiting his commander when he could. He placed the three trophies together and looked at us all before he continued. Somehow the colonel's voice, quiet and well-modulated, always surprised me, for one expected something explosive from the tense air of this man with eyes the color of steel in a well-whetted axe.

"Yes, sir, I will, but I want the boys to hear this." He pointed to the big scalps. "One of my men sighted these warriors and followed them. He wouldn't tell where it was, but I'm sure it was south of Augusta. He thought them up to no good and finally shot them; one had this little girl's scalp. No, we don't know who she was nor where she played with her dolls in the sun, but this is the way it must be."

Kelly looked at us sharply, his eyebrows drawn into a scowl, his voice grim and final.

"Two for one, if we'd make our river country safe for children. Two for one, until it gets too chancy for an Indian to take his hair down any of our rivers. So we must make it."

Knox gave a half-hidden grimace of disgust as Kelly wrapped the ghastly prizes in the buckskin from which he had taken them. Then the general picked up a rolled map from the floor and spread it over the table.

Kelly looked round and caught me glancing from the window. My face colored, and I was conscious of the long, newly healed scar along my chin. He grinned knowingly as I stepped to the table about which we now pressed to watch the trace of Knox's stubby forefinger.

"These rivers, gentlemen, give me the nightmare: your north and west branches of the Susquehanna. They rise in Indian country and carry bark canoes as easily as they do fallen leaves. They will bring the English with them, and we've naught strength enough to stop a determined raid getting clear through to the lower counties where they can wreck our food supplies, our gun and powder mills."

He looked up impressively, and I noted the smudge alongside his big nose to which he now raised the crippled hand.

"We beat the British at Saratoga, at Oriskany, and drove the Iroquois west. Our English friends will have to strike somewhere to keep their grip on their Indian allies who are as wild for revenge as tree cats."

The general had said the same thing several times before, but none of us offered a comment.

"His Excellency can spare not even a company from where his army faces Clinton in New York lest that general take it as an excuse to attack. You men—Kelly, Wigton, Simon here, and your friends in buckskin—must hold the west branch. God only knows we can do little for the North River; it's too easy a highway from the Cayuga country."

He made a wide, sweeping gesture, then fixed me with his watery blue eyes.

"Simon, you will take this map, which is of Pennsylvania, north to the New York border where the Tioga path runs and beyond which we cannot go. Study the rivers. In the margin, set down anything which would help to guide a general about the country as if he knew it as Kelly or you actually do. Rivers, fords, good ways to travel, strategic hills—note them all."

I watched his finger move on the paper and told myself he already had a pretty good idea of our north country, judging from the spots he touched where were shown creek mouths, lines of hills, and other features. He hurried on, instructing as a schoolmaster might.

"Put indicating figures on the map, your explanations on the margin. Above all, keep this map to yourself. Not only might its information be of use to the enemy, but even more important, it would indicate to him our interest in this territory—and that could well hasten an attack on his part before we were ready to meet him."

I nodded soberly, and when he had rolled up the map, he paused a moment and handed it to me over the table.

"You men will have troubles, but, believe me, one day we'll find the money for a fort and men to hold it. Then we can block any force coming down your river, and the Lancaster country where we fashion things for war will be safe."

He had risen and stood, a tremendous figure of a man. Between thumb and forefinger he took the lapel of my fine coat and looked into my face.

"Simon, for such a young man that's a long, lean, and dour face you have; also, there's a glint of red in your hair. Patience; push a quill for a time; and I'll engage to give you a chance to die in battle if it is that hankering that makes you solemn."

Loosing me, he snorted and waved to the others.

"Suppose this young fool had my girth and was condemned to paperwork for life."

Suddenly I liked this big, gross man, remembering the things he had done; the guns brought through the snow from Ticonderoga to thunder Gage out of Boston; his building up our Continental artillery; his loyal and generous friendship for Washington. So I joined the others in the sketchy salute we gave him as he clapped on his battered hat and strode toward the door, where he stopped.

"We'll give you a week here at Fort Pitt to wind up any business and to celebrate this return of the Lambs. There will be too much liquor, too many women, and too much talking. Remember, keep this map business quiet; get back to the Loyalsock as soon as you can afterward. Colonel Kelly and I will leave within the hour."

John Wigton waited until they were both gone before he commented.

"He gave no opinion on the horse patrol idea I talked about, but Kelly says he never forgets and that he thinks things over."

He smiled, showing his strong teeth.

"This general may be over fat for a lean country, but there's nothing slow about his mind. He really knows the threat that hangs over us, the destruction that waits only its time to fall." We tramped downstairs to where Fraser, the landlord, waited behind his bar, rubbing his palms together and smiling in false geniality.

"My reckoning," Wigton demanded, with nothing genial in his tones. He took the piece of paper tendered to him, studied it for a moment, then laid down some coins. "Fraser, you or one of your people was listening to our talk upstairs."

The landlord's hands waved in protest, and he started a denial to which Wigton paid no attention.

"I don't think you have the brains to make a spy, Fraser. But you are a dirty gossip, and I think all that happened will presently be common talk here."

He leaned forward suddenly, and the flat of his powerful hand went home on the side of Fraser's face with the sound of a slamming door. The man was thrown against the wall.

"That," Wigton told him, "is so you never again listen when I am about."

As we walked toward the fort, John cleared his throat. "Twice I heard him or someone outside the door, but I did not want to alarm General Knox."

Celine was there in the throng crowded into the wide room of the officers' quarters where they were about to feast and entertain the Lambs. Ever since I had met her months ago, as we of the Lambs prepared for our long journey, she had haunted my dreams. Our meeting had been brief, but her warm friendliness was infectious, and the name "Celine" had been music to me in the ensuing days of lonely danger. She had come down to bid the Lambs farewell on that gay morning, and I hastened to tell her now, as we walked along, how I had watched her when we drifted away from the dock until the faces on shore were no longer distinguishable. She had been standing well back on the wharf, some tall person beside her, but I had eyes only for her and treasured this last glimpse through all the months. Yes, I explained to her how I had seen in many campfires her dark hair with a bonnet pushed back, framing a small face, and she laughed the friendly, tinkling laughter that seemed half in fun, half in sympathy with my thoughts.

On our return, when we had left our boat, brave in the finery friends had brought down river to us so we could make a presentable appearance on landing, she had come up beside me, laughing and gay, walking with me as other women and girls did with Linn and the rest of the men. I could hardly believe that she had remembered me through all the intervening days, and her presence climaxed the joy of coming back.

"Celine."

That name had been ringing in my ears in all the hours since, and it had bothered me in the room where Knox had met us. It had been hard to bring my mind to the grim threat of our valleys, explained to us by the general and our own Colonel Kelly; and maps, for all their importance, were uninteresting as I remembered that she had left me gayly after promising she would be at the feasting. That afternoon, when we met, she had worn a dress of some flowered material, and her bonnet had swung from a small finger. Tonight, her gown was of dark cloth that left her rounded arms bare and her throat and bosom white between the blackness of the gown and the midnight of her hair.

This evening, she was different. In the afternoon, she had been a girl; now she seemed older, more mature; a woman, poised and sure. The transformation in her appearance was accompanied by a change in her attitude towards me, and I wondered if it was noticeable to others. I sensed that her friendliness had grown into a greater intimacy as she regaled me with tales of herself and flattered me with praise for my own exploits, about which she had heard.

We sat together at the great table ladened with food and liquor, where no glass was left empty, particularly if it belonged to one of the Lambs. Pitt was out to show its appreciation of what we had accomplished by bringing powder from the Spanish country so the fort could defend the frontier from the English and their Indian friends. Nothing was too good for us, and next to me was this woman or girl, Celine. I was conscious that she paid attention to no one but me. She was abrupt in her answers to others who addressed her and jealous of my conversation with anyone else. We drank glass after glass, and her eyes shone as they looked deeply into mine. When we leaned back to listen to the speeches and the toasts, I could not be sure whether the intoxication I felt came more from the wine I had drunk or the presence of Celine beside me.

Linn was speaking, and from the look of his face, he had been drinking hard all evening. He did not stand firmly, and his voice was not too clear.

"And now," he was finishing, "I give you the man whose face bears the scar of the knife meant for me when we fought side by side at Natchez."

He stopped, swaying a little in the candlelight, while he searched for my face down the table. There was laughter, for people saw he was far from sober. Glimpsing me, he raised his glass.

"I give you Simon Braide, first of the Lambs to be promoted. He is now to draw maps for His Excellency himself."

What he said was so startling that it cut through the fog of my preoccupation, and for the life of me, I couldn't guess how such news had come to Linn. I remembered Knox's caution, but the people were yelling, pounding on the table, shouting my name as I rose and spoke a few words.

Then in a few moments I forgot, for the time being, Linn's wild statement, for we were dancing. There was much heady liquor in me and Celine's warm stayless body in my arms. The room reeked of spilled wine and the air was heavy. Presently we were near a door.

"Simon," she whispered in my ear as I brushed her hair with my lips.

"It's desperately warm in here," she said, smiling at me, and I led her out into a night well set with stars. We strolled along, she drawing some sort of scarf about her shoulders, and soon we came to a bastion that looked out over a country where the moon was kind to the muddy rivers. I toyed with the scarf as we stood together.

"So," she said, "I have heard so much of you that I feel I have known you this past half dozen years. People have talked since we walked up the street together and you held my hand, but I didn't care."

I brought my head down so I could touch her hair with my lips. "What did they say, Celine?"

She laughed and reached up to rumple my short hair with her fingertips.

"So many things; that you are a wealthy trader with one John Wigton as a partner; that you have fought the Indians; that you are one of the Lambs. Now your lieutenant tells how you are close to the great Washington himself. Truly, you must be a great person, and I am so little."

I was drawing her nearer with a hand between her shoulders.

"And," she said, "I am pleased they say there are no women in your life, that—"

I had her close now, and her warm lips were answering mine until I thought I could never let her go.

"Celine," the world was whirling about me, and she was safely encompassed in my arms.

It was less than a block along this street to my rooms in Fort Pitt. Here I kept my gear, my clothing, and here I slept, in this empty house where we stored trading goods. To this place I brought her with an irresistible compulsion she inspired in me. As we stopped outside the door, she seemed to fall into my embrace. I swept her off her feet and bore her inside, slammed the door behind me, and after much fumbling, set a candle alight. She looked at me in the yellow glow. One arm came up and brushed the back of my hair. Perhaps she was a bit unsteady on her feet, but she shook her head slowly.

"Simon," she half whispered. "I am no tavern wench—" I knew what she was going to say and laid a hand on her shoulder in interruption. A fever enveloped me and I could not deny the sensation that now absorbed my whole being.

"Celine," I said, trying to keep my voice steady, "will you marry me? I told you that your face has been before me all these lonely months now—"

She looked at me, her lips slightly parted. Then she took one step forward and laid a small hand on each of my shoulders.

"Simon, we know that we love each other. It may be madness and the wine. But we will marry."

* * *

Brent was an old man, once an army chaplain, and we found him in his narrow quarters a little beyond the walls of the fort. Whatever surprise he felt he carefully concealed as he looked at us, then with a word of apology, stepped outside. When he reappeared, there were two women with him, plain souls who showed great embarrassment.

So, in that small room, he married us. There being no ring, Celine drew off one of hers which we used. Later, Brent wrote a brief certificate on which he put the names of the two witnesses and had them affix their marks. I gave each some silver shillings and to Brent himself, a gold piece.

"Simon Braide, bachelor, to Celine Barry, spinster," so the certificate had read, and with it we stepped out into the dark street.

* * *

This room of mine was no cheerful place at best, and the morning was overcast. My head throbbed from the liquor I had drunk, and it did not help matters when I thought of the step I had taken. Celine lay there, her small shoulders wrapped tightly in a blanket, and looking at her, I felt a deep sense of remorse. Now she stirred, and I crossed the room quickly as she sat up and pushed back her hair. My arms went about her, and she buried her face in my shoulder.

"Celine," I whispered, "are you sorry?"

She lifted her face and looked at me soberly for a moment before she shook her head.

"No—I have no people—no means. It was a wild thing to do but—"

She did not finish her statement. No means—I rose and crossed to the chest of drawers from which I took a roll of sovereigns and tossed it on the blanket.

"A wedding present, my Celine. Now you have something besides a clumsy husband."

She looked down; the paper had broken and the bright coins spilled out on the blanket. Her mouth drew into a round circle of sheer surprise. For a moment, I thought she might cry, so I put an arm about her shoulders and sat down beside her, but suddenly she threw back her head and laughed. After a minute, I joined her and the morning looked brighter. I could forget the months of danger and toil on the great river, the excitement of the homecoming. She was close to me and not unhappy.

Later, I did manage to find some food for us and a small gold ring to take the place of the one Celine had used before the preacher. We were very busy the remainder of the day, fitting up my rooms for living. There was a good fireplace, and Celine discovered cooking pans and pots. On our second morning, she looked at me a bit abashed.

"Simon," she told me, "please get my clothes from Mistress Whitmore."

She colored sharply when I looked at her, and I understood. She had left her lodgings for the celebration and had not returned. While I did not fancy the task, I knew it was one I could not shirk. I found a cart and a horse for hire, and it was not hard to locate the home of this hard-faced woman with the sharp nose who opened the door to my knock. With hat in hand, I bowed to her.

"I've come for Mistress Barry's boxes," I said.

Her nose seemed to wrinkle. "Young man, have you a mother?"

Perhaps I looked my surprise at her before I answered. "No, she has been dead a long time."

"Too bad, for you have great need of her. I am told that my lodger has married you."

I did not like the woman's tone. Had she been a man, I might have known what to do.

"Madame, I had the honor of marrying her. You are speaking of my wife."

Her sniff was like that of an old gray cat, suffering from a cold.

"That I would hope, young man. There is also a matter of two pounds ten pence owing in rent."

I laid the money on her table ungraciously, loaded the boxes into the cart, and took them to our place. I did not describe the encounter but lied carefully by saying that Mistress Whitmore sent her best wishes, after which statement Celine looked at me curiously; then she spoke dryly.

"Simon, you are either an excellent and gallant liar, or the lady with the sharp nose is pretty ill."

On the morning of the third day, I went over to Wigton's lodgings and was surprised to find Linn there; both men were heavily hospitable.

"We missed you, Simon. We thought you'd be over next morning."

Linn fidgeted a little. "Simon, I'm sorry for my drunken speech and the mention of the map—"

Wigton interrupted him. "Fraser's gossip, Simon. The map story is all over town."

I looked at these friends. Linn and I had gone through so much danger and labor on the river that it was as though we had known each other a dozen years. John Wigton had been with my father; he had been my friend since boyhood, and my partner in business for the years since father's death. In fact, he had come out here to liquidate our trading venture in this part of the state. Now, there was constraint about them both.

Wigton brought out some papers which I signed hurriedly.

"There's a good bit of cash, Simon—gold, silver, and British pound notes," he said. "What shall I do with your share?"

I looked at him, finding it hard to follow his simple statement; then I understood. "Oh, we'll take it back with us. It will be safe on the Loyalsock."

John nodded. "I'm starting home tomorrow; I go by the Shamokin Path since I'm in a hurry. Hope has been home from Philadelphia this past week, and I have not seen her in months—"

It was my part to be glad. I repressed now what I wanted to say, which was that I had expected him to travel with Celine and me. "Take the money with you, John. My wife and I will go by Bedford and Harris Ferry. You will remember me to Hope."

I thought of the girl now, how we had been such friends, this John and his daughter with the long yellow pigtails tied with narrow ribbons; and I remembered that I had not really seen her for two years, since she had been away at school a long time before I came to Fort Pitt a year ago. I was suddenly homesick for the bright waters of the Loyalsock and the lift of blue hills.

Wigton was speaking, his voice politely cautious. "Is your wife anxious to see our river, Simon?"

Looking at him, I realized that I had said nothing to Celine about leaving Fort Pitt, and I could not lie politely to this friend whose sober face showed concern. Then it was Linn, always impulsive, who brought the matter to a head.

"Simon," he cried, "you married her! Why in God's name did you do it, she—"

He stopped and breathed as heavily as though he had been running. He shook his head.

"Celine Barry, she of all women."

His backward step and Wigton's heavy shoulder saved him, for I had already started my blow. This man had saved my life and I, his; we had lived together, fought together.

"You," I said carefully, "talk too much. There was that about the map blatted to a crowd, a secret thrown open to all the Fort Pitt gossips. Now you spoke of my wife—"

And so I walked away from these two friends and came home to a domestic Celine wrapped in a long apron, her face rosy from the fire and her cooking.

"Simon," she said in my arms, "it's been such a short time, but already I am lonely if you are gone an hour."

With that as sauce, the meal she had prepared was excellent, though the cornbread was a little overdone. I told myself I would speak to her of our going to the Loyalsock on the morrow.

Early the next morning, Celine had gone about our small place sleepily, nor was she fully roused until nearly ten o'clock. It was then that she sat by the table, making out a list.

"These things, Simon, we will need for our housekeeping." I looked down at her small writing on the scrap of foolscap, and my heart sank, for she seemed so intent and pleased about the business of homemaking.

But Wigton had closed out our affairs; I was due on the Loyalsock, partly to complete the map, more to help in the defense of the rivers. I could not fail His Excellency, nor desert the mountain people who needed every rifle against the threat from the north, "But, Celine, we go in two days to the Loyalsock; no need to get things here for this short time."

She stared at me with eyes widening until they seemed dark pools in the whiteness of her face.

"The Loyalsock," she said slowly. "That river with the heathen name."

Her pause was only momentary.

"But your business is here; your factor says you have done well; you have money—"

I looked at her sharply, wondering what Kindore, who worked for us, had been doing. Neither Wigton nor I had liked the man, and I was glad that we were finished with him. He had too great an interest in the gossip of this place at the fork of the great river, was too much occupied with the women outside the town limits. But Celine, after interrupting herself, was hurrying on.

"Lieutenant Linn says you are to make a map. Simon, I cannot go to the wilderness; I cannot live in a cabin."

I tried to explain to her, tried to show her that I had no choice. But almost immediately she broke down and wept, nor would she let me comfort her.

* * *

Kindore was in the building we had used for our trading and looked up, surprised at seeing me. I did not know too much about coming to a matter tactfully.

"Mistress Braide tells me, Kindore, that you told her our business was good?"

The man rubbed his palms together. "Yes, Mr. Braide. It is so unusual for a wife to be interested in her husband's business that I showed her our books. She was much pleased—for you, of course, Mr. Braide."

"Kindore, John Wigton has had those books for days—"

I thought I had trapped the man in something, but he smiled unctuously.

"Yes, of course. Mistress Braide was in here the afternoon you Lambs came home!"

For a long moment I stared into the man's face, my fingers hungry for his throat. Yet, I could not let him see that I accepted the thought he was planting in my mind.

Certainly my new wife, who had for moments been reluctant, knew something of the man she had married so suddenly the night of the celebration.

CHAPTER TWO

KINDORE'S UGLY insinuation took me homeward in ill humor; yet I had walked most of that off by the time I opened our door and found the room we had fitted as our kitchen and living room empty. But a moment later, I found my wife sprawled on the bed, hair rumpled, her dress but half fastened. At my step, she sat up and stared at me with wide eyes, red rimmed from weeping. Brandy fumes filled the room; I noted the glass decanter by the side of the bed.

"So," she said, "he comes home, my husband who takes his new wife to the wilderness, perhaps as he has done with other women."

I stared at her, amazed at the savagery in her tone; and she swung her small feet round, then slid to the edge of the bed, her features twisted.

"He it is that fills a girl with liquor so he can bear her to his den like a filthy beast until she stands up with him before a minister to save her good name. Loyalsock! Who in the name of God has ever heard of the place where I must go to be murdered by loneliness or eaten by beasts or scalped by Indians!"

She snatched up the brandy bottle and would have thrown it had I not seized her; then her hand dropped, and she bit me on the wrist.

"Someday, Simon Braide, I'll make you truly sorry for what you have done to me—you and your mapmaking."

I tried to talk with her, tried to reason, but she leaped to her feet and walked up and down, shaking her mass of hair until wearied. Then she sank to the bed and buried her face in the pillow.

Part of her fury would be the liquor, I told myself, but she had been drinking to forget the dread of going into the wilderness. Yet, I had no choice; Knox had been specific. There was no doubting my place was on the rivers where war could blaze at any moment and where my rifle was needed.

That night, I lay awake thinking of things that might please Celine. She had mentioned liking horses, and I already knew she liked money. So, in the morning, I found and bought a small mare called Peggy, with a good side-saddle thrown into the bargain. Next, I located and hired a free Black woman named Abby to go with us to do our work. For myself, I had the horse, Salt, and two pack animals to carry our things.

I rode home on the mare and tied her outside. As I did, I noted a tall man on a gray horse disappearing beyond the corner, but thinking nothing of it, I went inside.

Celine was in the living room, looking tidy but a bit frightened. When I put my arm about her, she drew down the wrist on which she had wrecked her fury and kissed it.

"Come outside, Celine. I've something for you."

She slipped out the door, passing under my arm, and gave a cry of delight as she saw the little horse. She ran to it, flung her arms about its neck and actually kissed it on the muzzle.

"Name's Peggy, Celine. There's a saddle coming."

When we were back in the house, I told her we would leave next day at noon and, dreading another scene, I hastened to say more.

"You liked golden coins. John Wigton took my money home with him, but there will be a small bag of them, more of my wedding present, when we are home on the Loyalsock."

* * *

We left with a party of people going over the mountains to Bedford and, I thought, made a fine showing: Celine on her spirited little horse, Abby on one of the pack horses, and I on Salt, leading the animal that carried most of our belongings.

Travel over the mountains had become reasonably safe, but I did wear my pistols and heavy knife under the tails of my coat, unwilling to take a chance; and some of the men in our party carried rifles across their pommels. As for Celine, she became quickly acquainted with the women of our small company and, thereafter, had no time for her husband.

There was a dance in Fort Bedford the evening we arrived, and Celine in the low-cut black dress I remembered so well was the belle of the occasion. With her laughter, her grace, and her beauty, she was so thronged with admirers that I was permitted but one dance with her.

From Bedford to Harris Ferry our company was smaller: just another man, his wife, and we. Though they were older people, we got on well together, particularly Celine and the wife. I enjoyed our ride through this Cumberland country, so rich in fine crops and great barns. A fine settled country it was, unlike our wild hill country.

John Harris's Inn was better than any in Fort Pitt, for this was a country with a great many people passing back and forth at the Ferry. Here were great trading warehouses where my father and Wigton had often done business with either Harris or his agents. Now, the old trader himself was glad to see me and insisted on our coming up to his house as guests. His eyes admired Celine, and Mrs. Harris took her in charge immediately.

When the heavy evening meal was finished, Harris and I went out on the porch from which we could look over the river with its small islands midstream and the bar of hills beyond. He was tremendously interested in my recent trip with the other Lambs, and, as we smoked, I told him the story of the months on the Mississippi.

John Harris reminded me of an older John Wigton, wise in the ways of people and the land. He had been born here on the river and, through his life, had never been removed from the threat and promise of this country. Now wealth and satisfaction were his; yet his interest in what was going on was still sharp. He had led men against the natives, and he listened to my story, sitting there like an old gray eagle, dreaming of early flights.

"Knew George Gibson, your commander, when a boy," he said smiling.

"Never amounted to much; his wife still runs the mill down Cumberland, makes a living, rears his children. Now you Lambs and Lieutenant Linn have made him famous."

I had to smile and changed the subject, unwilling to talk about Gibson one way or another. I touched on the war, and he gestured widely.

"These rivers are a worry. If the British and Indians above us would put on a determined raid, there's nothing that would stop them getting through to the lower counties. Fort Augusta is weak; our Fort Hunter, rotten. A hundred painted Senecas could take Augusta as Shingas took Granville in the old war."

I smiled and spoke to him by his first name as he liked it. "John, you sound as though General Knox had talked to you."

He sat forward and slapped the arm of his chair. "That he did, but not of war. All the big glutton would speak of was a stuffed turkey we fed him and how we cured our hams. The man thinks only of his belly, which is truly a huge one."

"And Colonel Kelly kept laughing," I suggested.

He knocked the dottle from his pipe into his hardened palm, then flung it over the railing. He did not seem to wonder how I knew Knox and Kelly had been there.

"Yes, that and being busy every minute. When I'd get Knox about to talk sense, Kelly would interrupt, and he had the whole place upset. Climbed the flag pole when the lanyard stuck, was out back chopping in a race with axes, and beat my fellows sadly. In the evening, when I napped in my chair, he carried me up to bed, chair and all."

I wanted to laugh. Kelly's conduct was typical, for the man was never still. Yet, he had probably moved to a purpose. Likely Knox had not wished to be disturbed, and Kelly kept him from being questioned too closely.

* * *

From Harris Ferry north, our small party was alone. Celine and Abby had come to some sort of understanding which shut me out. One would have thought me the servant for all the attention I received. Yet, I was busy. This country was not too safe, and I was glad to give my attention to watching for those who might waylay us.

At Fort Augusta, I learned that Knox had ridden this way. John Harris had thought he had ridden eastward to Reading. The artillery man had gone upriver instead of to Augusta and had inspected the old cannon, later giving the men a lecture on how to care for them and fire them.

Here, with Celine helping a bit, I placed an order for supplies which would be sent by wagon up to my place next day. Then we rode on.

When finally we had passed the more settled land together with the great Challis farm where lived the man who was our greatest landowner, we struck into the wilder country, and I knew Celine was seeing it all and hating it with every mile. That she kept silent about it was some satisfaction. At last, we came directly across the ford from my place, and I pulled up my horse with the others crowding in about me.

Before us the water ran bright over the gravel, and beyond were the level acres held in the bend of the great western hill. A fringe of trees marked the edge of the fields along the water. It was very still; then from far across the cleared land we heard the measured drumming of a grouse. I touched my horse with my heel, and we splashed across the water and drew up before the house where I slipped from my mount to help Celine down.

She sat there for a time looking at the long, low structure which had been such a pleasure to me to build. All the logs were straight and true, well hewn. West of Challis Hall and possibly sparing John Wigton's place, this was the best house in these parts with its built-on kitchen, its good bedrooms, its smooth floors and real glass in the windows.

Finally she looked down at me and suffered my help in dismounting, but she was cold and stiff in my arms.

"I think I'll go in," she said.

Abby fitted herself into the place with no difficulty and was the only cheerful note about the house. But I did feel a lift of my spirit at being once more on my own land and listening to the chatter of my own river, so different from the great muddy western streams.

From the moment of her arrival, there was no kindness or sign of joy in Celine, and I had a suspicion Abby was helping to nourish her anger against me. When I set up my drawing table near a window, Celine watched with a sneer disfiguring her face. "Now my strong man plays his games."

She came close and leaned against the wall.

"He plays with his quills here where it is safe. I had thought young men went to war."

I wheeled to face her, then realized that she was baiting me and that she would do it whenever she could. Her promise rang in my ears: "Someday I'll make you truly sorry—"

She was right; she had shown me days ago she could do that, even before we left Fort Pitt. But I had promised something: She was my wife, at least in name.

* * *

The fourth day of our homecoming, the Wigtons came to see us, John bringing with him my share of the money he had brought from Fort Pitt, and he and Hope driving my small brown cow which had been left at their place.

As for Hope, I scarcely knew this poised woman with the straw-colored hair and wide blue eyes that seemed to change their shade with her expression.

"Hope," I cried when I had stepped close to her horse, "I scarce knew you after these two years."

She smiled a little. Certainly here was none of the friendliness of the girl I had known. When I put up my hands to help her down, she shook her head, slipped a foot clear of her stirrup, and was down with a whisper of skirts. Celine stood at the doorway.

"Celine," I said, "this is Hope Wigton. You already know her father."

Whatever her anger at me, Celine met Hope graciously, and she gave Wigton her small hand for a moment, then asked them both inside where Abby presently served tea. Wigton looked a bit doubtfully at his cup. Celine smiled and called Abby who brought brandy and poured him a small glass of it. To my astonishment, Celine drank tea, but I remembered that she had had several glasses of the fiery brandy earlier.

For myself, I could not help but note the difference between these young women. Both were about the same size, but there was such a difference in coloring: Celine with midnight in her hair, Hope with summer sun and the shade of ripe wheat; Celine with black eyes to match her tresses, and Hope with a blue that deepened with her interests. Both women were thoroughly alive, hope a bit the more restrained.

At length, John and I excused ourselves and went outside to the barn where we talked.

"Simon, Knox came up here when we were away. He left word that no unfriendly person was to see the map on which you work."

John Wigton was never very good at dissimulation, and now he looked everywhere but at me as I picked up a stick, worried it a little in my fingers, then tossed it away.

"John, no one in my household has the slightest interest in my map; set your mind at rest." My voice was probably hard for he placed a hand on my shoulder.

"Don't get your back up, Simon. We've lived and worked together too long to quarrel. You have your problems. I am hoping you will come to me—if they grow too sharp."

There was misery in me, deep down, and I knew he meant it as a kindness, so there was a sudden impulse in me to speak to him, but I knew that was weakness. I had made my bed; it was my business to lie in it without complaint.

John had brought me a good bit of money, much of it in gold sovereigns. There were two rouleaus of them that had been roughly handled, which we had picked up in Pitt. It looked as though someone had struck the edges of the coins with a dull knife, denting them a bit.

Hope was coming out of the house now and moving toward the horses. She told us she had some things to do at home and, I thought there was a coldness in her tones. But Celine was smiling.

As we stood watching them, when they had crossed the ford, the wife of mine stood very close, yet I knew it was for effect. She looked up at me, her lips twisted.

"Nice little white domestic—"

She stopped. Perhaps she saw the devil she had roused with her tone and the word I knew she would use. My hand had half raised, and I was shocked at the fury in me. But, after a moment, she smiled.

"Nice," she said. "Such a nice big girl for a playmate she must have been only a few years past. Such pleasant games they must have been."

Her words, her tones, cast a foul shadow over things as they had been. I thought of Hope, my wide-eyed comrade and good friend. However, there was nothing to do; this woman had been shackled fast to the things my appetite had demanded. I could plead no innocence through which her mockery would not pierce.

* * *

It was apparent to me in a short time that I did not have enough data to complete the map work, so I hunted up Ezra Lyman, and that seasoned man of our wild country came to help me and was often in and out of our house. With the instincts of a man who is natively a gentleman, he never seemed to notice Celine's lapses. If she was about the house in slovenly clothing or raised her sharp voice to fling a taunt at me, he paid no attention.

In only one way was Celine really my wife. One by one the people of our sparsely settled locality came to see us. Clarey Campbell and his wife, from twenty miles upriver, rode in. Larry Burt, from the creek we named for him, brought his Indian wife to whom Celine slyly gave whiskey so that Larry had to load her like a meal sack on her horse when he was ready to take her home. But to all these people, Celine was gracious, even kind, making them welcome. While the women visited, the men talked with me of the war and their quiet concern for the safety of these valleys.

One day I came in early from a short trip on the Tiadaghton with Lyman and found Colonel Kelly had come up from the White Deer country. The big man was seated at the table with Celine, and there was a bottle of whiskey between them. I looked sharply into the colonel's eyes, wondering what she had been saying to him, feeling sure it had not been to my credit for I was convinced now she really hated me. Kelly came outside with me to talk.

"There's been an express from Knox, Simon, about the river. He says he has some indefinite word from British Niagara that the Indians will strike somewhere. He feels it may be necessary to move all you people back to Augusta. There, we must hold."

He was picking at a piece of bark he had taken from one of the logs of the stable and looked toward the house. "The Indians are drifting about.

The other morning when my wife was away, there was one close to my house, watching for a chance at me. I buried him deep so there wouldn't be a blood feud. He was a Seneca way down on our Spruce Run. By the way, has your wife had any visitors? She must be lonely."

I laughed. "Off and on, the whole countryside has been in to see us, even Larry Burt and his squaw."

"I didn't mean that," Kelly said slowly, then aside: "If I were you, I'd keep that map out of sight; some Britisher'd give a good many pounds for the thing."

Kelly stayed the night but insisted on sleeping in the hay in the barn, and it was well past midnight when I lay wide awake in my room, thinking. A ray of moonlight made a bright path on my floor, and abruptly there was a light stir. Celine was there, her black hair loose over her shoulders, marble smooth in the light. She came to me like someone who is weary and nestled down beside me. Presently she slipped her warm arm about my neck, and it was as though there had never been quarreling or bitter words. Perhaps half an hour passed, and I saw that she was sleeping. I rose and covered her carefully with the blanket. The moonlight touched her sleeping face, and I thought I saw there a smile of satisfaction, so I went out of the room, out of the house, and down to the stream.

I knew something very clearly. Celine had reached me through the only channel open. I knew she did not love me as she loved the bag of gold I had given her or the mare, Peggy. Yet she had come to me. Now I knew that I hated the wife whom I had married in a moment of madness and haste.

* * *

Kelly left early the following morning. I was certain something had roused his suspicions. He had spent too many frontier years not to be alert to the slightest danger, and he had tried to warn me. Waiting for Lyman to appear on his shaggy, barrel-bodied pony, I had time to think of all Kelly had said. To the north was the black, threatening cloud of the Iroquois, savage as tree cats and hungry for scalps. The British must strike somewhere or lose their allies. Lancaster and the rich lower counties were far away, but their defense was here, and there were so few of us, our resources so limited, just a handful of men in buckskin with rifles.

* * *

Days dragged on. Celine would watch me at my map. Sometimes she would come and lean over my shoulder. Once I had drawn a tiny pine tree on the margin to show it was timbered country.

"Little trees, he draws. Little trees on little rivers. I'd think a big man would want them bigger."

I repressed my start. What did she mean by a big man? Did she know all about Knox, and who had told her back there in Pitt about him if she knew now?

Things grew worse: I knew she was often abroad on her mare, for I would find the horse with sweat caked on her smooth sides when I'd return. And Celine drank hard each day, more than any man I knew. To me, one of the worst things she did was to sit by the hour, fondling and examining gold coins I had given her. I think she knew each piece individually.

One evening I passed the tall mirror I had ordered downriver for Celine. Shocked, I looked at my own face. True it had always been a long one, but now it was thin, the scar showing red along the edge of my chin. Strain was there, in the shadows under my eyes, the lines shaping my mouth.

Sleep had become a torment. Often I would lie for hours trying to think of some way out of my difficulties. Then, utterly weary, I would sleep for a time and come awake with a start, thinking that she was watching me, that she was standing as she did that other night. Perhaps I feared her a little in that she could mold me so easily.

And I was finally to come to the point when I feared myself and what I might sometime do under this goading that did not miss a day nor an opportunity. Her prophecy had come true; the "someday" in which she would make me sorry was each day as it came.

CHAPTER THREE

THE DAY before, Celine had been drinking heavily, and this morning, instead of sleeping late as was her custom, she was awake when I prepared to go out along the creek of the Munseys. She would not be ignored and finally stood by the drawing board, her eyes somber.

"Someday," she threatened, "I'll burn this thing which keeps us in this awful country."

Her slim fingers worked under the edge of the paper where it was tacked down. My temper rose, and I stepped toward her.

"If you do, Celine, even though you're a woman and weak, I'll break your neck."

A pulse beat in the white column of her throat at my brutal words. She stepped back, caught up her brandy tumbler, and drained it. Suddenly, there was a madness in her eyes. Her arm whipped back, and she hurled the glass at me. It missed, smashing against the wall. I turned my back and strode out.

Old Salt, my horse, had an easy day, for I walked him along the stream as I took my notes, and later in the afternoon I slept for a while under a tree. A sort of numb hopelessness possessed me; no conviction as to what I should do came to my mind. I started homeward early enough to get there and do my chores before nightfall. About a mile before I reached the path that turns from the road and crosses Gunner's Hill, I met a man.

I knew him as soon as he stepped from the brush, for there was no mistaking the scarred head and the too wide mouth. It was Noah, one of Challis's black field hands, and sometime back, the Indians had given him a tough time with their knives. As he saw me, he stopped and stood there in the sandy road, shivering and clutching his wool hat to his breast. For some reason, he was horribly frightened, and I could not believe it was of me, but I leaned from my horse to reassure him.

"Noah, it's Simon Braide. What's wrong?"

The man tried to answer, rolling his eyes and twisting his neck. I could tell he knew me, but speaking distinctly was hard for him at best. In this fright he mumbled, drooling and gesturing with outflung arms.

It was certain the man could not be lost this close to his home, and it was possible he had seen a snake or some animal he fancied dangerous. I smiled reassuringly, took out a copper penny, and held it high. The man's frightened eyes followed the coin as if he had found a new interest, so I tossed it at his feet, touched Salt with my heel, and rode on.

For a while I had something else to occupy my mind other than the unfinished map, this long day in the woods and Celine's morning scene. I kept wondering why Challis, with his passion for efficiency, tolerated Noah and his crippled mouth and touched mind, for he was always getting frightened or ill. The fright the Indians had given him went deeper than the wounds they made with their knives.

We turned into our own path and climbed slowly along the side of the ridge, coming at last to the top of Gunner's Hill. Salt knew the spot too well and stopped, taking the prerogative of an old horse. I let him blow, swung one leg across my saddle, and sat, looking down.

From here I could see miles and miles of our small river and its valley which, far to my right, narrowed until the hills seemed to shut in upon it. But to the left, it widened to the flatlands along the Susquehanna, where our Loyalsock empties into it. A tumbled, twisted land it was, with small flat places along the bright water and high green hills lifting everywhere. But straight ahead of me and far below me was my own land, where a bend of the river holds the level fields against the loom of the western ridges.

Looking at it, the familiar stir this view always brought came to me, and I knew that no matter what happened, what dangers threatened, or how cold the welcome, I would always come back to this country as a homing pigeon will to its loft even though flames may have destroyed it.

It was getting late, far too much so to be coming home to a lonely farm, and there were chores to be done. The shadows were gathering under the pines and beginning to lurk at the bases of the western ridges. Swinging my leg back over the saddle, I clucked to Salt.

Celine would be down there in the log house, perhaps disheveled from lying in bed all day, or with eyes bloodshot from drinking. She might have been riding Peggy wildly and far. Whatever she had been doing, whatever her condition, her tongue would be sharp and bitter. Abby, the African woman, would cower until her mistress's rage was spent.

Dropping down the hillside, I tried to shut my mind against Celine and think about the data I had obtained this day, which must be added to the map. This stream had been the last I would need to explore. With a few days of peace, I could finish the job. Then I might snatch a few days and take Celine to Philadelphia, or wherever she wished, just so her tongue would be stilled.

I frowned as I remembered General Knox's warnings, Kelly's concern, Wigton's fears. They understood how critical things were along our rivers; they knew the danger that could come upon us at almost any hour. Not a man could be spared. I could not leave.

At the edge of the ford, Salt, usually anxious to get to his stable and food, checked his pace sharply and snorted, but I was preoccupied and paid no attention except to hurry him onward. In the middle of the stream, I caught it sharply—not the friendly smell of fireside smoke but the harsh, acrid fumes of burned refuse. I clapped my heels into Salt's ribs, drummed into the farmyard, and slipped from the saddle before the horse had fully stopped.

Major, the old black hound, had never been much of a hunter, and he was too amiable to be worth much as a watchdog. Now he lay beside the doorstone, lips drawn savagely back from his teeth, the white fletching of the arrow that had killed him sharp against the dark of his coat. I kneeled beside him a moment and laid a hand on his cold, stiff shoulder, knowing that only one thing could have roused the old dog to die like this. Then I looked up slowly toward the house itself.

Yawning windows and doors gaped at me as I stood and walked forward awkwardly like a man will when half asleep. Fire had destroyed my papers, scorched the lighter boards and furniture, and smudged everything with smoke. Slowly, my feet crushing litter under them, I went from room to room, but did not find what I dreaded—the horror of Indian killing and broken, mutilated bodies.

The floors were a revolting mass of smashed dishes, battered furnishings, bits of broken food, the ashes of burned paper and bright pieces of cloth that might have been parts of Celine's dresses. The wide drawing board had been ripped from its place and splintered into kindling, with bits of map paper still clinging to the tacks that had held the whole in place. The sight of it turned my thoughts to the map, which Knox had so carefully warned me to keep from hostile eyes. Likely the Indians had burned it, for they loved to see paper blaze. That was what I hoped, but I could not be sure.

Standing still finally, it seemed there was a light drumming sound in my ears, and it was as though I was apart from this Simon Braide, who, with his memory of the old wars, knew what this raid had been like. There would have been horrid gobbling noises blending as though they were the raucous clamor of unclean birds at an evil feast, and all the while, their small, bright axes would have been smashing everything in reach, like Celine's pier glass that had come upriver wrapped in straw and was now a mass of cutting fragments. While the wrecking had been going on, the women would have cowered, Celine screaming until a filthy hand had stopped her mouth; and Abby would have mumbled her prayers.

This man, who was myself but whom I seemed to watch, picked up a bit of the mirror and held it for a moment in broad, clumsy fingers, trained to point a lettering quill or to move steadily along a fine line. Slowly he turned the shard of glass as if he could catch a glimpse of Celine's gracefulness there before he tossed it into the remainder of the litter.

The place under the floor where Celine had hidden her precious leather bag of sovereigns which I had given her, keeping my promise, and in which she had taken such miserly delight, yawned open and empty. Her favorite brandy decanter was smashed against the masonry of the fireplace.

I went outside. The light was fading fast, but I could see the tracks of horses and moccasins leading down to the ford as if a half dozen Indians had followed the animals across the water. A quick circuit showed the print of a pair of moccasined feet and another of leather-soled boots directly beneath the small kitchen window.

Salt was waiting patiently outside his stable door. Mechanically, I stripped off the saddle and bridle, opened the door, and let him in so I could feed him. Presently I would need a strong horse.

Major's body had about hit the hard stiffness of a death that must have come early in the day. I broke the arrow from his wound, found a piece of blanket, and wrapped him in it carefully before I scooped a deep grave by the logs of the house he had died defending, and so buried him. Over the small grave, I lifted a heavy rock so he would never be disturbed again.

Still kneeling when I had finished, I looked at the bloody pieces of arrow for a little, then got up and went to the barn where I rebridled and saddled Salt. There was only one logical direction for these raiders to go—up the Loyalsock. Leading Salt outside, I swung up into the saddle and, as I passed the woodpile, bent and snatched the heavy, keen-edged axe from the chopping block.

It was already too dark to find a trail in this timbered valley, but Salt seemed to understand what I wanted and kept up a good stiff pace along the narrow way. I rode carelessly, thinking, the axe across my pommel. My mind was intent on what might be happening up beyond in the darkness, and in my heart was a sick guilt that I had brought a woman into a country where such an evil thing could befall her. True, she had not loved me. She had made my days a torment, but I had practically forced her to come. Now she would suffer with the natives, cringe from the odor of them and from their inhuman handling. Abby would fare better, since she was as stolid as one of their own squaws.

So I rode out the hours and covered the miles with no plan other than to come up with the raiders and take some of them with me before they cut me down. In the melee, there might be a chance for a mercy stroke at Celine, which would be better than what she faced.

The moon rose calm and placid, riding high over the loom of broken hills and spreading silver patches on the moving water of the stream. The valley through which I rode had become narrower and darker because of the crowding of the hills, and weary Salt had dropped his pace to a fast walk. Then the trail we followed swung sharply to the left, and I knew we were coming to the place where we would ford the now narrow stream to an old willow-fringed camping ground, beyond which was a sharp cut in the hills we call "The Slot." Sheer rage was now my master, for I was sure that a little distance ahead would be the camp of the raiders. If they were alert, they would have heard my horse coming for the last half hour since sounds carry far in the hills after dark. They would be waiting, ready, but I did not care.

We reached the ford, and then with a good grip on the axe handle, I sent Salt dashing through the shallow water. Half standing in my stirrups, I rode through the fringe of willows that hid the campground and burst into a moon flooded clearing. It was empty!

If the raiders had struck in the morning as it seemed, they could not have come farther than this place. I had been so sure all the way; now, in bitter disappointment, I slid from the saddle and fumbled about until I had a handful of dry ferns. These I kindled into a torch with which I examined the sandy ground that would have caught a trace of anything that had passed. Here was the sharp slot of a deer's foot, the small handlike print of a raccoon, and an indistinct smudge that probably meant a bear.

Disheartened, I tossed the torch from me and watched it burn out while I leaned against Salt's shoulder. Presently I turned, put my hands on the saddle leather, and rested my face on them. The moonlight brought no comfort. I knew I had used what time I had for pursuit. They had taken another direction, and likely my riding had only increased the distance between us. Spent and weary, I finally climbed into the saddle.

So we went slowly down the way up which we had come at such reckless speed, past the jutting rock shoulders that grudged the trail its meager width, through the swampy places, and past the silver flashing of the river. The moon went down, and one by one the stars lost themselves in the velvet blackness of the sky that comes before morning. There was a hint of gray in the east when we crossed our own ford.

Near the barn there was a sudden vague movement of a shape a little lighter than the shadow, a movement that brought me from the saddle, the big axe ready in my hand. There was another movement and a glint of white that meant a deer's tail; the animals had been feeding close, oblivious of the old, sour smell of burning that lingered here.

Salt was glad to return to his stall, to have the saddle off his sweated back and his ears well rubbed when the bridle was removed. He nudged me with his muzzle as though assuring me that he had done his best. Then I stepped outside and stood still for a while.

Weariness dragged at every bone and muscle of my body. I had been strong enough spare for the work and struggle on the great river with the Lambs, but there had been weeks of poring over a drawing board in the night time and the constant wear of Celine's nagging until I was almost spent. Yet, now, I could not allow myself the comfort of a bed in the hay in Salt's stable, and the house itself was impossible. Finally, I sat down and rested my head and back against the rough logs of the barn.

At first there was a merciful numbness that eclipsed all worried thinking. My head dropped forward on my chest, only to jerk up sharply when I fancied there was a movement in the shadow, something stirring that might carry a small bright axe and have a face crosshatched with paint. I listened, fingers groping for the axe I could not find. Then I realized that what I heard was the horse settling himself in his straw bed. Again sleep pulled at me, and I slipped into that borderland when half dreams come like the figments of delirium, dreams of the things which had brought me to this pass.

I saw stabs of orange fire at daybreak and heard the shaking gobble of the war whoop when young Parr, the boy of the expedition, had stumbled and fallen in the mud while a warrior leaped forward to take his scalp. My breath caught; I felt the tingling jar on my arm as my knife went home just in time, and there was warmth on my fingers that meant blood.

Then it was Linn, laughing, roaring in anger, working with those infernal small kegs that held the precious powder that meant safety to the frontier. Linn—I felt the strong hand on my shoulder snatch me from danger in that fight in the Natchez dive when British soldiers had died from failure to know how tough the Lambs could be.

My weary body sagged again, and a bit of breeze brought the stable smell to my nostrils. It became the stench of the Spanish prison where we crowded to the window, desperate for air but still not doubting that George Gibson would set us free, would not fail his Lambs.

Pictures crowded in: Knox with his crippled hand and soiled coat, his immense appetite for food. Now it was Celine with dark hair tumbled around her white face and smiling at me as she tripped beside me.

Celine—there had been magic in her smile, magic that could set aside all reason and bend a man to her will. Her voice had been small and timid.

"Well then, Simon . . . we will marry—"

The face changed, lost its laughter, was at first pleading, then angry, and finally disheveled as she shrieked her protests at going into the wilderness. Her pleading had almost made me change my mind.

"Simon," she had begged. "Oh no, Simon."

She was out there in the dark somewhere, and, if she was dead, I had killed her as though I had done it with a shot or blow. If she lived, the camps of the Indians would be a hell to her, and it was my fault.

I awoke wearier from this half slumber than if I had not tried to rest. Standing, I rubbed my sore, stiff muscles. The eastern sky was brightening, and about the place, things began to take on shape: the house, the barn, the low pole fences. Celine would be marching now, she who so loved to lie abed even when her temper was quiet. But she would be up and moving, bent under a pack of their loot and beaten by the nearest Indian each time she stumbled. Involuntarily, my hands closed. I knew they would never be satisfied until some day they closed on the abductor's throat.

With full morning, Salt nickered from his stall, and the small brown cow came placidly in from her pasture to be milked. It was odd that she should have escaped, for Indians delighted in killing or crippling livestock, likely because white people seemed to place such a value upon them. The demand of homely chores to be done helped. I fed the horse, milked the cow carefully, but Major was not here to enjoy his pan of warm milk. With all finished, I approached the house to make a more thorough inspection.

Celine's dresses were gone. The savages might either have burned them or carried them away because of their love of color. Dishes were smashed methodically, and I looked again at the charred pieces of my drawing board, which still held tacks and fragments of the corners of the map itself. Mercifully, the flames must have burned themselves out after the hurried flight of the raiders.

There were tracks in back of the kitchen, where men had watched, prints of moccasins and the one set made by soled boots. The tracks of moccasins and of horses' hooves still showed entering the ford, but beyond, there was nothing to indicate which way the raiders went, for there the ground was hard and rocky. That was another odd thing. A hasty glance showed that nothing had been disturbed in the barn where I kept my money, my hunting gear, and my weapons. I saw the stock of my rifle protruding from under the hay. Something must have frightened the intruders away before they finished.

The sun showed it was well past noon when I gave up the search and saddled Salt again. I had gone over the house, every foot of the dooryard, and a half mile up the trail without finding anything more. There was no sign of the map. The only tangible thing I had was thrust into my pocket—the broken arrow that had killed Major. Distraught, I turned to the Wigtons: John was my best friend, and Hope's ideas were always sensible. Even though she had been cold lately, she would not now deny me her judgment.

I rode down into the ford. Salt took his time drinking; then we went on, and I did not look back.

The ride helped to clear my mind, and as I veered off on the path which was a short cut to the Wigton farm, I pondered further about the map. It could have been burned, but there had been boot tracks, prints left by a white man; if he had wrenched away the paper—

I sat there on the old horse, my mouth open a little as though I had shouted a protest, and there was a faint booming in my ears like the distant beat of drums. Now I thought I understood. Knox had ridden far to survey the rivers and to call for their defense. He had given me the map to complete. The natives did not need the guidance of the talking paper to lead their long columns of painted and blood-hungry warriors through the forest. They could guide the British. Knox had spoken of "our interest in this territory." But the map must mean that General

Washington was actually making some plan of attack, else he would not have charted this forest country so carefully. My map, if it had not been destroyed, would warn the enemy, tell him where to place his defense. The enormity of its loss stunned me.

My thinking was clouded; had we overtaken the thieving crew at The Slot, I would not need to worry now—it would have been all over.

* * *

Hope Wigton was sitting on the porch that led round two sides of her father's home, and she was rocking slowly in the chair made carefully for her mother. Her yellow hair was loose about her face and stirred a little by the breeze. Her sleeves were rolled above rounded elbows, and her fingers were busy with something in her lap as they usually were. I slid down from Salt as she rose and came forward, surprise on her face.

"Simon," she cried. "What's happened?"

I stared dumbly at her, knowing it should be easy to answer her question and to say that Indians had raided my place, had taken away my wife, her servant, and the horses, that Major was dead, the house scorched by a fire, the map gone. But words would not come. It was as though there was a burden on me so heavy to carry that I had no breath for talking.

John Wigton came round the house; his sleeves were rolled up on his powerful arms and in back of him was wizened Ezra Lyman, with his old eyes quick and missing nothing. I looked at the three for a moment while humility and futility swept through my mind.

"Indians," I muttered. "They took Celine and Abby, tried to fire the house."

I stopped and stared at them, saw the shock on their friendly faces. The long muscles of my legs trembled.

Lyman jerked his head in a quick nod. The two men stepped forward, caught me under the arms, and led me inside to a rawhide-laced cot and pushed me down on it. Lyman bent quickly and slipped off my battered shoes.

"Sleep a while," Wigton said. "Then we will talk."

CHAPTER FOUR

IN SPITE of mental and physical weariness, sleep would not come at once, even after my body was relaxed, for I lay fighting back mental pictures of what Indians did to captives, especially to those who would cringe from pain as Celine would surely do. The little she might have seen of Indians about Fort Pitt would not have warned her of what these forest people could do in the way of creating human misery for the unfortunate in their clutches. Then, almost suddenly, weariness had its way, and I slept.

The room was full of shadows and the pleasant smell of cooked food when I woke, and through the doorway, I could see candlelight. These friends had waited to share their supper with me, and I walked stiffly out to the table where I turned to Wigton.

"John," I said, "there should be a warning out about Indians."

Wigton motioned me to take a seat at the table.

"Ezra and I have had two hours' riding while you slept; there's no sign of a war party anywhere near us. Sit down and eat."

I found my appetite so ravenous that I was ashamed, but none of these people paid any attention except to see that my plate was kept filled, nor did they bother me with talking until I had finished and pushed back my plate a little. Then Wigton spoke in a casual tone.

"Salt looks good, but it takes a lazy horse to keep fat. Now that Peggy mare is different."

His mention of Celine's mare was plainly a hint for me to tell my story, yet it was hard, even to these friends, to talk of Celine. I knew none of them approved of her, especially Hope, who had shown by her attitude when she came to my house how little she thought of the woman I had married. Of course, to Lyman, women were a matter of indifference. My hand knotted a little as it lay on the table.

"There was trouble in our house this morning—Celine had been drinking." I searched their faces with my eyes and saw that they probably understood what had been going on down there. The frontier permits few secrets and certainly none to these friends on the question of what went on with me or mine.

"It was a quarrel about the map, and she said she would destroy it because I had forced her to come to this country. She called it a silly bit of paper—"

I looked down at the floor, then up into Ezra Lyman's face, bland under its network of wrinkles. "Well, I probably threatened her a little, and she went into a rage, threw her glass at me, and I left."

I had to pause, remembering the embarrassment of that final scene, Abby crouching in the kitchen door, Celine, eyes blazing, her bare arm raised high. Now Lyman spread his wrinkled hands on the table with a slow gesture and took them off again. Hope's eyes had narrowed a little, but Wigton's bearded face had not changed.

"I spent the day along Munsey creek, working."

It was growing harder and harder to tell the story in this ordered room when I remembered the chaos in my own home. Most of my life had been spent on the frontier, but it had been in action where danger was danger, not this business of tormenting the mind.

"My papers were burned. Major dead at the doorstone with an arrow through his throat. There was ruin everywhere—glass, food, scraps of cloth. The women and the horses were gone, no trace of them, and the map had disappeared."

Again, I paused.

"There was but the one way they could go—I rode hard for The Slot and only wasted time as I am doing now."

Wigton's dark eyes were condemning, yet he knew me well enough to realize that a man whose boyhood had been spent in the frontier troubles could have done no less.

"You'd have known better in the old days than to have gone alone. Had you overtaken that pack they would have butchered you and to no purpose." When there was no reply, he spoke again with a question. "What of your map? Was it burned?"

I jerked forward in my chair and struck the table with my hand. "That I do not know. The board was splintered, scraps of the map corners were still fast on the tacks."

I came to my feet, hands clenched, and looked down at them with my almost sudden realization of what could have happened. "She hated it. Great God! You don't think that she—"

"Yes," Wigton said calmly and coldly. "I do think she would."

Plainly he had not said all that was on his mind. Truly Celine had kept her word to make me miserable if I brought her here, but I was still unwilling to believe she would destroy my work. Lyman took my sleeve, pulled me into my chair. Wigton's statement had first shocked me; now it was like the presence of another enemy calming me so I could watch.

"John, it would be better if she had burned it. If the British get it, they will know Washington has plans for this north country. That's the danger. True, most of the work's done; the data was on the margin, over my signature."

Wigton's somber eyes interrupted me. He seemed not to have heard what I said.

"So," he remarked quietly, "the British lovers of the Senecas will have a map to show them the way down our rivers."

He waved a broad palm. "However, it's little they need in that way; the rivers are pointed like arrows to the back of our colonies. They will be coming anyway one of these days, but with the map it may be too soon for us to stop them."

The big man was tremendously disturbed, and there was a restlessness about him I understood; he was this way when he did not fully understand. In action he was cool enough. "What of Celine's bag of gold, Simon, was it taken?"

"Yes, the place under the floor was open and empty," I replied. "There was naught left about the place but the arrow that killed poor old blundering Major."

I went to my hunting coat, took out the arrow, and laid it before Hope, for she was wise about Indian things and took some pride in what she knew. She took the pieces, studied the chipped stone head and the white fletching feathers a little before she looked up. "But, Simon, stone-tipped arrows in gun-and-powder days; it does not make sense."

I waited until she spoke again.

"Delaware," she said decisively, passing the war head to Lyman who merely glanced at it before he nodded his head in confirmation, and I stared at Hope, doubting.

"You must be wrong, Hope. There are no Delaware war parties in this country. It must be Iroquois."

"She's right, Simon," Lyman offered with conviction. "It's Delaware and very old."

"Nonetheless," I said grimly, "I'll go to Oswego or to Niagara where they take captives. Then I'll ransom my people and learn from Celine what happened."

John Wigton made an emphatic gesture.

"Simon, His Excellency put me in charge about here, and you'll wait until we can see Kelly and make plans. There's naught more we can do this night, but in the morning, we'll get down to your place."

Hope had risen and walked to the kitchen door where she stood, the candlelight making a nimbus of her hair, and I watched her dumbly while her father continued.

"You're a stubborn and brave young man, Simon, and you used to be steady; now you're upset. You must wait until we find the wise thing to do."

He might have continued, and I felt a rising resentment in his tone of command, but Hope had turned back into the room, walking toward the harpsichord which stood in the corner. The instrument had been her mother's pride. She seated herself on the broad stool, and with the first tinkling of the strings, Wigton was silent, spreading his broad palms on the arms of his chair. Lyman sat bolt upright. I stared at the pattern of the puncheon floor, thinking idly how well it had been laid.

Presently there was a tune I recognized, the air of an old English folk song, then the opening bars of a hymn, and she was singing softly, as if to herself, the words of Martin Luther's great militant song.

"A mighty fortress is our God . . ."

Farther up along this river, my house lay wrecked and foul with debris; this room was quiet, beautifully ordered, and the music was filling it. Perhaps it was a strange time to be playing and singing, but there was a change coming inside me, and I was listening with the intentness of one who clings to a precious thing lest it slip away. Again candlelight made a radiance of her hair, and the room was full of the sound of a mystic marching led by a rousing battle air.

She finished, but none of us moved, though I wanted to cross to her and touch her fingers where they rested on the yellowed ivory keys. Presently she rose and left the room.

Later, when John and I lay side by side on our cots, he spoke, referring to what he assumed was in both our minds. "She was like that from a little girl, sending courage through her music."

I wanted to say something in answer but could not phrase it, so I reached over and touched his shoulder, at which he seemed to understand for he was soon asleep.

Lyman did not appear at breakfast, and Wigton explained that he had gone a little after midnight to summon Colonel Kelly.

"They'll take the shortcuts, swim the river, and be here by late afternoon," he promised.

I said nothing, but his calm assumption that I would not leave this day irritated me. After breakfast we went out to where three horses were tethered to the hitching rail.

"We'll leave Salt to his earned rest, Simon." He was being tactful, for the old horse would not be up to traveling with the tall Wigton animals when speed might be a factor.

"Give me a score of horses like these," Wigton boasted, "and I'd mount a patrol that could keep this country safe."

He was probably right; certainly these tall animals were better under the saddle than pulling a plough.

Hope was dressed in a boy's suit of soft buckskin with her hair tucked in under a round cap, and there was a bright red scarf at her throat. When I stepped forward to help her mount, she laughed as she had years before at my awkwardness, but she did touch a small moccasined foot to my hand and went up light as any bird.

The Wigtons rode fast, as they always did, and I brought up the rear when we reached the path of the shortcut and had to go single file. This girl acted as though born in the saddle. Once, she swung clear down to snatch a spray of wild honeysuckle, which at this season makes our woodland sweet, and she festooned it over her shoulder so she could enjoy its fragrance as we went.

Wigton's first glance noted the brown cow. "I'll have her brought over to our place. Can't have her spoiled. Wonder why she didn't get an arrow?"

We went over everything together with Wigton, noting the drawing board more closely than anything else. The footprints in back of the kitchen held his attention for minutes. "I'd guess they were here before you left, Simon."

I thrust my hands deep into my pocket to hide rising anger. They had stood there like evil birds, waiting. And they had heard what had transpired, this white man—whoever he was—and the Indians who had stood by his side.

On inspecting the stable, Wigton noted the weapons still there and turned sharply on me.

"Simon, what did you take upriver?"

I shook my head and think my face reddened. "Just the axe, I forgot—"

"Great God!" he breathed. "You fair offered them a scalp."

*　*　*

I made a tight bundle of my belongings and gave Hope one of the pistols which had belonged to my father. Long ago, she had proven she could outshoot either her father or me with the long-barreled weapons. I also pressed upon her the shoulder pouch that held the powder, bullets, and mould for the weapon.

She smiled and tucked the long brown barrel under her belt, picked up the other weapon, and extended it to me. "See you carry that, Simon. It will throw a bullet farther than you can reach with an axe."

The far side of the ford yielded no further information, though we rode upriver as far as the creek we call Little Bear. Here, John Wigton, in a gesture not common to him, tightened the rein on his big horse so roughly that the animal went into the air on his haunches. When his mount was quiet, he spoke. "No use following, Simon. They did not come this way."

I shrugged my shoulders. "What does the way matter. She's in an Iroquois village by now, if she isn't dead. I must get to Niagara."

We turned our horses and rode slowly along toward the Susquehanna valley. Hope was beside me and presently asked a question. "You saw no one all day long when this happened?"

I shook my head, then did remember. "No, not until on our way home, then I saw that crippled man of Challis's, badly scared as usual."

Wigton looked at me and nodded decisively. "That's something; let's ride down and see what neighbor Challis has to say."

We followed the regular road, finally turning eastward until, after an hour, we turned into the smoothly graveled way that led through copses of woods and over a small bridge to the gray bulk of the Challis buildings. The hall was a huge affair of smoothly hewn logs, partly covered with painted clapboards. The lawn surrounding it was smoothly mown, and there was shrubbery in bloom. Beyond was a fringe of willows that shut out sight of the river. As we stopped, the wide front door swung open.

Of course we all knew the man coming toward us, but Hope and her father met him first. There was nothing unusual about this great land-owner and prominent Whig. In height and coloring he was ordinary, but his eyes were alert. Dressed plainly in brown coat and breeches, the only ornamental thing he wore was a pair of beautiful shoe buckles.

"Welcome," he called, holding out his hand to Wigton who had dismounted. Then he turned gallantly to Hope who used his help at dismounting. When I stepped down, he gripped my hand quickly and warmly. "It's an honor, neighbors. Mistress Challis is away and will be sorry to have missed Hope. Come on inside."

We followed him into a huge, beautiful room with walls hung with pictures, Indian curios, together with beaded quivers and strung bows. There was a wide fireplace, and crystal candle holders stood on its broad walnut mantel. Chairs and other furniture were in keeping with the room, all made of the same dark, hand-rubbed walnut.

When a servant appeared, we were offered glasses of a rich heady wine.

"John," Challis was saying, "some day I must have one of those tall horses you breed. They can cover ground."

Wigton nodded. Often a little blunt, he came to the point of our visit. "Neighbor Challis, is your boy Noah here?"

Our host looked at him, puzzled, and shook his head. "No, I sent him to Philadelphia with Mistress Challis. His nervous disorder seemed to be getting worse. I thought he might be better in town."

He paused politely to allow Wigton to explain his interest, and John did. "Braide saw him in the hills badly scared. When Simon returned home, his place had been raided; his wife, servant, and horses had been carried off, and his house partly burned. We thought Noah might have seen the raiders."

Every line of Challis's face showed surprise and shock. Yet I noticed that when he set down his filled wine glass, not a drop was spilled.

"God," he said softly, and the word was not profane, "deliver us all if they start raiding again."

He shook his head ruefully.

"Noah might have seen something but could likely tell nothing. Mistress Braide, she was so young, so lovely."

He spread his palms, then leaned forward to me.

"They might offer her for ransom. If you need money—"

"Thank you," I interrupted too sharply. "I have plenty of money."

Wigton asked a few more questions, then as we rose to go, said, "We think it better to keep quiet for a few days lest we unduly alarm the settlers. Do you agree?"

Challis thought for a moment and answered carefully. "Yes—unless someone saw the war party. Yes, and my place goes on a war basis this night."

It was apparent that we were all glad to be out of that beautiful room and in our saddles, once more hearing the crunching of gravel under our horses' shod hooves. Yet, none of us referred to Challis. Wigton had his head down, thinking; Hope hummed an air; and I kept thinking of that brimming glass and the steady hand that had placed it on the small table.

At Wigton's, all three of us stabled our horses and then went inside. Hope stripped off her gloves and threw them on the table.

"Father," she demanded. "Did you see the arrows?"

I remembered the beaded quivers as Wigton nodded. "Yes," he said. "All Delaware."

We did not have a chance at further talk, for Lyman and Colonel Kelly arrived, tired, wet, and hungry. After they were fed and more comfortable, Wigton opened the conversation. Likely Lyman had told the whole story, but the colonel listened again, gravely and closely. Then he examined the broken arrow, turning it about in his big hands which were scratched and torn by briars in some woodland foray. Finally, he asked me a question.

"What do you plan to do?"

I liked the fact that he assumed I would want to act; there had been too much delay. "Get after them, sir. Get to Niagara prepared to pay a ransom."

"And there they'll hang you promptly, Simon. Don't forget you were a Lamb," Kelly countered in a conversational tone. "Besides, you'll have to cross the whole Seneca nation country; you'll even be over the Forbidden Way."

He shook his head in finality; then Hope broke into the talk before I could say a word to Kelly.

"Father and I have a plan, since we know Simon will go anyway."

She looked at me, her small chin set in challenge.

"Yonido, the Oneida Healer, is on the Sinnamahoning where he watches for Father. He goes and comes as he wishes in the Indian country; the people of the Long House respect him, and this Indian and Simon are blood brothers."

I turned to Kelly sharply when she paused. "She's right; there is no question as to my going. I must know if my map is burned, nor will I be sure until I find Celine."

Kelly frowned. "It is too late to worry about the map. That they have it is dangerous in that it may warn them of Washington's plans. Yet, even we do not know them. Certainly the Indians know the rivers too well to need maps. But we cannot spare a man, nor dare we alarm the country lest a panic come. The settlers are jittery enough now."

He scowled and tapped the table with the stone arrow point. "This was no ordinary Iroquois scalp raid. There's some deviltry on foot; God knows what it may be. Someone may have wanted that map, though I doubt it. It may be—"

Hope leaned forward, strangely impatient, and interrupted. "Hear the rest. Simon will go to Niagara as a Tory who has lived on the Loyalsock where his neighbors turned on him so badly he had to leave. Father will make a proclamation and sell his things because he is a Loyalist. His house was raided by a mistake, one he is sure his British friends will right."

Kelly settled back into his chair with a different look on his face, and his eyes showed excitement.

"Then," he said, "he can learn the strength of the enemy and perhaps find when they will move against us. I would not send a man into that snake's den, but if he goes on his own errand, we can profit by what he might see."

Ezra Lyman, who had not said a word, now rose. "You men have both seen Indian deviltry; now you join with a girl to send a man straight to his death? It's like setting a baby to catch rattlesnakes. I've seen men burn, and I know what a Seneca squaw can do to turn a man's liver pale. Kelly, how much can a man see when his eyes are put out with a red-hot gun barrel? Them Delawares you played with—hell— they're school boys to a dumb Seneca. You folks are sending Simon to his death."

I reached out, caught the angry old man's hand and tried to get him seated again. "They're not sending me, Ezra. I'd go anyway."

Unmollified, he turned from us and strode out the door. Soon we heard the clatter of his small horse's hooves.

Sitting close about the table, we finished the plans by which Wigton would take me a good part of the way on horseback toward the Sinnamahoning where I would find Yonido, or he would find me; and the Indian would get me to Niagara if it was at all possible. It was plain that what Lyman had said had made them thoughtful. Hope said very little, and Kelly kept shutting his lips grimly.

Much later, when I thought everyone asleep, I stepped out on the porch to watch how the moonlight flooded the fields, touched the trees, and outlined the hills beyond the great river up which I would ride in the morning. Oddly, I felt at ease, sure I was taking the right course, and it did not matter what my feelings were for Celine. I had brought her to this country unwillingly, and she was gone. I could not this night feel she was dead, nor that she was suffering. In my heart I wondered if a woman could hate a man enough to do what I suspected she might have done.

I had been out there a good while before I saw that Hope, wrapped in some sort of dark cloak, was there. She had turned from the post where she had been standing and would pass me on her way into the house. I stood quietly, hoping she would say something. She did pause a little, and I caught the fragrance of her hair before she opened the door and went in. There were so many things I wanted to say to her—but tomorrow I would ride north. Beyond was the land of the Senecas; beyond that, a British fort. I had no business thinking about other things.

CHAPTER FIVE

COLONEL KELLY was gone early in the morning, having left word with Wigton that he would inform General Knox of what had happened. After breakfast I had time for a few things I felt I must do. First, was a trip to the stable, where I rubbed Salt's ears carefully after I had given him a mixed feed of corn and oats. Then, in the house, I took a sheet of paper and carefully listed the property I owned, a bit surprised at the extent of it. I directed, over my signature, that if I did not return, what I owned should go to the Wigtons and Ezra Lyman, share and share alike. This paper I placed in John Wigton's Bible in the book of Ecclesiastes where he liked to read. There was no doubt in my mind that I was engaging in a pretty desperate venture.

A little to my surprise, when we were ready, I found Hope was going with us and was dressed again in the buckskins and bright scarf with my pistol in her belt, which pleased me. This weapon threw a ball a bit better than the one I carried, and my initials were scratched on its walnut butt.

We were never out of sight of smoke coming from cabin chimneys until we crossed the Lycoming a dozen miles from our own river. Beyond, houses were few and far between, but these were those of the venture-some "Fair Play" men who liked their independence and believed they owed little to the colony founded by the Penns.

We camped that night in a hollow between two bluffs, where a brawling stream came down, having seen nothing all day which could be called suspicious, certainly no signs of a war party, not even at Great Island, usually a haunt of Indians. By noon of the following day, we had come to where the mountains crowded the river so hard that horses must turn back or climb the rough slopes to the flat land behind the frowning mountains.

None of us had much to say when parting. I would find Yonido near the Chimney Rocks which looked over the Sinnamahoning, or, what was more likely, he would find me, for he kept a sharp watch up there in the hills. I was traveling light, carrying only parched corn and dried meat in my war bag. I had left my other pistol behind with the better of the two rifles I owned. The one I carried was a battered looking piece, but a wicked thing to shoot in spite of its looks. I did carry my best knife, a long double-edged piece of steel heavy enough to serve as a tomahawk, and in my pockets were two rouleaus of gold coins.

Wigton shook my hand briefly, and Hope gave me her gloved fingers for a moment as she looked down at me. There was much in her eyes that I was not sure I could read, but she spoke lightly enough. "I'll take good care of Salt."

They turned back, leading the horse I had ridden, and five minutes later, when they were disappearing around a shoulder of mountain, one of them waved at me, but I could not be sure who it was.

It is not often that I feel lonely in the woods, nor was there fear in me, only an alertness so keen that it seemed to hold me motionless as when one listens for a suspicious footfall or another stirring in the bushes. The mountain lifted to my right; on the left was the boulder-studded reach of the great river; there was no sound but the fretting of the water against the rocks.

Some time passed before I freed myself from the obsession that held me. This river valley was a pretty dangerous place, and ahead, the big stream would presently make a wide bend. So I moved forward rapidly until I found a small stream, which I followed and which led me up and back into the high flat country. There I camped for the first night I was alone, being well pleased with the distance I had covered. I permitted myself the luxury of a bough bed, for later it was likely there would be scanty time for such things. Here, on this vast flat, I felt safe.

All the next day I fought the idea that I should travel closer to the river to note if canoes were moving, but that would mean slowing my progress, and I could do nothing about it even if they carried warriors.

This was great hunting country; I saw deer every hour, and grouse ran ahead of me before thundering aloft. Once I drew a bead on a fine wild turkey but was not hungry enough yet to risk a shot. When I found a place where a bear had turned over a rock looking for grubs, I stopped and looked a good while. It had been a long time since I had hunted the black fellows with dogs in the Loyalsock hills, where I had dispatched two at different times with the heavy knife in my belt. But in this country, I was the game, and my scalp would bring more to an Indian hunter than a bear skin.

"The wilderness and the solitary place shall make glad . . ."

John Wigton had so read from his Bible, but this vast wilderness held too many dangerous possibilities to allow a man to be very glad. However, the labor of fast travel kept me from thinking too much about anything other than how to find the best way and how to take advantage of the grades, avoiding the vast laurel thickets. At all times I must get the best out of my buckskin-clad legs and feet.

There is a tumbled pile of rocks, each the size of a good cabin, which woodsmen call "The Chimney," and it stands on the point of a mountain around which the Sinnamahoning curves. From this crest due can see both the big creek for miles northward and the Susquehanna as far as the eye can range. I saw the rocks from a ridge top a good half day's march ahead. Here Yonido watched. While he did not know I was coming, he was not likely to miss anything.

An Oneida, this Indian had been taken as a child into New England and there reared just as a white boy is, with the same training in the schools. Later, he traveled about with a doctor and acquired skill with wounds, broken bones, and other hurts. To this he added his knowledge of Indian herbs and simples until he was accepted everywhere as a healer, and so was safe to go and come. But his clan had cast its lot with our patriots, and Yonido's wishes were with us though he certainly never disclosed them to the Senecas.

A pleasant man, this Yonido, a bit older than I. He would grin widely, showing his wide, strong teeth, and he could never learn to whistle a tune though he tried at every opportunity. For some reason he disliked women, even Hope Wigton, whom he scarcely noticed when he visited on our river.

Careful scouting found me nothing, and there was no trace of the Indian. But it was near evening, and I could look for him in the morning. So I went back halfway down the ridge I had climbed, ate parched corn and dried meat, after which I had a good drink from an icy spring. Content, I found a bed in a hemlock thicket and slept like a log.

* * *

There was something odd about the birds in the morning. First, a wood thrush sounded a few bars, then a chipping wren had her impatient way, followed by the racket of a blue jay. When I was wide enough awake to realize this sort of concert was unnatural, the jay squalled angrily; I drew up my rifle, glanced at the priming, and, rolling over, brought the piece up. Just as I saw the figure outside my thicket, I remembered that Yonido, while he could not carry a tune, could mimic almost any bird.

I had not found the Indian; he had found me.

Yonido pumped my hand hard when I came out grinning sheepishly. He thumped me on the back, pulled off my cap and rumpled my cropped hair.

"Fine scalp, Simon—worth a good eight dollars." Then he was sober. "We'd best get out of here. Senecas went up yesterday. They hung around the rocks for hours."

Yonido's hiding place was a clever one—where a dead tree had fallen against a big rock. Small evergreens had grown up, and now there was a nice sheltered place under the tree and against the rock. Here he fed me hugely on roasted venison and excellent corn cake.

Sitting across the small bright fire from him, I told my story of the raid and of our plan made in the Wigton home. He listened quietly and made no comment until I had finished. Then he picked up a half dozen or so small pebbles and held one aloft between thumb and finger.

"It's good for a white man to see what's going on at Niagara. They don't want to listen to an Indian down your way."

There was nothing bitter about his statement. He was announcing a fact. The pebble was laid down on a cleared place on the ground. He held up another.

"Senecas no longer hunt with stone war heads. See?" He picked up his own quiver, drew out a steel-tipped shaft and touched the sharp point with his finger. "Nor would they go so far for so little. It's a long way from Little Beard's town to the Loyalsock."

The second pebble went beside the first.

"You are right about the map. When you find her, you'll know."

Now there were three pebbles in the row.

"Playing Tory might work, but it's a chancy business. Major Brevecourt at Niagara is a savage man. He might turn you over to the Senecas; their burning posts are empty,"

He seemed to forget the pebble this time, but presently he finished his comments.

"As for the women, I know nothing of them."

He gravely tossed the last pebble into the brush.

For a little, we did not talk. I ate some more of the venison, while Yonido filled his long-stemmed pipe with the tobacco I proffered him and smoked for a while.

"It'll be pretty bad getting you through the Seneca country. The woods are full of warriors driven here from the east. The Seneca has opened his lodge to Mohawks, Cayugas, all the people of the Long House."

Bending forward, in a small cleared place on the ground, he drew a small map with his finger.

"Here is the trail going west from Tioga to Olean. They call it the Forbidden Way. This side, a white man might be left alone; across it, he would surely burn. But we must go over. It is in my mind to travel fast to the gorge of the Genessee, up that a day's journey, then west to what the British call the neutral zone, which runs from lake to lake past the falls."

There was no comment I could make, for I was satisfied to leave things in his hands; and I was not impatient when he sat there and smoked his pipe clear through to ashes, which he dumped into his palm and gravely blew into the brush. After that he went into action.

Yonido had few belongings: a skin bag which I knew held herbs and other medicines, a thin blanket, a small war bag into which went the remainder of the food and his bow, quiver, and knife. I followed him out of his camp.

Inured as I was to forest travel, the Indian set a pace that called on everything I had to keep with him. For the most part, he followed ridges just a little way from the crest, but occasionally, we would creep to the top to observe. Near midafternoon, Yonido did this scouting alone. I watched him ease himself up over the top. When he turned and beckoned, I crawled up to him.

Far below us, five warriors in single file walked along the creek. We watched until they disappeared to the north.

"Hunters," Yonido declared, "carrying meat."

* * *

We made a tiny fire that night, and over it I boiled tea in my small saucepan. Yonido seemed to enjoy the hot beverage as much as I did. Squatting by the blaze, he held his wrist to the light and grinned. Then I showed mine. On each was a tiny scar. He and I had made ourselves brothers long ago by nicking ourselves with knives and touching blood.

"Brothers," he said smiling. "It's been a long time, Simon."

Lying beside him, waiting for sleep to come, I thought about the remark. Sometimes, in spite of his white training, Yonido could be pure Indian, as vague as any of them in their statements. I was sure he wanted to tell me something, either that I was passing into danger where I might need him and he was assuring me, or that there was something he wanted and for which he might ask at a future time.

Next morning, when the mists were rising, we crossed the ridge back of which we had camped and looked down on the long, rambling valley through which the great east-west trail ran. We could see the path plainly, for the most part straight, even though this was a country of brush and small trees. It followed the easiest grades and the dry ground well above the brawling streams that were now flowing northward.

An eerie feeling touched me as we lay, looking down and studying the land. True, we had been in Seneca hunting grounds for a long time, but across that line was the land sacred to the people of the Long House, where it was death to take a white face. Even the British respected this country, keeping to the lakes and venturing from them only when accompanied by their native allies.

We went down fast, but, on the trail itself, stopped a moment. Here the feet of many, through the long years, had tramped the trail nearly a foot deep in the soft ground. There were no blazes as there would be on a white man's path, but, when we were across, I saw a beech tree with the bark stripped for a space on which were painted odd looking symbols.

Yonido grinned at me and pointed. "It would do you no good to read," he commented and struck out at his fast pace.

In spite of the speed of our going, I observed the land which was parklike, with clumps of trees rather than the miles of pines through which I had come to Sinnamahoning. Along the bright river running north were great natural meadows. From hill tops we saw two or three small villages, and the odd thing was that we saw many horses grazing as though they were wild animals.

"British cavalry stock," Yonido explained. "The Senecas keep them in their pastures by the hundreds. They are now breeding horses."

Near evening, after detouring a large village, we came to where the river enters its long dark gorge that points to the north. Yonido did not slacken pace with nightfall but kept traveling, following the river closely, and I was glad when he finally called a halt. Both too weary to eat, we drank from the stream, then rolled ourselves into our blankets in the lee of a big rock.

Only our own Tiadaghton has cut a deeper gorge than this Genessee. The Tiadaghton hills may be higher, but they rise in an easier slope than do these great limestone walls which pitch upward from the narrow flat land along the stream itself. Twice, in our going the next day, we worked our way up and down past high waterfalls.

Yonido had thrown off his caution, killing two grouse with his arrows, and we had a good, hot meal of the birds. Again, he caught trout by working with his fingers under the overhanging banks of the stream. He was no more in a hurry.

"This country," he explained, "is almost sacred to the tribes, who hunt the gorge only in times of famine. Here the Great Spirit sometimes walks, thinking and listening to the sound of the waterfalls."

Two days of this easy travel, then our gorge turned eastward, and the hill walls became lower. We climbed the west side, coming into a country of broken hills and narrow ravines mostly covered with scrubby timber.

For the last hour or so of that long day's travel, we could hear, growing louder with the passing miles, the rumble of the great cataract of Niagara. Again, Yonido did not stop with evening, but we walked on into the night and some time, very late, we came abruptly into cleared land and slept at its edge.

We had reached the neutral zone, a seemingly strange idea of the British, where all native men were barred excepting the burden bearers or one accompanied by a white man. The Indians were children of the Great White Father, but the English were taking no chances with temperamental children in this vital area.

Here were two great traffic lanes, roads fully a hundred feet in width so carts and burden carriers could turn out from bad places. On one lane, the carriers moved north, on the other, south. Here were two-wheeled carts, pack horses, long strings of Indian bearers. It looked as though both roads were filled from end to end so great was the flow of British business, military stores and trade goods to the west, furs and Indian goods east.

We had entered the zone about half way from the lower lake to Niagara at the point where the land drops sharply and where the horses pulling the carts labored on the heavy grade. From where we stood, there was a tremendous vista that stretched to the blue of the northern lake. There was Fort Niagara, all but surrounded on its point of land by the river, and the lake, looking like a toy at this distance. To the east of it was the town itself, and northward along the lakefront, a second settlement.

Yonido was right, but then he knew this country intimately. He had said we would be in town by noon, and we were. There was no difficulty finding a room in a tavern, and almost immediately Yonido left me. He was back, though, in an hour to tell me it would be possible to see the commandant at three o'clock—so his informant had said—though Yonido was a bit doubtful.

A barber did his best with my short stubborn hair and shaved me closely, asking no question about the long scar on my chin. When he finished, he said he thought I might do, though I think he was doubtful of my worn clothing.

The fort itself had low walls of masonry blanketed with earth to break cannon fire, and I had to cross a good wide empty zone of fire to reach it, feeling a bit uncomfortable as I saw the British flag lazily slapping against its pole built like a ship's mast in the center of the parade ground.

A sentry challenged me at the entrance near the river and turned me over to a corporal whom he summoned and who took charge, taking me through a narrow passageway and over the moat to come out on an amazingly large parade ground. Our own forts were small, but here was room for a regiment to maneuver. Everything was in order, polished guns on the wall with neat piles of shot beside each, the grass smoothly mown on the parade, and across it loomed the three-story limestone building which I knew would be the old French citadel.

The corporal took me into the building, past a number of sentry posts, through a big room where officers lounged or looked out the windows. There he left me a scant five minutes before returning and stating that the commandant would see me.

This second large room into which I had been ushered was empty of all furniture but a table with a few chairs about it. Back of the table sat an officer in immaculate uniform with lace at the throat and wrists. His sword belt holding its pistol and rapier had been flung on top of the papers on the table. He wore the line insignia of a major. Holding my cap to my chest, I stepped forward.

"Major Brevecourt?" The corporal had given me the name of the officer whom I would see.

Being closer, I now had a better look at the man, and I felt a tightness within me. After all, I had come weary miles, had risked much for the answer this officer might give me, and I did not like the high-bridged nose, the thin cheeks, the air of affectation and boredom belied by eyes that were alive, alert, waiting. My mind flashed back to Natchez, to the opening door and the file of soldiers led by a slim officer. British soldiers had died that night in their fight with the Lambs. The man before me might have been that officer, though his wig fooled me a little.

He had not answered, but I bowed and continued. "Sir, I am Simon Braide, come from my home on the Loyalsock which was raided. My wife was borne away, and I have come in search of her."

The major's eyes had not ceased to study my face, and now he answered in a slow, insulting tone.

"Sorry, my man, there are no prisoners in Niagara—certainly no women—unless in the lower town."

So many miles, against the protest of all my friends, and yet I had been so sure; now all ended before this sneering officer in his red coat. About me was the might of England, this stone fort with its sentries, and before me was one man who could say yes or no as he pleased. Perhaps my eyes looked too long at the pistol lying there. Then I caught myself, took out a roll of gold, and held it in my hand, careful to speak in a deferential tone.

"Sir, I have come prepared to pay a ransom."

The searching eyes flicked to the roll of coins with real interest, and when Brevecourt spoke, the sneering was gone. "Mr. Braide, return in a day or so. Inquiries will be made."

I was half way across the room when he stopped me.

"Mr. Braide!"

The voice was sharp, and when I turned, I looked directly into the major's eyes.

"I think I have seen you before, but then there was no scar on your jaw."

I am not sure this man was ever certain about me, nor was I of him, yet there was an instinctive dislike between us. Now I bowed, partly to hide my face, partly to show my entire deference. "Unlikely, sir, I am a farmer on the Loyalsock. Once I was a trader, and I survey a little to help neighbors. I am a Loyalist."

His eyes went like searching hands over my worn buckskins, the linen of my shirt, the cap I held in one hand. They followed the knife scar along my jaw, received in that fight at Natchez, and rested for a lone moment on the coins in my other hand.

Finally he sneered. "You may be a loyalist, my friend. You may come from the place with the heathenish name—yes, you may be a loyalist, but before God, I am not sure who has your loyalties."

Crossing the parade ground, I was still occupied with my anger at the sneering tones of the commandant and what seemed the utter failure of my plan. It was not until I had passed out of the walled enclosure and was nearly across the fire zone that it came to me like a sudden chill wind that strikes one unaware between the shoulder blades, and, for the moment, I felt a prickling at the back of my neck as I realized that my life in this place was not worth a farthing, that I had just delivered my neck for the fitting of a British noose.

CHAPTER SIX

ALL THE long way back to the tavern I forced myself to walk sedately, lest I betray my fears. Now alone, I faced my plight. The cold-eyed officer back there would make up his mind presently if, indeed, he had not been playing with me. When I confronted him and his doubts, my mind had flashed to the fact that we Lambs had been in the British-held post of Natchez dressed as backwoods farmers. We had fought the soldier patrol that sought to take us, and we had killed two of them. Any British officer would have hanged any or all of us the moment they had us in their clutches for that and because we had managed the powder expedition successfully.

But, this was more. I had gone to the commandant claiming to be a Loyalist, asking for Celine. There had been a man with the raiders back there at my house who wore a soled boot, likely a soldier who would have taken the map or seen it destroyed. If that map had been brought to this post, I had surely placed my neck into a British noose with my first words to Brevecourt.

Concerned with my worry, I had not thought of the situation this way before, nor had my friends unless, like Wigton, they had been sure Celine had destroyed the map; but I realized that here, or wherever I might find my wife among the British, I would also find a cruel death waiting.

Celine—I thought of her. Of course, even if the raid was false, she could not have guessed the extremity to which I might be brought. There was no way in which I might have foreseen the trouble that taking this headstrong woman to my forest home on the Loyalsock would bring me. But my place was on the rivers with my neighbors, standing against the foe that could come out of the forest.

For a while I paced the narrow room. My impulse was to slip out of the town as quickly and quietly as I could, but I was soon ashamed of that course. If Celine had been brought here as a captive, I had a duty to her no matter what danger it brought me. Again, my home people expected me to know something of this fort and the plans against us. Certainly in my predicament, it was unlikely I would discover any plans, but I could look about me and learn from what I saw.

The town of Niagara was larger than that about Fort Pitt, and it was well furnished with taverns, stores, and dwelling houses. Here was transacted the big business of transportation between the lakes. But separated from this town across brush land and a meandering stream, in the direction of the lake, was another village. A short walk along its main street told me well enough the business done here would be at night when the candles in the windows would be lighted.

Beyond the edge of the neutral zone where the sentries stood ready, was a sight that shocked me. It was the Indian villages and camps. Knox and the others had told how the Iroquois had moved westward following our victories along the Hudson and Mohawk, and these people were here, whetting knives and planning deviltry. There seemed enough savage power here to destroy all our frontier country if it were well led or aimed. Here was a flood that could engulf us in pain and destruction.

Yonido came to the tavern late in the afternoon, seeming a bit dejected and doubtful at my first question.

"No, Simon, the women are not here, but there was a strange young man—not a soldier—who visited the commandant and quarreled with him about something he wanted to sell."

Yonido was earnest and leaned forward.

"Brevecourt is a gambler, hungry for money. He is both tricky and in debt."

The Indian stepped to the window and opened it as though the closeness of the air bothered him. Then he went on.

"One of Blanche's women wears a new scarf of great beauty. They say this young man was in that house a number of times."

There seemed to be in me two minds. One noted the oddness of this Indian in his battered travel clothes, a loon feather thrust in his hair, yet with precise New England ways. The other was concerned with what I had just been told.

The scarf—it was a slender enough lead—yet I was glad to clutch at anything since Brevecourt had so curtly dashed my hopes. Celine loved these things, had many of them. Yonido had no further information and became, for a little, the stolid Indian again when I pressed him.

"I know nothing of women," he reiterated, then grinned suddenly. Surely this Indian brother of mine knew me better than perhaps I did myself and had been sure of what I would do before he ventured his information.

"My brother would do well to let Yonido take care of his money for the lower town is a bad place when people are so hungry for gold, and nobody would think an Indian with holes in his moccasins would have money."

He gravely opened his medicine bag, redolent of many herbs, and I dropped in the rolls of gold after taking out a few coins to meet expenses. Yonido grinned at these.

"Gold," he said. "It will buy horses, murders, women. Yonido knows nothing of women and sometimes thinks his brother, Simon, may know even less."

With this cryptic enough remark, he drew shut the drawstring of the bag and left me, my mind too intent on this Blanche woman to pay close attention.

The second street in the lower town was dark in spite of candles showing at windows, and there were men about who moved in the shadows. I tried two houses; one door was slammed in my face when I asked for Blanche. At the second, a stout woman stood in the candlelight which showed over much of her.

"Blanche," she sneered. "She's a high-toned piece for officers and the bloods. Better bring your buckskins in here for sport that would fit you better."

Two silver coins dropped into her moist palm loosened her tongue.

"Last two houses," she directed. "If things are too cold or high toned, come back."

She jingled the coins in her palm and grinned.

"We'll put your money on account."

The last house was of wood and stone construction and boasted a heavy knocker which I sounded twice before a black woman, who reminded me of Abby, opened the door through which I could look into a long hallway, well furnished with chairs and settees.

"Madame Blanche?" I asked and dropped a silver shilling in the maid's fingers, at which she smiled.

"She's not busy; I'll ask if she will see you."

In ten minutes, she returned, took me along the hall, then ushered me into a room almost as fine as that in Challis Hall though not so large. The furnishings were excellent, and candles were everywhere, sparkling in crystal holders. Over the fireplace was a wide mirror, and I stood gawking at my own face, long and lean, with the lower part looking lighter from the barber's work. My short hair looked too red in this light, so that I passed a hand over it nervously. A sudden chuckling laugh back of me made me wheel 'round.

A woman was standing there, looking even taller than she was because of hair piled high above a slender neck and bare shoulders. Her arms were without sleeves, and her dress was made of a transparent net material from beneath which the tips of red slippers peeped.

"I did not see you," I mumbled.

She smiled, and I noted her mouth was wide with full lips.

"You passed me in the door," she explained. "You are Simon Braide, lately come to our town."

Her soft warm hand was in mine, and she smiled at my discomfiture.

"Such news moves fast in our small place, even that you saw Major Brevecourt."

She led me to a couch where we sat fairly close to each other, and the room seemed filled with the heavy perfume she used.

"I've come to see you about a scarf."

She leaned back a bit and looked at me through narrowed eyes. "Men seldom come to see me about scarves," she drawled.

One of my gold pieces was in my hand now, and I laid it on her smooth knee. She took it and turned the coin about in her fingers with a gesture that reminded me of Celine.

"These are scarce on the lakes, young man."

"One of your women has a new scarf; perhaps you can tell me about it."

She did not answer, seeming engrossed in the coin.

"My house was raided, my wife carried away. I've come looking for—"

Blanche interrupted me by rising with an indifferent shrug of her shoulders. In the play of the candlelight, she seemed to be unclothed, her slim body making her desirable. But my mind pulled back to what I had come so far to find. She tapped a small bell, and the maid appeared, received low voiced instructions, and left.

Perhaps ten minutes passed before the black woman returned, carrying a silk scarf which the mistress took and tossed carelessly to me.

"The perfume will be Bessie's," she said carelessly. "A young man who was a stranger here gave the scarf to her because he had no money."

I did not listen closely to her for I did not recognize the flimsy garment. Celine had many such things, some I had never seen her wear. Then, as I handled it, I saw the burned place, just a dark dot, but I remembered. There had been a spark from my pipe, and Celine had ranted because I had spoiled the scarf and she could not wear it again, though I thought it had been little harmed. I reached up and caught Blanche's arm, pulling her down beside me on the couch.

"Tell me," I demanded roughly, "what you know about this man, this scarf."

Her painted lips twisted until she looked hard.

"You poor fool," she said. "Did you love this woman so much?"

The sarcasm in her tone drained away my anger as quickly as it had come. Then I found I could not lie to her.

"No," I said carefully. "But she was my wife. I brought her into danger when she did not wish to come."

She took the scarf from my fingers and studied it a little. "The young man was a stranger, here only a few days, and it was said he tried to sell something to Brevecourt, but our commandant is so deep in debt he could not buy. As I said, this young man gave the scarf to Bessie for her favors."

This woman lived in the camp of the enemy, the friend of officers who would see me hanged without a qualm once they knew of my connection with the Lambs, or that I was here for information as to the strength of

Niagara. But I told her my story from the time I met Celine until this evening when I sat here, leaving out only the fact that I was told to gather information. And she did not once interrupt until I had entirely finished.

"First, I tell you, Simon, that I do not love the British, being mostly French, but my place is here. Now, you are a young man and strong—if sickness had carried off this wife, you would have grieved for a time, then forgot. Let it be so now; you are well rid of her."

She laid a warm hand on my knee and leaned closer.

"Simon, she was a woman like me, like Bessie, who used what she had to trap you. I doubt that she did anything with the map except destroy it; I'm sure the raid was a sham, something she planned."

Her painted lips were smiling a little.

"You are a blunderer, Simon, and need a woman you can really trust—"

There had been the sound of a harpsichord and a low voice singing, and there was another perfume like that of sweet fern on the hillside. But these were far from this bright room. "Find a woman you can trust." There would then be no need for such hunting as I did now, no danger such as now threatened me. To cover my confusion, I drew out a second gold piece and gave it to Blanche.

She looked a bit startled. "Have you more of these?"

I nodded. "They are all that Celine really loved."

"Listen." It was her turn to become intense. "You are not just a backwoods farmer and should understand. You showed gold when you offered a ransom. That could be your death warrant, perhaps it already is. That popinjay in the fort would sell his scrawny soul for money; he'd take what you have and toss you to the Senecas."

She rose, walked about the room, twisting her beautiful body like a dancer, then came back to me.

"Get away from this evil place—do it tonight. Norris, the spy, is here, who hates your people as he claims he does the devil. You saw the thronging Indians who will march when Butler returns. Brevecourt is cruel, but Norris is worse." Her head was on my shoulder now; I slipped an arm about her shoulders for she was trembling. After long minutes, she was still.

"Believe me," she almost whispered, "no woman—nothing—is worth the danger you will run into here, and they will find you out. So long as you are alive, you can hunt this woman and your map. But when Brevecourt gets through with you—"

Her bare shoulders shrugged, she slipped from my arms and stood up before me. With a slim hand she drew me to my feet, then went with me through the hallway, talking as we went.

"I think you are stubborn, very much so, my friend. Butler will see me—if you get into trouble—"

She did not finish, but we were at the door; now she rose on the tips of her scarlet slippers, her hands pulled down my head, and she kissed me gravely and tenderly on the forehead.

"Go ye with God as the Spanish say, my foolish Simon, if you will not get away from here—soon."

I had heard that old saying down in New Orleans, and it touched me now as I walked from this house into the night. Certainly I would need such help.

Most of the lights in the windows were gone, but there was a sound of revelry back of some doors, bits of singing, high, shrill laughter. I was soon clear of the town, moving through the bushes in the direction that would take me to my tavern. I might have noticed that I was being followed had I not been so deep in thought. A hundred yards from the town, two men leaped from a clump of shadows at me.

This I could understand; here was a clear course with no debating. For a long time, violence had been storing up in me, and there had been no chance to release it. Now the first man went over my head and struck the ground with a solid thud; my knee jerked up into the other's groin, bringing a shriek of agony, after which I mauled him down with savage blows he could not fend off. It was not fair fighting, but it was the sort of thing George Gibson and Linn had taught us Lambs so we might keep alive on the river.

The first man was getting to his feet. For a moment I thought of closing with him and breaking his neck in a way I understood, but instead, I hammered him until a too hard blow dropped him unconscious. My other attacker was groaning so I dragged him to where the light was better. He shrieked when he saw me draw my knife, but I did not scalp him. All I did was notch both of his ears before I flung him into the bushes.

All the rest of my way tavernward, I felt better for the relief the conflict had brought. My knife haft had felt good in my palm. I did not then wonder why these men had followed; I was a stranger; they had no way of knowing that I had money.

Yonido showed up in mid-morning, and I told him what had happened. He became very serious.

"Simon, it is in my mind that we should get away from here, that you are in danger where I cannot help. Let us go."

I pondered the suggestion. There seemed little reason to stay here, yet I had seen a scarf that had belonged to Celine here in Niagara. But if she were here, I felt either Yonido or Blanche would have known something about it.

I was still thinking what to say to Yonido when there was a tramping on the stairway. The door was flung open and in came three soldiers in uniform, one of them a sergeant who addressed me.

"Major Brevecourt ordered us to bring you to him at once."

At his nod, the two soldiers moved about the room gathering my belongings. One picked up Yonido's medicine bag, but the sergeant scowled.

"Let that alone, Grimes."

He jerked his head toward the Indian. Then, with no further explanation, they marched me out of my room, across town to the fort, and again into the room where I had been before. Brevecourt was back at his table. With a salute, the sergeant and his men left the room and me to face Brevecourt alone. There was temper in his eyes this morning, threat in his voice and movement.

"Do you know a man named Norris?"

"No."

"You still claim that you are a Loyalist, that you come from the Loyalsock. You are a liar; you come from Fort Pitt. You are not a follower of His Majesty."

I bowed, unwilling to trust my voice, and his temper broke all bounds.

"You come to me with a cock and bull story of a raid and deny ever seeing me. You claim to hunt for your tavern slut of a wife."

He was a quick man, even in temper, and was out of his chair before my lunge reached him, the blade of his sword whipped out, his pistol in the other hand. The point of his rapier pressed against my chest.

"Braide, I would love to spill your rebel guts on the floor, but before I have finished with you, my friend, you will be begging me to take a ransom for your hide. You thought to fool me."

The stone cell in which they placed me was in a cellar, the single high window letting me see just a scrap of sky. There I was, left with no hope except that whatever was going to happen would be mercifully quick.

* * *

Day after day for a week, Brevecourt came down into the corridor, saying nothing but staring at me until I felt the man was mad. My fingers were hungry for his throat. Finally he tricked me.

This particular day, when I watched him standing out there, I saw that the key had been left in my door. In a moment, I had turned it and was outside in the corridor. Then the trap fell. Men rushed at me from a side corridor. They beat me and kicked me savagely with heavy shoes. When I was down, one with a bandage about his head under his hat kneeled upon me and beat my face while the others held me fast. Sometime after merciful unconsciousness came to me, they must have carried me into my cell for there I came to, and a surgeon was working on my cuts and bruises.

Days afterward, when it was still hard for me to move about, a soldier opened my cell. I did not step out at once. There seemed to be no one with him, so I finally did, and he took me up two stairways and once again into that big room I hated.

Another man sat behind the table today, an officer with a heavy face and body but a bit short in stature. He wore a green uniform with the insignia of a colonel in the Ranger Regiment familiar to the colonies. He looked up. I noted that Major Brevecourt stood at a window.

"You are Simon Braide."

The colonel's voice was rasping; it did not ask a question but suggested a reply. However, my battered lips were still painful, and I merely bowed. He continued in the same tone and manner.

"Your home was raided, your wife taken; you came here to find her?"

"Yes, sir." This time I answered, and his eyes bored into mine for a moment. Then he bent forward, wrote rapidly on a sheet of paper, sanded his work, and rose, pulling down his coat with stubby fingers before he came round the table and stepped close to me.

For minutes he studied my scarred and bruised face, even glanced at my hands. His lips closed into a straight uncompromising line as he turned on Brevecourt.

"Major, be good enough to summon Cloud and Bennet. I am taking this man with us."

Brevecourt was probably an excellent card player. There was no expression on his face in spite of the fact there had been menace and threat in the colonel's voice. He bowed and stepped away.

"Braide, I am Colonel Butler of His Majesty's Rangers. You will be in the charge of the two men I have called."

They came in as he finished speaking, Bennett about my height and as broad but older and with heavy lines on his face. Cloud was younger, and what he lacked in height he gained in breadth of shoulder. Both seemed pleasant enough, and they wore the coats and caps of Rangers, but their trousers and moccasins were buckskin. I noted, too, that both carried excellent rifles, not muskets.

The two men fell in beside me, and we came out on a parade ground crowded with men in green uniforms. They were everywhere, lolling about, sprawled on the grass, some in groups talking. Colonel Butler appeared at another door, and a young Ranger who walked two paces back of him sounded a small silver whistle that glinted in the sun. The men in green began at once to take formation, urged on by the noncommissioned officers, while Butler waited there a short distance from the door.

Before we moved, another man appeared back of the colonel, a tall man dressed in green, wearing a chaplain's insignia. We were close enough to hear what passed; I saw the man point to me, and I caught the last of his words.

". . . But Colonel Butler, the man is probably a spy."

Butler's answer was frosty and strong with finality, apparently ignoring what he had been told.

"Chaplain Norris, if you appear again for services wearing side arms, I shall put you under arrest."

The tall man stood for a moment as if undecided, then unbuckled his sword belt and passed it to the young Ranger who had sounded the whistle and who now, at the colonel's order, gave another signal. The men formed facing the doorway where the chaplain stood.

I know that I have never heard a more beautiful voice than that of this man Norris who spoke briefly in normal tones and then began to harangue the men.

"Come on," Cloud muttered. "I don't want to listen to that bloody-minded devil any longer."

Outside the fort in the open space were long lines of carts, hundreds of pack horses. Over at the neutral zone, the redcoated sentries stood less than ten feet apart, keeping back a thronging mass of Indians, some of whom were warriors. Some were mounted; many were with the women and children.

Cloud left me with Bennett while he went to bring our belongings, and as we waited, the Rangers began filing out of the fort and taking their places in long lines on either side of the baggage train. The wheels of the carts started to creak. The whole force—carts, pack animals, Rangers— began to pass through the sentries and along the wide Indian trail that I knew ran to the Genessee. On either side of the moving, disciplined body, the Indians followed like children do a band until it looked like a migration rather than a march.

Desperation seized me as I realized what this force meant. Blanche had told me to get out of this country. Yonido's warning might have still given me time. Now I had lost the chance for which I had been allowed to go by Colonel Kelly; there would be no warning the frontier. A glance at Bennett showed he was alert.

Blanche—I thought of her and her sharp warning as well as her strange remark about the man who was leading the force. Had she talked to him? How else could he have known of my imprisonment? And presently I saw him. At the zone line, he was joined by a tall, corpulent Indian who wore a single eagle feather drooping over one ear. Bennett nudged me and pointed.

"That's the one they call Old King or Old Smoke. I can't say his Indian handle, but he's chief of the natives that march with us."

The line of march stretched out a good half mile. When Cloud joined us with our things, I took my bag. He looked a bit doubtful.

"You look pretty peaked to carry that," he commented, and I grinned and heaved it a little higher on my shoulder. Then the three of us swung forward, there being only the one slight satisfaction to me that I was leaving Niagara.

One thing was quickly apparent about Butler's march. He would permit the Indians to cluster on both flanks of his Rangers but would not allow them to follow in his immediate rear. He had a few mounted men, and they were riding back and forth. I saw them handle two or three Indians roughly, and it was in this rear that we marched.

"Why," I asked the men, "is the colonel fussy about the rear?"

Cloud looked at me with a grin. He was chewing sassafras leaves mixed with tobacco. He spat far to one side.

"Stragglers," he said. "Remember a Ranger scalp would look just like one from your folks. Butler just won't let them Indians have their way."

Near evening of that day's march, the first incident happened. I supposed that my guards had moved slowly out of consideration for my condition. We were well back, for here the carts raised much dust and were passing a long line of heavy underbrush. Suddenly my hat was ripped from my head, then came the report of a rifle, and smoke bloomed in the thicket. But even in this split second, Cloud had fired. A man broke cover, trying to reload his piece as he ran. Bennett's long barrel swung with the hurrying figure. In another second or so he would be behind a tree. Then the rifle spoke, and the man rolled over as a stopped deer sometimes does.

Cloud had reloaded and shook his head.

"Can't be getting you killed. The colonel wouldn't like that. Let's get back and see what we have."

I recognized the man as I looked down at him. It was the fellow whose ears I had cropped and who had beaten my face in the corridor. He was dead, shot through the throat. Bennett turned the body over and searched the pockets, finding a pipe and tobacco, a clasp knife, and a little silver. In the man's bullet pouch, wrapped in a bit of soft buckskin, was a single gold sovereign, and I saw something that startled me more than the shot. The coin was nicked like those Wigton and I had found. The money had been a part of Celine's hoard!

I was sure she had owned all the marked coins. Yonido had none of them with my money. There had been a scarf, now this coin. But I was helpless, unable to make a move.

"You know him?" Bennett queried, and I shook my head.

"Seems you ought to," Cloud commented, "He went out of his way to get you. The fellow is one of Brevecourt's pups."

A knot of Indians, attracted by the rifle fire, appeared. My two guards raised the body and tossed it into the brush followed by his rifle. The two Rangers looked at each other.

"Buzzards," Cloud said. Bennett looked up to the sky and nodded gravely though I could see nothing. Then I understood their calloused point of view. The body of the man would be found scalped. That would close the matter save that it might make some trouble for Old King if Colonel Butler questioned him.

* * *

The second day took us over hills that slowed down the baggage train measurably. Here Butler divided his force into a heavy guard for the wagons and a fast column to move ahead. Marching with the faster group, we sighted the bright waters of a lake to our right and at dusk saw a river and a big bark village.

"Little Beard's town," Cloud said. "Colonel'll let them dance off their deviltry tonight."

CHAPTER SEVEN

EVEN BEFORE the Ranger baggage train had arrived, the eager Indians had started their dance. Their provisions for the celebration were quite simple—a cleared place with a pole topped by a dog's skull in the center and a number of skin-headed drums for rhythm.

Once his transport was up, properly placed and guarded. Colonel Butler had three kegs of rum broken out and set up with a guard of a half-dozen hard-faced Rangers standing by. The warriors came up in long lines, and each was served a small drink of the fiery stuff. This procedure was repeated twice during the dance, by which time, thoroughly excited and smelling horribly of grease, the reveling natives began to get out of hand. A mob of them surged up to the rum kegs demanding more liquor. Weapons were brandished, and there was a lot of wild yelling.

I had thought Colonel Butler was in his tent, but now he stepped from the shadow and stood by his men. A huge warrior with a scarred face leaped forward and waved his tomahawk over the head of the officer who did not flinch a single inch from the threatening weapon. He rapped a sharp order, and the soldiers lowered their bayonets and moved forward, walking shoulder to shoulder into the screeching mob. Some of the Indians were badly nicked in the scramble to get out of the way of the keen steel.

"I figure the colonel just don't like the boogers," Bennett commented with a grin.

"Hates the smell of them," Cloud added, "and he's got to have that Old King close all day long."

East of this place, Butler turned his march southeastward, following a stream Cloud said was called Cohocton. The possibility of escape had never left my mind, and on this day's march, there was an occurrence that sharpened both my uneasiness and my desire to get away, almost at any cost. Most of our carts had been left behind at Little Beard's town; now at the noon halt, the remainder of them were unloaded and a long file of about a hundred warriors came to where quartermasters were sorting the contents of the carts. Ammunition, blankets, and food were issued until all were equipped. Then the long line, accompanied by a white lieutenant and a sergeant, swung off to the south. There was a feeling like a fever in me as I saw this force disappear into the woods. From the direction taken, I was sure the band would strike our West Branch River, and by now, I felt pretty certain of Butler's objective.

That afternoon, when we had been marching along a sort of hog-back to escape the mosquitoes, Cloud called a halt to rest. We sat down, and he turned to me,

"Braide, I've been watching you and figure I know what's going on in your mind. You want to run for it. Now look." Below us the soldiers marched toward a break in the hills, and over everything was a faint blue haze like powdered smoke. The green lines marched in perfect precision with the tips of set bayonets catching glints from the sun. In back of the column, the pack animals moved at exactly spaced intervals, and on either side of Butler's men as far as the eye could reach, in the timber and brush, were the Indians.

"If you was to cut for it, you'd have to get through a half mile of Indians, either way. Besides, Braide, even though we like you, we'd shoot you down if you ran. We wouldn't fail the colonel; we've been with him a long time—neighbors before this war."

I nodded, but I was sick at heart. Those I lived with and the country I loved would be at the mercy of that flying column moving up the valley of the Genessee.

That evening, around our own small campfire, we three talked, and I told much of my story—of the raid, of my treatment by Brevecourt. They had already heard of Norris and had seen the attempt on my life.

Bennett nodded soberly.

"Simon, you seem sort of unlucky. I can't figure why so many want you in real trouble."

Cloud waited until his partner finished.

"Me and Bennett don't talk about it much, but we lost everything, kith and kin along with all we owned when Pontiac took Presque Isle in the old wars. We've had our tough times, and a man just sort of pays for living. Bennett and me figure we've paid a heap just to sit round a fire and eat dried meat. The colonel had had his troubles, and he must have had a reason for taking you from Brevecourt. He sort of put us in charge of you because he knows we hate Indians and would like this job better."

He leaned forward grimly and pointed his finger.

"Just the same, we'd shoot you; that's what we're here for. Simon, there's no manner of letting the folks on the rivers know about our coming. Besides, there's no force down there that could stop us no matter how long ahead they had the word."

What he said was true enough, but it could not quiet the sense of futility in me or the feeling that I had failed my people. Something of the pain and death that would strike on the rivers could be laid at my door.

* * *

Next evening, I was summoned by Colonel Butler himself. He looked up when I entered his tent, his heavy features friendly enough.

"Braide, what do you know of the two branches of the Susquehanna?"

"Our Loyalsock empties into the West Branch, sir," I replied. "It's just a big forest river. I don't know much of the North Branch; the people over there came from Connecticut." A slight smile twitched the grim corners of his mouth. "Most Pennsylvanians do not like them, I am told."

Before I could answer, he shook his heavy head.

"These Indians will sweep those lands clean, Braide, But it's war, and, since Burgoyne was taken, we must have a diversion. This is it, and because I am not given enough white soldiers with bayonets, I must use native people with war axes." From the long silence following, I thought I was dismissed and had turned when he spoke again.

"Braide, I have been told the story of the raid on your house and the loss of your wife. I can tell you it was not done by Senecas or Cayugas for we have tabs on them. It does not sound right—it is strange, and I have thought about it."

His keen eyes missed nothing; now they noted that my hands had clenched when he spoke of the savages.

"No, Braide, I do not like Indians either, but, as I said, this is war, and I follow orders from those who think those men useful."

He tapped on his table for a little with a blunt forefinger. "Perhaps it may help you to know, young man, my own wife and little girl are prisoners in Albany."

My mind was confused; I knew this man was trying to help me, and I wanted desperately to ask questions, to get more information. Since he seemed to know so much of me, he should have known had Celine been taken to Niagara or Oswego. Yet, he said definitely the Senecas and Cayugas had not raided.

He gestured my dismissal but stopped me at the tent fly. "Brevecourt wanted to hang you; Norris seems to hate you for obscure reasons which he does not state. So—I brought you with me, feeling there was, perhaps, enough death in the world. Simon Braide, I do not think you a spy, but I agree with Brevecourt in one thing and no other—you are not a friend of His Majesty's cause."

* * *

From where the Cohocton empties into the Chemung, Butler's force took with it every canoe that was to be found, and when we were pretty well down this river, where a big creek entered it from the north, we were joined by another band of painted warriors.

"Another dance tonight," Bennett speculated. "Likely the colonel will let them work off steam."

Our camp was pitched in the "Y" formed by the streams with the tents of the soldiers down near the point. For some odd reason known only to himself, Butler relaxed discipline markedly this evening. Soldiers strolled about watching the Indians clear a dancing ground. Bennett had been right in his speculation, and we went up to watch.

This time, their central post was not a large one, and it was sharpened to a point. Two Indians dug a hole for it, using their knives and fingers,

getting plenty of advice from bystanders according to their chatter. When
the hole was finished, a dog, one that traveled with an Indian group,
came up, and one of the Indians grabbed it by a hind leg, swinging the
animal into the air. Then a second warrior took hold, and they laid the
struggling beast on his back; a third Indian snatched up the pointed pole
and impaled the dog with one savage thrust. Together, the three raised
the pole and settled it into the hole they had dug while the impaled
animal shrieked out its life, and blood and filth ran down the pole. Near
me, I heard a young soldier retch, then mumble.

"Some day, by God, I'll kill me an Indian."

* * *

With evening, there was an issue of rum all round the camp and to
the Indians in larger quantities than in Little Beard's town. The dance
was soon in full swing, the warriors moving round and round with their
everlasting bent-kneed motion. Occasionally one would leap in and attack the post with his knife or hatchet. This evening it seemed to me that
most of the Rangers were watching, and Cloud and Bennett certainly did
not act vigilant to me. Each man carried a pistol, but their rifles were in
our tent.

I did not do any real thinking, and certainly I had no plan except
to get across the Chemung. I would have to run for it. Edging slowly to
one side, I reached the outskirts of the crowd, then darted away in the
direction of the white camp.

They missed me before I had gone fifty yards. Someone saw me and
yelled just before I reached the tents. The Indians joined the rush after
me with a howl like a huge wolf pack. It is frightful to be hunted by a
few men, and even more terrifying when nearly a thousand take up the
chase. I doubled about the tents, making pretty good headway. I could
see the water of the Chemung when I glanced back, and in that instant a
tent rope tripped me. Before I could rise, a knot of Indians was upon me.
Dragging me to my feet, then beating and prodding me toward the dancing ground, they pitched me into the clear space at the foot of the pole.

It was plain the savages considered that I had become their game. A
solid ring of warriors was about the small space, and every man showed

weapons. The light of the big fire illuminated the place and the angry faces in the circle.

While I lay for minutes, fighting to get back my breath which had been kicked out of me by moccasined feet, a huge warrior stepped into the ring, and I recognized the man who had threatened Colonel Butler at the other dance. He carried a small bright axe that glinted in the firelight, and his face was hideously painted in crosshatchings of red and white. Plainly he considered himself my executioner, and he began to pad round the circle mumbling some kind of chant and occasionally taking a leap in my direction. I had become some sort of forest beast; he was the hunter.

Slowly I came to my feet, testing my muscles as I did. My head was clear. Down on the rivers those I loved might be dying under other hatchets since I had failed to warn them. My map might even be leading Colonel Butler for all I knew. I would die here on the Chemung in the center of these howling, smelly beasts. But I felt strong; my muscles tensed to my wish, and I had a tremendous sense of freedom. I had to die, but that was all. Nothing more could be expected of me. And I knew I would take this stamping fool with me.

He had narrowed his circle each time he came round. Between us, the earth was bare and dusty from the dancing, though I noted some small pebbles and a bit of scuffed moss. Little puffs of dust rose each time the warrior's moccasins patted the ground.

He was very close, and I spread my arms wide like a wrestler may do when getting into action. I moved forward while he gave ground a little. The axe was swung up high. Then, I stumbled, going down almost to one knee. They had taught us this trick in New Orleans, saying it came from the French, and all of us Lambs practiced it. I spun round, my heel swept up, and the force of the kick stretched the Indian flat on his back. I was upon him like a cat, wrenching the axe from his hand.

Dead, shocked silence was on the faces of the ring for a moment, holding them motionless for the minute I needed. As the axe went up, the man under me shrieked his abject terror; the bright steel whistled down, missing his skull but shearing away most of one of his ears. Dropping the axe, I grabbed the man's head and beat the ground with it, hoping that I might get it on a stone and so crack the skull. All the while, he was gasping out his awful cries, and in me was a savage delight at humbling him. He, at least, was paying for what was happening on our rivers. Once more I snatched the axe. Then there was a rush of booted feet about me, and a big sergeant snatched me off my victim, hissing in my ear: "Come off—you want to kill the bastard?"

The file of soldiers, bayonets ready, closed round us, and the sergeant had another word.

"That's Old King's son, Pigeon. You want us all to get scalped so you can chop up their stinking crown prince?"

I cursed the sergeant fluently, but he just grinned as they took me down to the center of the soldier's camp.

Nobody officially took me to task for the escape or what followed, but my liberty ended at that point. Cloud, however, did comment mildly:

"It was all right to us to clip Pigeon, but we don't want the running away. You see now you haven't a chance."

From now on, I was somewhere in the center of the marching column where the route step was shorter than mine and so tiring, because when you move with marchers, you must keep step. At night I slept under a fly with Cloud and Bennett on either side. It seemed strange to lie so close with men who would shoot you the moment you ran, yet who shared their blankets with you in the chilly nights.

* * *

The Chemung is a lazy river, turning slowly in its course to the south along a line of hills that grew higher and more broken with each mile. We marched along this stream day after day until the monotony of the everlasting flow of the green column, the rising dust from many feet striking in unison, the swarms of deer flies about our heads, grew to be almost as unbearable as the uneasiness within me for my people whom this march would destroy.

Past the Painted Post with its cabalistic designs like those Yonido had shown me at the Forbidden Way, we turned more sharply southward and, in another day's march, reached the junction of the Chemung with the North Branch of the Susquehanna. Now I knew the heavy blow would fall first where I had guessed when canoes were collected. This force would drop down the river; there would be blood and tears in the Wyoming Valley.

That night, Cloud and Bennett, wearied from marching, slept soundly beside me, but I lay staring into the darkness. Suddenly there seemed a crowding in the shadows over me, something caught a faint ray of light, perhaps from the camp, and glinted. I set my teeth and tensed my muscles for a spring when I caught the unmistakable odor of an Indian, and my immediate thought was of Pigeon with his ear shorn away. Someone bending forward between my sleeping guards was directly over me, and my upthrust arm was gripped and held for a moment. Then a finger touched me lightly on the wrist, and I understood. It was Yonido, smelling and acting like a Seneca. He drew me to my feet, and I stepped outside the fly with him.

"Yonido," I whispered, and he placed his fingers over my lips, then whispered in my ear.

"Listen, I have marched lately with the Senecas, and tonight I go to warn Wigton. Wyoming would not listen to an Indian. Now get back to your bed; stop grieving."

His fingers thrust something into my pocket. He found and gripped my hand, then was gone in the darkness. When I lay down, one of the guards stirred.

"Where were you?" he asked sleepily, and I answered, "Outside," which seemed to satisfy him.

* * *

Colonel Butler put all his men to work at the river junction, building a strong corral fence for the horses and throwing up bark shelters for the stores that would be left behind. All canoes were repaired and wide rafts of dead logs constructed. With that work done, soldiers were used as guards, and it seemed to go without saying that Cloud and Bennett would remain with me.

* * *

On a bright morning, Butler's officers marched the Rangers down to the canoes and rafts while the savages followed, using what crafts were left. More than a thousand men were moving, and those for whom there was no room in the boats and on the rafts marched on the bank of the river. I watched the embarkment, and as Cloud and Bennett had told me, there was nothing I could do. As they had also said, there was nothing downriver that could stop an expedition like this which could strike clear through to the lower counties if it wished.

Tedious days of waiting succeeded each other. My guards relaxed, knowing it was now too late for me to escape, and I had nothing to do but sit about and think. I was trying to put things together. I could not place the young man whom Blanche had named, but Celine's scarf and one of her treasured coins were in Niagara. I could understand the vindictive things done to me by the commandant but not why Chaplain Norris should take steps against me. Surely I was not important enough to have set in motion so many things that seemed to wish to destroy me.

Then my thoughts turned away from my own affairs to others who were dear to me. It scarcely seemed possible that Yonido could reach the river valleys in time. The flying column had left us days before. It was certain my friend would be far too late for Wyoming.

On the evening of the tenth day, a runner appeared with the news that the Wyoming settlements had been destroyed and that Colonel Butler wanted the pack train put into condition so we could march immediately on his return. Then at noon two days later appeared the first canoe bearing wounded, and soldiers marched along the banks as guards. The Rangers and the canoes moved together, and after them, the Indians, jubilant, with scalps hanging from many belts, the wet bloody things slapping against naked thighs.

I saw something as the soldiers swung into their camp. An Indian jostled a Ranger, whether accidentally or on purpose there was no telling. The soldier did not hesitate but knocked the Indian sprawling with a reversed gun butt.

Colonel Butler walked quietly among his officers, none of whom seemed to have much to say, and that evening there was an assembly of all soldiers, officers, and pack train men. Sentries were posted with bayonets ready to keep the Indians at a good distance. Butler spoke to the assembly in a shocked voice.

"Men, for the last time I have marched with Indians unless we whites outnumber the foul beasts. You saw what was done down there after we had won a clean victory, and that blood will never be entirely washed away."

In the dead stillness he looked down for a moment, then up at us.

"Nor can any of us ever forget what happened to put such a blot on British arms."

When the commander had moved away, one of the captains held up his hand for attention.

"Men, no straggling. Those warriors are scalp- and blood-hungry and will lift the hair of any white man they find alone."

* * *

Next morning, to my surprise, Butler summoned me. He was sitting on a stump outside his tent looking grimly toward the Indian camp. His heavy features looked weary, shocked.

"Braide, I'm sick of killing. If I take you back to Niagara, Brevecourt or Norris may insist on your being tried as a spy. Tonight Cloud and Bennett will give you arms, take you out of camp, and turn you loose."

He smiled a little, then I abruptly thrust out my hand to him. I liked this grim soldier.

"I'm grateful, Colonel Butler."

His strong fingers gripped mine for a moment, then his lips twitched.

"Few of your people will ever want to believe this, Braide. They will never know how hard we tried to hold those beasts of ours in check."

Going back to the big fly which Cloud, Bennett, and I occupied, I passed a big open tent in which there were wounded and saw an Indian dressed in hunting shirt and breeches working there. When he glanced up, I recognized Yonido. That evening, he found our tent.

During the meal we ate together, he was stolid Indian and then, under questioning, became his voluble self. He said that he had reached the West Branch before these British Rangers to find the people already warned and fled from the country. Few scalps had been taken in that region, and he had not seen the Wigtons.

Neither Cloud nor Bennett seemed to resent the fact that a warning had been taken. Cloud spoke.

"Wyoming; what of it?"

Yonido shook his head.

"I got there after the battle and things were bad, all bad. The Senecas went wild after the surrender; they had the taste of blood in their mouths."

He talked for most of an hour with his gift of presenting things graphically, and all of us listened eagerly. He told what he had heard of the small Tory fort that had opened its gates to Butler, of the short, savage battle and the surrender. Butler and his officers had risked their lives, but the Indians wanted scalps and spread murder over all that once peaceful country like an evil mist.

Shortly before dusk, Cloud and Bennett carried out Butler's orders, equipping me with a knife and gun, food, and a blanket. When they looked these things over, they were not satisfied but went back and returned with a pistol. They saw to it that I had spare flints, that my knife was sharp, and my powder and ball to their liking. As we went out of camp, I saw Indians watching and noticed that one was Pigeon, who carried two small scalps at his belt.

We marched eastward, following a good path. I had made up my mind that I would see and talk to General Washington or one of his officers before I ever returned to the rivers. I wanted to tell of the strength which could be brought to bear by the British and Indians and show how it would be easy for them to break through our lightly held area.

* * *

Sometime before midnight, we went into camp where a good spring bubbled. In the morning we ate together, and it was time for parting. I believe that these two Rangers were genuinely sorry to lose me and cared not a whit that I was going to the patriot army, which fact they must have guessed. They shook hands soberly, and when I pressed on each one of the gold coins which Yonido had returned to me, they demurred until I insisted. After all, they were poor men. Cloud had the last word when, after we had shaken hands for the second time, he said:

"Be sure to watch your back track, Simon."

* * *

It was mid-morning before I was sure I was being followed, and not by my former guards. Then I had some luck. My pursuer, intent on following my trail, was puzzled when I circled a wide clump of trees and showed himself in the open for a moment. I recognized Pigeon, even from this hilltop on which I watched.

A wild feeling of elation swept over me for I hated this man who seemed to typify, for me, all I disliked in Indians. I had seen children's scalps at his belt, seen his arrogance to Butler, had waited for him to kill me that night when I clipped his ear. Now he was hunting me and doing it clumsily. So, for a mile I left a plain trail, not too plain to rouse suspicion, but enough so he would not miss it. I had watched Bennett load the short musket I carried: a huge ball and three buckshot.

The man was eager. After all, he wanted this business finished so he could march with his people back to Niagara. So it was easy for me, lying in back of a lichen-mottled rock. Pigeon saw me only once—when I raised the musket. No, I did not give him a chance; he was dead before he fell, his head half torn away.

The two little scalps were fast to his belt so I cut a piece from his leggings and wrapped them securely. I did not touch the man's belongings or drag him from the trail but left him there for the buzzards.

* * *

The two weeks that followed were a nightmare of dreadful travel, of sleepless nights nearly encountering small Indian bands, of briar and laurel thickets that ripped my clothing. Again and again, I lost my reckoning when the mists were in the mountains hiding the sun. But in two weeks I achieved the goal for which I traveled. I reached Washington's army and the camp of the Commander-in-Chief.

Incredibly dirty, bearded, clothing in rags, holes in my moccasins, there was still a fever upon me that would not let me wait, so I approached the sentries at that white painted house near the Hudson and found it surprisingly easy to see the general himself.

George Washington, Commander-in-Chief of our armies, sat in back of a table in the big kitchen of a farmhouse. His shoes dried before the fire, and the stockings he wore had been darned. General Knox occupied a corner, where he sat in a tilted chair, but I had eyes only for His Excellency. After all, I had not seen him since I was little more than a boy.

He had aged tremendously; the planes of his face were flattened and grim, but there was life in his deeply set eyes, not arrogance; the quiet assurance of a man who has learned to trust his own judgment. His eyes studied me gravely; I saw there was recognition in them before he spoke.

"You have had a hard trip."

"Sir," I began, "the map—"

"John Wigton has told me of its loss."

The room was still; both men were watching me. Washington stooped, slipped on his shoes, and I was suddenly so desperate that I took out my buckskin parcel, as Kelly had done, and tossed the children's scalps on the table, not turning when I heard a startled exclamation from Knox.

"Sir, I took them from an Indian who had been at Wyoming. I have just come from Colonel Butler's army. I have been to Niagara. For the sake of every child on the Susquehanna, Your Excellency, destroy the Iroquois."

Washington's coldness met my heat, and his level eyes gave me no peace.

"You went to Niagara for your map?"

"Is it true there are no good maps of the Iroquois country north of the Tioga Path?" I asked without answering his question.

"Yes."

He leaned forward and pointed one long forefinger like a pistol barrel at me.

"You failed to guard your map, and the enemy may profit by it. Your loss may have warned them, may make it harder for us. We cannot afford failures."

The cold voice was probing, and my anger was rising. I had not planned to have things this way, and I had tramped weary miles in constant danger. Half a dozen times my life had hung by a thread. Now this tall, calm man was talking of failures. Even as the blood mounted to my face until I could feel my scarred chin, the great man's features relaxed.

"Simon," he said softly, reading what was in my mind, "they have not killed your spirit as I thought at first. General Knox will talk with you later."

I walked from the room a little proudly. After all, I was a young man, and Washington had done me the honor to remember me and to understand. No wonder I held my shoulders square under the broken seams of my hunting shirt.

CHAPTER EIGHT

"GENERAL KNOX will talk with you later." On these words of His Excellency, I waited a full two days to see this trusted artillery general who had advised and instructed us at Fort Pitt so long ago, and in this waiting period I, at least, had time to think about my meeting with our commander. He had been grim at first, then seemed to know all about my wanderings. Truly this man had a mind for details, as he showed by knowing there was no map of the forbidden Iroquois country north of the Tioga or Forbidden Path. He had chided me but was kind in the end.

The morning of the third day, when my patience had worn thin, the sentry admitted me to see General Knox, who was expansive and congenial, even giving me a mug of sour cider to moisten my throat as I talked; and to him, at his bidding, I told my story from beginning to end and explained the anxiety under which I had labored for so long.

"Most of the West Branch folks are safe," he assured me. "That of course includes the Wigtons."

It was on my tongue to ask specifically about Hope, but I did not like the intent look in the general's eyes. He went promptly into a series of questions on the post at Niagara, its garrison, its position and the way to get there. Naturally, my engineer's eye had noted many things at the fort and on the long way down the Chemung and the Cohocton. It was noon by the time I finished, and he bade me return at one o'clock. I did not receive, nor had I expected, any invitation to lunch.

In the afternoon, his questions first touched on my own map and what data I had gathered. I explained how I had followed his directions as carefully as I could.

The general raised his maimed hand, examined the fingers critically, then shot a sudden question at me.

"Who took your map?"

I had told him my long story in the morning; now I was restless, eager to be up and about and done with this talk. I shook my head.

"Of that I cannot be sure. It may have been burned, as I hoped at first. If ever I find my wife, I expect to learn just what happened."

He shook his shaggy head decisively.

"Simon, your dog was killed with a stone arrow; there had been a booted foot in back of your kitchen. The house itself was not burned, nor the barn of livestock disturbed. John Wigton told me there were some tracks going away from your place but no other signs of a raiding party. I think, young man, you are the victim of a very real plot or—"

He interrupted himself with a shrug of his shoulders that threatened the seams of his coat. Then he held up a long forefinger.

"Of course, the British and Indians could come down without a map. The danger is that, if your map went north, it would warn our enemy of our interests in your forests. So they would be prepared for us; men would die because of that piece of paper."

I answered him scathingly,

"You are too late for the upper rivers, general. The British and Indians have destroyed the Wyoming. There is no one left on the West Branch of the Susquehanna."

Knox showed no offense at my tone though he probably knew I was trying to annoy him. His brow went up, making his face a greater expanse of well-stuffed skin.

"It's the main rivers that matter. The forces of the enemy must not pass Fort Augusta and so get at our backs in the lower counties where we fashion ammunitions."

He heaved a long sigh, fiddled with the papers on his table a little, then gave me his widest, most ingratiating smile.

"Simon Braide, you are a Godsend to us now. It is true that your first map was destroyed or stolen, and His Excellency thinks you may have served your personal interests in trying to find your wife rather than helping your country."

He let that sink in, and it did not help my temper. I wanted to get away from here back to the Loyalsock to see my friends or be there alone if necessary.

"But," he said pompously, "more than anything else, we need good maps of this country through which you came with the infamous Butler. You will be given assistance but—forget all about everything else—your wife and friends will be cared for properly. You will do us this map through the winter months that lie ahead. I shall go to His Excellency."

My temper boiled over. This man was a major general in the Continental Army; I was a civilian in badly patched clothing.

"Sir," I roared at him, "you can go to Hell. I'm going back to the Loyalsock."

He looked at me as blandly as though I had just made an interesting observation about the weather.

"Well," he commented dryly, "I am quite sure we are both mistaken as to where we are going. Certainly you will not leave here until we are ready, nor will I worry about my place in eternity until the chaplain so bids me."

I was on my feet, striding up and down, almost pleading. "For months I have had little peace, General. There was the raid and the responsibility for bringing my wife to that dangerous country when she hated it. If aught evil happened to her, it was my fault. I have marched for hundreds of miles, been bullied and beaten by the British in Niagara, have marched with the wolves that tore Wyoming apart. I could not warn my people. Now I am to sit by a table making fine lines with a quill? Sir, I want to get back to my river and there kill every native man I see."

He leaned so far back in his chair that I was concerned for its legs, and he spoke musingly, undisturbed by my heat.

"So George Gibson called you Lambs. If the others were like you, what a flock it must have been, and what a beastly thing shearing time would be. No wonder Hugh Mercer had you locked up in Williamsburg."

He dropped the chair; now he was grave.

"You have endured aplenty, but you could not warn the rivers. They were warned, but we had nothing to stop Butler. As for mapmaking, you are now nothing but skin and bones on which your clothes hang as though on a drying rack. It's time you rested. Then, though I cannot tell you before spring, your chance will come."

He shrugged his heavy shoulders and fussed with papers as he had done at Fort Pitt.

"And plop no more scalps before His Excellency. He does not like them. He—makes me bury them."

So, perforce, my temper having burned out, I was ready, knowing that what I had seen would look well on a map. In two and a half months I had completed a route map up the West Branch over the timbered divide to the headwaters of the Genessee, then through the gorge and over the flat land to Niagara. Secondly, I did Butler's march, putting in small figures, trying to make the information useful to an army officer, and also, by keeping busy, refrained from thinking too much of my own problems.

A week after Knox had turned over my new charts to His Excellency, I was summoned to headquarters. The room was pretty well crowded with officers, and I was pleased to see my map spread on the table where the great Virginian sat. He seemed in high good humor, and, remembering that he had once been an excellent surveyor, I hoped this mood was due to my craftsmanship.

"Simon," he said gravely, "I understand you have been advising General Knox as to his spiritual condition."

My face must have reddened; then I saw that Knox stood in a corner and was looking uncomfortable also.

"Well," Washington continued, "I have worried about the same thing for years, but it seems to do little good."

He tapped the map with a long forefinger.

"You are wasted in the field, my friend. You must go over more of our maps and put them in better shape. Now tell me, what is this land along the Cohocton and the Chemung like, say, for corn?"

I did not need to hesitate, for the country had made its impression on me.

"Sir, it is a gray land where our colony is green. There are too many small rocky hills, and the streams wander all over the flat lands, making new channels after each fresh set. Now the Genessee land is wonderful—high grass, natural meadows. There Indian corn grows as high as a man on a horse."

Washington was listening, oblivious to all about him, and I felt he was thinking of his own fields and how they would be neglected. Before me sat the greatest landowner in the colonies now that Sir William Johnson was dead and George Groghan in difficulties. He nodded his head and began to roll up the map while he glanced at his officers.

"Any questions, gentlemen? Mr. Braide has come through the Indian country and may have information you wish."

A trim little officer with extraordinarily large eyes stepped forward, and I saw him look over my worn clothing. He glanced at the Commander-in-Chief.

"With your permission, sir."

When Washington nodded, this man, who was a colonel, put his question, the other officers falling silent as if they deferred to his ideas.

"How many warriors, Mr. Braide, do you think the Six Nations could muster?"

Cloud and Bennett had talked loosely on the long march from the lake to the Susquehanna. In spite of the hordes about Niagara there had been less than eight hundred warriors with Butler. So I did not hesitate.

"From two thousand to two thousand, five hundred, sir. Not more, and they are so poorly organized that I doubt their getting over seven or eight hundred into a battle line anywhere."

The doubtful looks and the buzz of excited whispering that followed my answer indicated their lack of faith in what I had said. Now the small colonel smiled, but there was no real mirth in his expression, rather it was patronizing.

"My man," he said, "surely you would not have us feel they are that few, for we know better. The Senecas alone can muster five thousand warriors."

I bowed, determined to make no scene here, for Knox stood quiet, and I had been offensive enough to him. His eyes followed me.

"Sir, there are not five thousand women, children, and warriors among the Senecas. I have been among these people, have seen them on the march."

I tried to smile.

"Of course," I added, "it is sometimes an Indian custom to count the roll of the dead, but I assure you there are not that many alive in Seneca country."

The officer's face clouded with anger, then Washington's calm final tones cut through.

"Colonel Burr, this is a controversial subject in our military family. Mr. Braide has been among the Seneca for months. I believe we will now excuse him with thanks for his fine map of the country of these People of the Long House."

"They will not listen to an Indian." I remembered those words of Yonido, spoken in calm and from experience. Nor would they listen to a white man who had been up there. To these officers, the dark land of the Iroquois was a cloud that could not be penetrated, and no one yet had tested what a small determined army might do in humbling these arrogant woodland citizens.

* * *

With the Iroquois map finished, I continued in Washington's camp and worked on the regular military charts, either redrawing them or making smaller sections for officers' use. Mostly, these were of Northern Jersey or Southern New York where His Excellency watched Clinton and wanted his people familiar with all bits of country where an attack might come.

One day, when the winter was beginning to wane, I had a welcome surprise when I emerged from the small house where I worked. I nearly collided with a big officer who grabbed my shoulders and shook me hard before I realized it was Linn, now resplendent in a new captain's uniform.

We pummeled each other, forgetting the scene in Pitt when we had nearly come to blows. He had been with Clark in the West, had slipped into Detroit as a spy, and had worked about Pitt, concerned with Tory agents. Then he came east into the Lancaster area, checking on the safety of our gun and powder mills there. Now he was assigned as a sort of intelligence officer directly under the command of His Excellency himself.

Once more I had to retell my story, and when I talked about Celine, I did it with all the circumspection I could muster. At once he had his doubts of the raid.

"Simon, there are rotten, dangerous things moving, and I think the archvillain in Pennsylvania may be the man, Norris, as the man is in this country."

"A clergyman?" I asked, thinking of Niagara.

He nodded.

"Yes, a tall white-haired man with a beautiful voice and a genuine hatred for rebels. They ran him out of Pitt shortly after you left. Probably he went north to British posts."

Linn filled and lighted his pipe. When it was drawing well, he leaned forward, pointing with its reed stem.

"Simon, the picture seems to be taking shape. The map business is bad if the raiders came to get it, and it is, of course, too bad about your wife. But I feel the important thing is to get you and other men back on those rivers and make plans to stop raids like that on Wyoming and down the West Branch."

He got up, walked to the door, looked out, then returned and spoke seriously,

"I have reason to believe, Simon, that His Excellency will strike a blow at Indian power. But that is all I know, excepting that he pores over a map you made for him. Knox knows his plans but will not talk. I have a notion that you will be sent home soon for the plan should be about ripe."

* * *

Linn and I did a good bit of riding around the country in the days following, and it was pleasant to be abroad once more, even

though the early spring weather was wet and raw. We talked of the Lambs, of the Wigtons, but whenever I brought up the name of Norris, Linn would look disturbed. Once he spoke half in fun.

"I'm not too afraid of any army of the Lord that man might raise since I believe he is out of favor there, but I am afraid it's just a fanatic like Norris who will be given a chance to lead painted men against our frontier."

Knox summoned me again, and when I reported, he was bland, affable, talkative, but wary of giving important information. He smiled broadly when he finally offered me a chair.

"I noticed the other evening that you did not like to be addressed as 'my man.' It is a very British expression, is it not?"

I grinned ruefully, remembering Brevecourt, and he went on, as he usually did when he had a chance, to monopolize the conversation.

"This time we will not discuss the possibility of my going to Hell, but I do have orders to send you home to your Loyalsock."

He rubbed his hands together, examined the crippled one critically, and probably read my pleasure from my face.

"For once I have seemed to please you, and a smile goes rather well but lonesomely on your dour face, Simon. Get back to the Loyalsock, help Wigton get as many of the settlers back as possible, and send John to me in a month for instructions. You stay on the rivers and watch—nothing untoward may happen for some months; then some of your worries may vanish. Wigton will bring you further instructions."

We stood and he gripped my hand warmly. I did not understand this man, Major General Henry Knox, but realized he was fine metal.

* * *

Linn was not surprised at my news. Now that I was leaving, I wanted a favor from him yet scarcely dared ask it.

"Your men get into New York occasionally?"

He looked at me sharply. I walked to the small mirror hanging on its wall and went through the motions of adjusting my stock.

"If they do, ask them to look about a bit. Celine might be there."

His eyes were stern as he looked at me, then he raised his hand and pointed it, pistol fashion.

"You do not think she is there, Simon, or you would have gone into that city sometime during these months. Yes, I'll have a man look. The fact is, it has already been done."

With that small crumb of information, I asked about a horse, and through his help secured a tall bay mare of doubtful disposition but of power and speed. She looked as though she would match John Wigton's tall horses. With a cavalry musket across my pommel, a pistol at my belt, I was willing to take chances riding southward and over the mountains until I struck the Indian trail that led down the North Branch to Augusta.

There I stopped for a full half day and was dismayed at the condition of the place for here, if anywhere, we must stop the invasion of our valleys. I was told that some of our people had returned to their homes following the exodus, and that raised my hopes.

With a good feed of grain inside her ribs, my new mare made excellent time upriver. I passed the loom of Challis Hall at twilight and wondered how it came to miss the destruction which had fallen on the valley. But when I rode into the fields which John Wigton had kept in such excellent condition, I could see the neglect, even in the dusk.

When I reached the place where Wigton's big friendly house had stood, a Mecca for neighbors and travelers, there was nothing but the stones of the cellar wall.

Shocked, I slid down from my mount and sat on these stones.

This house had meant much to me, it and the friends it sheltered. I thought of the harpsichord and the battle hymn played on it that night when I had come here all but beaten, the pleasant room where we had gathered about the table to eat together while we argued about plans. Now the land below me toward the river was empty, deserted, hopeless, and I remembered that I had not seen candlelight in any window since dusk had fallen. Perhaps the whole valley was abandoned.

Presently I thought of my own house which would be even more empty than this place, though the logs still stood. I had built it with a pride that Celine, with her bitter tongue, had managed to kill, but she could do nothing to my love of the land, the singing of the river, or the play of light and shadow on our hills. So I put my foot into the stirrup and swung myself up.

Riding slowly, savoring the scent of the pine and hemlock, which made the breeze down the valley such a pleasant thing, I came to the rocky road, then to the ford, and I was half over this before I noticed. There was candlelight in a window.

A darkened house may hold a threat or loneliness, but candlelight means a welcome, so I dismounted, took the reins in my fingers, and walked toward the door. Only then did I see the dark figure standing in the shadow cast by the walls, and my heart leaped as I recognized him by the outline of his heavy shoulders and his beard.

"John," I said, "so it is you with a ready gun and a candle in your window."

"Simon," he yelled, then had me by the hand with fingers that gripped like a clamp while he beat me between the shoulders with the other hand which had dropped the gun. I felt as though in the grip of a bear.

"Hope," he called. "Simon's come home."

The door swung open, and she was there with candlelight making the same radiance of her hair that it had done on that last evening. Loose sleeves fell back from her arms, and she ran forward until I had both her firm small hands in mine. All three of us turned to enter the house, the mare trying to follow me. John Wigton could not stand that.

"I'll put up the horse."

All traces of the raid had passed. Floors were newly laid and the Wigton furniture was in place. With gladness, I saw the harpsichord in the corner. Hope and I faced each other over the table.

"We'll wait for father," she said. "He's been so anxious." I could not deny the sudden hunger in me to take this girl into my arms and hold her close. I had been misled by laughter and by a woman infinitely wiser than I. But there was nothing for me but to hold my feelings in check and to look about the room. When Wigton came in and saw me looking, he grinned.

"Welcome to my house, Simon. You know a tough Loyalist used to live here, but he was run out and I took over. Then, when we got the warning of the Indian raid down the main valley, I slipped our goods over here. The Indians passed us by."

"John," I demanded, "that warning, how did it come?"

"One of Kelly's men came over the mountain. Most everybody got clear but lost their houses and goods. They say Yonido came down but was too late. The people are coming back, though. I'm helping all I can."

The story of my journeys and troubles had come to be an old thing to me from many tellings, yet I had to repeat it once more, this time using sticks, as Yonido had taught me, to mark the periods. Once the candle burned low, Hope replaced it. The hours dragged on until I finished and had answered all the questions asked me.

"But," I said, "that's enough of me. What happened here?" Wigton waved his hand.

"I said we were warned and lucky enough to get our things up here. Some other people, like the Forneys in the Nippenose, did not go. It was a fast-moving column that stuck pretty close to the river. I saw them several times. There's been no threat since, and we have used the horses to bring folks back." The big man was excited about getting to Washington. Now he rose and walked about the room.

"So," he said, "I'm to get to the camp in a month."

He crossed to the fireplace and made a mark on the stones with a bit of charcoal.

"There it begins, Hope. We'll make a mark each day." Hope smiled at me.

"He needs excitement, Simon. My father thrives on it and grows stale when things are peaceful."

One by one I asked about the settlers and learned who were safe. All evening I had been expecting Ezra Lyman because he was usually about Wigton when he could be, and I remembered how he had left the room in anger that night.

"Ezra," I asked. "Where is he tonight?"

Wigton looked at Hope who dropped her eyes when I stared at her.

"Dead, Simon. One of the few."

Ezra Lyman, dead, a man we would need on these rivers and with whom I had shared so many quiet campfires, so many miles on the trail. Wigton cleared his throat.

"It was in back of a rock on the Lycoming. There were signs that he had dropped two of them when one must have slipped round back of him and shot him with an arrow. He was not scalped for some odd reason. We buried him where he had fought. I used the horses to pull a big rock over his place."

"Simon," Hope said gravely, "Father showed him what you left in the Bible." Then her mood changed. "Ezra was very proud. I think, too, that he would have chosen to die in battle."

The death of this good friend saddened me, and later I stepped outside and listened to the talking of the river among the rocks. So much had happened. I thought of the great blue lakes up there in the Iroquois country, of the nicked gold piece, the burned scarf, the hatred of Norris. I felt that I had offered myself freely either to ransom or rescue Celine, who for so short a time had been my wife. Yet, I was no nearer the full truth of what happened now than when I had started up this river with an axe across my pommel.

CHAPTER NINE

WIGTON TOOK me on his patrol as far west as Great Island and the place where Reed's Fort had stood, pointing out the great shelf of rocks from which one could get a good look at the river for miles either way. But his mind was not on this scouting business; he was thinking of getting to Washington's camp and was counting the days. There was finally no holding him; he left three days before the month had elapsed, taking two horses.

Hope and I were left alone in the house on the Loyalsock for, in spite of what John had said, there were actually few people yet returned to stay permanently. Men had come and worked at their cabins, but most families were still down the river, waiting.

Spring was early this year, and occasionally Hope rode with me as I followed her father's routine of patrolling. We watched for the new flowers almost as much as we did for Indian signs. I kept telling Hope that snow would still lie deep in the great pine woods, that real danger, if it came, would come in late May or June.

Of the flowers, the arbutus seemed to give this girl of the frontier most pleasure, perhaps because it was early, perhaps because of its fragrance which is so elusive it never cloys. But we did find the windflower, the liverworts, the dusty trilliums which we call Jack-in-the-Pulpit, and she laughed when I squeezed this bloom near its base, saying that the tiny squeaky noise was caused by Jack's shoes pinching. When the wild honeysuckle appeared, she had great sprays of them in the house.

"I like flowers to be fragrant," she told me, and I stored that away in my mind with all the other things about her that made her so different from anyone else I had known.

She seemed pleased when I did things about the house, like making shelves or fashioning outdoor seats. I felled a great pine across the end of our ford and hewed it flat on the upper side so that it formed a bridge. She laughed.

"Those who used to come to this house had to wade. Now a bridge will make it easy for the neighbors."

And neighbors were coming in the bland spring weather, hardy people who wanted to get land in shape early. The Kings, near the Lycoming, had three cabins about finished. Bratton Caldwell was said to be on the opposite side of the river near where Fort Horn had been, though we had not seen him; and Simon Cool, deserting the Nippenose, already had his family with him a mile east of the Tiadaghton.

The new bridge pleased me so much I fixed a hand railing on it, and it was pleasant in the evening to walk out there and watch the reflection of the moon on the water.

Hope had kept the broken arrow that killed poor Major, and it lay on the fireplace mantel where no one touched it, reminding me of all the trouble that had come since. It was also a sort of barrier, indicating that the old carefree days when Hope was a good comrade had passed. As for her, I could not complain for want of her kindness. Yet, there was something, a sort of coldness about her, that seemed to shut me away. I was a good friend, nothing more.

Our tally of days showed that Wigton had been gone a full month, and both of us were a little uneasy about him though we did not talk of it. He had a disregard for danger, and one man with two good horses would be a temptation to either stray Indians or marauders abroad near the armies. So when we heard a hail from the top of Gunner's Hill, we dropped things and ran. Hope outdistanced me in spite of her skirts. Wigton was riding down the hill and swept Hope up beside him. I mounted the horse he was leading. And so we came home.

* * *

Wigton dearly loved going away, and more, coming home to place his long legs under his table and tell all he had heard and seen. So when I had stabled and fed his horses, I brought in a bottle of wine, which had been hidden in the hay, to aid our celebration.

John's stories were complete to the last detail and some of them very amusing.

"They would not let me see Washington at first so, after trying a couple of things, I just walked in. He was slicing meat with a long knife and pointed to a chair when he saw me. That man, Knox, was there and could have helped, but he just laughed. They did not give me any of the meat."

But both Washington and Knox had talked to him, and the news was both startling and gratifying. A Colonel Boone and a force of axemen and Rangers were to have moved in far up on the West Branch, from which place they were cutting a road to the great lake of the Eries. Supposedly, they were already at work. Then, a great army was to march against the Iroquois from the east and pin the tribes against whatever force moved up the new Boone road. Wigton pointed at me.

"Your orders, young man—" He grinned. "That's what Knox kept calling you. Your orders are to get to Boone and tell him there's no time to waste. He is to hurry and close the western door. They kept me down there until they were sure of things," he added.

"When do I go?" I asked, and Wigton scratched his head with his pipe stem.

"Why, at once, I guess. The word was hurry, and that's what I'd do."

That night, after Hope and her father had gone to their beds, I made my preparations which, after all, were simple. No directions had been given me as to how I would find Boone, but the river would lead me to him, and the message was plain. For the moment it looked a bit foolish, all this elaborate message bearing. First, I had been sent home with a vague suggestion that things were to happen; then Wigton had waited one month and spent nearly another until he was given a message that I should carry, and it was nothing more than that a man named Boone was to hurry with his brush and tree cutting.

Sitting there by the table on which my gear was spread, my thoughts were of Hope sleeping nearby, and I was suddenly bitter about her coldness. I had known her so long, and now she must realize what was moving within me. Perhaps I had not appreciated her until I saw her contrasted with Celine, but now I knew how blinded I had been by my own appetites back there in Fort Pitt. I thought bitterly that I had paid for my mistakes, but that did me no good.

So in an unreasoning mood and with no word to either of these good friends, I left the house a bit after midnight. I would not have them bearing me on my way or saying another casual goodbye. Besides, Wigton had been away a long time, his horses were tired, and the order was to hurry.

Boone was to close the Western Door. I wondered if either Washington or Knox knew what the magnitude of that task might be and wished that they had seen the gathering of the Long House people at Niagara.

* * *

It was pleasant to be on the march again when I had walked out the darkness and traveled in the freshness of the morning, noting how most of the buds had already broken. The hickories, which lately had carried what looked like masses of cotton inside the brown bud cases, now flaunted leaves, and there were plenty of scarlet maples showing grenadier colors along every stream.

I had passed the King places too early in the morning for anyone to be astir, but I did see smoke from the Cool cabin near the Tiadaghton, and that stream made me a deal of trouble trying to get over with dry buckskins. All this country through which I moved was rich land waiting, needing only resolute settlers. And these would come and stay once the cloud of danger to the north was destroyed.

Three good stiff days' traveling should take me to this man, Boone, if my calculations as to where he was were correct. I did not follow the river valley but went up on the ridges a short distance above the Great Island. There was fog along the big stream; up here on the hills it was comparatively clear.

I did not come down until I struck the creek we call Young Woman's, and that night I slept near the old Indian camping ground. Intent on my mission, I was careless about my camp, and because the sun was hidden, slept late the following morning to a most rude awakening.

The heavy kick of a moccasined foot jolted me from sleep and rolled my blanket-swathed body clear over so that I lay on my rifle. Three hard-looking men in buckskins and battered hats stood over me, reminding me exactly of the hard-bitten Tory scouts who marched with Butler and his Rangers. Looking at them, my thoughts were bitter. I had failed at Niagara; I had lost the map; I had not found Celine; now I had a definite mission for Washington which looked as though it would end in a matter of minutes. My pistol was in my belt, but it was one shot against three. I flung back the blanket and leaped to my feet.

"Now," I announced grimly, "if the cowardly son of a white mule who kicked me will wiggle his ears, I'll engage to feed them to him."

My three captors looked at me, their rifles all trained carelessly on my stomach. Then one man with wide shoulders and a thin slit for a mouth moved his thumb. I read the message in his eyes before he could draw back the hammer of his rifle.

My leap was too quick for him, and my headlong dive sent him rolling, his rifle flung yards away. The others jumped away to escape us for I followed and pounced on the man, hammering his face unmercifully until a rifle butt crashed home on my head, and the world exploded into blackness.

One of them must have thrown a hatful of water over me, for when I became conscious, my head and shoulders were dripping. My hands were tied securely behind me, and there was a looped rawhide strap about my neck. Four other men had joined the trio which had taken me, and a thin, well-shaven man seemed to be the leader, but I saw no Ranger insignia.

"Miller," he said bluntly, "lead the turkey cock and see he don't break his neck stepping into a hole or something. We'll see what the colonel says."

I walked along back of the big man they had called Miller and kept remembering that he had a scar on his face just under one eye. I thought of it every time I stumbled and the noose tightened, shutting off my breath until I gasped in desperation. We were moving westward at a fast pace, and I do not think that Miller once thought of the captive that he led like a cheap dog through brush that twitched the strap, and the stumblings became more and more agonizing.

There was only one satisfaction; we seemed to be moving into the country where I had expected to find Boone. These men might well be a part of a force sent to attack the road builders.

In mid-afternoon we came over a sharp, pointed hill and onto a scene of remarkable activity. Here was a huge camp spreading from the river well up the side of the hill, and along the river was what looked to be a small shipyard where a force of men worked on canoes or double-ended batteaus. Here were piles of tools: axes, augers, saws, grindstones, and rope. I realized that must be Boone's camp, that the men who had taken me were under his command.

Few paid any attention to our arrival, and we went up the hill to a large lean-to where some men sat on upended blocks of wood. At our approach they rose and left us facing a man in worn buckskins who remained seated.

The shoulders of this man showed the dark stain that comes from carrying a rifle. He wore a battered hat pushed well back on an unruly thatch of hair already dusted with gray. The remarkable feature of his face was its calmness, and the steady gray eyes reminded me of His Excellency.

"Colonel," the man with the strap jerked me forward, "we didn't obey orders today; we brought this fellow in."

The man on the block finished his inspection of me, then spoke in a low voice to the one who headed the party that had captured me.

"Well, Miles, it ain't too late."

I stared down at this man to whom I had been sent with a message, knowing that I was facing Boone and that he had just sentenced me to death as casually as he might have directed the killing of a snake. Perhaps I could tell him I was a messenger, but a bitter sense of disgust was nearer choking me than the noose Miller held.

Miller dropped the strap, bent, and picked it up, and I knew I should announce myself, but that seemed as impossible as escape. I thought of the scar on this man's face, of how he had dragged me through the brush. Then there was a yell, and a big bearded man pushed through the group.

With one gesture he threw the noose from my neck and pushed Miller back.

"Hell, Colonel," he roared, "what are you doing to Simon Braide? He was one of Gibson's Lambs, and you've got him tied up like an Indian dog."

The quiet colonel was on his feet as my friend cut me loose, drew me back, and rubbed my wrists.

"Just in time, Coley. These bloody-minded hellions were going to shoot me," I said, trying to keep my voice steady.

My rescuer had known me for years. He was John Coleman who had worked with my father on the trading strings, and it was like him to behave in this highhanded way.

Blood was stinging in my wrists. Abruptly I caught up the leash from where Coleman had thrown it. Miller went down before my first hard-driven blow, and I stood over him, lashing at him with the doubled thong until they pulled me away.

Coleman was grinning, but I noticed his hand was on the buckhorn haft of his knife. The colonel spoke, addressing me.

"Name's Boone. We got work to do and orders to keep live folks out of this country till we finish. The men was following orders. What's your business?"

We looked straight into each other's eyes, and there was no wavering on the part of either of us. My lips twisted; this was the way I was always received—by Brevecourt, by His Excellency. I even thought of Hope and her coldness. I wanted to turn away, to withhold my message. Then I remembered Knox fidgeting about in his too tight coat.

"I'm a messenger from Washington."

Boone turned from me to the men.

"There's daylight left. Better get back to work."

Alone with me, he gestured with a wide hand toward the moving men. "This is a hardish kind of crew, and we don't aim to let any news get out."

That was the closest this man ever came to an apology for the treatment I had received, and while I was not mollified, I could see some point in what had happened.

"Mister," the frontiersman continued, "you're still mad. If it would pleasure you to take a fall with me, I'd oblige, though I'd guess you could spot me a stone and a half, and I've heard that them Lambs was pretty tough sheep."

Then Boone's smile broke the rugged lines of his face and had its way until I threw back my head and laughed, partly in response to him, partly from thinking what would have happened to me had I put on this show of violence before one of Washington's martinets or a British sub-altern. This man who laughed with me was in charge of important work, commanded some hundreds of hard-boiled bordermen, yet he proposed a knock-down-and-drag-out struggle with me just to cool my temper. After all, my chief hurts had been to my pride.

Sobering, I passed along Washington's message, explaining how it had been brought to me, and about the big army which was supposed to move against the Iroquois. Boone knit his heavy brows and stopped smiling.

"Yes, I know about that army. Sullivan will lead it, and he's to go up the Chemung and beyond. Yes, there's real need for hurry if we're to get through to the lake."

He used a long forefinger for emphasis.

"Braide, this crew will cut road as fast as an army but—it's just too long a job. They didn't figure right. Now if I was to take the men I have through the brush, we'd get through with time to spare. And what's the use of a road with none to travel it."

He shook his head as if trying to rid his mind of its perplexity.

* * *

In the next few days, I learned a great deal about this work the colonel had been called from his beloved Kentucky to accomplish. The road began at the river and flung itself over the hills, with no regard for grades, and across the valleys in a direct line for the lake of the Eries. Light troops could use it to block the escape of the People of the Long House if they were pushed from the east by an army, for the Senecas would have the other tribes rolled against them.

Boone would have his troubles out there on the Niagara, facing British troops and hordes of desperately fighting warriors. Yet, looking at his men, I felt he would give an excellent accounting, for all those he led were tough fighters and used to the sort of odds they might encounter if the colonel were allowed to lead them. But, to me, the best thing about this force was the fact that raiding Indians could not come down the river while it was there. Here was a body of men and a commander who could have stopped Butler and his Rangers when they raided the Wyoming valley.

A man named Allardyce managed the boatyard where light craft seemed to grow like magic. Presumably these boats and canoes would be sent downriver to bring up any force planning to use the new road. But it was the road itself that intrigued me. Stumps were cut low to allow the passage of wagons or guns; soft places were bridged with corduroys of poles, and two streams were spanned, the stringers being great white pine logs over which were laid smaller timbers and the whole covered with earth to make smooth going.

The big trees that had to be felled were cut directly away from the road itself, so there was no breastwork along the highway to shelter attackers. On the hills was something that chilled me a bit. At points where one could look long distances each way, riflemen were posted. No man could move along this road unless he was in range of a well-placed patched bullet.

Boone took me out to where the axemen labored in pairs. Tall, powerful men these were. They would step up to a huge pine and swing their heavy axes alternately into the cut they were making, and it took them but a few minutes to drop a three-foot pine. As I watched, it was to marvel at the precision with which their heavy, keen tools were used. During daylight, the sound of the axe blows was never stilled. Boone spoke of this particular body of men.

"Them's hard ones, and they need some hellin' around every once in a while. It'll be hard to hold them 'gin another month goes by."

Apparently Boone liked to have me with him and asked me to take some compass sights on his construction. He was pleased when I showed him how accurately he had worked, using only his eyes for the sighting. But he did not like his assignment.

"It ain't the sort of job I like, Simon. There's too many men. There ought to be a general or somebody like that here. I'd rather be out with Coleman, watching for the Indians."

I had one chance to talk with Coleman, who explained what he did.

"We just rub out what we find, and we've handled two fair-sized war parties and a scattering of others. We shoot careful and bury them deep. If the Senecas got word we was here, they'd be down on us like white-headed hornets."

He took me into his lean-to and opened a small box from which he took odds and ends of things to show me: bear claw necklaces, stone pipes, weapons. He picked up a small buckskin bag.

"One of the boys got the fellow that owned this pretty well north of here. Look what he had."

He turned out on his broad palm some delicately colored beads, perhaps a dozen of them, a bright piece of cloth that might have been part of a white woman's dress, and a single golden sovereign which I took from his hand to examine. But there was no tell-tale nick in it, nothing to connect it with Celine's hoard.

That evening when I sat with Boone and Coleman out at a watch point where we had cooked our supper of meat and corn pone, I began telling them of the Indians about Niagara. Boone leaned forward abruptly and asked:

"Why was you up there?"

There was a vague edge of suspicion in his tone, and I told enough of my story to explain—the wrecking of my house and my haste to try to ransom my wife, and how I had been caught in Butler's raid. Both plied me with questions, and Boone delivered his opinion, so like that of others that it did not make much of an impression on me.

"Don't look Indian to me. Those devils has to spill blood. Mebbe they was after something else."

* * *

Boone's fears about keeping the men in order showed they were well founded two evenings later when he and I, with several others, were seated in his lean-to. A commotion started well down the long camp street. The colonel's rifle leaned in a corner, but his knife was in its sheath. He rose promptly and walked in the direction of the noise. I followed.

The trouble was at a mess tent where the cook and two helpers cowered in back of a board counter, facing two of the big axemen, one of whom had the cook's boy helper by the hair. With the other hand, the man brandished a knife. The second one held an axe.

"Liquor," the fellow with the boy demanded. "Liquor, or this pup gets scalped."

To me, it appeared that the men had already been drinking.

Boone edged through the ring of watchers before he was noticed. The boy's tormentor yanked his victim closer to the cook, and his knife arm, held aloft, was directly in front of the frame that held open the front of the tent. Boone's movement was quick as lightning; his own knife was thrown with such force that it pinned the axeman's arm against the board support. The man who carried the axe leaped forward to drive his keen-edged weapon through Boone's skull, but the colonel dived low, plunged forward, and threw the attacker sprawling.

The circle of watchers moved back, firelight shining on their surprised faces. Boone crossed to the tent and picked up a heavy oaken stick used to stir the big soup kettles. The thing was fully six feet in length and all of two inches square.

The man with the arm pinned fast had loosed the boy and stood whimpering while blood ran down his arm. Boone stepped up to him, yanked out the knife, wiped it on the fellow's shirt, then sheathed it. Methodically he beat the wounded man with the stick until he dropped to the ground and was still. The second man tried to crawl away, but Boone caught him and administered the same kind of beating. Finished, the colonel returned the stick to the cook and spoke quietly.

"Better bring all your cooking liquor over to my lean-to."

I noticed that Boone was not even breathing deeply after his swift actions, and it was plain that he, of all the men I had ever met, would be the most dangerous to have for an enemy. I was glad I had not been fool enough in my anger that day to accept his proposition of trying a fall with him.

Yet, within a week, this big gray-eyed frontiersman showed me a side of his nature that was radically different. Leaving Allardyce in charge of the whole operation, he and I scouted miles ahead of the axemen where the forest was heavy with giant rhododendron, flaunting their high blooms in the shadows of the pine woods. On the more open hills, laurel bloomed and columbines spread their dusty purple. I saw that Boone noticed and liked flowers.

"I like summer flowers," he told me gravely, "but witch hazel means most to me because it blooms last, when the leaves are down. It kinda shoves winter back a little."

Returning to the chopping, we were more than halfway back to camp beyond the second ridge when Boone's hand jerked to the battered hat he always wore, and immediately the crack of a rifle sounded to our right. One could not have counted three before there was a second report; then above us we heard the light thump, thump of a rifleman reloading his weapon.

We found the dead man lying on the spot from which he had fired, a round hole through his forehead. It was the man with the knife Boone had wounded and beaten, the bandage still on his arm. We walked on up to the watch point where the trail watcher was priming his piece.

"A little high, Walker," Boone said, "unless you was sure."

The marksman corked his powder horn, spat into the brush.

"I wuz sure, Colonel."

Again, I felt something like nausea at the entire lack of feeling shown. Probably Boone had been in Indian country so long he, like the natives, had no feeling for pain given or taken. The wilderness is a remorseless place. Such a man as this road builder was good at fighting because of his chilling lack of feeling.

Coleman shared the evening with us. Boone was talkative, explaining how he had brought this force in from Fort Pitt, over the mountains with the equipment packed on their backs, under orders from Washington. Since that time, he had only contacted the outside world once, when a paymaster and his guards had appeared. He worried aloud about the road.

"You say, Simon, the Iroquois can't muster more than twenty-five hundred; Sullivan had ought to send a fast column this way and take to the woods. We'd get through and keep things hot till the big army came up, and the Indians would be finished."

No man knew better than I did the long way to the lakes. This road was moving at excellent speed, but it would be months before it was completed, if it even were possible this summer. I thought of Butler who cut no road, of Clark in the west. Later in the evening, Boone made his decision.

"Get to Sullivan, Simon. Tell him there just ain't enough time, but if he'll send me a light column. I'll take it through to the big lake. I'll send boats down to bring his men up here."

In the morning the colonel personally selected a canoe and stood by until he saw that I had food and that my equipment was in good shape.

"Don't take any chances, Simon. You saw how things is up here. I'm hoping this big general will be faster than some, or there's likely to be no road, no door-closing, and mebbe no Boone."

He was still standing there at the landing when I started round the bend. When I waved a hand to him, he gestured awkwardly as a man will who is unaccustomed to such things.

And gratefully I carried my "safe" feeling with me. Those men and those rifles were a stone wall so long as they remained on these upper reaches of the Susquehanna.

CHAPTER TEN

THE TRIP downriver was uneventful enough. Had it not been for the screening force of Boone's men in the hills, I would have needed to watch for ambush at the bends or where timber and brush came down to the water. But that fear was gone, and it was a comfort to feel easy about the river people who had returned to our valleys. The colonel's men played roughly enough, but they made excellent frontier guards.

There was little for me to do but think as I slipped quietly down-stream, and I turned my personal problems over and over in my mind. I could see now more clearly why Washington had told Knox to have me draw that first map which might have been useful either to Boone or Sullivan. It was some comfort to know that, after the misery of that march with Butler, I could make a chart of territory our men could not know otherwise—the dark Iroquois country.

Then I thought of Celine and why she had married me and seemed so content at first, then had become a harridan at the mention of leaving Fort Pitt. There was small reason a girl who loved light and gaiety should be so attached to a place of small dirty houses and cramped quarters. There were only a few shops about the fort, and parties were few and far between. My feeling of guilt at having brought her to the Loyalsock was fading, for I could not believe her the tormented victim of savages, nor dead in the forest.

Thinking of Celine brought me round to Hope. Before she had gone away to school, which was months before I left to go west to join the Lambs, she had been like a cheerful, friendly sister. Now there were seldom flashes of the old friendliness. It was hard to face the possibility that my infatuation with Celine had disgusted her and cheapened me in her sight. Certainly I had no claim on her, nor aught else. She would, and did, give me the kindness due anyone, and particularly friends of her father; that was all.

* * *

My logical route would have been to follow the Susquehanna to the mouth of the Loyalsock, then up past my home and beyond to the North Branch of the Susquehanna, which would lead me to Sullivan and his army. But hungry as I was for a sight of level fields, I held to the mountain by the river. I beached my canoe in a thicket at the mouth of the Lycoming and struck across country to come to my own valley north of my farm.

So, traveling too fast to be cautious, I encountered John Wigton and Yonido in the narrow place where the valley is crowded by the hills. I did not see them until they were too close for me to escape by climbing the hill, and I could not hide near where they would pass because of the keen eyes of that Indian.

John Wigton was glad to see me, though we both remembered that I had left that morning without word to him. When I dropped my hands from the Indian sign of peace and came forward on the trail, he rested his crossed hands on his pommel and sat for a moment,

"You've just come upriver, Simon?"

"No, John, I cut over the hills from the Lycoming. Is all clear below?"

"Yes," he said shortly and dismounted, followed by Yonido.

"Tell us about your trip, Boone and his plans."

With the horses tied to brush, we sat down, and I gave these friends a brief summary of my adventures on the river and of Boone's work and perplexity.

"So," I finished, "I'm to get word for Boone to Sullivan, wherever he is."

Wigton sniffed, making almost as much noise as one of his horses doing the same thing. "No trouble there. Just follow the burned villages and corn fields."

He allowed that remark to sink in, then continued. "Since Clinton joined him, he has nigh five thousand men somewhere on the Chemung. He fought the Indians in one battle, but there was only a handful of them and they ran at the sound of the cannon."

"Cannon?" I questioned.

"Yes, he even has siege pieces with him, and he's built a big fort where the Chemung enters the Susquehanna. Now he's marching, burning villages and crops."

Disgust was strong in Wigton's tones. To this big horseman, destroying food was both a calamity and a crime.

He glanced at Yonido, who, so far, had no opportunity to speak. "My brother remembers the man, Norris, does he not?"

I nodded, and the Indian hurried on.

"Before Sullivan marched, he was trying to get a raid on these valleys started. They listen to him in Niagara, but Colonel Butler would not march with the Senecas. Sullivan has stopped such raids only for a time. Norris is said to hate these valleys."

Wigton nodded.

"We have more, Simon. We do not think Challis is a good Whig as he claims. There are stories that people come and go from his house at night, some of them in the wrong uniform, some with feathers in their hair. We have watched but have seen nothing—so far."

We stood up, and Wigton, now that he was talked out, seemed to forget his coldness. After all, we were close partners in business, and before that he had been with my father. He had known me since I was a boy. Impulsively, he placed his hand on my shoulder.

"Simon, I have a feeling you're in danger, but I cannot explain why. It looks as though something or somebody wants to destroy you. Watch that general to whom you go."

I smiled, trying to be assuring, but Wigton seldom spoke that way without good reason. Yonido and I clasped hands ceremoniously, touching the scars on our wrists with a hidden motion of fingers, then I moved out on the trail and had traveled a good way before I heard their horses moving down river.

* * *

The backwash of an army is an unlovely thing, and I encountered that of Sullivan's force about ten miles below the new fort where an old Indian village used to stand. Here in the field was broken equipment past mending, horses buried in too shallow graves, fragments of paper, bits of cloth, and the inevitable discarded hats. Between this place and the fort, I came to the camp of two women and a man, as definitely a part of the army debris as the scraps of paper. They were civil enough to give directions, and presently I had my first glimpse of a part of the great expedition, one of the boats far out on the river that would be bringing up supplies. It made slow progress, and I watched the work of those who poled it for a while.

The new fort amazed me for one of the most powerful armies the colonies had so far put into the field was moving against a people who could not muster half its number; yet, here in the rear, was a bastion strong enough to stand cannon fire. It stood where the Chemung and the North Branch meet, almost at the site where Butler had his camp. And it commanded both rivers with its guns.

The collection of well-built cabins near the fort housed the wives and officers, and there was an excellent place for wounded soldiers. I felt I had no time to visit here, but I did find a private who had been badly burned in the destruction of a village. He informed me that the army was far to the north, that the general was not well, that the men were unhappy about destroying grain. He was indeed a loquacious and eager fellow. Next morning, he located a Sergeant Garth who, with two troopers, was taking medical supplies to the army. I rode with them on a borrowed horse.

Twelve miles out of Fort Sullivan, we encountered the first devastation where all that remained alive of what had been a village was a swarm of flies. The corn was down, apple and peach trees girdled. Garth informed me that even the dogs had been shot.

The army had built a better road than the one on upon which Boone labored, but here the grades were mild, though they had more trouble with swampy places and river crossings. We four mounted men made good progress following the road and, late in the afternoon of the second day, came upon the army at its work.

There had been another village here with long low communal houses that had won the name of People of the Long House for the Iroquois. It was now a mass of smoking ruins, and the soldiers were spread out, plying bayonets in the corn and axes on the fruit trees. We rode through the workers at a slow pace, stopping occasionally when challenged by some officer.

Beyond the scene of destruction, on a hill, was the army camp, and Sergeant Garth pointed to the big headquarters tents. There was a big staff attached to the three major generals, he explained, and any number of brigadiers and colonels. Boone had told me that Hand, who had commanded at Pitt, would be with Sullivan. I had seen him out there, a big florid man noted for his patience, but I had never known him personally.

When I had been turned over to a sentry who, in turn, summoned the officer of the guard, I stood, while waiting, admiring the long, straight camp streets, the neat tents, the stone cooking places.

A lieutenant of the Line appeared, a young fellow wearing a good buff and blue uniform.

"I am a messenger," I told him, "come from Colonel Boone on the Susquehanna to General Sullivan."

The young officer saluted smartly, then looked uncomfortable when he noted that I was a civilian, and afterward he seemed a little irritable. He went to the tents and rejoined me in a few minutes.

"The general will see the messenger this evening at eight o'clock, after he has dined."

This time the young man did not make the mistake of wasting a salute when he left me.

Of course there was no reason for the feeling of irritation I had. A major general in charge of a great expedition is a busy man with each hour of his time taken for crucial decisions. I had traveled far and knew that Boone was desperate for some word to guide him; yet I must wait on military formality.

Promptly at eight, having had the services of a camp barber in making myself presentable, I waited just inside the main headquarters tent.

The big marquee blazed with candlelight, and it was thronged with officers, some of whom sat at small tables while others stood about talking in low tones. At the far end of this tent, in back of a table, a man was seated who seemed to be in authority because, from time to time, others would approach him, speak a word, or lay a paper on the already littered table. Nobody paid any attention to me after I had been admitted, and I had this chance to study General Sullivan, whom I assumed to be the man at the table. He was tall with badly powdered hair that showed reddish in the light. His forehead was high and went well with his long sharp nose and closely set eyes. Altogether, it was the face of a quick, impatient man, and deep down within me, I felt a stirring of caution. Bad luck had certainly followed this general at Long Island, relenting at Trenton, reasserting itself in his relations with Congress. He was, however, a friend of Washington, a loyal one.

The general's quill stopped its loud scratching, and he looked up with a frown as I stepped forward and bowed to him politely. His voice snapped at me like a trap.

"Why don't you salute?"

Of all the questions this man might have asked me, this one was probably the last I could have expected. My face colored, and I felt the scar along my chin. Nearby an officer smiled at my evident chagrin. "Sir, I am a civilian come from Colonel Boone with a message."

Sullivan twisted his lean body in his chair; it was plain some other trouble had irritated him before I faced him. Now he needed a whipping boy, and my appearance gave him his chance.

"Great God," he snarled. "The fellow is a civilian and has followed us into this heathenish wilderness. He does not salute; he says he comes from Colonel Boone."

His stress on the word "colonel" showed his contempt for the man who labored with his difficulties high on the West Branch.

"I presume," he went on sneeringly, "you have come for soldiers to defend your miserable log cabins, perhaps for money."

"Sir," my own voice sounded brittle and sharp, "I can defend my own cabin, and I do not need money."

To one side of the tent, there was a badly covered chuckle. I could not turn to see who it was but hurried on, feeling sure that sound had not helped my errand.

"Colonel Boone received a verbal message from His Excellency to close the Western Door, and Boone now asks for a flying column to lead to Lake Erie because he feels sure he cannot finish his road in the time expected. He feels that troops must hurry to stop the Indians you are driving westward, and light soldiery could get through the forest."

Sullivan was glaring down at his clenched fist on the table. Now he leaped to his feet and paced back and forth.

"So," he roared, "a backwoods colonel sends advice which he presumes to state comes from His Excellency by a civilian. I am to divide my forces in the presence of the enemy on the basis of this excellent planning."

I stood quietly through the tirade, waiting until he would listen again, but when I did speak, I seemed thoroughly to arouse the man and remember too late the controversy in Washington's headquarters, the one started by Colonel Burr.

"General Sullivan, there are not more than twenty-five hundred warriors among the Iroquois, and the British muster far less than half that force at Niagara. You can—"

I got no further for he stopped me with a roar of anger; then he put his question:

"Niagara—were you there?"

I faced the man, feeling sure I had talked myself into real trouble, but, after all, I felt I could have expected a decent hearing. I was only telling the truth. His face wore a look of gloating that crowded the anger from it like a man who has stalked his prey and sees it trapped. I had said I had been in the fort of the enemy. He stepped round the table, a hand half raised.

I felt he planned to strike me. This was worse than Brevecourt, than the trouble getting to Boone, and the interview with Washington. Each time I had tried to be of service, I had encountered violence or disbelief.

"Answer me, you lout!"

There are army officers who think they terrify when they roar at a man, but I felt no fear, only disgust that a man leading a great army could stoop to insult and browbeat a messenger. Perhaps my expression revealed my contempt to him and the watching, listening officers. When I spoke, I crowded every bit of anger I felt into my tone, but I kept my voice down as I addressed this man, whose face was livid, his hand raised to strike me.

"If you touch me. I'll break your damned neck!"

Stillness dropped in that tented room as it comes after heavy snow falls. Before Sullivan could speak or I add to my effrontery, an officer who had stood close behind me stepped forward and faced the irate general.

"General Sullivan, sir, I know this man. He is Simon Braide, one of Gibson's Lambs of whom you have heard. He helped bring the powder up to Fort Pitt from the Spanish lands."

The officer grinned, showing his white teeth.

"Braide is a mapmaker for His Excellency; some of the charts we are using are his work."

I recognized the officer defending me as Major Parr, who was my neighbor at home, living south of us along the river just over the ridges. A big, powerful man, his grip when he laid his hand on my shoulder was almost like the snap of a bear trap.

Surprisingly, General Sullivan returned to his chair as if his outbursts had exhausted him. Major Parr walked back to his place at the tent wall. I realized how much this man had done in risking his military reputation to face down his commander in defense of me, who had insulted the general in the presence of his staff.

The tent was silent. Sullivan sat staring down at the paper that littered the table. Once he raised a hand and moved an ink pot, he paid no further attention to me but sat as a man will when he feels himself alone with his thinking. I no longer existed to this commander of the army sent to destroy the Iroquois.

There was nothing to do but turn and walk out of the tent. The colonel held the door open for me and grinned, but whether in sympathy or derision, I had no way of knowing.

Parr found me later and took me to his tent where we talked for hours. The big rifleman was both optimistic and gloomy. He knew this army could destroy both the Iroquois and the English at Niagara, but he was sure it would not press things home as it could and should.

"Sullivan's sick, as you saw tonight, and the sickness is of the heart and head. God knows the devils that drive the man. Some say it is money trouble, some say it is because this big army was detached from Washington's slender command and sent on this far expedition. Sullivan knows His Excellency feared to weaken his army by sending even a company to defend the frontier lest that tempt Clinton to attack. Sullivan will not risk this army, nor will he feel any ease until he has it back in Easton again. Simon, what's this Niagara business?"

Again, I had to unfold the story of my wanderings, of the manpower of the tribes, of Boone's troubles, of the apprehensions of Knox. Parr shifted about in his chair.

"Simon, I've learned to leave the strategy to the generals. I lead my men in, and we shoot it out."

Impatiently he unsnapped his belt and flung it with the heavy sheathed knife and wicked pistol onto the table.

"This expedition will turn back after we reach Little Beard's Town on the Genessee."

I stared at him, aghast at what that would mean to us on the frontier.

"Turn back!" I cried. "Great God! They can hear Niagara's sunset gun from there."

"Yes," he insisted, "I should not have told even you, but Sullivan already has orders to go no further than that."

He grinned broadly. "And we've dragged heavy siege pieces all the long way from Easton."

"Well," I announced, coming back to my own problem, "it was hard to convince them in Niagara that I was a Tory; Boone's hellions all but shot me; now your red-faced general yowls at me like a tree cat when I give him a message. Next time I carry word it will be from someone who will write it down."

Parr sobered abruptly.

"Simon, get out of here as soon as you can. Nothing you can do will help Boone; nobody could do that. This army will turn back, and Boone will leave the river. Then God help our West Branch country. Get back, Simon. Round up everything, every man and boy who can shoot. Watch the trails. The scalpers will be down on our valleys before this army's in Easton."

CHAPTER ELEVEN

NEXT MORNING, I sat before the tent Parr had assigned to me, and in which I had spent a comfortable night once I shut my mind to the unpleasant things of the evening and gave myself over to sleep. But now I was thinking about the scene which my coming had precipitated. My concern was for Boone and whether I had wrecked his plans in presenting them. Surely if the retreating savages were not stopped at the lakes, this great force Sullivan led would do little more than the devastation they had now accomplished.

"Close the Western Door." That was Washington's word relayed to me by Wigton. If it were not done—

My thinking was cut short by the arrival of my lieutenant of the previous day, who now stood before me in all his dignity so that I had to repress a smile. "Mr. Braide."

I rose and looked at him.

"General Sullivan directs me to advise you that he has sent messengers to the man, Boone, directing him to take his men out of the woods at once. His orders are that you remain with this army until he directs you otherwise."

I stared at the fellow, aghast. "That is impossible. You must be wrong."

The young officer said no more but turned smartly and left me to hunt Parr and pour the news into his ears. The rifleman was not surprised.

"I told you last night, Simon, things would happen, that we have orders to turn back. So Sullivan sends Boone out of the woods. What the hell does he care if there's no protection for our country?" He tapped me on the chest with a huge forefinger.

"Mark me, too, Simon. It won't all be Sullivan's fault. You and I will never know what goes on among the big boys, what they plan. We fellows who run the errands and shoot the rifle guns are just like chessmen on the board."

He spat carefully into the dust and left me to go about his business.

* * *

Through rich summer days I traveled with this army, marveling at the efficiency of it as a destructive machine which could make a village a black scar in a few hours or level standing cornfields in even less time. The soldiers spoke of this corn:

"Got nothing like this down home—stalks fourteen feet high, two ears—planted closer'n ours."

Parr took me with him and a squad that reconnoitered northward to the great lake of the Senecas where it lies between low bluffs, blue as any unclouded sky. Here, grapes grew in profusion in thickets that bent under the weight of the vines. Wild plums hung ripe and tangy for the taking, and the groves of chestnut trees looked like planted orchards.

Several Indians had been captured here, among them an old crone who seemed to have been abandoned by her people. She sat at the door of a small hut we set up for her and smoked a vile laurel wood pipe on which was carved the rude likeness of a snake. Altogether, she was sheer animal, snatching up food tossed to her and squawling like a cat at anyone who came close. When Parr and I approached, she looked squarely at us, then abruptly pointed a dirty forefinger at me and jabbered something. Parr grinned.

"Your friend seems to know you, Simon."

"What did she say?"

He shook his head. "Couldn't get it at all; it was something about smelling death—fortune-telling stuff."

He did not say more, but I noticed he looked at me queerly several times, to my amusement, because I did not think the big rifleman would take any stock in a fortune teller.

* * *

The army moved north and westward, past the greater lakes, through the forest country into the parklike Genessee country, where the grass grew higher than a man's waist and tired a man pushing through it. Corn-fields were everywhere, and villages dotted the land so that the sharpened bayonets and torches of the soldiers were seldom unused.

We were touching places now where I had traveled with Butler and finally reached the point on the river just above the gorge up through which Yonido and I had gone on our mad journey north. There had been scattered firing ahead late in the afternoon, and reports were that two soldiers had been killed, the first since we took the village of Kendaia.

My patience was at a low ebb; for months I had encountered nothing but failure and frustration. The map was gone; I had failed with my warn-ing; Boone had been sent from his labors. I knew I should hunt Celine, but I could hit on no plan other than possibly trying to get to Oswego. But finding her among the British and coming to an understanding with her meant risking another noose. Perhaps I had risked enough.

Suddenly I was resolved. I would follow this monotonous march of destruction no farther. Not being a soldier, certainly I was not subject to Sullivan's orders. There was relief in packing my gear that evening there in the tent. Pistol, rifle, axe, knife, and warbag, all were ready, and a squad cook filled a bag with parched corn, dried meat, a small package of salt, and another of cornmeal. He asked no questions and was glad to get a silver shilling for his pains, but he did say dourly: "Mark me well, this army will have empty bellies before it gets home."

At my agreeing nod, he continued.

"The men say there is a broad road homeward, and the folks there need the corn we burn each day. You marked the cribs at Kendaia where it burned like cannel coal, and if you destroy, you'll want. I've no time for Indians, but their good corn ought to be carried home."

Everything was in readiness, and I was debating whether to tell Parr when the inevitable lieutenant appeared. He always seemed to hit on the times of my decisions.

"General Sullivan wants you in his tent."

The place was certainly familiar, just as well lighted as before, most of the same officers there, even Parr looking grim, and I recognized General Hand whom I had seen at Pitt. He stood close to the table in back of which sat Sullivan whose face was set in a scowl.

"You are Simon Braide?"

I simply stared at him. He knew who I was, but I sensed the tension in the air as he continued.

"You claim to have done map work for His Excellency?"

"Yes, sir; I am familiar with northern Pennsylvania and did some work on his maps."

It was evident that Sullivan's questions were pointed to inform the listening officers. Suddenly he leaned to one side, snatched up a roll from the floor, and flung it open. It was a map of northern Pennsylvania and purported to be also of southern New York. I glanced at it swiftly, then shook my head and pointed to a line of hills.

"The map is incorrect, sir. Misleading. The Burnett Hills are wrong."

He nodded, drew the map to him, glanced at the bottom, then thrust it back at me. On the lower right-hand corner was a signature—my own!

He whipped up another roll from the floor, flung it out, and showed the signature again.

"Sir," I almost stammered, "this is not my work. Military maps seldom bear the signature of the man who does them. They are incorrect, misleading."

Again, the nod and the lips pressed tightly together. "Exactly. They are misleading, Braide, though they came through regular channels. I thought you merely a poor engineer until—"

Now his face showed an unholy triumph as he placed before me a triangular piece torn from a map. It was the lower right-hand corner of a chart; there on the margin were notations in my own hand, the explanations of the tiny figures on the map itself. Below was written:

"Data to military map added by Simon Braide." Tremendous excitement gripped me as I recognized this portion of the map that had caused me so much trouble, so many dangers and doubts. I felt the blood pounding in my temples, and my hands shook as I tried to take the fragment from the general's hands.

"Sir," I said, "that map was on my drawing board when the Indians raided my home, carried away my wife and servant, killed my dog, partly burned my house. Where is my wife? I have gone to Niagara; I have—"

My words had come close to shouting when Sullivan's voice cut through.

"You were in Niagara?"

"Yes."

"When?"

"Just before Butler's raid on the Wyoming. I was taken along—"

"And brought no warning to the settlers in your own valley?"

There was something monstrous here; all the officers were listening, and Sullivan's voice carried the dry threat of a rattlesnake about to strike. Celine—this man knew something. He tapped the map fragment, and I saw Parr edge nearer. What control I had snapped.

"Where is my wife? I do not care a damn for your foul suspicions!" I roared. "This map was taken from a dead British civilian who, with others, attacked one of our scouting parties this afternoon. It is undoubtedly one of our own military maps supplied to the army and on which you worked. As for your wife—I venture she is happier with another more—"

Parr's mighty arms saved the general as I leaped forward with no other thought than to tear that gloating face and stifle that derisive voice. I felt as though I were wading through a deep river or a mighty snow, and my breath came in gasps as they pulled me back.

"Therefore, Simon Braide, you will be hanged by the neck thirty-six hours from now on the charge of giving aid to the enemy. That will be the day after tomorrow morning, my violent friend."

The tent was still, the officers standing stiff as ramrods. No one seemed to have expected the matter to go this far. Likely they had thought of a court martial, forgetting that I was not a soldier. I still strained at Parr's grip, and he had my mouth covered with his palm as General Hand stepped forward.

"Sir, I commanded at Fort Pitt and know something of this man's services. I demand a fair trial for him."

Sullivan was up, his face apoplectic.

"Day after tomorrow morning, this man hangs. Not a soldier, he will receive no court martial. He is a civilian taken while aiding the enemy."

Hand, his voice still calm and showing no signs of whatever emotion was in him, stared a long minute into the face of his irate superior.

"General Sullivan, I would not treat a trapped Seneca as you have treated this man a few days ago and now. If you and I are in the army six months from now when the campaign closes, you will answer to me for this action."

* * *

There was a crude log house a little distance from the main camp, and here I was taken and locked up with another prisoner who proved to be a weathered little man, seemingly morose at the idea of having company. When he had taken one look at me in the light of the guard's lanthorn, he crawled into his bunk and pretended to sleep. An hour later, he was more civil, said his name was Jedediah Sledel, though everybody called him Jed. He was in the guardhouse for shooting an Indian baby in a burning home. At my expression of disbelief, he explained.

"The house was fired before we knowed it was in there, and you could see it through the fire in one of them frames. I shot the brat so it wouldn't burn."

"But," I demanded, "why jail?"

He laughed bitterly. "I'm to get a hundred lashes, when and if they get around to it, for not letting it burn."

I did not have too much faith in this preposterous story, but a little later the guard appeared and took Jed outside. Then he ushered in Parr. The rifleman was extremely angry and disturbed so that his voice shook when he started talking.

"Sullivan is nigh daft, Simon. He's so sure you are a spy that there is no reasoning with the man, and enough of the officers are with him to make his death sentence stick. You see, none of them knows your story, and there isn't enough time to get to Washington and back."

"Well," I said, "at last I do have something settled. They raided my house for the map, whatever else they may have wanted. My wife must be up here somewhere. The finding of the piece of map proves it."

"No," Parr demurred, "I doubt if she's up here, or your offer of ransom would have brought something out. Who of the neighbors down home knew you worked on military charts?"

I shrugged my shoulders.

"Everybody, likely. You know there are few secrets in a country like ours."

"Challis," he said shortly. "You're the sort of damned fool that trusts everybody. Now, I don't. Your wife hated that country; she had money, and there was a valuable map in the house. Challis with his odd friends lived close. I never trusted that man; he's too smooth. They say Norris was once seen there."

"Norris!" I cried. "When?"

He studied a moment. "Some time before the war, I guess, but he was at Challis Hall."

I jumped up and paced back and forth in the small room. Norris in our valley, Challis doubtful, Celine and the map, but where was the rest of the chart? What had they done with it if they did take it, and why did the man who died on the Genessee carry only a part of the map? I thought of Celine, the iron will behind her seeming softness, and her way of destroying a man's judgment.

Parr's rough voice stopped me. "You got any money?"

I showed a half dozen gold pieces, of which he took three without explanation.

"Hate like hell to have a neighbor hanged, especially one who helped my boy. You see, I remember how you saved him on the big river from a savage death at the hands of an Indian warrior. Watch around midnight, and if anything happens that you get away, take Sledel with you. He's deserted twice, and a hundred lashes would cripple him. But remember—if you get away, all the officers will be sure you are guilty. The other way you'll be dead, and that kind of man looks bad and is no manner of use."

We looked at each other in the poor light of the lanthorn, and both wanted to say more. Parr had shown his courage in defending me, risking a court martial. Now he dared more, if I understood what he planned.

"Gibson told me about the boy, Simon, how you risked your own hair for his. He's quite a lad. If you get out of this mess, sometime when you're on the White Deer, come and drink a cup of cider with us."

Sledel was full of talk and veiled questions when he returned, but I was in a poor mood to talk to him for my mind was on Parr and the risks he might be taking. Furthermore, his hints about Challis and Norris bothered me, especially because they checked with Wigton's suspicions.

"It's a Delaware warhead," Hope had said, and she had seen more of these arrows in Challis Hall on our visit.

Nostalgia gripped me. When a second morning came round, I would die, and tonight I wanted to see the clear river again and hear its song among the rocks. I wanted to watch a deer fling up its head and see its flag vanish in the timber. And, even more, I wanted to see the level fields against the hill. Guiltily, I thought of another picture, Hope in the doorway with her sleeves falling back from rounded arms and the breeze having its way with her loosened hair.

I missed my breakfast by oversleeping in the morning, but the noon meal was good enough. Sledel talked a lot, mostly about horses and his wonder that Sullivan had not seemed to find or destroy the strings of British cavalry horses kept among the Indians.

"Our gun teams is about shot, and them British horses are good. I've seen them," he insisted.

When he had eaten to repletion, he belched loudly, and I must have frowned for he grinned.

"Funny, that's polite among Indians, and the housewives down our way expect something like it after a big meal."

With careful deliberation, he filled and lighted a short black pipe, and the cloud of smoke he produced drove me to my own briar in defense. Sledel was using Indian tobacco which is pungent stuff.

"Could I get clear of this place," he said musingly, "I'd get me back to Berks County fast. I've got a little farm down there and had two horses I was forced to sell when I joined the army. But I couldn't get away from here, even if they'd open the door. The woods would get me if the Indians didn't, and I kinda believe they'd make it hot for any straggler they picked up."

I nodded, and Sledel chuckled. Then he was suddenly sober. All the fun was gone, and he struck his brown hands together smartly.

"All I want is to get me out of the grip of that nasty . . ."

The man's profanity was straight Dutch, and therefore I could not follow it closely, but it concerned Sullivan, and from the occasional English word Sledel used, I felt I was fully in accord with it.

CHAPTER TWELVE

RAIN BEGAN sometime in the afternoon, the drops coming in the leaky roof until we were compelled to shift our bunks a number of times in order to keep reasonably dry. The evening meal was a sketchy one shoved in by a bedraggled guard anxious to have his chores finished. During the long evening, the downpour increased in violence until it roared on the clapboards outside, and rivulets coursed across our floor. Stepping anywhere meant wet feet, so we clung to our bunks.

It seems odd that a man who has only a few hours to live should be drowsy, but I did fall soundly asleep sometime in the evening and woke to a room that was still because the pounding of the rain had stopped. There was nothing to be heard at first but water dripping from the trees outside. Then, after a minute, I could hear the measured pacing of the guard. While I had no way of knowing the time, I remembered that I was to be alert about midnight, so I slipped from my bed, untangled the flimsy blanket, and crossed to the door, not being sure whether Sledel slept or not. At any rate, there was no sound from him. I found the door after some groping, and my fingers conveyed the startling fact that the leathern loop which should have been on the outside was inside, and when I pulled it gently, the door swung open as the wooden catch raised.

The sentry's pacing had stopped, and I stood for a while with the hair prickling along my neck for this door should have been barred. After some minutes, my eyes became a bit more adjusted to the darkness, and I could make out the dark loom of hills to the west and, beyond them, the faint reflection which would mean the army's campfires. In the other directions there was nothing but darkness.

Still, I hesitated to move because of some instinct of caution. The dripping from the trees had slowed. Since I did not hear the sentry, I imagined that he had heard me and stood somewhere with his musket leveled, ready to fire when he saw a movement. But I took a long breath of the fresh rain-washed air.

"Watch around midnight." Those were Parr's exact words. Then I remembered that he had told me to bring Sledel with me, and I turned to reenter the place when fingers caught my wrist. There was no mistaking the reek of Indian tobacco or the slight form beside me as that of Sledel.

He led me round the corner of the building, seemingly with no thought of the sentry, and then about a hundred yards over ground so soggy from rain that our moccasins made little sucking sounds. Suddenly, men were about us, and a feathered head was momentarily silhouetted against the skyline. I caught the rank sweetish odor that meant Indians, a mingling of rancid bear fat and unwashed body odor.

The eeriness of the situation made my neck hairs prickle. It was true that in the morning I was to hang, but that might be much better than what Indians could do to me—if they had time.

No one spoke, but Sledel, who seemed to see better than I in the darkness, kept fast hold of my sleeve, riding me. The little man gave no indication of fright. We were moving fast. By another trick of light, I saw a smear of paint across a man's cheek and then heard guttural whispers that might be the Seneca tongue. Then we were walking into timber, and the light diminished.

Still no checking of the pace—those who surrounded us seemed to know exactly where we were moving. My feet told me we were dropping downhill; I heard running water and was surprised to find myself so thirsty that the roof of my mouth felt parched. In a moment, we were in this water, and I snatched up a handful of it, finding that it tasted of roots and swamp plants. Then stiff heavy leaves and rough branches tugged at my hands and clothing, and I realized that these were rhododendrons— we were passing through some sort of swamp.

Ten minutes more, and we began moving in single file. I kept a grip on the tail of Sledel's hunting shirt until we stumbled from the water and climbed a hill, descending on the far side of it to where I heard the sound of horses moving and stamping.

"Well, boys, that's that, I guess."

The voice after the deep stillness seemed unnaturally loud, especially here in the thicket. There was nothing Indian about it. Rather, it was mostly Irish, and, best of all, I recognized it.

"Tim," I said. "Tim, it's you!"

A hand like a ham clapped me on the back. "Who the hell else would Parr pick from his company for his dirty work but Tim Ehlerson and boys from our parts! Tell me, Simon, how was the smell?"

They crowded round me, saying their names: Keller, Wert, Carson, and others, until a full dozen had spoken-names familiar in the country from Fort Augusta and on our way up the river.

"You stood up to Sullivan," Carson said, "so we was glad to turn stinking Senecas for the night. Sledel, you Dutch horse thief, you knowed we was coming."

Ehlerson took charge. "No time to waste. Your gear is on the horses, and they're bridled but not saddled. We had to let on the Brutes had strayed."

I slipped a coin into Ehlerson's hand. "Treat the boys, Tim, when you have a chance. I remember your Irish dislike of strong waters yourself."

The rifleman snorted. "There's a full keg bought already with your money, Simon. Enough to keep this crew near drunk for a month."

But he took it when I pressed it upon him. These men had so little money that a gold coin was a fortune to them. They closed round me, shaking hands. Then they were gone in the blanket of the dark, so silently that in minutes there was no sound at all from them. I stood motionless for some time.

The Indian smell in the dark—there had been Yonido that night on the Chemung, now these friends. Warriors seldom moved in the dark; Tim Ehlerson would have thought of that. I would remember the rough hands that had gripped mine and the keenness of these men. It was worthwhile to spend oneself making the homeland of such people as safe as one was able.

The horses were restive, hard-mouthed brutes likely taken from some Indian herd, but with Sledel up on the smaller of them, we were moving, and apparently the little man knew his directions for he chuckled.

"Wisht I could see the Old Man's face when he sees his guard tied up and his prisoners gone to make a Seneca pot roast."

"Was the guard in it, Jed?"

"No, but all he got was a crack on the head after he'd seen feathers and paint and got a whiff of Indian stink. He's kinda dumb and will be thankful to keep his scalp. Come—I get the shivers when I think what Sullivan would do—after this—if we was caught."

In an hour's riding I began to feel better, for my sense of direction was good, and it was not as dark up here in the hills. We were moving a bit to the south and east. When I had a chance, I rode up beside my companion and spoke of it.

"Yes, we're cutting crost country to the army road. We got to get feed for these beasts before we turn into the big pine woods, and the only grain left will be where the army's stuff is."

Whatever Sledel might have been down in his home country before he joined the army, he was not the man to mistreat a horse. That was apparent this night from his talk and his riding. If we broke south and came into the timber where there was no grass, we'd ride our horses to death.

Before dawn the sky cleared and the stars shone briefly. We camped for a rest as soon as we could see our horses' ears, and then fed them a sort of mash we made from the cornmeal we found in our packs. They refused the food at first; then Jed rubbed their noses with the paste, and they finished eagerly what we gave them.

Jed admired them as they ate, and they were good animals with stout barrels and long legs, typical cavalry stock though a bit pot-bellied from grass feeding.

"Good stuff," the small man declared. "Straight from a good British stud."

By afternoon we saw the military road with the dark scar of an Indian village near it, and Sledel showed that he had a professional knowledge of what we must do. First, we tied our horses securely with knots that would slip easily if we yanked on the ends of the straps. Afterward, we blacked our faces, turned our hunting shirts, and then hid in a roadside thicket to wait.

In an hour, what Jed wanted appeared, a small pack train with two men riding—one ahead, the other to the rear of the string. The pack animals between them were laden with bags. When the leader was opposite Jed, he stepped out, rifle ready. At the small man's gesture, the fellow slid from the saddle. My man tried to bolt, but I stopped him with a smart blow of my rifle barrel. Sledel tied both of them with a rope taken from one of the packs.

Some of the bags held shelled corn, and we threw two of these into the brush. Jed pointed to the saddles of the two men and grinned. When I nodded, he took both from the horses and tossed them to the bags of grain. While I watched our victims, he brought our own mounts down, saddled them, and tied the corn sacks securely in place. Then I did the talking.

"Tell your bosses that two honest King's men needed your corn. We'll be waiting for your Sullivan on the way back, enough of us to give him real trouble."

We cut them free, and I gave each a shilling.

"Drink to sweeten your story."

The train moved off at good speed, and while Sledel looked after it, he shook his head.

"Risky."

"But necessary, Jed. To men like us, a little highway robbery don't mean a thing."

With good horse feed available, we struck south and rode hard clear into the night until we reached the big timber where we camped.

Sledel slept peacefully within minutes of the time he had rolled himself into his blanket, but things were not that easy for me. Bitter events had happened, and trouble had followed me from that night in Fort Pitt when I had suddenly married a not too reluctant Celine. It was as though I had surrendered my peace in payment of a reckless act. Staring upward into the blackness of the pines, I knew she would rejoice at the punishment I had taken since I compelled her to come with me, home to the Loyalsock.

Wigton, Parr, Hope, Yonido—all had doubted the raid. Celine had hated the map and showed her contempt for it. I wondered what white man had stood near our kitchen that morning. If I knew that, I would understand everything.

Desperation kept me awake. In the Iroquois country I would burn for the killing of Pigeon; in Niagara, I was a spy, as I was with Sullivan. In every direction, forces moved that would destroy me. I envied Sledel, his quiet sleep, and his lack of worry now that we had put miles between us and Sullivan.

There was no longer much danger of direct pursuit so we rode leisurely. At each camp, Jed worked on the horses with pinecones as curry combs, and the animals looked better each day. I told Jed about Wigton and his love for horses. He turned to me.

"If that Genessee country was closer to Berks County, I'd get rich with Indian horses in a month or so. There's a real market down there for stuff just like we're riding. A while back I deserted for a couple of days, and I saw some of the Indian horses. I'll bet I could sell a dozen mounts right down there in that fort where the rivers come together."

"Augusta," I supplied, and he grinned.

"Knowed a woman of that name. She was English, tight as a drum, and folks say she bossed her husband to death. Well, as I was saying. I'd sell horses to folks who'd organize a fast patrol that could watch for Indian parties. Not many folks on your rivers, and horses would double what they could do."

Jed's idea was interesting in that it was the same one Wigton had talked of for so long and had attempted to get General Knox to support. Once an Indian band was robbed of its chance to surprise, especially with a patrol that could strike quick and hard, it would lose most of its destructive power. But it meant a lot of horses, weapons, and feed for the animals, and Sledel and I were outlaws.

On the fourth day of our leisurely riding, we came to a small stream which I recognized, and we followed it down to "The Slot," where we camped for the night. It was the spot to which I thought the raiders had come after the raid. Sitting on opposite sides of our little fire, we talked a long time that night; and I told the little man some of the things that had first sent me wandering. He heard me through with little comment. Nor did it seem important to him that we were both outside the law.

"Wasn't your fault, Simon. I figger when a man ain't to blame things will jest natcherly come right."

There was good reason in getting back to the river country where the both of us could be of use. If Sullivan did withdraw as Parr said he would, the tribes would follow the retreating army back to their former homes and from there strike quick and hard. Every man would be needed on the rivers, and there would be little questioning of me or Jed; it would be enough that we were two more rifles.

The clatter of our horses had brought John Wigton across the ford and to an ambush behind a big rock, from which he stepped as we came close enough for him to recognize me. Then he set his rifle against the rock and ran forward, yelling his welcome. He took one good look at Sledel, then shook the slight man by the shoulders.

"Jed!" he cried. "Jed Sledel, you old horse thief! Where did Simon find you?"

Jed showed some signs of embarrassment, and Wigton explained that he had known him years before, down country.

"Jed may have his secrets, Simon, but he is number one with horses. Both of you are welcome at Tory Hall."

Hope welcomed us kindly, shaking hands. But she drew hers quickly away from me when I held it a bit too long. Her face was flushed, likely from her hearth fire.

"Come in, all of you. Supper is about ready," she invited.

The interior of this house had changed a great deal. There were more vases of wild flowers, and there was a white homespun linen cloth on the table now laden with food, the odors of which filled the room.

"Venison," Hope enumerated on her small fingers. "Then chestnuts boiled in milk, for the little cow gives us plenty of that, and potatoes roasted in the coals as you like them, Simon."

I was pleased at the fact that she remembered the things of which I was fond. Jed was diffident, but he proved a valiant trencherman, and Hope complimented him on his appetite, at which his face grew red.

John and Hope kept up the conversation. It was mostly of the farm, the buildings, and the horses, also the rebuilding of their own home which had been started.

"Hope and I are getting the people back. She talks to the women; I lend the men stuff they need, like seed and sometimes a bit of money."

So far, we had been asked no questions, but when we rose from the table, Hope said to me abruptly, "I've something to show you, Simon, now that you've finished."

She went swiftly out the door, with me following closely, and led the way over the field, into the woods, and along a path.

"It's a mother grouse, hatching late, and she's right by the path. Look at her as we walk past but keep moving."

The bird was there at the foot of a small oak, the nest pressed deeply into the leaves, the bird's feathers blending with the brown of the forest floor. Her small head turned slowly as we passed casually, and she did not flush, even when we returned. A short distance on, I spoke to Hope.

"You know I've seen many a grouse nest; why did we look?"

She faced me.

"Just for a lesson. If we had blundered along, she would have flown. Had we searched for her, she would have escaped. That's the way it has been with you, trying too hard for whatever you want. If you'd be content to wait, maybe the answers would come to you."

I looked away for a moment, feeling what she said was probably true.

"You loved her, Simon; when you are alone, you think of her?"

I stared at Hope, surprise stirring within me. The woman, Blanche, had asked this same question. I could not tell this calm girl standing here before me and whose face looked out at me from lonely campfires what I scarcely admitted was in my heart.

"No," I said, "I never did. I knew that well long before she went away. But I brought her here, was responsible for her safety."

"Pretty soon, Simon, it will be too late for these desperate ventures of yours."

"That is true already," I said, and we went into the house where Wigton was alone, with the word that Jed had gone to the stable where he could sleep in the hay.

"Sullivan would not hear you," Wigton said soberly.

"Did Jed tell you?" I countered, and he shook his head.

"No, but you always find trouble for yourself, and it was there in the Genessee country or you would not have appeared with Jed on strange horses. He, too, has a faculty of getting into wild scrapes. Are the troopers after you?"

Immediately he jerked forward, caught my arm impulsively. "Forgive that, Simon. We're concerned for you and that which worries and follows you. Remember, this is your home, and we do not care if all Sullivan's army is after you."

John Wigton had a discernment almost as great as his native kindness, and I felt the momentary edge of temper pass. Then I plunged in and told the story of Boone's message, Sullivan's rage, the appearance of the map fragment, the sentence and escape. Wigton was silent a long time.

"Simon," he said slowly, "I worked with your father; you and I have done well together; Hope sort of grew up with you, and we're about all the family you have. Now this."

His face went hard.

"If I had that woman who brought all this to pass here, I would strangle her. Simon, she is evil; her touch brings misery. She is a disease of which you must be cured. All that has happened traces back to her, even to the death of poor old Major who did not like her."

He shook his head, and I could find no answer and no resentment for he had voiced the thing which I had seen in my own mind. He changed the subject.

"I cannot understand Sullivan. It is surely strange that men like Hand and Parr stand against him."

"John," I answered, "Parr is worried about the valleys when Sullivan leaves the Iroquois country. And now Boone is gone."

"Well," Wigton commented soberly, "we have a few more rifles now, that's something. We'll take things as they come." I closed my eyes and could see Butler's long green column winding down the narrowing valley into the mist. I could see the bright tips of the bayonets, the pack trains, and the hordes of natives on either side. Also, I would never forget the return from Wyoming Valley, with Indians trotting through the woods like wild dogs, wet scalps dangling from their waists.

Involuntarily I shook my head. When Sullivan was gone, nothing on the river could withstand a force such as I had seen, if it were launched. The whole defenseless side of the colonies lay open, and here we were but a few score rifles.

As for Hope, she had listened through the whole long story, saying nothing. Her full lips were pressed in a straight line, and I could not guess what was going on in her mind. Her eyes looked darker, but that may have been a trick of the light. In my own thinking, there was a resentment because I felt she might have said some little thing which would be comforting.

CHAPTER THIRTEEN

WITH NO set occupation and no task demanding completion, the days dragged heavily on my hands here on the Loyalsock. There was decidedly too much time for thinking, especially since it seemed I could make no plans that did not end against the wall of the fact that I was a hunted man.

Wigton finished his task in the fields and turned to work on his new house. I was glad for the heavy labor of cutting logs and drawing them down the hill to the stone foundations. After long hours of toil, I was able to sink into the deep sleep of weariness when evening came instead of having to lie awake and think.

Quite openly I envied Sledel's ability to fit himself into the life of the small farm. He showed no inclination to leave us and go on home. He seemed to find something interesting or challenging to his ingenuity each day. He began by fitting up a room for himself in the stable where he constructed a comfortable pole bed and two chairs, together with a table which was so well made that Hope threatened to steal it for the house. Most of the time he spent with the horses, and he taught tricks to one of the animals we had brought with us which proved to be a fine young stallion. It learned to rise on its hind legs and come at a man with every indication of extreme viciousness. But it was really a gentle horse and would answer to Jed's whistle, following him like a dog. More than anything else it was his love of horses and the work he could do with them here that prevented Jed from pushing on immediately to his home in Berks County.

"You know," he told me one day, "I always wanted a horse like that. Now if our man Sullivan sent for me, he couldn't get within a mile of that fellow's flying legs."

He glanced at me sharply, his little eyes bright.

"Friend," he said softly, "you don't look worried enough."

I looked at him without understanding; then he developed his point.

"Me, I was only a kind of whipping boy. They won't bother about me for long because it wouldn't pay. But that Sullivan won't pass you up, young man. He'll send for you one of these days for he wouldn't be fooled into thinking the Senecas got us that night, and he'll learn about the pack train that was robbed. You don't get to be a big general by letting things slide."

Seeming to think he had said enough, Jed whistled to his horse, then lay down on the ground while the stallion rolled him over. When the trick was repeated, he gave the knowing animal a piece of maple sugar, probably wheedled from Hope.

That evening, when the talk about the table shifted to Boone and Sullivan's summary dismissal of both the man and his labors, I became indignant.

"Washington should know," I insisted. "I could ride to White Plains—"

Then I remembered and stopped while my listeners looked as embarrassed as I felt, and Wigton finally spoke.

"Yes, Simon, you understand, and something has to be done. You can't hole up here in the mountains like a bear for the rest of your natural life. You—"

Suddenly, with no other warning, there was a knocking at the outer door.

We had neighbors down along the big river, but none here seemed to think this a casual visitor. Wigton rose and, without a sound snatched down his rifle. I saw Jed glance toward the back door, and I hurried to catch up my own weapons from the pegs on which they hung.

The door opened softly on its oiled hinges, and Yonido stood there framed against the darkness. I heard a faint sound from Hope and glanced at her in time to see her replace the pistol, which I had given her, on its peg. The Indian regarded us with a wide smile which probably concealed his real thinking.

"So," he said, "it is still war on the Loyalsock, and my friends talk and grow careless when Senecas could be their guests at any minute."

Yonido was making one of his unannounced visits to us, having just made a quick trip through the Iroquois country to which the evicted owners had returned in the months since Sullivan's withdrawal. The general had made a quick job of that and had even burned his fine new fort where the rivers meet. Practically all he had accomplished was the destruction of a harvest.

The Indian was hungry, as most of his race seem to be at all times, and ate what food Hope set before him, thanking her politely. He could not completely hide the fact that he really disliked all women. They might be necessary and deserved routine politeness, but that was all. I think Hope enjoyed the man for all that, asking him with politeness that matched his, about some herbs, with full knowledge that he did not like to speak of his healing work. Finally, having eaten, Yonido turned to John Wigton.

"There are many horses on the Genessee, John. You should see them for yourself as Simon has. Perhaps you could get some of them."

Wigton shook his head.

"If I went up into that country, there could be a raid here while I'm gone."

Yonido shook his head. "No, they are too hungry and busy getting settled. Later they may come, but now is the time to get horses—when they think the raid on their country is over."

Jed and Wigton had listened closely. This was the thing that captured their interest for they were both real horsemen. But Wigton did the talking when Yonido had finished his suggestion.

"Jed and I have figured. Counting Simon's Salt, we have seven horses now, and we have some extra feed. How far is it to the Genessee country?"

I thought rapidly; the idea appealed to me for the formation of a good patrol would do much to protect these threatened valleys. "We could cut across the high pine timbered flats instead of following the rivers. Say a hundred fifty miles, John, and fair going if we dodge the stony ridges."

Jed broke in now. "We could carry corn as Simon and I did coming down. Four men couldn't handle a herd, but we could take six or eight head, and Fred Forney could pasture them in the Nippenose."

John Wigton was a man who loved action. He pressed Yonido to give up his trip southward for the time being, and late the following morning, we four men rode up to Long Island, crossed the river, and went up through the grim bastions of Antes Gap to the mountain-locked Nippenose. I was always glad to get through this defile. On the left, the mountain pitches up sharply but is all rocks and loose stones. Then there is the creek, and another point lifts, covered with the dark of hemlocks and pines which darken the defile even at noontime.

* * *

Ben Forney liked the idea and showed us some of the small natural meadows where grass grew as rank as in any tilled field. The Forneys came here as young men with their father and knew each square yard of the valley and had not left it, even in the Runaway. We had a place for the raided animals; the problem now was to get them.

On the morning of our start, Wigton dispatched a most unwilling Hope downriver to tell Colonel Kelly what we were about. Angry with her father, she was kinder to me. I held my hand for her small moccasined foot when she mounted her tall mare, and, settled in her saddle, she leaned toward me until one end of her bright red scarf brushed my cheek.

"I wish I was for the Genessee, Simon."

She gestured toward her father who was tightening the lashings of his pack.

"Take care of him; he's so like to be—"

Her little hesitation reminded me of the days when she was a small girl and seemed about to use strong language. John Wigton used to tease her about "profane silences."

"—foolish when he sees horses," she finished.

She dropped her hand, touched me lightly on the shoulder, walked her big mare through the ford, then clapped heels into the ribs of her mount and was away, riding like Jehu in her father's Bible.

For myself, I thought I could feel the warmth of her fingers through the tough buckskin of my coat, and I kept her little gesture in my mind for a long time, trying to read in it some concern for me.

Three days later we were riding through the pine country that lies east and north of the Sinnamahoning, Yonido having led us straight as the crow flies over the forest miles where his woodcraft saved us a deal of lost time and travel. We had hidden some of the corn we carried at several points so we would have feed for the horses on the return.

Beyond the pine land we struggled over a number of small stony ridges, coming finally to a small stream flowing north. Yonido pointed.

"Genessee."

He continued to lead us forward until we finally had a good look at the country ahead from the top of a hill. Below, the stream we followed was joined by another larger one, both flowing into a great valley that widened in the distance. The country was parklike with meadows and trees. Forty or fifty miles to the north would be the place where Sullivan turned back, and between this Genessee Valley and the lakes would be country seething with the hordes of the dispossessed people of the Long House. The Western Door had not been closed, but the council fires of the Six Nations had been extinguished, and the Indians lived on the bounty of the English at Niagara. Certainly this country would be highly dangerous for any white man who ventured beyond the Forbidden Path.

We left our mounts in thick brushy woods, and Wigton lost when we cast lots to see who should stay with them. Yonido, Jed, and I went down into the valley, and luck was with us for in a few hours we saw horses. As I watched and helped with what followed, I saw how valuable Jed was, for the small man knew this business thoroughly.

We stalked the animals where they grazed in a meadow. Each time a horse raised his head, we stood still. Finally, Yonido moved some of them past where Jed stood near a clump of brush with a big rawhide loop in his hand. With this, he caught one animal round the neck. Then he made himself a hackamore bridle, mounted bareback, and in less than an hour we had three good-looking but wild horses on our hands, taking them back to Wigton.

It was too dark for a second try that day. We rolled into our blankets after a cold supper for we did not risk a fire. This was Seneca country, and we dared not advertise our presence in it.

* * *

Next morning, before the dew was well off, we had three more animals, two bearing the British broad arrow. Wigton thought we had enough to handle on the long way back, but we had not ridden a mile on the homeward trip when Jed stopped us.

"Listen, folks, we've come a long way, and we'd ought to have done better. John, you and Simon stay with the horses; Yonido and I'll go back."

I had an objection in my mind even though things had gone so well, but each horse meant a mounted man on patrol so I said nothing, nor did Wigton, and the two rode away, Yonido grinning. This time, Jed must have felt it better to work from horseback.

Wigton and I spent what was left of the morning trying to get the new stock to eat corn and finally succeeded. John took one of our saddles and put it on a branded animal. It was frightened for a little but then handled docilely. These were certainly not wild horses though they did need currying.

Our two friends had ridden away about mid-morning, and the day dragged into the afternoon. About four o'clock we heard a shot, or thought we did, but could not be sure, and it was not repeated. Just at dusk, we heard them coming—fast.

Jed was apologetic; Yonido, amused; and they had two extra horses, the best we had taken.

"There was an Indian back there," Jed explained. "He didn't want us to take the stock, and we tied him up to a tree near the water. We was going to loose him on our way back."

He rearranged a halter carefully, glancing at Yonido from whom he received no help, then to me.

"Well, the fellow had been tied to a sapling real close to the water. Likely he tried to work loose and fell into the river and drowned."

Wigton and I looked at Jed and realized that we would never really know what had happened down there along the stream.

Both Jed and Yonido would have known that if this Indian reported the presence of horse thieves, our chances at more horses later would be slim—also it might mean pursuit. Neither man would be troubled in his conscience by one less live Seneca, but there was the matter of the shot, and Jed certainly was uneasy and hurried.

"I figure it would be good to pull out since it's a long way home, and driving horses is sort of slow work," he said.

The pace he and Yonido set in getting to our grain cache showed that both were restless about what had occurred. On the pretext of blowing his horse, the Indian kept a good watch on our back track, Wigton seemed engrossed with the horses.

Before midnight, we reached the grain and camped there, though we did go to the trouble of setting a watch. Two slept while the others watched.

"John," I told Wigton, "this lot of horses won't be missed, nor are there enough. We'll have to put on a real raid, gather men, and come up for, say, a hundred head, getting to the main herd on the Genessee."

He agreed but found a difficulty. "Be hard to come by enough men for such a trip. We'd have to have those who could handle horses and who could fight."

He looked at me quizzically, then pointed to the sleeping Indian and Jed. "Them fellows had real trouble down there, and don't you believe anything else."

Next morning, I was riding along trying to figure out a bigger raid when abruptly an idea came to my mind, and crowding up to Wigton, I nearly lost the animals I led.

"John," I called, "I have it. We'll stampede a herd, chase it east, then turn what we can into the Tiadaghton gorge. A dozen men could hold back an army there. It's a chute ready and waiting."

Wigton whistled softly.

"Simon—you're acting human again. You're thinking."

* * *

Four days from the long grass country of the Genessee and the lurking shadows of Seneca horse guards, we pushed our string of horses into the river at Long Island and left them there under the care of Jed and Yonido. John and I hurried on homeward, for I knew he was uneasy about Hope. Darkness overtook us just beyond the Lycoming ford.

This night on the way up our Loyalsock, I kept thinking of the time I came home at dusk to the trouble that had followed me. When we came to our ford and no light showed, a cold hand took hold of my heart and squeezed it. We had no business leaving a girl, even as resourceful a one as Hope, alone in these times.

We splashed over the water, and I slid from my saddle, but Wigton raised his fingers to his mouth and whistled shrilly. I thought an echo answered; then I heard the sound of hooves. Minutes later, Hope galloped into the yard and swung out of her saddle before I could help her.

"They about again?" Wigton questioned grimly.

Hope tossed her reins up to her father. "I thought so. I took a blanket and Becky to the upper field; the mare's better than any watch dog."

John insisted on taking our horses to the barn, and I helped lay fires and light candles. Supper was well started before he came in, and then Hope explained.

"Father and I have the notion that this place is watched. Once we found indistinct tracks—white man's shoes, and sometimes, when the night is still, we think we hear things."

She tossed her head in a gesture strange for her. "But I like to sleep outside with Becky on guard."

Neither she nor her father seemed to wish to talk about the subject any further. Wigton was excited and pleased with our raid, telling Hope all about the horses and sketching plans for a full-stage expedition.

"It should be soon, John," I offered, "before those villagers come down with hatchets."

Wigton nodded and smiled. "Down the gorge itself. We'll comb the herd out of their valleys, drive hard to the upper Tiadaghton, then run them down the gorge like a chute."

I glanced at Hope sitting there where candlelight touched her rounded face with both light and shadow. She might be thinking of the raid, but I doubted it when she leaned forward and cupped her chin in her palm, her round elbows on the table.

"What about that bad place in the gorge, Simon?" Wigton asked.

"We'll lose horses, John, maybe a lot of them, but it's war. What worries me is men—a good dozen. I'll start to scout the gorge tomorrow."

Next morning, Wigton left on an errand of his own, and Jed appeared with the word that the horses were now safe in the Nippenose where the Forney brothers would care for them. He was also concerned about corn, in case we secured a larger number of horses.

"There's plenty the army missed up above, but it would take another army now to get it," he said ruefully.

The small horseman gladly promised to stay with Hope while I left for the scouting expedition up the Tiadaghton mounted on Salt, now pretty fat from long inaction.

The lower reaches of the big creek presented no difficulties, and the higher I ascended the stream, the loftier were the ridges lifting from the narrow defile. I camped the first night in a small meadow where Salt eked out his grain supper with late grass. It was eerie down here at night, and full daylight seemed slow in coming.

At midday, I reached the ledges which concerned Wigton, but Salt went up them, scrambling like a cat on the smooth rocks. The place could be dangerous, but any good rough country animal should make it, and the Indian horses had not been too carefully treated; surely they could come over.

I followed the gorge until it ended abruptly where the stream came in from the west. Here were sharp low hills on either side, and on the northern one grew two tall pines which could be an excellent landmark to guide us coming in from the west.

I was satisfied, after riding some little distance west, to find a rolling country stretching away toward a line of dim hills. Then because I did not wish to endanger Salt's legs a second time, I took a roundabout route to the main river valley.

Riding along now, I thought how pleasant it would be if I were really coming back to a home. Hope had been kinder lately, I felt, almost her old friendly self. Then, when I was closer to the house on the Loyalsock, another thought came to me: I was a fugitive and must approach home furtively lest there be someone waiting there to claim my forfeited life.

I thought, too, of Hope and her horse sleeping in the fields, and of the guarded talk between her and her father about whoever seemed to be watching them. Furthermore, I had an idea of what and whom they suspected. Abruptly, I stopped Salt and sat thinking. It had occurred to me that I must do something, and without too much delay.

CHAPTER FOURTEEN

JOHN WIGTON did not return until the day after I came back from the Tiadaghton, but as soon as I turned up, Jed developed a sudden and deep concern for the horses in the Nippenose and left us. For my part, I had no idea of leaving Hope alone to watch for herself and perhaps to sleep in the fields.

Wigton was pleased with what I told him of the gorge. At the least, it would give us a good forty miles during which our pursuers could approach us only from the rear. Our main problem seemed to be finding men who would venture sticking their heads into the possible Indian trap on the Genessee.

More settlers had been coming, especially into the main valley of the Susquehanna, and the big horseman was delighted. The presence of such people was vital to defense, and besides, Wigton had a tremendous faith and love for this land as a home for farmers. He had no wish to live without neighbors. In my own heart, I was not too anxious for people to come—not until the land was safe.

Wigton had left home without explaining his purpose to me, so I had no compunction going out that night without explanation other than to say I was going to take a ride up toward the Lycoming. And I did go that way until dark, then turned and rode down the main river. No one was to know my business this night, and I wanted no company, except possibly Yonido, and I knew he was in the Nippenose if he had not decided to take his trip south as he had planned earlier.

I was ready, at last, to couple the Challis place and the men who came there with my own misfortunes. Parr claimed one of these visitors was Norris. Perhaps he had been there before the war, but I was suspicious, the more I learned of the man, about the time of this happening. Parr might have been misinformed; perhaps he withheld something he knew. But the presence of the clergyman, whenever it was, would indicate that Norris knew something about our country which, in itself, was a danger. Challis was supposed to be a good Whig, which I doubted. It was my notion he wished to be with the party which would win this war; my mind went back to our little visit when his hand had been so steady with the wine, even though he claimed to be so greatly shocked at the news we brought.

At this time of year, Challis was usually in Philadelphia or somewhere on the seacoast looking after his business ventures. The probabilities were that I would find no one at home, but I did mean to look through that big house. Perhaps I might learn something of the prowler on the Loyalsock who watched the Wigtons; at least I would look again at the quiver filled with Delaware arrows.

A further thing drove me—the craving for some sort of action now that any attempt to locate Celine appeared to be out of the question. At Sullivan's orders, my life was forfeit; yet I was not willing to give myself up to the tight grip of circumstances.

Salt was a patient and quiet animal; yet I tied him securely in the brush a good distance from the silhouette of the great house, just off the main road. In my belt I carried my pistol and the heavy two-edged knife I liked. Outside of that, I had nothing but a short length of candle and a good tinder box. A lanthorn would have suited me, but taking one might have excited Hope's suspicions.

The night's chill made me shiver. From beyond the little bridge, I studied the big house, dark against the willows between it and the river. The stars were bright enough so I could see the shutters were closed; no light showed at the barn where the servants' quarters were. I had watched a good quarter of an hour when I thought I detected a faint flicker at the crack of an upstairs shutter, as though someone had carried a candle past some narrow opening. Again I waited, but since it did not reappear, I set the incident down to imagination and approached the house, keeping well in the shadows of shrubbery and trees.

The first shutter I tried opened easily with the aid of the broad, heavy blade of my knife, and the casement window inside yielded to a gentle push. Just as I was about to swing my leg over the sill, a sound caught my straining ears. Indistinct and far away across the fields, it was unmistakably the sound a horse makes in stamping on the ground and then blowing through his nostrils.

I closed the shutter and stood with shoulders against the house while I listened. Finally I concluded it was Salt tied down there in the bushes. Even light noises carry far in the night here in the quiet of the country. Easier in my mind, again I opened the shutter and stepped into darkness.

The interior of a darkened house presents an atmosphere that sets the nerves of an intruder on edge. It is as though the blackness closes in and hampers progress like a dragging blanket. As I groped about this room, I wished I had brought the lanthorn. A door opened on oiled hinges, and I was in another room, but there was no finding anything in this dark. I fumbled for flint and steel. When the small flame of my stub of candle lifted above the tallow, a great relief came to me and my nerves steadied.

This room was part of a kitchen. Outside I found a hallway and stairs up which I climbed to another hallway from which smaller rooms opened. The doors of two of these opened easily, but I had to use the knife blade on the third. This proved to be a room that was entirely bare save for one item which startled me. Here by the shuttered window was a table that supported a drawing board. I closed the door behind me.

A wide sheet of mapping paper was tacked fast to the wood; at one side lay quills and the other instruments one uses on a map. There was a full pot of ink and a tiny keen-edged knife used to point quills. Nowhere about the room was any sign of finished work; all there was lay before me—work to be done.

Something of my first start passed when I remembered that this man Challis, through whose home I prowled, was a great land speculator. Naturally he would have maps and have those who would do mapping.

But my mind would not shut out the picture of a boot track in back of the kitchen window, and I saw again the piece of map in Sullivan's angry hand. Shielding the candle with my palm, I stepped out of the room.

A few steps down the stairway, I sensed a stirring too light to define, like the soft flight of bats or night birds. The thin candlelight showed a well of darkness below me; then from behind me a hand grasped my shoulder. The strength of the grip pulled me half around and sent me spinning down the stairs to strike with force against the wall of the passageway. My head was whirling from the bump it took, and vaguely I knew the sound I heard was the snicking of a gun lock. Then the darkness above me split with an orange stab of fire, and the whole place exploded into a crash of sound.

Half stunned by the fall though I was, I had presence of mind enough to lie still. Someone had hurled me down the stairs and had shot at me. I did not propose giving away my position in case he had a second pistol. How long I lay was hard to estimate, but it was likely a full quarter of an hour, when distinctly I heard the measured trotting of a horse on the graveled way. I had been mistaken about Salt's making the sound I had detected before I entered this house.

Presently I eased myself up from the cramped position into which I had fallen and, with groping fingers, found the candle. What I wanted now was bright light and escape from this house of heavy shadows. With outstretched hands, I walked slowly forward, finally pushing open a door that admitted me to a room smelling faintly of spirits and tobacco. As the door panel closed in back of me, I knew I was not alone. There was the sound of breathing, the quick intake that comes before action. And whoever stood across from me held a closed lanthorn, for there was a faint glow a short distance above the floor.

There was nothing to be gained by hesitating, and I did not feel like waiting for a second pistol shot in the darkness. As I plunged forward, there was a click, and a lanthorn beam shone from the open slide. Behind the light I glimpsed a face, and then came a burst of fire. A red-hot needle passed through my shoulder, and as it met the bone, I crumpled down into a darkness deeper than that of the room.

Nothing more came to me but a faint feeling of being carried, then a soft sifting and the cold of sleet on my face, that and agony in my shoulder.

There was a borderland in which I was living; faces would appear; sounds would come, then vanish. I struggled against great masses of thick gummy fog that threatened to smother me as it filled the room where weights held my body fast against the thong lacings of my bed. Above all I was cold, as though standing naked on a winter hilltop with wind searing me like an icy flame.

There were times when I knew vaguely that I was in my own house on the Loyalsock, that the faces were those of John Wigton and Hope. There had been someone else, a stranger who had done things to my shoulder while I writhed under his hands.

Two faces leaned over me, and dim as they were, I could see the anxiety on them, hear a woman's voice tense with fright. When I tried to raise my body, a numbness held me fast. And the cold wrapped me more closely than the blankets.

An infinity of time seemed to pass. Then, against the candlelight, was an aura of radiance, a fragrance, and I was no longer alone in the blanket-piled bed. Warmth began to steal through me; my sluggish blood stirred. Now I dreamed that warm arms were about my neck and that I was being drawn against a soft, warm, fragrant body to a comfort such as I had never guessed. Desperately I clung to this comfort lest I wake to coldness again. In the warm happiness, my body relaxed; it was safe to sleep.

When I opened my eyes, Yonido sat by the bed looking down at me, and I tried to smile.

"You—"

"Lie still, my brother," he said softly. "It is a good time to sleep and get strong."

With a broad hand under my shoulders, he lifted me high enough to make me drink some villainous stuff, and when I scowled, he grinned. When he laid me back, he got up and crossed the room, unsuccessfully trying to whistle as was his custom when he was happy.

From then on, my mending was rapid. I gained strength under Yonido's nursing and the evil decoctions he made me swallow. But it was not until a week after the Indian appeared that John Wigton told me the story of what happened that night when I invaded Challis Hall.

Neither Wigton nor his daughter had been fooled by my excuses that evening. They even guessed my plan, but I had thrown them off the track by riding upriver, and the time they wasted before they turned was probably the same as I had spent in entering the Hall and having my adventures there. They did find Salt for he whinnied when they came near him. Sometime before midnight a sleet storm had set in, and they hunted me several hours before they found me thrown into a thicket with a sword cut in the shoulder from a thrust that had just missed the heart and which my attacker probably thought was fatal. More damage had been done by loss of blood and exposure. The surgeon brought from Fort Augusta had wanted to bleed the patient.

"But I would not let him," Hope said. "Why weaken a man who has already lost so much blood?"

Yonido looked at her and nodded, which was quite a concession for him to make to a woman's opinion.

Pneumonia had set in; I had been unconscious for days, and Yonido could not then be found.

"I did get him," Wigton explained, "on the night we both thought you would die. I left you with Hope, and you were better when I came in from the Nippenose where I found Yonido. You were sleeping."

I was pensive and did not look at any of them for a moment.

"How long have I been sick?"

Wigton smiled broadly.

"We figured it was taking you a long time to die. Something over a month, Simon."

My start of surprise brought on a fit of coughing, and Yonido threatened me by taking a cup and moving toward the small iron pot that hung over the fire. Then it occurred to me that I had never told them what had happened in the Challis house, and I proceeded to do so in detail.

"John," I asked, "who was it? There were two of them for one left on the horse; the other wounded me."

He nodded, reflecting before he spoke.

"There are the stories of a tall pale horse which sound much like old ghost stories. I do not trust Challis. God knows it is bad enough to have the Indians from the north hungry for our scalps without evil scheming among our neighbors."

We had to leave it at that. After all, we could not ride down to Challis Hall and demand an explanation. I had been the invader. Whoever had hurled me down the steps had power in his arms; yet I did not think him the same man who had used a sword.

This house with curtains at the windows and the crackling of a good fire was a cheerful place in which a sick man could get well. Wigton, Jed, and Yonido kept me company. Occasionally Hope visited with me for a few minutes, but she had a lot to busy her. Sometimes it was pleasant just to lie relaxed, to think about nothing, to forget that I was really a fugitive and that I had problems to solve.

Wigton said there had been heavy snows, but the horses in the Nippenose had come along well, for there were small open meadows in the mountain-walled valley where they were kept. Some of the newer settlers were already drilling themselves as a small mounted patrol.

For a man who had been with the Lambs and who could travel from dawn to dark with little weariness of the body, this convalescence was a surprising experience. At first it was labor to walk to the stable and visit with old Salt. I had to sit down in Jed's room before walking back to the house.

One sunny day, I sat by the west window in the room where John and I slept, and his battered old Bible lay on the shelf above the head of his cot. There was no one else in the house at the time. I picked up the book, and it fell open at Ecclesiastes. There was the note I had left so long before and a notation on the death of Ezra Lyman. There were other papers—John Wigton's marriage certificate and a small strand of light hair tied with a red thread that reminded me of the scarf that Hope loved.

A little embarrassed at having looked at these intimate things, I was about to return the Bible to the shelf when I noticed a tiny edge of paper marking a leaf of the book. I opened the Bible again. It was not the stories of battles and leading men in battle that held me, but the one in which the virgin Abishag lay beside the aged King David to keep his body warm.

Abruptly, as understanding came to me, I stood up and, with fingers that trembled a little, replaced the marker and put the worn Bible where it belonged. She had shared the warmth of her body and her health with me. Turning back to my chair, I saw my face in the mirror on the wall and stared at the thinness of it, the high cheekbones, the livid scar along the jaw, the puzzled eyes. Surely there was nothing about this scarecrow that he should be called back to life by a kindness that was beyond me to fathom.

Hope had entered the outer room. She was humming a tune as she worked. When I walked out of the bedroom, she glanced at me.

"You look almost well again, Simon."

"Yes," I said smiling, "it is really a wonderful world, if one is alive. . . ."

* * *

Yonido had been restless for some days. He had started twice for the south; the second time he had returned to the White Deer Valley where someone had told him John Wigton wanted him. That was when he had come to heal me. Now one evening, when the air was full of the suggestion of spring, he left the house without telling us how long he would be gone. He was riding the tall horse I had brought home from General Knox's camp and which I had given him.

At noon the following day, John Wigton came in greatly excited. Challis Hall had been burned!

John had been riding down to see some settlers who had camped below the Hall, and the ruins were still smoking. There had been no signs of life, nothing but the smoldering beams of what had been our greatest and finest house.

Neither Hope nor her father deplored the destruction. As for me, I thought of the dark rooms, the one with the drafting board all ready for someone who would work on a blank sheet and make it into what the Indians called a "talking paper." Also, my mind was on that stairway and the wait for the second shot that did not come, and for the flicker of steel in lanthorn light. Yes, I was glad the place was burned for it truly seemed evil.

CHAPTER FIFTEEN

SPRING WAS upon us with a rush that year, swelling the Loyalsock until it roared past the house, voicing a threat to overflow its banks and inundate the level land. Scarlet maples flamed in every direction one could see from the house, and Hope had found early arbutus as soon as the last snow had melted. Even the horses knew that winter was gone, for Old Salt elected to take a good roll in the barnyard, getting himself so muddy that it took me a full hour with a curry comb to make him presentable again.

With the kindness of the weather, we realized that it would not be too long until danger threatened from the north. When the rivers were still full but with the flood stage past, canoes could bring the Indians down either branch of the Susquehanna. Of course, the fact that spring would be later in the high pine country gave us some days of grace.

Our talk was mostly of a second raid for horses, and now that I was getting strong again, I was eager for it. A few days in the saddle or on the trail would tune my muscles, but John Wigton felt we should wait until there would be better footing for horses moving along streams, and none of us knew what the upper Genessee might be like at this season.

Then Colonel Kelly came, and I viewed his presence with a good bit of misgiving. After all, he was a commissioned officer in the Continental Army, and I was an escaped prisoner. It would be his duty to arrest me. Jed, also, was a fit subject for the attention of the big backwoodsman, though that small and wily man was abruptly excited about some horse-shoeing which must be done in the Nippenose for which he departed in some haste. I saw Kelly's veiled smile; he knew as well as the rest of us that even Jed and his stallion could not swim the West Branch at this season if half of Sullivan's cavalry were after them.

Very soon it was apparent that the colonel was ignoring Simon Braide, the fugitive, and was so concerned for the river that he counted me an aide. He was also tremendously interested in the burning of Challis Hall and my encounter there.

"Simon," he asked earnestly, "you've been in tight corners before and have learned to be watchful. Couldn't you get some idea who the man with the sword was?"

After a minute and a glance at Hope and her father, I spoke carefully. "Colonel, I don't like to point a finger unless I'm pretty sure, and that I can't be in this affair. But—it's likely that only one man knew that house so well he could get about in it when he carried a closed lanthorn. The man with the sword had the height of—"

"Challis," John Wigton said with conviction, and Kelly's eyes lighted as he nodded and spoke.

"People, if I was sure, I'd hang the man, but all I hear are stories— guesses. Yet he's no friendly Whig; he's trying to play safe with both sides. If the house were standing, we could investigate that drawing room. We do know that a tall man on a gray horse came to the place occasionally; he may have been Norris."

What Parr had said to me that night on the Genessee flashed to mind, but I said nothing. There was no use connecting anyone with my escape. But here was Norris mentioned again. He had been everywhere: at Fort Pitt, Niagara, now here. The man was assuming a stature in my mind. Kelly was speaking again.

"Norris used to be a surveyor. Likely he was a good man with a map."

I kept my eyes steady, feeling sure that this big man in the worn buckskins, with eyes that were now kindly as he looked at me, knew everything of my encounter with the irascible Sullivan. He continued:

"Challis has been up here since his house burned, and there's a good bit of sympathy for him in Augusta. Understand, the man has a right to go and come as he pleases—he's apparently a good Whig to Congress and the Philadelphia folks."

Wigton changed the subject by asking about the raid. "When do you figure we could go, Colonel?"

Kelly considered for a few minutes. "I'm not sure, John, but not for a couple of months anyway. Then I could come up and patrol for you or send a man. By the way, I want to have a look about your country today—visit some of the upriver folks."

The pair of them, Wigton and Kelly, left without inviting me to go along, and Hope decided at the last minute to accompany them. I tried to be affable but did not like it when Kelly, instead of holding his hand for Hope's foot as she mounted, picked her up bodily and swung her into the saddle. Hope laughed and she did not wave as they rode away. I told myself that I was getting childish.

Kelly stayed the night, but there was little talk because he and Wigton got out the chessboard and the two played, forgetting us. Hope sat in a corner with candles close and sewed for hours until I thought I had never seen her look so exasperatingly domestic.

* * *

Kelly did have a word for me the next morning when Wigton was down at the barn saddling the horse and Hope was in the house.

"Simon, keep clear of bear traps. We need you."

He fussed with a saddle girth, and I stood by, exasperated. Yes, they needed me. I was another rifle, another pair of eyes to watch, that was all. I was not a human being as other men were, nor supposed to hunger for the things other men wanted—home, peace, quiet labor. No, I was the man to run errands, to face these damned generals and stick my neck into nooses. All the luxury of self-pity I ordinarily denied myself welled up in me.

Hope was approaching from the house, Wigton from the stable, and Kelly was already mounted. He leaned toward me.

"I think they've a trap set for you at Augusta," he said gravely.

Thoroughly angry, albeit I did not fully understand what he meant other than to warn me of something, I spoke savagely.

"So," I gritted, "I'm bait again. That red-faced Sullivan—"

I remembered the night in the leaky hut with Jed, and before Hope got close enough to hear it all, I hurled the Dutch words at Kelly as my full description of Sullivan and all his works. When I finished, he flung back his head and roared with laughter. Hope and her father were close. He leaned farther and patted my head as one would that of a small boy.

"Fine, Simon, fine. I certainly agree with you, only your Dutch is so damned bad."

He was saying his goodbyes to the Wigtons, and I was wondering how it came to be that all these men of the frontier had big, powerful hands and strong wrists. But when I glanced at my own, I saw that I had them, too.

For nearly a month more, we had quiet days while John and I split rails, worked at fences, and made repairs to the barn. Then he and I went over to his own place and worked there, getting his building further along. This time he planned a bigger barn but a house much like mine.

"John," I asked one day when we were resting and stood, our hands on the axe helves, "why don't you just keep my place? You could farm both, and I think Hope likes the house."

He straightened, lifted his axe with one hand, and clipped a bit of bark from the log on which he worked.

"Simon, you love that house too much for us to crowd in. Things won't always be for you as they are now. One day, the house on the river will be home for you again."

John Wigton was an odd man. Under the rough demeanor was a quality of looking deeply into the motives that made men think and act. In what he said now, there seemed to be so much confidence that I came close to believing him.

* * *

On the tenth day of May, Jed returned from the Nippenose, because he said I had promised to go to the valley with him to inspect the horses before the middle of the month. So, to satisfy him, I saddled Salt, and we started out the next morning.

Somewhere, the small horseman had obtained a canoe, and I had no notion of asking him where he had gotten it. He was capable of going up to the Great Island and stealing it from peaceful Indian fishermen or traveling halfway to the Sinnamahoning to find one. Its value to him would depend on how much trouble he had getting it.

We left our horses and paddled across the stream, then walked through the grim Antes Gap which I studied carefully as we walked. The steep upthrust hills, the dark of evergreens, the rocky side of one ridge, all made the place a bit oppressive, and I was glad when we came out into the open land of the valley.

The Forneys were sociable men, glad to have us and to show how well the new horses had come along. Full fed, these were tractable, easily managed mounts that any man would be glad to own, not the fearful, haunted animals we had taken on the Genessee.

"Three horses are out," Ned told me. "Those men are training for Wigton's patrol and keep the horses with them. Saves corn for us."

It was very quiet at the house on the Loyalsock when we arrived at noon the next day, having spent the night with the Forney brothers. When we went to the barn, we found that the Wigton horses were gone and their saddle gear with them. The house was in excellent order, but Wigton's best clothing had disappeared from the room we shared. Instead, I found a note pinned to my blanket.

> *Kelly will send a man to help.*
> *J. W.*

I came out of the house angry and shook the note under Jed's nose. "What do you make of the damned thing?"

Jed took the paper, examined it on both sides and then passed it back. "I don't know, Simon. I can't read."

What the Wigtons did was not my business; yet I resented their leaving me summarily without a word save this note which I did not understand. Frequently John and Hope would go to Philadelphia, but that was in peaceful times. Now they might have gone to Lancaster or even Fort Augusta. When they did not return in two days, I realized they must have gone farther than Augusta anyway.

I was afraid of cluttering up the immaculate house with my housekeeping so I moved in with Jed, and we cooked outdoors over a small stone fireplace. I think Jed liked it, but I found the whole setup almost intolerable. Hope had made my house homelike, comfortable, and I missed her presence and her singing. In the morning her songs were light things; in the afternoon, soberer.

It was natural that I connected the timing of Kelly's visit with the absence of my friends. Furthermore, this keen officer had warned me of some kind of trap which I associated not too clearly with other recent events. "Keep clear of bear traps . . . set for you at Augusta."

On the fourth day of the Wigtons' absence, a man appeared. What he lacked in breadth, he made up for in height, a beanpole of a man with a voice pitched in the lowest registers. He seemed to hesitate to use it, and Jed and I were soon to learn how incredibly taciturn he was.

"Name's Abel Struble," he announced. "Kelly sent me." Jed gave the man up promptly after one or two attempts to talk to him, and I settled him in the house since the quarters Jed and I occupied were crowded enough. The man was certainly on the job, for he was out on his small, sturdy roan horse during most of the daylight hours. In between times, he kept house well and was almost as neat as Hope herself.

Jed and I worked hard, spading ground for corn and squash in back of the barn where it was hard to maneuver a plow. I was tired that evening, but Jed was full of questions. He seemed unusually anxious to know what I would do if they—whatever he meant by the word—came after me. That exasperated me for I had no plan. Just at the moment, I wanted to get those Indian horses and, for my personal problems, had a sort of apathy. There simply did not seem to be anything I could do about them.

* * *

It must have been close to twelve for I had slept a while and now lay awake, staring at the shadows in this stable room. Outside the barn door was a pool of moonlight, and there was little or no sound for both Salt and Jed's stallion were in the upper pasture.

Suddenly there was a soft noise of something moving, followed by a light metallic clinking on the far side of the ford, then a splashing. I sprang up, thinking the Wigtons were returning, though I could not imagine their traveling at this hour. Before I got out the door, Jed had me by the sleeve.

"Get your things on, Simon. That's cavalry."

Now I knew what his sharper ears had detected; the clinking would be the sound of the chain martingales the troopers used. Both of us dressed rapidly, and Jed handed me my belt with the loops supporting a pistol and knife. After that, he tossed me a bundle tied with thongs.

"Hold that," he hissed.

There were six troopers. We could see them plainly between the ford and the front of the house, with glinting jackboots and horsehair plumes in their caps. An officer crowded his horse close to the door and hammered on it with his sword hilt.

The second time he knocked, the door opened, and Struble stood there, disheveled, half dressed, holding a candle high. The officer stared down at the odd figure, at the long-tailed shirt which was his only garment. "Who are you?" he demanded curtly.

"Corporal Struble, sir, with Colonel Kelly."

The reply was military enough, but the officer was gruff. "Bring out Simon Braide. Tell him Lieutenant Barr is here with a warrant."

Struble shaded his flickering light with a broad bony palm. "Can't, sir. He ain't in here."

The officer cursed, then swung himself from the saddle and stepped close to Struble who blocked the doorway and spoke in his deep tones. "A lady lives here."

The lieutenant checked himself and half turned but again Struble spoke.

"But she ain't here tonight either. You can come in."

I stood beside Jed, taking in the entire scene and marveling at the way Struble was killing time. He had told only a half-truth; I was not in the house. He was obviously stalling for every precious moment.

"Simon," Jed shook my arm, "take you and that bundle over the footlog and then go to Wigton's. You'll have to foot it. I can't get Salt."

The troopers blocked the ford that I could see, and the lieutenant was just inside the house door, showing plainly against the candlelight. The belt of shadow cast by the trees along the stream was not enough shelter to hide me, and one horseman was close to the footlog bridge.

Jed whistled so sharply that I jumped; then he pushed me out of the door, and I dodged into the meager shadow.

There was nothing planned about my leap; it was merely the instinct to get out of sight of the troopers who must be looking our way. Then I understood, for from up the fields came a faint drumming that quickened into the beat of a big horse galloping fast. Jed's stallion had heard his signal and was obeying it.

In minutes, certainly before the troopers could realize what was happening, the animal pounded into the farmyard and swerved at Jed's second signal. Somehow the little man swung up on the stallion, and the next instant the vicious beast charged the troopers, caroming into one of their horses, and sending it and the rider sprawling. A pistol flashed, and Jed, howling like some wild creature, was away down the narrow path that runs through the rocks on our side of the river, ordinarily used only in daylight because it is so dangerous.

Jed had made his diversion for me. In the confusion, I did what he expected, darted over the footlog and ran along the river with none of the confused troop the wiser. As I went, I could hear the sounds from across the water, the measured drum of Jed's stallion going like the wind on that perilous trail, and the noise of the soldiers in pursuit. The little man was a superb horseman but, had I been he, I would have preferred to stop and fight it out rather than to ride as he was doing. Minutes later, the troopers turned back; the going had been too bad for them.

Jed was waiting at the Wigton place when I reached it half an hour later; he was busy rubbing the legs of his horse. He laughed when I came up.

"Pretty good without a saddle," he boasted, and I stared, remembering that he also lacked both bridle and reins.

"Thanks, Jed. I'm getting deeper in your debt every day."

"Regular troopers," he commented, ignoring my thanks. "Some of Sullivan's men who stopped over at Fort Augusta, is my bet."

I made no comment but stood thinking while he finished with the horse. My escape had been made a year before; it was odd that this was the first time they had come after me. Jed must be mistaken for all of Sullivan's men would have long been out of the country. Kelly had said I should look out for a trap; he had hinted it would come from Augusta where he said they sympathized with Challis.

I had escaped tonight, but if they kept up this hunt, planning the big raid for horses would be hard, almost impossible in fact.

Jed threw away his bunch of grass.

"That Struble was good," he commented. "Takes a smart man to act that dumb. Why did he do it?"

I shook my head for that was another problem that I could not solve at the moment. There seemed to be no reason why one of Kelly's men should stall in my interest.

"Jed, let's get some sleep, then see if they're hanging about in the morning."

We slept well enough, feeling sure the stallion would warn us if anyone approached. In the morning, however, our scanty breakfast of parched corn and water left us in a dejected mood. It certainly was not pleasant to be run off from one's own property in the night and then be compelled to sneak back in the morning.

Everything looked peaceful, but when we got closer, we saw a strange horse tied near the barn. Struble and his roan were gone apparently, and the man was probably out on his patrol. Certainly there was no one in sight—outside at least.

Both of us reconnoitered and, through the kitchen window where the raiders had watched me and Celine that morning, we saw a trooper with his chair tilted against the wall, his mouth wide open in deep sleep. Equipment lay on the table. Jed looked at me and grinned, malice on his face.

"Let me handle this, Simon. He just mustn't see you." The wily little horseman certainly had some sort of penchant for deviltry, and I sometimes wondered about his life down country in his beloved Berks County. He ran to the stable and returned with horse blankets and rawhide straps. One of the blankets he turned into a bag by catching it at the corners.

"Grab his legs if he fights," he directed, "but if he opens his eyes, dodge outdoors and leave him to me."

We moved inside quickly. Then Jed approached stealthily and jerked his blanket over the young fellow's head and shoulders. I grabbed the flailing arms while Jed tied the man securely, after which I carried him outside and dumped him down before the door.

In a matter of minutes, Jed returned from the barn with the trooper's horse and his own saddled. When he mounted, I boosted the prisoner into the saddle and tied his legs fast under the horse's belly.

"I'll get rid of him and make him talk," Jed whispered as he rode away with his victim.

Two hours passed, and I was a little uneasy as to what Jed might do with the soldier. I remembered the Indian on the Genessee who had fallen into the water and other things. The small horseman could be vicious and direct when he wanted something.

Eventually, Struble appeared without showing surprise at seeing me. He stabled his horse and came toward the house where I sat on a bench outside the door.

"That lieutenant last night said a man named Challis, or something like that, told the commandant at Augusta that an escaped prisoner was up here. There was to be a reward if they caught the man."

I thanked Struble and went into the house. So Challis, who was a good Whig, was concerned about me. I thought again of the darkened room, the flash of the sword, but all I could clearly remember was that my assailant was about my own height and that he moved about easily in the dark with no resort to his lanthorn until he ran me through.

I glanced in the door, but Struble was frowning at the kitchen's disarray. Likely there would be no further information from him.

* * *

Jed's face wore a suspiciously satisfied look when he appeared. His stallion had put on an act in the barnyard, going up on its hind legs and whinnying shrilly while it fanned the air with its wicked front feet. Finally, Jed pulled him down and dismounted.

"Simon, our young man felt he'd ought to get back to Augusta. He got the idea one of them Doane robbers from down our way had caught him, and them fellows is all Tories who like to slit a soldier's throat."

He took off the horse's saddle, slipped out the bit, and slapped the animal smartly on the rump. My eyes caught the fine short carbine in Jed's leather boot.

"You know, Simon, he was really a good boy and wanted to pay for the blanket he took with him so I did keep his gun and some little things he won't really miss."

That was exactly all I ever got out of Jed about the matter, and he had failed to get any information. Struble appeared, now that he had the kitchen looking all right once more.

"It might be wise," he said earnestly, "for you boys to get to the Nippenose. Them soldiers is likely to come back."

Jed did go, but I wanted to stay closer and wait for the return of the Wigtons, so I rode up the river to the Little Bear Creek and camped in an old lean-to we used when we hunted in that locality. Each day I rode down to reconnoiter, and no more soldiers came, but the third day I saw Hope's big mare in the pasture.

I did not think of myself. I wanted to see Hope and her father so I dashed over the ford and dismounted. The door stood open, and I heard Hope's voice. Struble appeared, carrying a bag.

"You really kept the place well, Corporal," she told him, "and I'll tell Colonel Kelly how pleased I am when I see him." The tall soldier beamed his pleasure, then went round the corner of the house where his roan was tied. Hope saw me, walked forward, and gave me her hand for a moment. "Struble says you had a bad time, Simon."

Her concern was friendly enough, but I wanted something more and, as the corporal came round and mounted, I went to him. Money would likely have displeased him, yet he had been of very real service to me. So I gave him the small stubby pistol I carried in my saddle bags, and his dull eyes lighted as he handled the weapon, then thrust it into the breast of his hunting shirt. He beamed.

"I'll tell the colonel you're offering a reward of five pounds for Challis' ears."

Hope stood on the wide doorstone looking toward the barn and smiling. Behind me, Salt was trailing his reins, and now he nudged me with his nose as I looked toward the stable. Almost involuntarily I turned toward the horse, picked up the reins, and threw them over his head.

John Wigton had stepped out of the barn, and behind him came a man in the buff and blue uniform of a captain in the Continental Line. There was no mistaking the hawklike face or the swing of those shoulders. This man was chief of Washington's Intelligence Service.

It was Linn!

CHAPTER SIXTEEN

WHEN THE two men had come a dozen steps from the barn, I pulled down the reins again and stepped clear of my horse, watching them approach. Neither man was smiling, nor was I.

Captain Linn had been my best friend on that faraway river. Time and again we had pulled each other out of danger, witnessed by the scar on my chin. Linn, whose foolish drunken speech had started the gossip in Fort Pitt about the map, was now an Intelligence man. The Wigtons had been gone long enough to bring him here from Washington's camp, and bitterness swept over me. Linn spoke first, his tone a bit bantering.

"You're a hunted man, Simon. You're careless."

Hope was walking forward to meet the men. I, with Salt at my back, formed the third point of the triangle made by the house and this group who I had thought were friends.

"No," I answered him, "it was just that I thought friends lived here."

"Come into the house, Simon," John Wigton said, and his voice sounded tired.

I looked sharply at Linn. "Captain Linn's in uniform to make the arrest. Will it be now?"

My rifle was inside the house, but I did have my pistol and the heavy knife I had used at the Challis house in my belt. Linn showed no weapon. But—perhaps for the first time—I felt the full force of being hunted. Linn would arrest his brother or stand by and see a friend hanged if he believed that to be his duty. There was no doubt in my mind that he had come for me.

It was Hope's turn, and she spoke as I turned again and set the toe of my moccasin into my stirrup.

"It's not his fault, Simon. I went for him—"

That was what I had thought, but I had not expected to hear her admit it. I left the horse, stepped up to her, and stood looking into her troubled face. I was under sentence to hang, and this girl standing before me, straight and slim with the wind tugging at her loose hair, had just told me she had brought one of my best friends whose only purpose could be my arrest.

I thought of Celine who had hated this house and me and whom this girl had despised for treachery—Celine who herself had been soft and warm and charming, when she chose.

John Wigton looked on until Hope dropped her eyes but not before I saw the hint of tears in them.

"Come inside, all of you," he directed, and I followed the three of them through the door of my house, once wrecked, now made tidy and beautiful by this girl. We seated ourselves at the table, and by common consent, I had the position where my back was to the door.

Linn cleared his throat loudly. "Simon, all your friends think it high time this hiding and hunting came to an end."

The bitter irony of what he said possessed me so strongly that I placed the palms of my hands flat on the table and watched the knuckles grow white under pressure. There was only one way it could end, on a rope or, by mercy, before a firing squad.

"Has it been my choosing?" I snarled. "I've been a stranger to peace and quiet for years. I've prowled the woods and stuck my neck in a British noose. My house was broken, my wife carried away."

I looked sharply at Hope and continued. "It was not my fault that the map was stolen and that I'm under sentence because your damned general found it on a dead thief. Iroquois want to burn me; the British have a scaffold waiting. They send troopers after me from Augusta. I am left for dead by a strange swordsman who wishes me destroyed."

I rose fighting back the anger that choked me. "I'm the simple Simon, Linn, who goes about offering the penny of his life to set things right. I wish I had taken your red-faced Sullivan by the throat and choked the truth from him about the maps. As it is, if I sleep, they send troopers; when I am awake, they send you."

Reckless and aching only to hurt somebody, I leaned forward over the table. "Linn, I've even felt coldness in my own house from people I have known all my life, and now you sit here."

The captain's face went dark with anger. Hope and her father, sitting close together, stared at me.

Linn struck the table with his palm. "Sit down, you great fool; sit down. They have tried to help you. Before John and Hope left, they had Kelly send a man up here to watch for the troopers, to keep you safe."

So that was what the presence and action of Struble meant. It disarmed me a little.

Linn hurried on. "Sullivan's out of the army, ill. Washington has sent an express to him stating that the maps of his expedition were made by you, and the story of the raid on your house was also sent. But His Excellency will not clear you without Sullivan's word. I've come to take you to Boston."

Hope and her father were nodding as Linn glanced at them. "They've done all in their power to help you. Hope and John went—"

He stopped at Wigton's gesture to be silent, cleared his throat, and then finished. "We need you free for the work on the river. I've done what I could, even if my drunken speech in Pitt did make trouble—"

Hope started to say something but stopped at what she must have read in my eyes. Nor could I understand what was in my own mind about her, but I did know that nothing either Wigton or Linn said mattered. What did concern me was the question of whether I now hated this girl whose face had been so often in my dreams and whose opinion, up until these hours, had become the most important moving influence in all I did or thought.

I turned slowly and walked out.

Salt was waiting at the stable door and whinnied softly to remind me that I had forgotten him, so I took off his furnishings and made him comfortable in his stall, with plenty of good food before him. Jed was still in the Nippenose, so I took the small horseman's room and bed.

There, in the darkness, with the homely sounds of the barn about me, I fought out my battle, the bitterness fading after a while and a hopelessness taking its place. I had gone here and there over this great north country, taking any risk to solve the problems that had been thrust upon me. There had been times when I felt Hope had a deeper feeling for what I was passing through. There had been that night when she played and sang until I had courage again. Then, wounded, almost dead, I believed she had given me my life with a kindness one could not measure.

* * *

Sometime in the night, I got up and stepped outside. No light showed in the house, and there was no sound but that of the river and the horses in their stalls. I walked a little way toward the house, wondering. Likely Linn slept in my bed, and John Wigton's self-discipline would prevent his sleep being disturbed. But what was Hope doing?

Once more back in the small room with its rude furnishings, I made my decision. The present situation was hopeless. I could be of very little service toward the safety of this river country with the shadow of arrest hanging over me. The possibility of a pardon seemed out of the question, but I might win a reprieve long enough to last while danger threatened this home country. Perhaps, if I went to Sullivan, he might grant that.

After my decision, strangely enough, I fell asleep.

Salt's whinny woke me early, and I went to the stream, slipped off my buckskins, and swam in the cold water for a while. Then I shaved carefully and donned a clean linen shirt taken from my warbag. Afterward, I walked slowly to the house, tapped on the door, and stepped inside.

The three of them were seated at the table, and Hope, at sight of me, rose and placed another plate on the cloth between her and Linn.

"I'll be ready to ride when you are, Captain."

There must have been something strange or final in my tone for John Wigton looked down at his plate. Linn nodded soberly, and Hope, who had not seated herself, stood for a long moment. I saw her take the plate from the table as I went out the door.

An hour afterward, we were ready. Wigton had one of his own horses saddled and explained briefly that Linn wanted to travel fast and Salt was too old for that. Rather than argue with him, I put my own belongings in these saddle bags and mounted while Linn made his farewells, holding Hope's hand too long, I thought. He crossed the ford first, and I followed, remembering how, on another occasion, Hope had told me she would care for Salt while I was away.

We rode hard, neither of us saying anything until we reached the main road and the dark pile of burned Challis Hall was behind us. Then around a turn came three cavalrymen on lathered horses. They pulled up with a jingle of equipment and saluted as they saw Linn's uniform. The sergeant spoke. "Yes, Captain Linn, of the Line."

"Captain Linn?"

My companion nodded and returned the salutes.

"Colonel Hunter sent us, sir. He has a message from Colonel Chambers downriver that Norris, the Tory spy, escaped his guards near Reading. Chambers needs you, sir, at once."

Linn looked ruefully at the messenger, pulled his worn boot out of the stirrup, then replaced it.

"Very well, we'll pass through Augusta. Follow at your own pace; your horses look hard pushed."

Excitement leaped in me at the mention of Norris. They had captured the man whom I wanted to see, the man I had vaguely imagined might have been in Challis Hall that night.

"Part of my job, Simon," Linn explained. "It will delay us."

He glanced down at the sandy road frowning, then back to me.

"Simon, there will be no foolishness about a parole between us. But if you want to ride straight for Boston, it will be all right with me. It might save time and this trouble below isn't yours."

I grinned at him. "No man's in a hurry to hang—let's get after Norris."

* * *

The Fort Augusta sentinel stopped us a bit after dusk, and we hurried to the house of the commandant where Linn went inside and I waited with the horses. He was out in a few minutes accompanied by Hunter with whom he exchanged a few more words.

Then Linn saluted and swung up on his horse. "We'll ride for it, Simon. Chambers has gone to Galbreath's for a couple of days and we'll catch him there."

Beyond the fort, the road was wide enough for us to ride side by side and talk, Linn commenting on what Hunter had told him. "The colonel is nervous. He sympathized with Challis and the loss of his house. Now that he suspects our Whig friend of harboring Norris on a number of occasions, he's flustered and apologetic."

I made no comment, although Linn seemed to expect one. There had been two men in the Hall that night, and up to very recently, this Colonel Hunter had trusted Challis; witness the troopers sent for me. Now Linn talked on as if refreshing his own memory.

"From all I hear, Norris is a queer bird, really holds a commission in the Royal Americans, but he hates the American cause with a bitterness hard to understand. He is a great swordsman and, in spite of his cloth and age, a ladies' man. He fears nothing but the possible success of our cause."

We spent what was left of the night at McKee's tavern, which we reached very late. The place seemed homelike to me with the sound of the river fretting among the rocks. Rising early, we rode through Harris Ferry about noon and turned eastward toward Reading, After two hours more of stiff riding, we crossed Swatara Creek and approached the huge rambling inn known far and wide as Galbreath's. From here, a man can turn southward toward Lancaster or northeast to Reading town. Our road time had been excellent.

Colonel Chambers was a much older man than I expected, which explained some things, and he was extremely worried. At the sight of Linn, he seemed pathetically relieved. He was courteous to me when Linn introduced me as a friend. After an excellent dinner, Chambers talked at some length.

"They had Norris in the Carlisle jail, safe enough, but a deputy from Newtown came to take the prisoner over there for some sort of military trial. Having only one deputy was a bad mistake in handling a person of Norris's wit and importance. Near a tavern called the Black Horse, two well-mounted men appeared and captured the deputy after which they rode away with Norris, leaving the officer tied to a tree."

"The Doanes?" Linn questioned, and Chambers nodded.

I had heard something of this band of robbers that infested the lower counties, but this was the first direct contact with them I had. Jed often mentioned them. To a man, they were Loyalists, particularly when it served their pocketbooks, and British gold was more plentiful than our own, even in this rich region. There was a story that once The Doanes had planned kidnapping His Excellency and selling him to the English.

Chambers continued. "Likely by now, Norris is with the British; he had help enough and not far to go. I've less than a dozen men in these parts, Captain Linn. It's up to you to try to get the man. You can manage if anybody can."

Linn smiled. "Thank you, Colonel Chambers, but you put it too strongly. However, Simon and I will do our best."

The older officer seemed content with that thin promise and went on talking.

"The country's wild about here, what with too much money in every hand from working in the gun and powder mills. There's drinking, wenching, fighting, and the country constables are mostly old men anxious to keep the peace. It is little wonder The Doanes ride and rob at will."

The colonel's talking delayed us so much that we reached Reading late the following afternoon, and then my horse had to cast a shoe. When I looked, it was to find a second one loose, and Linn was doubtful about the wisdom of continuing with an animal in that condition.

"Can't risk laming one of John's horses. Hunt a smith and follow me east as soon as you can. I want to see this Black Horse tavern. Ask for me there."

It took me an hour to find a shop with an open door, and the smith who did the shoeing was at supper and could not be hurried in that important business. Then, the big brown horse proved hard to handle, which slowed the job. In all, I lost three hours, the last of the smith's work being done by lanthorn light.

He told me, in answer to my question, that the road to the Black Horse tavern was a lonely one, but it saved fording the river if one was bound for Philadelphia.

"A shortcut it is," he said, rolling his eyes, "but most men ride that way in the dark, for the business in that direction is best done by either moonlight or a single candle."

I was busy adjusting a strap and had not heard all the man said.

"What?" I asked, and the smith waved his hammer.

"Don't tell me, young man, it's not the girls up there that take you galloping along dark roads. There's better liquor in Reading, but Landlord Fife's daughters . . . Son, if I was not now getting old and the father of five, I'd joy a ride with you, I would."

So with gossip in my ears, I rode out of Reading on a road that ran a little north of east. Whatever the blacksmith's interest, I wanted to overtake Linn, though it was a bit amusing for a prisoner to be following his captor. I did not want to miss what little chance we had of coming up with Norris.

When the road I followed descended a long hill, I rode through a scrub pine barren and splashed through shallow streams on two occasions. Then, when I topped a gentle rise, I saw the first light since I had left Reading. It was perhaps a half mile farther on, and I clucked to my horse. Linn would be impatient.

* * *

The house, a big rambling building, stood north of the road in a grove of what appeared to be high walnut trees, judging from their shape against the sky, and after I drummed over a narrow bridge, I came to a wide porch. Just as I leaped from the saddle and brought my rein forward, the door of the place opened, spilling candlelight, in the center of which stood a man.

"Good evening to you, sir." The voice was deep and pleasant, and I followed him into the wide room not too well lighted except in back of the bar. To my surprise, a woman was seated at a table, but she did not look up.

"John Fife, landlord here," the man explained. "Can I do something for you?"

"Yes," I answered, "I was to meet a friend here."

The woman at the table raised her head, and I saw she was young, just a girl. Her eyes were sleepy above a too short nose and a loose mouth.

Fife looked at her with an odd expression on his thin, lined face. His small body was erect as a ramrod. He turned to me.

"Yes," he said. "Perhaps you'd like a little cheer. I have good whiskey and a little rum—"

The girl had risen and slouched over to the bar when I spoke again.

"He should be here, landlord. A big man riding a black horse. He wears a captain's uniform."

The girl laughed contemptuously.

"You think stuck-up captains'd come here?"

Fife silenced her with a scowl. "Sorry, there's been nobody over the road this evening but country boys who have all gone home by now. Likely your friend took the other road out of Reading."

The man annoyed me, but there seemed no reason for it. The girl chuckled deep in her throat. Suddenly Fife wheeled on her, every inch of his small frame tense, menacing. If this was his daughter, he was most unfatherly.

"Be still, you baggage."

When he spoke to me again, he was civil. "Ride on, turn left at Amity crossroads, then in a mile or so, you'll be at the White Horse. Your friend may have mixed the color of his horses. Men get that way at times."

He came out on the porch with me and waved his hand as I cantered away. The girl stood in the lighted doorway where every line of her ample figure stood out boldly.

What I considered five miles farther on, a second light appeared, this in a tiny house to the left of the road, and I pulled up, dismounted, and knocked at the door. An old man with an immense shock of tousled hair appeared, holding a candle high so he could see my face.

"Now who are you?" he demanded querulously. "Well, I see you ain't a Doane; guess I know all them hellions by sight. Come in; I've got some cider I was sitting up with."

I smiled and thanked him. "No, I just wanted to know if an officer on a black horse passed here this evening."

Before he could answer, we heard the sound of a horse galloping fast from the direction I had come. As we waited, the horseman loomed in the moonlight and dashed by us so rapidly we could see little of him. Certainly it was not Linn.

"Nope," the man answered. "That fellow in a hurry was the only one this night. You and him."

I stood thinking so long that the garrulous ancient cleared his throat loudly and lowered his candle. "The cider's good stuff, mister. Put it up myself in whiskey barrels, leaving some of the Monongahela in them for seasoning. A couple of pounds of maple sugar goes in through the bung. Man, it's even good for the 'hair on the dog' when morning comes and regular cider don't set too well."

I laughed, liking this man with rumpled hair, standing in his bare feet. He was simply making conversation. I spoke my thoughts aloud.

"Fife said my friend must have come this way."

My informant cackled and turned toward his door.

"Sonny, you think any army officer'd ride past Fife's place and its women, then you just don't know the facts of life. Get back to the Black Horse where I'd bet a pint of cider your friend's bedded all right. You're a sort of solemn looking cuss, but they might have a place there for you."

I was irritated. Fife might have lied to me, but there seemed little purpose in that, and I did not think Linn, on an important errand, would stop for a wild night at a tavern no matter what entertainment was offered. So I shoved some shillings into the man's palm and mounted.

"I heard tell the one they call Agnes is the best," he called after me when I had turned my big horse and it had lunged forward. His ribald cackling followed me until the pound of hooves covered it.

Now no sign of life showed at the Black Horse, and all was quiet in the grove of high trees. The barn was even bigger than the house, and I walked my horse round it twice before I heard the sound of another animal inside.

The padlock did not matter much for I had my big knife, and the door opened to give me the rich smell of hay, grain, and stabled animals. When I walked in quietly, a horse nickered.

"Blackie," I whispered, and the horse answered, knowing my voice. This was Linn's horse, and working with caution, I found the saddle and bridle, put them on, and led the black outside and tied him beside my own animal.

This time, when I came round the front of the inn, I saw I had been mistaken. There was a light; a single candle shone in the big room.

CHAPTER SEVENTEEN

MINUTES SLIPPED away while I watched this building deeply shadowed by the trees. It is not a pleasant thing to contemplate breaking into a man's house, and I had taken bitter medicine for that same act not too long ago to have forgotten. Linn's horse was in the stable; that deception was the only thing I had directly against this man Fife other than his extremely unfatherly attitude toward the girl. It amused me a little to think of Linn inside with some girl because he had been so outspoken about my weaknesses.

The door was locked, and I stood before it, balancing the big knife in my hand. Then I grinned; with a number of nooses waiting to stretch my neck, a little thing like housebreaking should not deter me, for I had achieved a very doubtful freedom of action.

One twist of the heavy blade worked the wooden lock, and the door opened until it was stopped by a short length of chain. Abruptly impatient, I hammered with the haft of my knife, no longer caring who heard me or how unreasonably I behaved. A muffled voice from somewhere on the second floor called.

"Effie, send that damned fool away and get yourself to bed."

Fumbling, uncertain fingers loosed the chain, and the door opened a foot wider, but the girl I had seen earlier stood blocking it, outlined by the candlelight behind her.

"Fife says you're a damned fool. Go away. I'm drunk anyway."

I set my shoulder against the panel and pushed while the girl tried to hold it, but there was little strength in her.

"La," she mumbled when I was inside. "You're strong, let's drink to it."

I tried to push her aside for I had caught a glimpse of Fife on the stairway, candle in one hand, a heavy pistol in the other. The man's voice was charged with malice and threat when he yelled:

"She told you to get out. Step aside, Effie, while I blow hell out of him."

There was no doubt the man intended to shoot; the pistol hammer was set at full cock, and there was a half crazed look on his thin face. With one sweeping motion I snatched a stool and hurled it just as the pistol roared. The thing had done its work; the weapon was thrown from Fife's hand, and the next instant I had him by his thin shoulders and shook him until his mouth gaped open. Holding the man against the wall, I snatched the apron from the girl who had come close and roughly trussed my victim securely.

"Fife, now I'll search your shebang, and if anything's happened to the captain, I'll cut you apart as one does a fowl," I said and slapped him hard with the flat of my broad blade.

Effie was laughing and mumbling. Sometime in the evening she had been drinking hard, and I had a sick memory of Celine and her brandy. I took the girl by the shoulders and marched her ahead of me, the candle in her uncertain hand.

There were half a dozen upstairs rooms, all empty, and I wheeled my captive around until she faced me.

"Where is he?"

Weaving back and forth, spilling drops of tallow on the floor from the melting candle, she chuckled. "He means the beautiful captain. Where but in bed with our Agnes." She pointed a shaky finger toward the door at the end of the passageway, and I strode forward and pushed it open.

There was a candle in a bracket on the wall. By its light I saw a wide bed pushed against the wall in which, resting on her elbow, was a half-dressed girl. On the floor beside the bed, securely bound and with a gag in his mouth, lay Linn, dressed only in his uniform trousers.

I crowded Effie into a chair, drew my knife, and moved toward the bed. The girl screamed in fright.

"Get up, you, and untie him."

She came off the bed in one smooth motion and, down on her knees, fought with the knots of Linn's bonds. The gag was untied first, Linn spitting out some lint and threads.

"Watch for Fife, Simon!" he gasped.

Presently the captain was free, rubbing his wrists and ankles where his captors had used rawhide. He looked shamefacedly at me a couple of times. "Don't know what happened. The liquor was heady, and they carried me up here."

He turned on Agnes. "Where's my coat?"

She crossed the room, found the garment, and put it in Linn's hands while I watched closely. Linn thrust his fingers in the pockets.

"Gone!" he said with an oath. "The letter to Sullivan and my own commission."

He walked toward the cowering girl, and I remembered the fury of which this man could be possessed. With one pull, he ripped a slat from a chair, then doubled the girl over his knee and laid on the improvised paddle while she screamed and twisted. Over and over the stick rose and fell until she was gibbering when he finally stopped and let her slip from his grasp.

"Where are my papers?"

She spat at him like an aroused cat, and he turned toward me.

"Your knife, Simon."

The keen blade glittered in the light. He tried its edge on his thumb while the girl watched him fearfully.

"He gave them to Joe Doane."

She said the words grudgingly, her eyes on the steel, and I remembered the speeding horseman. Linn caught my arm. "Come on; it's Fife I want."

Our unwilling landlord had just about freed himself from my lashings and was working in a cold fury of haste. Linn seized him and stood him erect on a chair. In back of the bar was a stout bell pull rope and, at Linn's gesture, I cut this loose and gave it to him. Presently the captain had a noose around Fife's neck, the free end flung over a ceiling beam. All ready, Linn tightened the rope until Fife stood on his tiptoes.

"Now," Linn demanded, "where are my things?" His voice was broken and brittle from anger.

Fife made the mistake of shutting his lips together, muttering profanity. Linn's quick hand tore away his shirt. The captain still had my knife and set the point against the landlord's quivering chest. The point made a red mark before Fife screamed. "Joe Doane has them—everything."

Linn slacked the rope; then his captive talked rapidly.

He was a victim of The Doanes who planned holding Linn for ransom since he was a captain and the bearer of important letters. The British would pay a good price for Continental officers. Yes, Norris had been taken to the British by The Doanes. Likely he was in New York. Shaw, the deputy in Newtown, could give us particulars.

While he was talking, the girl Effie appeared and flung Linn's saddle bags over the railing of the stairway. But Linn had not finished.

"Why was I in the girl's room?" he demanded, and Fife had a ready answer.

"If soldiers came, we'd say you were with Agnes, drunk. We had to tie you to sober you."

Linn snorted. To me it seemed that the full truth had been told, but the angry captain had not finished. He still held my knife and now tested it on his thumbnail while his victim writhed. He grasped Fife's ear between his forefinger and thumb as if considering cutting it off. Abruptly he seized the rope and drew it taut until Fife stood once more on tiptoes to prevent being choked. Tying the loose end, Linn caught up his saddle bags and stalked toward the door with me following. But as we went out, I saw the girl Agnes hurrying down the stairway to release the hanging man. The fellow would not die, and it was possible that, caught between two fires in this disturbed country, he might not be too much to blame.

"Can't forgive myself," Linn insisted as he mounted. "I stopped at the place, asked a few questions; then I was served strong ale. One of the girls sat across from me, drinking when I did. I guess it was Effie. I was reeling in my chair, and they took me upstairs."

He glanced toward me, but I could not see the expression on his face. "Don't remember much else, but a second man helped carry me."

We rode a little distance before he said anything more. "That girl dumped me on the floor when she came up."

I laughed, and he did not like that very much, but he seemed to realize he had it coming. After all, it was a humiliating experience for a man who did intelligence work, and who had a prisoner in his charge.

In Newtown, we found a grim, red-headed young man who said his name was Shaw and who was profane about The Doanes. He gave us a good breakfast at the jail house and told of his experience with Norris.

"The man didn't seem dangerous, just rode along, singing hymns softly as if to himself. I had him locked up in Reading overnight. Next morning, we went on but stopped at that infernal Black Horse Inn where Norris bought me a drink." He shrugged his shoulders. "Two miles farther along, they came out of the brush; Norris just sat on his horse while they trussed me to a tree. I still can see the tall devil look down at me from his mount and hear his deep voice."

I listened with some amusement at the way Norris succeeded in getting people to underestimate him. Well I remembered the deep voice haranguing Butler's men that day in Niagara.

"Now listen, men. Word came an hour ago that three of The Doanes are at their cabin on the Tohicon. Would you help round them up?"

Decisions were up to Linn. After all, I was a prisoner. Whether Linn recovered the letters to Sullivan or his commission did not matter a great deal to me, but Linn sprang to his feet.

"We surely will. I want to get the fellow that—"

He stopped. After all, Shaw did not need to know what had happened in the Black Horse, but I knew Linn well enough to realize how much he wanted to even the score.

* * *

Shaw found a Colonel Burd in the town, and there were two others who held a grudge against The Doanes so, early in the afternoon six well-armed men rode north on the route that would take us to the London ferry, running across the Delaware. Since the colonel had served in the army, he was our commanding officer.

Seven miles out of Newtown, we stopped at an inn called The Plough, where the landlord was civil but disclaimed even knowing who The Doanes were. The man was plainly lying, but he did admit that there was an old cabin on the Tohicon and that sometimes his neighbors said strange young men came there.

When we reached the sluggish creek, Burd divided his forces. Half of us, including Linn, were to move down the stream. The rest, with whom I went, were to make a detour through the hills and approach at a different angle.

In an hour, our party reached the river at a point where the creek emptied its muddy water. Here the country was covered with brush and scrub timber that made good cover until we saw a clearing with a small cabin set almost in its center. The place looked like a farm, but there were no outbuildings, no signs of tillage, and certainly no evidences of life about the place. It looked deserted.

Burd, with our group, fired a pistol shot, and the door of the cabin opened. A tall man wearing a wide flopping hat stepped outside, looked about, sighted Shaw and his squad, then jumped inside and slammed the door.

Both our groups now ringed the meadow, and we moved forward slowly until two shots from the cabin stopped us. Then a third shot crashed out and a man in Shaw's squad screamed, dropped his rifle, and clutched his arm. It was a signal for all of us to drop prone and, from this range, pour our fire into the cabin, answered every few minutes by shots from the flimsy log structure through which our bullets must be tearing.

It was Linn who precipitated the real excitement. More than an hour of this delusory business had slipped by. I was not close enough to the captain to hear him, but he was on his feet, running toward the cabin. He had covered the first fifty yards when he stumbled and fell. I saw the smoke bloom and a spurt of dirt fly up from the bullet not a yard from the captain. He kept down and edged himself forward until he was sheltered by a boulder. Twice we heard the whining sound as bullets ricocheted from the rock that shielded him.

We kept up our fire and crept forward at Shaw's and my signals. Then we saw something else. A narrow draw ran from close by the building to the brushy woodland. The cabin door jerked open; a man clutching a gun leaped out, then a second.

I do not think it was my shot, but someone's bullet must have struck the first man's gun stock, tearing the weapon from him. He cried out, then held up a hand dripping blood and walked toward us. A man near me aimed at him, but Colonel Burd struck up the barrel of the musket.

The second man was running. I saw Linn and Shaw both on their feet following the running man with their rifles as one will a bounding deer. Five yards, ten yards, perhaps twenty, then both pieces spoke as one. The running figure leaped into the air, fell, and scrambled for an instant before it was still.

There were only two men in the cabin—Mose Doane, now dead, and our captive, Joe Doane. When we had him tied securely, we searched the premises and found two horses tied in the brush a full five hundred yards from the cabin. Both animals were recognized as having been stolen. In the cabin, under a pile of firewood, we found an old trunk which we dragged into the open. Burd spread a blanket on the ground and dumped the contents of this leather-covered box on it.

Linn's letters and commission were there, and he pocketed them promptly. Here were watches, weapons, rings, bracelets, pieces of fine lace, and some coins, probably the loot of years. Then abruptly, I leaned forward and took a coin from the blanket. My fingers trembled as I turned it about and saw the tiny dent on its edge. It was one of the coins John Wigton and I had found in Fort Pitt, one of those that had been a part of Celine's hoard.

Standing there in this meadow close to the Delaware, with the others looking curiously at me, it seemed that, at last, I was looking through a partially opened door to the solution of my problems. With no preliminary, I stepped close to our prisoner, seized the breast of his shirt, and held the coin before him.

"Where did you get this?"

He glanced at it stubbornly, and then must have seen something in my eyes for he answered, "Norris."

So it was—a scarf and a coin in Niagara, then part of a map on the Genessee. I had thought Celine was in the north country, and perhaps she had been. But this was different. Here was a coin on the Delaware. Norris had her money, or some of it, and I knew Celine would not have parted from her gold lightly. Norris must have some powerful hold on the woman who was my wife—or else she was dead.

I wished for Yonido and his trick of organizing his thinking with pebbles. Linn might help, but I was suddenly reluctant to confide in him. After all, if our mission to Sullivan failed, I might hang. I was his prisoner for all that he trusted me as a friend.

There had been a drafting board in Challis Hall; Norris did surveying and therefore could make maps. Challis was a prominent Whig, Sullivan had false maps. There had been one pair of booted feet among the raiders that had carried Celine away and killed Major. All these things would make a pattern; somewhere there was a key to this maze of happenings, but I was sure that all of them were part of one whole.

We buried Mose Doane in a shallow grave by the cabin, and the brother looked on unemotionally as we finished the job and patted the soil in place. It was not until many years afterward that I learned that The Doanes had once robbed Shaw's father, having tortured the old man with coals to make him reveal the hiding place of his money. No wonder he claimed that his bullet had cut down Mose Doane.

Our return to Newtown did not occasion much excitement though a few people came to the jail to see Joe Doane. I went into the man's cell and tried to question him.

"You know more of this man, Norris. What can you tell me?"

He looked at me doubtfully until I showed some money at which he smiled.

"Wouldn't do me much good, Mister, seeing as how they'll hang me in a day or so."

I winced at the irony of the fact that a similar fate might be awaiting me. It would all depend on a red-faced fury of a general.

"Well, I'm in trouble, too, and money always helps," I declared, pressing a sovereign into his palm.

"That's generous," he said, pocketing the coin. "But I don't know much. We got word to take a man from the deputy and that we'd be paid well to get him to British friends. So, we did. The folks that sent word knowed just about where this man would be and where they were taking him."

He was silent until I asked another question.

"What is the man Norris like?"

He smiled. "Mister, Mose and I figured he was cracked for he offered us ten pounds if we'd set fire to Reading town. But we've got friends there. He's a big tall man, gray hair, and you can't forget that deep voice. It's sort of like music, even when it's saying devilish stuff."

The outlaw tapped with his finger on the side of his cot. "Mebbe I shouldn't tell you this. But this man really hates you folks along the rivers. He said to Mose and me that when he finished, he'd make the Susquehanna a race track for the Senecas. Anyway," he concluded, "we don't want them Indians down here; it would sure spoil our business in this country."

He did not seem to realize for the moment that his raiding was likely over, and I thanked him as heartily as I could before leaving him. I had not learned much that was new, but I more than half liked this young man, Joe Doane.

With our business concluded, there was nothing to hold Linn and me any longer; we rode north until we cut into the Reading-Easton Road. There Linn left me in a tavern while he rode into Easton for some information. There would be many soldiers in that town, and he thought it would be risky if I went with him. Certainly at no time did the captain seem concerned that he had in his charge a dangerous, escaped military prisoner. He even allowed me to pay most of our reckoning when we stopped at inns or had the horses fed.

CHAPTER EIGHTEEN

WHEN LINN rejoined me, we rode north in a country that grew ever more suspicious, with the marks of marching and countermarching armies deeper and deeper on the land. Not far south of White Plains, a dour ferryman took us over the Hudson, one man and a horse at a time. When he took my shillings, I asked:

"What's your party?"

He tested the money I had tendered him with yellowed teeth and grinned when he pocketed it. "The one that has the coin, every time."

That spirit was common. We had to pay and pay well for everything we needed, from water for the horses to food for ourselves, and the hardest part was to be watched with suspicious eyes while we ate or baited our mounts. Hospitality had vanished somewhere in the war cloud that hung over this land which had once been friendly.

Both of us liked to ride fast, and we covered distance rapidly. Linn had a good animal, and John Wigton's horses were hard to beat either for speed or stamina. Late one afternoon, we rode through a country of mixed farms and woodland, a pleasant place with its glimpses of bright streams and an occasional small lake. We were nearly across a wide valley when Linn pulled in and pointed.

Some distance down the valley and along the side of the ridge was a black knot of horsemen, and as I looked, something flashed in the sun.

"Field glasses," Linn commented. "They're watching."

We rode forward perhaps a hundred yards; then he stopped again and laid his hand on my knee.

"Simon, back in your country the man to watch is likely Norris. Challis simply plays along with him. In this country and North Jersey, our man is Mason. Lucky the two don't play together. Anyway, our Mason is bad, active, and has a brain like a whip. Maybe he's over there on that hill with a bunch of British cowboys. Shall we ride for it or hunt a place and stop?"

I grinned at him. "Natives or cowboys, whichever they are, I don't like to turn tail to them."

Linn threw back his head and laughed. "Coming to life, Simon, that's what you are, and it sounds like the old days on the big river. Look."

We had topped the ridge and looked down into a small, pleasant valley that reminded me a bit of the Nippenose. To the side of the road and well back from it was a brown log cabin with a big barn behind it, both set at the edge of well-kept fields.

"Looks a good place," I commented. "Let's get down before it gets dark."

We cantered down the road and turned into a grassy lane that had been carefully mown with a sharp scythe. Everything about the cabin was neat; flowers showed in beds and a nearby field was rich in the bloom of red clover. In back of the house were rows of straw-thatched bee-hives set on some kind of frame. There seemed to be no one about as we dismounted.

When we approached the back door of the cabin, Linn pointed and smiled, for high in the panels was a loop hole for rifle fire. As we stared at it, there was a light cough behind us, and we turned smartly. A small man in snuff-colored clothes, with a brown, weathered face and brown hair flecked with gray, stood there. In his hands he held a short, preposterously big bored rifle, the hammer at full cock. He was smiling.

"Thank you, gentlemen. Most who ride up beat my poor back door with pistol butts or sword hilts. You, I believe, were about to knock."

He lowered the hammer of the gun, opened the door for us, and stepped aside so we could enter. Before he followed, he tied our horses securely. In minutes, the dim room bloomed with candlelight.

"I was about to get my supper when you rode up; I hope you are both hungry."

There was something familiar about this man with his courtesy, his easy manner and the hint of a smile at his lips as he moved about, but I could not place him. He put a kettle on to boil water and then lighted a lanthorn.

"Now, we'll put up the horses while the water boils. I would leave the task to you, but the hives are so close to the pathway, the horses could be bothered by the bees."

The barn was of good size and as neat as the house. Here were stabled a heavy draft horse and two cows. But there was room for our mounts, too. He looked curiously at my horse. "Did you breed him?"

"No, a friend named Wigton does. He likes tall and strong horseflesh."

Again, there was that hint of a smile. We went about caring for the horses and then returned to the house.

"We have an ample cold roast of beef, some newly cooked mush, plenty of milk and, yes, honey from my hives," our host promised.

The three of us settled about his table, and Linn and I, at least, ate our best meal in days. The honey was strained and clear as spring water, the milk as yellow as the cornmeal mush over which we poured it. When we had feasted to repletion, our host rose.

"Now, we'll have our warm drink."

He put a small handful of dried green leaves into an earthen teapot and poured in hot water. Instantly the room was filled with a fragrance that made me think of a peaceful, sunny hill looking out over the world below, a smell more elusive than that of pine needles or warm sweep fern.

Slowly, Linn rose out of his seat, his eyes alight with glad surprise. "Great God of the Mountains! I did not recognize you until I smelled the tea that so often bubbled over your campfire. Lew Coleman, did you know me?"

Our host threw back his head, and the room reverberated with his laughter. "Yes, from the first I was sure of you, Linn, and I felt sure the younger one must be Braide. He wasn't with us until later."

We shook hands all around while Linn continued. "So here's the man that outshot the Lions at that match at Williamsburg, the one who fought with Sevier and Boone, the man who brought the word east that Pitt was shut in by Pontiac."

Coleman raised his hand. "That's gone, boys, and I'd rather folks didn't know where I am—too many Indian blood feuds. I had to watch so much to keep my hair that I moved up here and until lately, I've had peace."

The tea, sweetened with honey, was as good as it smelled. True mountain goldenrod, the stuff was never found in fields, and only a few woodsmen knew the plant and its excellence. Coleman tapped his mug.

"This particular tea comes from a place they call Sand Mountain down in Colonel Kelly's country close to where the great path crosses. I go down for it once a year, even in war times."

I sat and listened to Linn and Coleman talking. Linn had been with the Lambs longer than I and knew more of this woodsman. While I had seen him, watched his uncanny accuracy with a rifle, his deeds, to me, were almost legendary. At Linn's suggestion, he took down his heavy piece from the Deerhorn rack,

"See," he said, "the barrel's stiff and heavy, easier in the brush, and I like the weight of lead it throws. It drops a bear in his tracks."

I took the weapon and found, in spite of its weight, that it came to my shoulder as though I owned it. Then I noted the notches on the stock and glanced at Coleman who shook his head with a laugh.

"No, not notches, they're just nicks so I can hold it better when the hands are wet."

Somehow this evening, for the first time in long months, I felt completely relaxed. Finally, Linn turned my way. "Simon, suppose you tell Lew what has happened to you. It will make a wondrous tale for him, and he may help you."

I hesitated for a little, but our pipes were going, the candlelight was soothing, and the small fire on the hearth spluttered softly. I told the whole story from the time of my marriage until now.

Both Linn and Coleman listened, intent as hunters waiting for game. Linn was surprised to hear about the gold piece found among The Doane loot. When I finished, Coleman played for a moment with some small sticks upon the table, arranging and rearranging them until I thought of Yonido and his pebbles.

"I hope, Simon, you will not be offended. I think your marriage was some kind of a trap, that Norris or Challis raided your home for the map.

You have had a hard time, but I doubt if your wife ever went into the woods. Likely they just took her to other Tories."

I had heard doubts about the raid so often that I made no comment. Yet nothing of this sort of thinking freed me from the feeling that I must one day face Celine and hear from her the whole story.

Coleman looked down at the tabletop for a moment, then spoke slowly.

"I have heard tales of this man Norris, that he is dangerous and capable, but he belongs in Pennsylvania and western York state. Now this man, Mason, belongs to us and is just as dangerous."

He paused for a moment, then continued.

"I had not meant to tell you because I had no way of knowing you would come to my house. My neighbors and I trust each other and because I help them, I get news. The grapevine story is that Washington's Chief of Intelligence would go through this country to Boston and that a man with him had to visit General Sullivan."

We stared at Coleman in amazement; he held up his forefinger.

"It is said that George Mason, the Tory raider, is about, looking for these men. Clinton would pay well for a capture such as that, and Mason is always hungry for gold. Simon, since hearing your story, I wonder if they know you are with Captain Linn, if they want to keep you from Sullivan—"

He shook his head, poured more tea, and spoke in less strained tones. "But here I go, talking like a fortune teller. You men will ride carefully in the morning, watching both in front and back as a wounded bear does."

Our beds were fine, and we slept relaxed, trusting to the care of this brown man who had been such a power on the far-flung frontier and who now peacefully followed his plow and pruned his fruit trees.

In the morning, I woke to the pleasant odor of bacon and nudged Linn into wakefulness. Both of us went outside to wash under the spout that led from a hillside spring.

The morning was fresh and bright; already bees, humming peacefully, were at work on the nearby flowers. We cared for the horses and returned to the house.

Our meal was finished when we heard the rapid approach of a body of horsemen. They were about the house before we could do anything. Coleman looked at us.

"I'm sorry," he said. "I thought they had stopped bothering me. Perhaps this is meant for you."

Both Linn and I prepared our weapons. Coleman was using his loopholes carefully.

"Near a score of them," he told us, "and George Mason leads them. Come here."

I was first to the loophole and looked out to the small back yard thronged with horsemen. One of them, a big man with a broad handsome face, wore a red silk scarf tied about his throat and sat his big horse within yards of me.

"Mason," Coleman whispered. "Presently they will be at my door. It is high time I summon my friends to take care of this business."

"Watch!" Linn was looking out the loophole in front. Now Coleman bent down. Near the floor was the end of a piece of light rope that passed through the logs. He pulled on this, and as I looked outside, I saw two of the straw-covered beehives tilt sharply, then fall, and the angry insects stormed out by the hundreds.

Suddenly there was wild shouting and confusion as the bees impartially went to work with a will on horses and riders. Another hive went over, horses began to run, men cried out in pain. From the west window loopholes, we watched them, riding at a mad gallop to escape the angry small pursuers. Coleman sat down in a chair and laughed; then Linn and I joined him.

"The only thing is," Coleman explained, "that it will take the small warriors an hour or two to settle down. You two will have to sit tight, or they'll mistake you for Mason's riders."

"Mason," Linn said, "What do you know of him. Lew?"

Coleman shook his head. "Not much. He comes from upstate somewhere and has gotten a reputation as a daring partisan raider. He likes the color of Clinton's money, has no conscience, and will torture a man for information just as an Indian will do for fun. The whole country is shot full of spies; likely Mason is in touch with most of them. He's truly a dangerous man."

While we remained indoors, Coleman went out among his bees, setting up their hives, and when he thought it safe, we joined him.

"Last time, I let loose the little Jersey bull when they came. I lost him, but it was worth that much beef. Twice, my neighbors and I hunted down small bands of these destructives. That's why I think Mason was after you because the downriver people have been letting us alone for a long time."

We were reluctant to ride away, but before we did, I left some money with Coleman to be used in the community either for powder and shot or medicines and seed, whichever was needed more, and he was grateful for the patriots had become abjectly poor. From the main road, we looked back at him, a spare, tanned man alone among the growing things and his bees.

Both of us heeded Coleman's warning, and we rode for the most part a rod or two apart, one watching ahead, the other to the rear, a lesson the great old woodsman had learned from the bear.

I had some new misgivings, for if Mason and his men were really after Washington's useful officer, it was my problems that brought him into the danger. Yet he had proposed the journey. Down inside me I was beginning to be ashamed of my sullenness and reluctance. After all, I was not of so much importance that so much trouble should be taken for me.

The huge granite boulders and the small lakes and ponds of New England began to appear after we had climbed through the hills of western Massachusetts. Things looked better in this country which had been free from actual war now a good many years, ever since Washington had driven the British from Boston. The small farms here were better tended; people were more friendly than down in Jersey, northeastern Pennsylvania, and the troubled country of southern New York.

Twelve days out of Newtown where we had helped settle the Doane business, we rode into Boston, and neither of us was impressed with the town. It was smaller than our own Philadelphia, and its streets were both so narrow and so crowded that they seemed entirely inadequate for the traffic carried at nearly all hours.

We had never seen so much activity or so much business as we observed in this town which was evidently making up for the years lost when the presence of the British had all but stifled trade. Houses were being built, ships unloaded, warehouses filled and emptied. The clatter of iron tires on cobbled streets made an unholy din. Over everything was the smell of the sea.

Linn located a tavern that looked good to both of us, and we went up to see the room that was offered. There was a high canopied bed with a flowered screen about it. Leather fire buckets stood on either side of the small grate which must have burned some kind of cannel coal. Certainly it was too small for wood. Linn pointed to the bed with a sheepish grin.

"If anybody's in that thing when I come in, see that it's you. I'm bound to be a little shy when I think of the Black Horse. Wonder if our Agnes sits easy as yet."

He strode to the window and looked out a while, then turned to me.

"I can't forget that frowzy girl. She sat across the table, and when I'd drink, her mug would come up. I figure for every sip I had, she took a swallow—"

He waved his hands, grinned widely, caught up his hat, and left. We had agreed that I would not appear on the streets until we had seen Sullivan.

CHAPTER NINETEEN

ON THE second day, Linn returned from his regular trip downtown with the word that Sullivan was ill and likely could not see us for the remainder of the week.

"Can't hold you in the room longer, Simon. Take the risk and walk out. There's nothing much of the military about the town anymore."

Naturally I had been getting tired of the confinement, and my first walks took me to the outskirts of the city. I liked the quaintness of the old buildings and their air of having been here a long time, in which they differed so radically from our frontier homes, where the sap from the logs oozed out on hot days. But finally I turned my steps to the waterfront, for an inlander is always curious about the sea. Down there in the taverns, I met seafaring men, most of them disgruntled because the war lingered on, shutting off their means of living.

One old ship master wore a curious ring, and when he saw that I looked at it, he asked me to come with him to his room where I sat for a good hour, fascinated by curios he showed from many lands. Here was a bit of black stone which he said was Chinese jade, there a tiny piece of olive wood which had come from the Holy Land. Finally I opened a small box made of sweet scented wood, and there lay a bracelet of silver carefully and intricately fashioned so that it looked to be a circlet of tiny joined leaves. I looked at the man as he lighted his pipe.

"Would you sell this?" I held up the bracelet.

He took it in his brown, knotted hands, and there was a faraway look in his eyes.

"It was—"

He checked himself almost in mid-word, and his lips set in a straight line lest he be tempted to tell the story of that bit of silver. When I laid down a golden coin, he picked it up and slid it into his pocket as though he wished to hide dishonest money.

One other thing I did buy from the old man, but that one he was eager to sell. It was a small pocket compass with a case hand fashioned from ivory. I meant this as a gift for John Wigton.

In my room, I studied the bracelet carefully. Perhaps Hope might like it; perhaps I should offend in giving it to her. But before she had gone away to school and before my trouble, I had brought her things, even so common a trifle as a "glass stone" from a mountain brook where I had found it when taking a drink. She had said that these stones reminded her of diamonds.

Before Linn came in again, I had etched her name inside with the sharp point of my penknife, making the letters as precise as only a mapmaker can. On the leaves at either side of the name, I made tiny drawings of pine trees. Also, I put the date there.

Inside Wigton's compass cover, I drew a simple map of our Loyalsock and Susquehanna country and was busy with that when Linn returned, this time jubilant. General Sullivan was better and would see us the following evening in his home here in Boston.

"Now, Simon, whatever happens, keep a civil tongue. True—letters have been sent to the general but—it still may be a matter of life and death. We've come a long way; your friends are anxious. You did well among the Spanish downriver. There the stake was powder; here it is—"

"A rope," I countered wryly, and he did not like it. He held up his hand.

"You'll be talking to a sick man. Remember, he resigned because of bad health when he returned from the Iroquois expedition. Remember, too, you have had about enough foul fortune since you met Celine. She tricked you close to death, my friend, entirely too close for the rest of us to stand by and do nothing."

What he said of Celine did not rouse my resentment as it once probably would have done even a few days before. The fact that her gold had been in Norris's hands had opened my eyes a little, though, of course, I did not see too clearly yet. However, I now had more of the old feeling I entertained for Linn in the early days. Oddly, his next words were of that time.

"Sometimes, my Lamb, I wish we were back on the river with nothing to bother us but bad currents, sand bars, Indians, cutthroats, fever, and a little hunger."

My laugh joined his. Linn seemed even more anxious than I that this interview should set things right.

That next day of waiting dragged abominably, and I am sure Linn was in and out of the room a dozen times for one excuse or another. For myself, I took a long walk, hoping to tire myself, but that was hard to do in a town for a man with muscles like my own. So I returned to the room and set down carefully the things that had happened up until our visit to Boston. Linn approved of this heartily. With the paper in his hand, he asked a question.

"What will you do if he clears you?"

"Get back to the Loyalsock," I answered with no hesitation, and he drew his heavy brows together, fiddling with a quill before he looked up again.

"Hope?"

I stared at him with some of the old bitterness rising. All I could keep in my heart was the meaning of her name, nothing more. His question reminded me that what I had in mind about Hope was as impossible of attainment as it would be to take moonlight from moving water and hold it fast in one's hand.

"No," I said after a long pause. "I want to raid that Genessee country for horses and help John Wigton get his patrol going so our Susquehanna and Loyalsock country may be safe."

"And then?" his voice and question probed my thinking, but this time I had no plan.

I shook my head. "I don't know. Perhaps I shall join the army, perhaps try once more to find Celine and settle things."

Whether Linn was satisfied or not, I did not know, but we spoke no further of the matter, instead going down to a dinner made up mostly of fish for which I do not care too much unless they are our mountain trout. But they do cook the things of the sea well here in Boston.

This time I did not go to a huge headquarters tent set to one side of a vast encampment where torches flared and sentries with fixed bayonets stood on duty. Instead, Linn and I arrived at an immense house, painted white and set well back from the street in a yard surrounded by a white picket fence. There was a heavy brass knocker on the dark wood of the door, and minutes after Linn sounded this, a black man, dressed carefully in white shirt and dark clothes, answered our summons.

"Good evening, gentlemen," he said, bowing. "The general is expecting Captain Linn and Simon Braide. Come right in."

Five minutes after he left us, he was back.

"The general will see you—this way, please."

I thought of the embarrassed lieutenant back there in the forest camp as we were ushered into a beautiful room where soft candlelight spilled over mahogany tables and chairs, where crystal gleamed on a broad mantel and a soft carpet muffled the fall of our feet. My first glance was for the room; then I saw the man over by a window staring out into the street. He turned.

The buff and blue uniform was gone and with it the harassed look. There were marks of illness, but now there was peace on the thin-featured face. Lace showed at his throat and wrists; he wore a dark coat, black satin breeches gartered above white silk stockings; the silver buckles on his shoes glinted in the light as he walked. The reddish hair was unpowdered and pulled back so harshly that his features looked even thinner. He did not limp as he came forward, but he did use a cane. It was evident that he was quite weak.

"I welcome this visit," he said simply as he smiled at Linn and bowed to me. "First, Mr. Braide, I have been eager to apologize for the boorish and unfounded remarks I made about your lost wife. There was no excuse but the horrid strain I was under and the start of my illness."

The man's smile transformed his face. Here was something boyish, eager, ingratiating, and before I could think of bitterness, I took the thin outstretched hand, finding a surprising strength and warmth in the fingers that closed round mine. He gestured toward chairs and took one facing us.

"Further, I have talked with His Excellency and know your hardships with Butler resulted in the maps which we used in the Iroquois country. I have made other mistakes which illness kept me from righting until this evening."

He leaned forward, not wasting time nor words, and he spoke in the manner of a man accustomed to handling affairs.

"The map General Knox turned over to you on his inspection trip was to help me get quickly to the Indian country. Of course we could not then tell you of its purpose, but we did need the data. The worst of losing it to the enemy was that it gave some idea of our purpose, that we might come at them. So, a heavier force had to be sent to meet any possible resistance. The theft of your map cost us a deal of effort." His brows knit; his lips drew into a straight line. "Persistent efforts were made to mislead us, false maps furnished, bad information."

He tapped on the floor with his cane, and the black man appeared carrying some rolled maps. Evidently Sullivan had planned this interview carefully. He spread out one of the charts, and we leaned forward to look at it. I recognized this as one shown me that evening in the generals' tent on the Genessee. The second was like it, and my signature was on both, done so cleverly it was hard to deny it was mine. Sullivan tapped the maps.

"These are false, as you know, Braide. But I am not so concerned with that as with the way they came to me at the beginning of the expedition. Men, these came from the camp and files of General Washington himself. He thought them genuine; so did Knox."

He nodded grimly and rolled the maps.

"We know now that a prominent Whig—who was your neighbor, Braide—had a finger in this, though we do not know exactly how. This man has fled to his British friends in New York. It was Challis!"

I stared at the general for things were becoming clearer. The map room in Challis Hall was explained now.

Linn spoke. "General Sullivan, sir, I think the man who drew these was Norris, the Tory spy who made us a deal of trouble. He had been seen near Challis Hall before it burned."

Sullivan nodded. "I've heard of the man, Norris, who must be hanged when we take him. Challis Hall was burned. I understand it was quite a show place."

Linn smiled. "And was likely to be the death of Braide, sir."

Sullivan looked sharply at us both. "Gentlemen, I must hear Braide's full story. Pipes and tobacco will help Linn and me in our listening."

While the two officers relaxed, puffing away at their long clays, I told my full story, glad that I had it in such good order. When I spoke of my coming up the Susquehanna to the Loyalsock, however, I was kind to Celine in the telling. Then I described my trip to Niagara and Butler's march together with my dismay at and Butler's abhorrence of what the Indians did at Wyoming.

The critical time came when I spoke of Washington's sending me to Boone and then how I came to the general's camp. Sullivan seemed to realize my trouble for there was a quizzical look on his face. He spoke to me by my first name.

"And then, Simon—go ahead. Tell everything though you may withhold how you did get away from my guardhouse."

He turned on Linn.

"These woodsmen are as hard to hold as the body of a bear. Yet had he not been clever, I fear he would have been a dead man instead of sitting here telling this wondrous story."

I went on, recounting the horse raid, the trip to the Challis house, and the wound I received.

"Then, sir, my friends would have it that I come to you, though I was unwilling and said some hard things about you."

Sullivan's grin was like that of a boy. He tapped my knee. "Most of them true, I will be bound." Then he sobered. "Truly, Simon, you have had an unhappy and dangerous argosy like nothing I have ever heard before. I know something of your feelings, for the English captured my brother and held him a captive until death freed him. They tormented him, trying to get him to betray our cause or to trick me into turning to them. I would love to burn New York as you would doubtless like to do to Niagara. Yet I would wager your wife is in New York. It looks as though plotters were all about you, Simon."

He rose abruptly and walked to the table without using his cane. There he wrote rapidly, his quill scratching. When he had sanded the sheet, he read it through, folded it carefully and gave it to me. Then he took his chair again.

"I feared I might overlook that. Now, gentlemen, that expedition I led was truly a devilish thing, planned more to destroy a general than the Iroquois. First, urged by Gates, Congress furnished too large and unwieldy a force to be handled and supplied so far from a base. Our provender had to come upriver in small boats. I was furnished a sledge hammer to drive a tack. You did not know, Simon, that even before I struck at Newtown, the Iroquois were passing through the Western Door bound westward. They and the British were fully informed as to each move made."

He waved the pipe he had picked up again. "Boone was never meant to get through to Erie, but he did serve as a foil which would prevent the escape of the Indians southward. I did not destroy the People of the Long House; I merely ruined a harvest and compelled England to feed its native brethren through a winter. Believe me, I turned back heartsick, the sound of the Niagara gun mocking me."

His hands came up slowly covering his face, and he bowed his head. The black man, who had evidently been watching, came to him and touched the bowed shoulders. The hands came down, and the general smiled at the servant's solicitude.

"Don't worry, Tim. I'm all right. It is a great evening. Gentlemen, I hear that gun in my dreams. But when it first sounded, I had orders in my pocket to turn back when I reached the Genessee. I think I see the hands of my enemies in that; I would not be allowed to make a real success of what some said was an impossibility.

"I see the mangled bodies of Boyd and Parker there in that evil glen where stood Little Beard's town, but even our fire could not cleanse that place. Gentlemen, I believe Hell is full of Iroquois squaws—they know so well the evil torments that turn a man into a shrieking shell, filled with pain.

"Sometimes the forest calls over all these miles for me to strike again, and I dream that I struggle with an enemy that yields like mist but returns in the same manner. I hear the complaints of officers, the jangling of the soldiers."

Sullivan was panting now as a runner will when almost spent, and this time Tim brought a glass of something which revived him.

"I was meant to fail, and the blame is not on His Excellency but on those who ruined Arnold, those that tried to defame our great commander."

He rose, once more smiling.

"Gentlemen, I have run on past all reason, but you brought the frontier to me, the black swamps, the dark pine lands, the stench of burnings. Had my health not failed, I might have erased my memories in battle."

He pointed his finger at me.

"Washington believes in you, young man. His Excellency watches Clinton, but his men are sullen, almost mutinous through the follies of Congress. Spies abound as did the flies in your woodland. They, with devilish planning, came within an ace of hanging you, Simon. Hunt them out and kill them. There will be no more great battles here in the north, but the gnawing from within could destroy our cause."

Tim approached again, and this time the general took his arm.

"Linn will go back to the army. You, Simon, get back to your lonely rivers but do not be lulled by their quiet whisperings. Watch for men like Norris and destroy them as you would wolves. I would you could strike a blow at that cloud of native fiends to the north before they come down upon you in their mad-dog packs seeking revenge for burned corn and villages."

He leaned more heavily on Tim, but his eyes were bright. "No, Washington cannot spare regiments. Single men like you must take the place of companies, and you dare not fail lest the enemy butcher us from the back. Make the land safe!"

The soldier looked feeble leaning on his servant's arm, but in full candlelight there was something unbeatable in the eyes, something neither disease nor evil fortune could conquer. Each of us took his hand for a moment; then we bowed ourselves out of the room.

We reached the tavern without saying a word, each under the spell of the man we had seen and heard. Nor did we think of the paper until we were partly undressed, and I heard it crackle in my pocket. I produced it sheepishly because I had actually forgotten, for the time, what had brought me to see the general.

General Sullivan has reviewed the case of Simon Braide and finds he did nothing treasonable in connection with military maps. He therefore revokes the sentence passed upon him and recommends that he be restored to all rights and confidence due him.

Furthermore, His Excellency concurring, it is recommended that the said Simon Braide be returned to the Loyalsock and Susquehanna country for service there.

"Well," Linn commented dryly, "you are once more a reasonably honest man in the sight of the law and a free citizen of a somewhat misguided country. You should get back to your stamping ground at the best pace that long-legged, hard-mouthed beast of John Wigton's is capable of delivering. For once, you'll carry good news."

I winced a bit at this last remark, but it was true enough. The only thing I had borne home these last few years was the record of my troubles.

We rode rapidly on our homeward way, but my mind was not so much on the release which had come to me as on the general back there in Boston who had led a great army and who had held in his hand a force great enough to break the threatening power north of our valleys. He had been hampered, turned back, nearly broken in mind and body by the evil meanness of men who had envied his courage. Surely I had not been alone in troubles, and the way this man bore them helped me.

Both of us wanted to see Coleman and his beehives again, but we had been absent too long. Linn should get back to his post. I should get home and then after those Iroquois horses. So we took a shorter way, crossing the Hudson directly west of the sharp hills through which we had ridden earlier. On the far side of the river, we began to see camps of detachments from Washington's army, strung out a long way, watching the river up which the British ships could sail. At headquarters, we were referred to General Knox.

The big artilleryman was as cordial as usual and well informed about everything but the whereabouts of His Excellency. Yet, he did have a note from the commander to Simon Braide, and he found it after a brief search. As I read, I saw that Washington had known what the outcome of the visit to Boston would be.

Pass the bearer, Simon Braide, on confidential service. He is to be given full aid and comfort by members of the armed forces and those who supply their needs.

GEO. WASHINGTON

Knox waited politely while I read; then he examined his bad hand, looked surprised at its condition and thrust it into his pocket.

"Simon, get back to Wigton. Tell him the horse patrol is good if he can get the Indian horses, for we have none to spare. If it did happen that we had a fat horse, the men would have roasted and eaten it instead of letting it carry a horseman. Watch for Norris as we do for Mason. Both are dangerous, but we suspect Norris is planning something unpleasant for you folks on the rivers, your Susquehanna mainly."

He frowned heavily, fumbled with papers on his table as if embarrassed; then his expression changed to something like exasperation.

"Tell both Wigton and Kelly we have no troops to spare unless the emergency is dire. There will be a fort built near you to end this menace, but I cannot promise how soon."

We had risen to leave when he thought of something else.

"Tell Kelly if he has any more lousy scalps, he's to bury them. They ruin my appetite for days after I've seen them."

This man's digestion might be weak, but he looked like a rock seated there, a rock against which rivers might divide but which they could not move. I had the notion that an Iroquois fire would draw nothing from the man but contempt.

They quartered us that night in a small barn where we spread our blankets on moldy straw, and as we rolled up, Linn chuckled.

"Full aid and comfort, the paper says. But there's at least one corncob beneath me, and I suspect this straw has served many a horse before it came to us."

He was quiet for a little, then raised himself on one elbow. I could see him pretty plainly even in the faint light. He spoke in low, earnest tones.

"I'm fearful, Simon, for evil things are breeding. Too many watch us; you heard what Coleman said about our trip. Sullivan spoke of the unrest among the soldiers. You hurry home, get things settled there on your rivers, and come back to me. You are wondrous stubborn and blind about things, but I'd like to have you at my back in the days ahead."

It was odd to hear this man who knew so little about fear talk in this vein. He seemed possessed of some great dread and to lack confidence. Before he slept, he spoke again.

"You saw Mason at Coleman's; I didn't see his face. You remember it carefully. Norris and Mason are the two most dangerous men we're likely ever to face. Both are clever, both afraid of neither man nor devil. When you meet one of them and are sure, shoot first; it's the only safe course."

We did not refer to the conversation in the morning, but Linn gave me careful instructions to remember him to the Wigtons. When he spoke of Hope, I felt a faint touch of irritation at this man who, on her urging, had done so much for me, and I wondered if he did it for me or to please her.

CHAPTER TWENTY

ALTHOUGH I had just ridden along the banks of three great rivers, the valley of the Loyalsock, as I came down it on my homeward way, still seemed the fairest I had seen. This had been a well-watered summer. The stream ran full, and every mile or so I could see long stretches of river where the water moved, deep and quiet, between walls of hemlocks and pines. Again, there were places in which the stream broke into white foam around rocks where I knew great trout would lurk, waiting for luckless grubs to drift into their yawning jaws.

Once, I saw a family of deer, a lordly buck, his antlers heavy with "velvet," and a sleek doe with two fawns just out of their spotted coats. Grouse flushed at each turn or scuttled across the path, and a flock of wild turkeys took off in great rising slants that carried the heavy birds to treetops across the stream.

No one could find a fairer land. Someday, farmers would use the rich bottom ground along the water. There would be enough of them for defense against the Indians and for sharing the heavy labor of harvesting and building. Thinking of this, my mind went to the responsibility placed on the few men now here to hold back the dark power threatening from the north.

John Wigton's big horse was tired when I rode him across the ford at my place a little before dusk that evening into a too quiet farmyard. The doors on both barn and house were closed; no sign of life showed, and I felt something like the cold touch of a hand between my shoulder blades, thinking of that other time.

The horse was my first care. He had carried me well over many long miles, so I rode on to the barn before dismounting. The place was in perfect order but entirely empty. Salt's stall was neatly cleaned, but the horse was gone, and no small brown cow chewed her cud in the lean-to which ordinarily sheltered her. Hurrying a little, I finished grooming the horse and went to the house.

Here the rawhide latch string dangled outside as is customary in our country when we are not at home. A pull on this double thong raises the wooden latch which holds the door closed. When we are inside sleeping, or want privacy, we draw in the leather loop, and those who want us must knock or call out.

I stood for a little before I seized the latch string. There was no indication of danger past or present, only emptiness. With a tug at the strap, the door opened, and I stepped into a room where again things were in excellent order, even the ashes having been removed from the fireplace and a neat pile of kindling stacked there. My first glance showed most of the Wigton furniture was gone; no harpsichord stood in the far sunny corner. But on the mantel stood one of Hope's wooden vases, the flowers it held now withered and drooping.

My steps rang loudly on the floors as I went from room to room, finding each one emptier than the last. However, the laced cot in the room I shared with John Wigton remained, and it belonged to him. There was a brown linen sheet on it, and the blanket was folded back neatly, ready for when I wished to sleep.

The lift to the spirit which had been with me on the ride down the river passed as did my satisfaction in the news I carried of Sullivan's pardon. Sitting in my chair before the cold fireplace, I knew the Wigtons had returned to their own home, for, after all, there had been little warmth at our parting.

My judgment told me how much these friends had helped me, but they had also hurt me, even in their kindness, and I sat there wondering how, in this long stretch of months, I had managed to twist my life so badly. Surely I had paid well for those mad hours in Fort Pitt with the violence and danger that had since met me at each turning.

Whatever anxiety I had for Celine's safety had largely passed, for I felt sure wherever she was somehow she would contrive to have everything under control. Certainly she had made good her threat to make me sorry for bringing her to this forest home of mine. Yet, I must see her and have an accounting even though I knew that the woman Blanche had advised me correctly when she told me to forget Celine as one would the dead.

I did not light a candle but sat in the dark, thinking that Hope had lived in this place and had taught me how homelike it could be by her presence. Discovering finally that I was weary, I went out to the barn and slept in Jed's small cramped room.

John Wigton was puttering about his new barn when I rode up there in the morning, and he pointed with pride to the fact that his buildings were finished.

"The neighbors came—we had a big party and house raising. Everything was so shipshape here that we could not wait for you to come home—we moved in. Salt and the cow are here where we could take care of them."

We did not go into the house until John had shown me the stalls and fittings and we had groomed the horse I had used. I explained carefully how well the big animal had performed.

Hope met us on the porch, giving me her small hand in friendliness as she would to any of her father's guests. The noon meal was ready so, perforce, we sat down and ate together, making pleasant conversation during which I passed along Linn's good wishes. They received my news quietly, listening with constraint to my account of the interview with General Sullivan.

I was hurt that they had moved from my house and knew they had been offended at my attitude on leaving; therefore, they had hurried the work on their own home.

Presently Wigton pushed back his chair.

"Well, Simon, we start for the Genessee tomorrow afternoon."

I looked at him sharply, for I had hoped to have some hand in the planning of that expedition. It was to be my first move after I was cleared by General Sullivan, and after all, I did carry the recommendation of that officer as well as the direction of His Excellency and Knox.

"Jed and I scouted the Tiadaghton. There's only the one bad place, of which you told me. Yonido is back, and the men who ride with us are in the Nippenose." Holding up his fingers, he checked them off.

"The two Forneys, Jed, and Yonido, you know. Then there's Scott Stoner over from Penn's Valley with his two men, Abel Jones and Melan Reif. We also have Matthew McNeal and his son, Bob, from below on the big river. Then, of course, there's you and me and Hope."

I did not answer, shocked that Hope was included in this desperate business. Usually John Wigton had sound judgment, but I doubted it now. The men he had named and whom I knew would be fine for the business; Stoner and his people likely would do, but it was no venture for a woman, and an Iroquois stake waited for any who might be wounded or captured up there.

Wigton continued. "Colonel Kelly will send some men to patrol while we're gone."

He got up and, in his enthusiasm, walked about. "We have the men for the raid and we've collected horse feed. Once we have the horses, the patrol will shape up. Maybe you and I can get some more weapons at Augusta."

His sudden look of embarrassment made me half smile. I drew out Washington's commission and showed it to him, at which his lips shaped a soundless whistle of surprise.

"Well, Simon, that does it. Hunter will have to help us. You're practically an officer. Here, Hope."

She read the note carefully, but there was no change in her expression until she handed it to me; then she smiled. But that did not quench the rising irritation in me. She might have made some comment.

"Who stays round the house, John?" I queried, and Wigton frowned.

"I'm not sure, one of the Forneys likely. Why?"

"No particular reason, but I'll leave the cow here and ride Salt home. Thank you for the dinner, Hope."

I found my cap and went out toward the barn with Wigton following. When I had Salt saddled and bridled, I turned to him.

"John, in God's name, why take Hope? Remember, some of us—it could be all of us—may not come back. One slip up there, and we're likely lost. The Senecas are like mad wolves; anybody they take will burn—slowly."

He looked at me, and I noted the lines on his face. He walked to Salt, tested the girths and made a slight adjustment to the bridle.

"I know the hazard; so does she. That is what moves her. There is so much of what looks like real stubbornness in both of you that all I can manage is to stand back and worry."

I laid a hand on his shoulder.

"Listen, John. I have money; so have you. Take Hope, and you two get down to Augusta and buy arms and equipment for the patrol. We'll run the horses. I can't see her ride on such a venture."

But Wigton did what I expected he would do. He shook his head slowly and for a little, looked so much like an old man that I had to say something to cheer him.

"When this is over. I'm going to try to clear things up. Sullivan cleared me in Boston, but I must find Celine, have the truth from her and my freedom."

Reaching in my pocket, I took out the things I had brought from Boston, still wrapped in paper, and gave them to him. Then I mounted and rode back to my empty house.

My first impression next day was that we made a hard-looking crew gathered there in Wigton's farmyard. Yonido kept a bit apart from the others, sensitive of the average frontiersman's dislike for Indians. Scott Stoner was a stocky, powerfully built man with cold eyes and a step as light as an Indian's. His two men, wearing mixtures of buckskins and army uniforms, were undoubtedly tough customers. Reif was the older, a man with a weather-wrinkled face. Jones, the younger, already bore the stamp of hard living on his face. John Wigton named us all to each other, and afterward I had a chance for a few words with him.

"Stoner and his men look pretty rugged."

He nodded.

"But Stoner's a horse dealer out for some profit, and his men are horsemen as you'll see. They'll be good in a bad pinch. By the way, Reif rode Jed's stud yesterday."

I looked at the man with more respect, for it really took a horseman to ride an animal Jed had trained.

With the exception of the Wigtons, we rode horses taken in the former raid. I was not going to risk Salt's old legs on the mad riding we might have to do before we finished this business, so I rode one of the Indian horses.

In back of his saddle, each of us carried a good-sized bundle in which there was grain for the horse, some food, and extra weapons besides lengths of good hide ropes and spare halters. With these men, no inspection was necessary to see that their gunlocks were in repair, their flints sharp, and their pans well opened for priming. Lives might be risked on dull knives.

We filed out of the Wigton barnyard, leaving Ben Forney standing glumly on the front porch of the house. Hope and her father led the procession. She was riding the Becky mare and was dressed like a boy in buckskins with a bright scarf at her throat. It pleased me to see that the gift pistol was in her belt and that she carried across her pommel the short horseman's carbine which Jed had taken from the trooper. Yonido and I came next, and after us the rest in ragged column. As Hope mounted, I saw something that made my heart leap; her sleeve was pushed back and on her smooth arm was a bright bracelet.

After a dozen miles of riding along the main river, we had passed most of the settlers' places. Beyond Great Island we stopped and looked across to where Fort Reed had stood. Then we rode hard until we turned at a break in the hills to the north about five miles beyond Great Island. Here we began climbing the ridge which would put us out on the great timbered flats we must cross on our way to the Genessee.

Of us all, Hope was the lightest hearted. Sometimes she hummed a little tune or whistled, at which Yonido would turn to me and grin because I knew how often he tried the same thing with such poor results.

The Indian was what John Wigton would call a "sloppy rider," in marked contrast to the girl with her straight back and small moccasined feet thrusting her stirrups out at right angles. Yonido simply slouched in his saddle, making himself as comfortable as he could. To him a horse was something one rode to avoid walking.

Young Bob McNeal was excited, accompanying his father and asking questions, while Stoner and his men just made a business of their riding. It was work to them. Jed had the rear and at times seemed to be straggling.

He, of course, rode his trained stallion, one of the horses on which we had made our escape from Sullivan's guardhouse on the Genessee.

Our camps were crude things, nothing more than a tarpaulin shelter for Hope and a couple of small cooking fires. Sometimes one or two of the men would fix bough beds, but there was nothing elaborate about them, just piles of hemlock or pine branches. We were concerned not for comfort but to get this dangerous business over.

When we struck the pine country, Yonido, by common consent, moved up. In this land of great trees that almost hid the sunlight at noonday, it was extremely difficult to keep a straight course. There were no landmarks, just mile after mile of the red-brown trunks of giant pines. On the evening of the third day, Yonido halted and pointed before him. When we rode up, we saw that the big timber was thinning and before us was the small winding stream which would be the headwaters of the river we were seeking. Even the stolid Stoner broke down enough to tell the Indian what a good job of guiding he had accomplished.

At this place we made our final, regular camp, building our fires carefully so they would burn out before nightfall, and we set a guard. Yonido said he would scout ahead, but when Jed volunteered to accompany him, I frowned on that, remembering the other time when a tied-up Indian had drowned. Before he left, Yonido spoke quietly to Wigton and me.

"Hold the men. Don't get careless. The Senecas are brutal. If we make a slip, we'll burn—even Hope."

The wily Indian did not return until well into the next evening. Our men were nervous from waiting, but they did keep quiet. Most of them were rolled in their blankets when Yonido appeared, slipping in from the shadows like some forest ghost.

It was not very dark; we could see that he was terribly weary, his clothing in tatters, his moccasins worn through, and there were briar scratches on his hands and arms. I fed him cornbread and meat while Stoner opened his own pack and supplied a new pair of moccasins, insisting that we should not bother the scout with questions until he had finished eating.

"The horses are there," Yonido said. "But not in the main valley."

He picked up a stick and, at his nod, we built a tiny bright fire of kindling and leaves about which we stood or sat while Yonido made a map on the ground.

"Three ridges run north and south, two valleys; the one to the east is small, and there's a gap in the east ridge of that. The herd is in the small valley, but there is a village there—five or six houses."

He tapped with his stick.

"There is just one way. We must run the horses through the village where the men and boys watch, if we'd get them through the gap."

He stood up grimly and shuffled his feet in the new moccasins.

"We must march tonight, get closer, lie up tomorrow, strike when the dark comes again."

Before the men could get to their horses, Wigton stopped them. "From now on, Braide takes charge."

That was what I wanted in spite of the responsibility, but I was a little surprised for ordinarily Wigton liked to lead.

It was eerie business, this breaking camp in the darkness, making sure nothing was left behind, and then moving out into the night in single file, leading the horses and keeping close to the man ahead.

There was a hint of dawn in the east when Yonido finally called a halt, and the word came down our line. We had followed the crest of a ridge and now were in heavy brush and stunted timber. Here we eased girths and hobbled our horses. Two guards were set, and then we tried to sleep.

Yonido could get along with amazingly little sleep and long before noontime, he routed me and Jed from our blankets. We followed him farther down the ridge until we could look into the little valley with its village and see the cut in the hills to the eastward. Below the cluster of bark houses, some hundred yards from it, was a wide, natural meadow through which a stream meandered.

Now he guided us up over the head of the valley and along the ridge until we got a good look at the gap. A wide game or Indian path went through it and stretched away to break in the lower ridges farther to the east, the direction in which we must drive. On our way back, we saw the dark mass of the horse herd at the end of the meadow.

Before he lay down for another of his cat naps, the Indian led the others out to our first viewpoint so they could all see and know where we must go. Jed went along the second time.

"Godfrey," he muttered to me when he returned, and his fingers were trembling. "The horses were moving. I counted sixty-eight, not mentioning a sway-backed gray to boot."

At first dusk, I outlined our strategy.

"We lead our horses down this ridge and to the left of the creek. Let them drink a little as we cross it. Then we'll string out in a long line, still to the left of the creek. At my signal, we'll go forward to bunch the horses and get them moving fast so they stampede through the village toward the gap. No gunfire. That sound may rouse the lower valley and bring help, but not for us."

Then I gave them their stations—Jed and Yonido on the ends of the line; Wigton, Hope, and me in the center; the rest on either side of us.

Stoner listened carefully, but his heavy fingers kept breaking a small stick he had in his hand. Hope seemed restless, but the others stood stolidly, blankets over their shoulders, for it was cold here on the windy ridge and a man chills quickly when he waits with tense nerves.

An hour later, I stood and cinched my saddle tight, first making sure the saddle blanket was smooth and feeling to find if my things were in place.

"All right, men."

In five minutes we were moving, and I passed back a final word.

"No shooting—drive for the gap—push the stock hard."

I knew all weapons were ready and that worried me, for we were about to pass through a hornet's nest, and I remembered what had been done to Boyd and Parker when captured down this river. Each man carried a double leather rope to use as a quirt on the driven horses. That had been Jed's idea.

The glow of fires in the village showed clearly as we angled down the ridge, but there was no telling how many people were there or how many guards might be in the meadow where the horses grazed or slept. So after we crossed the stream, I sent Jed forward for a look, and he was back in a few minutes with the word that all was clear.

We formed our line, centering the village with the gap, and took our places. At my signal, we pushed our horses into the creek, and across it we were immediately among the scattered Indian horses. Some were lying down, some grazing, some getting up, disturbed by our appearance.

"Hup, hup," the words were coming softly, and the crack of leather on horse flanks seemed loud. "Hup, hup." A wide dark mass went before us, and I could see that, even now, the animals were bunching a little.

In fifty yards they were trotting; in fifty more they were galloping, a mad roar of hooves sounding in the quiet night. These horsemen with me knew their business. Now I realized how light the night was; I could see well.

A dog barked in the village; others joined him, and the glow of the fires at the houses seemed brighter. Then came the thing I had dreaded and hoped so much to avoid, the crash of a pistol shot and a spurt of fire. It was far to my right. Someone with us had fired, and the horses were stampeding.

The thundering herd struck the flimsy village like a hurricane. One animal knocked a bark house clear over, and it fell across the fire. In a moment a beacon of flame shot high, showing Indians running, trying to escape. Our riders were shouting.

Excitement mounted in me, and my own horse was on a dead run. I knew I must be yelling but could not hear my voice. Then I thought of Hope and edged toward her. She was standing in her stirrups, the big mare stretched out as if racing. She was waving her rope above her head and yelling, transported with excitement. Then gunfire burst out again, and I saw a running Indian drop and roll. Another shot, and he lay still. I seized Hope's bridle and crowded her horse to the left.

We were nearly past, the horses crowding each other but going toward the gap which was sharply silhouetted against the sky. Then a mounted figure appeared close to the village. I saw an arm sweep up and heard another shot. In that glimpse, I knew the man was either Reif or Jed, judging from the size.

On either side, the riders were closing in, using their straps viciously until a long stream of dark animals was pouring upward to the gap. Wigton, Hope, and I pulled to the side, watching them go and trying to locate our men.

When all seemed to have passed, we three waited a while with rifles ready. We saw figures moving down at the village. Three or four started in our direction and then turned back. Real pursuit would not start until morning.

All the rest of the night we drove the captured stock along the trail which was narrow but good. Jed and Yonido had worked their way up front. Again Wigton, Hope, and I were the rear guard with Stoner riding just ahead of us.

Dawn found our cavalcade out of the ridges in rolling country to the east. Under the new sun, but so far away as to be indistinct, was a faint line indicating the hills along the Tiadaghton.

Stoner was excited out of his calm when we talked to him.

"Nigh onto eighty head. Lordy, that would be a fortune in my country."

I smiled at his excitement. My concern was for the shooting that had been done, but it was too late to remedy. I did think I saw both Reif and Jones recharge their pistols, but Jed, if he had any such need, would have done it more slyly. Ten minutes later, he galloped back to us. His horse looked tired.

"Hardest job's ahead, Jed," I admonished him. "Ask the men to rest the horses a couple of hours in the first good meadow. Then we'll push them again. That gunfire last night will rouse every hornet on the Genessee."

Jed made no reply but dutifully turned his horse and left to pass the word along.

CHAPTER TWENTY-ONE

BY MID-FORENOON, after we had rested for three hours, grazed the Indian horses, and fed good grain to our own, we were underway again, moving eastward over a gently rolling country made up of timber in clumps and small rocky hills. Our men showed the strain of the night, but they did their work well. Since the captured stock was still tired, it was not difficult to keep the animals from straying; and so it went through the day, the long slow shuffle of the horses and the occasional low calls of the men.

Two hours before sunset, we found a meadow rich with grass and hidden from the west by one of these freakish little hills. Here we camped. The men fed and groomed their mounts well; the tired Indian horses grazed slowly. Before dusk we built bright fires and cooked our first real meal since leaving the pine lands. With the cooking over, all fires were extinguished so as not to furnish a beacon for pursuers.

Planning to set a watch of two of us at a time, we drew lots, and I was delighted when I was paired with Hope; and when we drew a second time for the night watch, she and I got the dangerous two hours just before dawn. Hope was shivering a little when I roused her in the morning, and I tossed my blanket over her shoulders as we walked to our post.

We had watched for a little over half an hour when I became dissatisfied.

"Too close," I said in a low tone. "The sound of our own horses keeps me from hearing anything else. Let's go farther back."

About a half mile from our camp, beyond the hill, there was a low, grassy swell where we stopped. As Hope said she was no longer cold, I took the blanket, spread it on the ground, and we lay there listening.

After several minutes, she whispered. "Do you think the worst is over?"

"I don't know," I answered. "But I'm sure we're closer to the Tiadaghton than I expected to be. A day should get us there."

She seemed satisfied with that, for we all knew once the horses were in the gorge, our chances improved immeasurably.

We lay silently for a long time, and I was acutely conscious of her nearness. I could hear her quiet breathing and occasionally caught the scent of her hair. Now she was like the girl I had known years ago, the good comrade. I wanted to talk and straighten out whatever had come between us which was crowding us more and more apart. In the dusk, I wanted to reach out and touch her.

She moved a little, coming closer, and her hand fumbled until she found mine with warm fingers.

"Simon, listen," she whispered with lips close to my ear.

I pressed her hand to let her know I understood and lay tense trying to hear, but there seemed to be nothing. Then I took out my knife, plunged the blade into the ground and laid my ear to the haft. Almost immediately the vibration came to me, and I sat up. She could see what I had been doing and pressed her ear to the knife handle.

"Horses?" she questioned.

"Yes," I agreed, jumping. "A lot of them, coming fast. Hurry."

I snatched the blanket, and we ran until we found Wigton and roused him. Hope told what we heard, and in minutes, we had the others out of their blankets, fumbling for equipment, saddling their mounts. Wigton told us that his watch gave us an hour until dawn as we moved out slowly, the men eating cold cornbread and meat as they rode.

The plan now was to gain as much distance as possible, for the pursuers would make better time than the herd. Yonido was out front, ready to turn the horses once we reached the gorge. Stoner, Forney, Jed, and the two McNeals did the driving; the rest of us, when first light showed, turned back a quarter of a mile or so until we reached a rise of ground.

There we left Hope with the horses and moved forward on foot until we could see well back over the broken meadow and brush land.

We had not long to wait until we saw a long irregular line of horsemen coming fairly fast but evidently slowed down a little from a long night's ride. Reif and Jones carried the heavy long-barreled rifles common to the frontier, the only pieces we had that could have reached; yet at Wigton's signal, we all fired, and the pursuing column broke like flushed game into whatever cover could be found.

So through the morning, we held them with a shot whenever a horse or man appeared. I was pretty certain that Reif and Jones had scored with some of their shooting, but we had been untouched by their return fire. Some time after noon, we moved back to the horses, leaving Reif to watch.

It was fortunate that we made this move for we were scarcely in our saddles when we saw, to the north of us, a small body of horsemen disappearing behind a clump of trees. The terrain was kind to us as we dashed forward, knowing that body was trying to cut between us and the herd, for we came up behind one of the hills scattered about this country like the huge boulders in New England. Dismounted again, we climbed and were just in time to see five Indians and a man dressed in the familiar Ranger uniform, coming forward at a full gallop.

Our volley took them by complete surprise with one Indian rolling on the ground, the Ranger clutching his arm, and another native weaving in his saddle as they took cover. They had not fired a shot, and we could not locate them even though we scouted about a little.

Hope had stuck closely to us, though I felt she did not like the horse-holding business, but I was satisfied that was safer and she couldn't well urge herself as a substitute for one of these riflemen.

Reif was waiting.

"Rangers with them, maybe a dozen and a good score of Indians."

He swore viciously.

"I hate them green coated—I'm taking some of them when I get the range."

Through the long afternoon, we kept up this same business of riding, then dismounting and firing back. We had Jones and Wigton far out on our flanks to guard against another attempt to divide us. Close to evening, our spirits were lifted by the sight of a clump of trees marking the start of the gorge, and in a half hour we were riding along the Tiadaghton. Leaving the others, I hurried forward to overtake the herd.

Closely bunched, the horses were being handled almost like one animal. The ground was rougher here, the horses tired, but they were moving, and I could see ahead where we would turn southward. Far out, I saw Yonido who waved his blanket to turn the first of our captured stock.

Then we had our first real accident. The old sway-backed mare we had seen in the meadow was with the captured horses. Now she stepped into a hole, broke her leg and went down kicking, squealing, and scattering the horses. Bob McNeal shot her, but precious time was lost rounding up the other frightened animals. There was no use for me here, and I was uneasy about our rear, so I turned and hurried back.

Whoever led our pursuers knew that the time to push an attack had come, and they were riding in a long-curved line, firing as they came, but as yet I thought them ineffective. Then something inside me seemed to die out. Reif was closest to the riders, but Hope was not far on the safe side of him, and her big mare was turning circles while the girl seemed to fight madly with the bit. After a moment, the horse bolted directly toward the Rangers and Indians, and I could hear them yelling. Out of the corner of my eye, I saw Reif's horse fall, saw its rider roll, scramble up, and then one man in the line pitched forward as the big rifle spoke. Reif started in a stumbling run for the clump of trees that had been our landmark.

John Wigton had made a real horsewoman out of his daughter. Somehow, she swung the big beast to the left more and more until she was headed away from our attackers. I did not stop to count my responsibility or to reason, but swung my own mount and was after her.

The girl's horse was bolting now, likely with the bit clamped in its teeth, and it was going like all fury but with a weaving sort of pace. Hope's cap had come off; her hair was flying in the wind. Then I realized another thing; we would be cut off from the gorge entrance and a glance back told me our pursuers understood, for a dozen riders detached themselves from the main party and were after us, their yelling and firing coming to us on the breeze.

This area, like most of the country through which we had come since leaving the mountains, was open, but to the south and east of us was a lone line of trees marking the edge of the gorge. We were getting closer to it with every leap of our horses.

I drew near enough to see the great red weal on the mare's hip where a bullet had seared and set the beast mad with pain. Hope partly turned and jerked up her hand in a frantic gesture. She realized the same thing I did in another minute; the crazed mare would take both itself and its rider over the edge of the gorge.

Behind us, the yowling was louder, and I did not need to turn to know that those who followed us were Indians. I lashed my mount with the reins and drummed his ribs with my heels. We were gaining a little, but I drew my heavy wide-bladed knife and brought it down on my straining animal's flank.

This last frantic spurt drew me closer alongside of the big mare. Foam was blowing from her mouth; blood from the wound was coursing down her leg. Hope turned, and I saw her kick her feet free from the stirrups.

For just a moment or so, both animals were running side by side. I leaned from my saddle and snatched Hope clear with a wrench that all but unseated me. Her mare seemed to fly forward, then plunged over the brink. The sound of an awful crashing fall came back to me as I pulled in on the reins of my own spent horse.

We had only escaped one danger, and our time for evading the other was being reduced to minutes. Hope was a dead weight in my arms as I slid from the saddle and laid her on the ground. With frantic fingers, I loosed my saddle, dashed to the brink of the gorge, and pitched it over. Then I ran back, slung on my rifle, picked Hope up in my arms, carrying her, and returned to the edge.

There was no time to hesitate and pick a way. I simply went over and down that terrific slope, slipping, sliding, falling, catching myself, trying to take the falls on my shoulders to save the burden I carried. A hundred yards down we tumbled over a big rock, and I heard a sound above us. Huddled there in the shelter of the boulder, I saw a feathered head against the skyline, but by the time I had loosened my pistol, it had disappeared.

We resumed our descent of the slope, and a nausea tugged at me for it was already night in the gorge far below us; and the ground, the rocks, the brush dropped away so sharply they seemed to move. I shoved my pistol back, picked up Hope, and started, anxious to get down before all my courage passed.

It was like a battle in which one turns from adversary to adversary. So I fought the slope by clutching at branches, by clinging to rocks. Again, I slid on my shoulders, having a momentary thankfulness for the toughness of the buckskin I wore. After the nightmare of all this had been repeated over and over, I was suddenly on level ground and, because it seemed to rise up against me, I stumbled, falling heavily.

Hope was on her knees when I gained my feet and stood, but I could scarcely see her in the gloom.

"Simon," she called, her voice sharp with fear. "Where are you?"

I found her and drew her close for she was shivering. A branch had whipped her face, drawing blood which I found when I touched her with my fingers. The sleeve of her hunting shirt was torn away so that my hand rested on the warm softness of her shoulder and arm.

"Simon," she said desperately. "Don't leave me. I'm s—so—"

Her arms were about my neck, and I bent my head forward, forgetting all my stubbornness—all the things that stood between us, all the coldness, all the heartache—in the warm sweetness of her lips.

She had been so close to death up there on that mad horse, from the hands of our pursuers, and from that murderous slope. I strained to pull her closer to me, forgetting the strength of my arms, and her fingers went up to caress my cheek.

"Hope," I said brokenly, resting my face against hers, now wet with tears. "Hope."

She had come to me at last out of the shadow of danger.

After a little while, knowing no enemy could come down that slope in the dark, I found some dead pieces of brush and built a fire near a big rock that would reflect the heat. I made her sit down while I took up a burning branch and walked a short distance along the stream to find where we were. By a stroke of unbelievable fortune, I stumbled upon my own saddle which I had flung over the cliff. To it was tied my blanket roll, and in the saddlebags were food, a short length of candle, dry tinder in a metal box, a bit of linen to be used as a bandage or to patch bullets, and, wealth untold, a small box of the balsam salve Yonido had prepared for cuts and bruises. I dragged the whole back to Hope.

"I've everything, Hope—food, medicine, blankets."

We built the fire higher and added to its light that of the candle. Truly we had made a wonderful escape, mostly because of the tough buckskin we both wore. There were scratches but none of much moment, and Hope managed to draw together the torn shoulder of her shirt and secure it somehow.

I left her fussing with things and collected an armful of evergreen boughs which I piled against the rock. Over this and my saddle, which would serve as a pillow, I spread the blanket, and Hope dutifully got into this bed when I told her to. After a few minutes, however, she sat up.

"Simon."

I went to her, dropped on my knee, and her arms slipped round my neck.

"I'm still shaky, perhaps if you will—"

I sat down with my shoulders against the rock and took her in my arms, wrapping the blanket close about us. For a while her body twitched sharply and her fingers tightened on my arm, but finally her breathing was so regular that I knew she slept.

Before us, the fire burned low, but I knew by Hope's warm nearness I should never be entirely cold again.

Sometime in the night I must have dozed, for I was roused by what seemed many voices high in the dark sky over us. Hope stirred at my start, and I smiled to myself realizing that what I heard was the chatter of wild geese on their long flight. Those birds knew their way through darkness, storms, and daytime light. Thinking of it, I was aware that at last, I, too, knew my own way.

Daylight was tardy down here as I had learned when I scouted the gorge, but we were up with it and breakfasted on cold meat and cornbread heated a little over our fire. When we had finished, Hope insisted on moistening her kerchief in the stream and then cleansing my cuts and scratches. For my part, I reprimed her pistol and told her she must stay here until we worked the horses down. Catching up my badly battered rifle, I started out.

Half a mile upstream I met Stoner and Bob McNeal with the horse herd, and they seemed amazed to see me, wanting to know how I got there.

"Over the bank," I said shortly. "Hope Wigton is just ahead of you. What of the rest?"

"Forted up a couple of miles back. Take a horse, if you're going there," Stoner explained.

I noticed both look up at the tremendous lift of the hill over which we had come, and Stoner shook his head slowly.

The canyon entrance was a wide meadow with the stream itself close in toward the looming hill. Here I turned loose the animal I had ridden bareback and went forward carefully, hunting for Wigton whom I found a short distance ahead.

"Hope?" he demanded anxiously. The big man's face showed the strain of the night's anxiety.

"Safe, John. I took her over the cliff, and she's all right."

He heaved a long sigh of relief. "Saw her go and you follow, but I couldn't get clear over from where I was. They got Reif down at the point. He was wounded but helped cover us a good while. We're pretty hard pressed."

We edged forward through the cover until I could take in the situation which was at a standstill, with pursuers and pursued lying back of cover and firing occasionally.

"How many?" I asked.

"Less than we thought, about eight troopers and maybe a score of Indians."

I laid a hand on his arm. "We'll have to move; they may get help. That's why they are trying to hold us. I'll get Yonida and Jed and slip round back of them. When you hear a shot from us, all jump up and run as if retreating. They'll come into the open, then pour it into them."

Wigton managed to get the word around. Yonido and Jed joined me. With the Indian to lead us, we came around behind the attackers nicely. When I felt sure of our position, at my signal, Jed fired a pistol.

We could see all that happened; Wigton and the others sprang up and ran. Instantly, the Rangers and Indians were on their feet, moving forward. Then we struck them from behind, and Wigton's party turned and delivered their fire.

With a half dozen men down and caught between two fires, our pursuers broke and scattered, some of them reaching their horses tied in a grove out of rifle shot from us. Jed thrust his rifle at me. "More horses, tied in that other clump of trees."

When the little horseman was a scant ten yards from the tethered animals, an Indian guard rose up, but Jed shot him with his second pistol. In minutes he was back to us with six horses, all as good as any we had taken, and three of the animals were saddled.

Mounted, we scattered the enemy even more and picked up an additional saddled horse. There was little chance of our pursuers getting together, so we took our time.

When we reached the landmark trees, we scooped out a grave for Reif with our knives and buried him, Wigton saying a short prayer. Indian killer, deserter, whatever the man was, he had died fighting as he probably wished to go, and we left him there in the shadow of the tall trees where he had made his last stand.

We all moved down the deepening gorge, coming on the horse herd and its guard near where I had left Hope and where Stoner and Bob now had a good fire going. Bob, an excellent hunter, had slipped down stream and killed a small spike buck. The men were ravenous, and we prepared and ate the best meal we had enjoyed for days. We camped for the afternoon and night about a half mile farther on where there was a big meadow. The men used the time to groom their own mounts and to catch trout by feeling for them under the edges of the stream banks.

Wigton and I went upstream and a quarter of the way up the bluff found Hope's dead mare from which we took the saddle, the hand tooled bridle, and saddle bags. Hope almost broke down when she saw them, but she was glad to have her things.

The big rock ledge was merely an incident, Wigton going down first. Only one horse fell and that one not badly. The rest of the trip was simply the monotony of travel; yet we were all delighted when the sides of the gorge fell away in either direction and we could look ahead toward the distant line of high hills that marked the other side of the great Susquehanna.

We emerged on the east side of the Tiadaghton, here a big stream, where its west tributary entered it. We drove the herd to a place opposite the Long Island, then forced the animals to swim the first channel and left them to graze on the long grass there. Jed, Forney, and Yonida, who told us he wanted to travel again, remained with the stock.

All of us were pleased with the results of the raid, for we had counted ninety-four good horses though they did show the effect of hard travel. Stoner said little about Reif's death, and Jones nothing at all. I believe all appreciated the fact that we had come through with such little loss. We had raided a most dangerous country. We had crossed the Forbidden Way and robbed the Senecas. Certainly the loss of so many horses would bring reprisals, but we justified our risk by the safety a mounted patrol should bring us. Wigton's dream was coming closer to realization. Our rivers could be made safe.

CHAPTER TWENTY-TWO

THE NEWS of our success spread like wildfire even in this sparsely settled region and brought us visitors from up and down the valleys. Amos Jett and his two boys crossed the Susquehanna at old Fort Horn and tramped down the long miles; Colonel Kelly came up from the White Deer. All the nearer neighbors gathered promptly. These people seemed to feel it was worth a long tramp just to hear about any discomfiture of the Indians.

Those who came remained to be fed, at least, and the Wigton home was like a tavern, both John and me helping Hope with the interminable cooking. Jed relieved us by coming and telling the story of the raid with gusto to all who would listen to him, and the tale lost nothing in his telling. When I listened to him, it seemed I could hear the drum of the running horses and the cries of the drivers.

John Wigton was in his element; naturally a hospitable soul, he liked people to gather at his house, and his friendliness helped in the business of getting recruits for the patrol. Kelly hinted that he wanted any suitable extra horses we could spare for a patrol in his own country.

Our horse dealer, Stoner, had ideas. Some of the horses would make draft animals, and in a week he, Jones, and Wigton took a string of such animals over the Old Buffalo Path which eventually reached Penn's Valley. They were back in a fortnight, delighted.

Stoner took some money for himself as he had been promised, but I was pleased at his moderation. Our share went down to Fort Augusta to be laid out for what arms and ammunition were available.

These days were not too pleasant for me. Hope was too occupied to give me much time, and she was often so tired I had not the heart to intrude. The hard work of breaking and training the new horses had to be done, and I worked at it although impatiently, having little of Jed's enthusiasm, for I wanted desperately to get in touch with Celine and obtain my freedom. After all, she was still my wife legally. It was my notion that she must be in British-held New York.

My thoughts went back to her repeatedly. It was certain that she hated me, and I was sure there was some connection between her and Norris and, perhaps, Challis. But I could not bring myself to believe she had much part in the theft of the map. She had no interest in it except her annoyance at seeing me work on it. The magic of that which had come to me and Hope up there in that great mountain gorge made risking my neck to a British rope seem not too great a thing if it would bring the freedom I sought. I would go—even into New York.

Settlers were moving in, even this late in the season, some to reclaim their destroyed homesteads. John Wigton found time to help others locate lands along the Susquehanna Valley and even on our Loyalsock. But he did try to keep them all east of the Tiadaghton for better defense purposes.

Then, on a bright snappy morning, my quandary as to what I should do ended. I was swinging a heavy axe at the woodpile on the Wigton place when a horse clattered up the hill. A trooper in a nondescript uniform slid from the saddle and approached me while his tired horse hung its head.

"You'll be Simon Braide, sir?"

I nodded and he hurried on as if afraid of forgetting something.

"Captain Linn told me to look for a big man with reddish hair and a scar on his jaw. Said I'd likely find you in some sort of trouble, and I was first to help you out, then bring you to him. Are you in trouble, sir?"

Wigton, who had come up in time to hear the trooper's question, joined in my laughter.

"Yes, I'm Braide, and I'm not in trouble—not at the moment."

The young fellow fumbled with his battered coat and produced an envelope which he tendered me. The note was short and typical of Linn.

Congratulations on the raid. Knox is pleased. I need you. Mason's on the prowl.

Linn

The soldier introduced himself as James Marshall, a private in Linn's company. Wigton led the weary horse to the stable while I took the man into the house where Hope made him welcome, to his acute embarrassment. While he ate, Hope and I had a moment together, and I showed her the note.

"I'm going, Hope. Linn needs me, and it's near New York. It may be that I shall learn something,"

She looked at me a long moment, her blue eyes turning to watery pools.

"I am afraid I have waited too often—" she murmured.

She stopped, and I did not understand the finality in her voice, but Wigton was coming in and Marshall had finished eating. Wigton read the letter again and passed it back.

"We'll have the troop in good shape by the time you're back," he promised.

Two hours later we rode down the hill toward the river road and then to Fort Augusta from which we would take the Warriors' Path along the North Branch of the Susquehanna.

Trooper Marshall might have been a cavalryman, but he certainly was not a horseman. A dozen times on the trip I wished for a third horse to save the time needed to "blow" his mount when he had crowded it too hard. But we managed to make Linn's camp, which was pitched a little north of the village of Seffern in northern New Jersey, shortly after noon on the third day of our travel.

Linn, looking thinner and more worried, seemed extremely glad to see me. Later in his tent, we talked.

"Things are really bad, Simon. It is reported that the Pennsylvania Line is about to mutiny. Its commander, St. Clair, is away, and Wayne commands. Since I sent Marshall for you, the report comes up from Mount Kemble, Wayne's headquarters, that the mutiny has actually started."

I stared at him aghast, for this same Pennsylvania Line was the backbone of the patriot army. The men were veterans of nearly every major battle of the war, almost professional soldiers, in fact. Wayne had been their idol, leading them in the desperate fighting at Stony Point, at Germantown, and at Brandywine. Some of them were in the frightful massacre perpetrated by Charles "No Flint" Grey at Paoli.

Linn continued. "If we lose the Line, we lose the war. Now you get down there, Simon; see what's happening and report."

He had tilted himself back in his chair. "I wonder," he said musingly, "what would happen if Mason got into this mess."

* * *

After two hours of sleep, I was on my way on a fresh horse which, though rawboned, was an excellent traveler. I was riding over ground familiar to me from my map work when Knox had me under his official thumb.

As no purpose could be served in arriving at the camp of the soldiers by night, I found a room in a small inn five miles out, where I slept well, rising with the sun.

So it was that I reached the big camp early in the morning. The great bulk of the encampment lay in a "Y" made by two streams where the men had built a small city of low log huts well daubed with clay. Off to the left and possibly a half mile distant, was a grove of trees under which one could see the outlines of a big house which I knew was called Mount Kemble, for which the camp was named. Nearly three thousand troops were here, I had been told.

My first care was to locate a sergeant named Sherman who hailed from Lancaster County and who had worked for my father on the pack trains when Sherman was little more than a boy. His hut was on the edge of the camp, and he was civil enough, but gloomy.

"You come at a bad time, Braide."

He did not seem suspicious of me but rather welcomed an outsider who would listen to grievances.

"The men are in bad humor—pay, food, enlistments. They're ready to break out at any minute. Congress will be made to pay; so will some of the officers."

He looked at me sharply. "Braide, I know you've come for information. I'm smart enough to see that. But if something breaks, get out of here fast. The men of the Line ain't children, and they'd play rough with anybody they think might carry news."

I looked at the sergeant's rawboned height, his determined face with the blue scar on the forehead, and was inclined to agree. He looked hard, unhappy, and determined. I could make but one comment.

"Sherman, if anything happened to the Line, it would be almost the end—worse than losing a half dozen battles."

He nodded.

"Yes, but men can't dress themselves in sunshine and eat wind. If the country can't feed or clothe us, is it worth fighting for?"

* * *

It grew chillier with the evening, and I had remained in Sherman's hut all day, sharing with him and a grizzled corporal the food I had brought. Sherman was in and out a half dozen times and kept telling me not to go down to the main camp. Then, about four o'clock, things exploded. From some place on the main camp street, a volley of musketry sounded.

Sherman jumped up, grabbed a corn cake, and started eating it while he strapped on his bayonet belt and thrust a primed pistol into the breast of his coat.

"Twigg," he directed the corporal, "get Braide out of here fast."

He half smiled at me and thrust out his bony hand which I grasped. "Sorry, Braide; next time you see me I may wear a rope neckcloth."

He was gone at a run, and the corporal had his own musket, with the bayonet fixed, in his hand.

"Got to travel, Mister. Don't make any trouble."

Leading my horse and accompanied by my guard, who limped a bit, I left the camp where the firing had grown sharper, spreading over the entire area. As I glanced back, I saw an officer running. Then squads of soldiers converged upon him from two directions. There was a melee; I saw steel flash. The corporal rested the point of his too sharp bayonet against me.

"Travel, Mister. It surely ain't safe for the likes of you about here."

His voice had been ferocious, but a half hour later when he said he was turning back, he was civil enough, especially after I gave him a little money to share with Sherman.

"It's not that the men want this thing," he advised me soberly, "but it's just got past standing; that's all."

* * *

Linn was naturally disappointed by the meagerness of my information, but he sent the news on to Washington by a courier. All next day, rumors filtered in; the soldiers had butchered all officers; they were robbing and raping through the countryside, seizing food, money and women; Wayne had been hanged. So ran the stories.

"Get to Wayne," Linn told me in desperation. "I'll have to stay here and clear what news comes through."

He looked me up and down. "Anyway, you're in buckskins, Simon. An officer's uniform wouldn't be a good calling card down there, I figure."

Ten miles out of Pompton village, I rode up to the big house on the Beverwyck estate and pounded on the door for most of five minutes before a black man answered. At my questioning, he said General Wayne often came there for dinner, that he had been expected yesterday but had sent his regrets.

"Yes, sir, he said as how he was detained and was sorry."

That would be like Wayne to remember to send regrets for missing a dinner at such a time. The person who had stormed Stony Point was a man of parts and a stickler for good manners.

From the driveway on this estate, I could look across and see the village of Whippany, which I avoided by a wide detour, thinking some of the mutineers might have come there. Then I rode up along Primrose Brook so that I could approach the Kemble mansion from its rear to learn how Wayne did, if he was still alive.

The big house bulked huge among the trees, and I tied my horse with a knot that would open at a tug if I were pressed for time. There was no one outside and no sign of a sentry, but I heard the sound of horses in the stable. After minutes of watching and relying on my civilian garb to protect me from the soldiers if they were here, I walked boldly up to the front door and sounded the brass knocker.

Five minutes passed, then ten, and I thought I heard the sound of distant yelling from the direction of the camp. Something moved in the shrubbery, and I loosened my pistol. Just as my taut nerves were about to get the better of me, the door opened, and I saw a man inside.

"Simon Braide," I said, not knowing if the house had been seized or whether I should meet Wayne and his officers. A strong hand reached out and drew me inside. The door closed and there was the sound of a chain dropping into place.

"Sorry, Braide," the man who had pulled me in greeted as he opened a lanthorn. He wore a colonel's uniform, but my attention was drawn to a cocked pistol which lay on the table.

"Colonel Stewart, Mr. Braide. We are compelled to be a bit cautious about visitors tonight, but I do know your name. I have heard General Knox speak of you. The general will be glad to see you."

General Anthony Wayne was the best dressed and best looking officer I had yet encountered in the Continental Army. A tall man, he still limped a little from some old wound, but everything he wore was immaculate. His hair was neatly clubbed, and there was even a bit of lace at his throat. He took my hand and then gestured to a chair.

"We've heard of you from Knox, Braide. He's quite taken with you and has told us some of your experiences. You are with Captain Linn?"

I thanked him and told of my experience in the mutineers' camp and Linn's concern lest he was killed. The general laughed shortly.

"No. Tell Linn Colonels Stewart, Butler, and I are still alive." He nodded to each officer, presenting them with a wave of his hand.

Butler asked about Colonel Kelly; Stewart said he had known John Wigton.

"Both good men," Wayne commented. "Braide, this thing down here in the camp is the worst defeat our cause has yet suffered; worse than Long Island; worse than Germantown. We stand to lose three thousand of our seasoned veterans. It means the long fight is near its end."

It hurt to hear an indomitable man talk in this vein. He struck his chair arm.

"The men are good soldiers, but they have been shamefully treated. Congress has loosed the whirlwind with its parsimony."

Abruptly he smiled, and the lines disappeared from his face. "They played with me today, fired a volley over my head—Indian stuff. But if we do not bring them to see reason, I pray next time they may shoot lower."

Rising, he poured a glass of wine and gave it to me, motioning me not to rise. He passed a hand over his forehead. "You will excuse me now. Occasionally I have a headache, and I fear one is coming on now."

He grasped my hand warmly, nodded to the two colonels and walked out of the room.

Stewart did the talking, speaking in a low voice. "That head wound taken at the Point bothers him, Braide; his head gives him almost constant pain."

Butler nodded soberly with a quick glance at the closed door. Stewart continued eagerly. "Braide, this is for you and Linn. We have talked this over with the general. The grave danger is that the British general, Clinton, who must know our trouble through his spies, will send agents to the mutineers with promises of British money and heaven knows what else. It will be enough to tempt hungry, unhappy, desperate men. Do you understand?"

I nodded, remembering Linn's last remarks.

"Get back to Linn and tell him to spread a net along the Jersey coast. Mason would be Clinton's best man for the job, and I'll wager he will be sent. Do you know him?"

Again, I moved my head in assent, remembering Coleman's farmhouse and the bees.

"Tell Linn to kill the man on sight and take whatever papers he carries afterward. While Mason is a boaster, moving with a swagger, he is shrewd, afraid of nothing, and dangerous as a coiled snake. I knew something of him back in York State."

I rose, anxious to get back to Linn. "Captain Linn will be waiting, gentlemen. I take it time is pressing."

Both officers rose and shook my hand.

Butler smiled. "Someday, Braide, I want to hear your full story of which we have been told parts. Even His Excellency has mentioned it."

The bolt snicked home when I was outside, and I was glad to mount my horse and ride away. Danger seemed to hang in the air like mist, and it was very real when men such as these two colonels and Anthony Wayne sat in a house with the shutters closed and barred.

* * *

Linn, looking more drawn than before, heard all I had to say soberly and without comment until I finished.

"Mason—that's why I wanted you, Simon. You saw him at Coleman's; I saw only his back. But I have other news for you."

At his summons, a man stepped into the room and stood quietly. He reminded me of Challis, but he had no particularly distinguishing features. Dressed in sober brown, his shoes and stockings were filthy with mud, and the rest of his clothes showed the marks of hard riding.

"Simon Braide," Linn said formally, "this is Thomas Ogden from New York. Clinton uses him as a confidential man but—he is with us."

Ogden smiled and gave me a hand strangely strong for its size and smoothness.

We three seated ourselves before a small map which Linn opened up, and Ogden spoke. "Six British agents will be dropped at different points from a schooner tomorrow night. Each will carry a message to the mutineers which will be promises of money, pardon, and protection to the men at Mount Kemble."

He pointed to the map.

"Here will be the places." Most carefully he placed dots where the agents would be left while Linn and I followed closely.

"But Clinton's main agent, Mason, will get off at Raritan Bay. My task was to have secured guides and horses for these agents. Captain Linn says you know Mason."

Ogden leaned back in his chair and looked at Linn as though asking to proceed. The captain nodded.

"Mr. Braide, as I told the captain, we know something of your wife."

Celine—I stared at him incredulously. Excitement surged in me until there was a drumming in my ears.

"A Mistress Celine Barry came to New York from Philadelphia when the British left there. She was friendly with Norris and even Mason. The story is that she came to this country to locate a wild younger brother who was killed up country somewhere, shortly after she found him."

Ogden stopped for a moment as though hesitant to go on, but Linn gestured impatiently.

"The lady was very popular. Challis entertained her; Norris was with her constantly when he was in the city. We know of her because we watch any friends of the three—Norris, Mason, and Challis."

I could contain myself no longer and leaned forward, clutching Ogden's arm.

"In God's name, Ogden! Where is she now?"

He looked at me as though sorry to tell me. "A month ago, Norris left; we think to go to Niagara; and a week later, the lady sailed for England."

I was on my feet striding back and forth. I knew that she had slipped me at last, that she had taken my hopes for freedom with her. The manner of her going did not matter now, nothing but that she was out of reach. For so long I had thought that when I found her, things could be cleared up. Her friendship for Norris did not concern me, or any part she had played in the matter of the map. For the moment my only concern was the personal one—my hope for happiness.

Linn looked sharply at me. I stopped pacing and he spoke. "Simon, I knew Celine was in New York."

His hand went up to stop my interrupting him. "We knew she was there but did not tell you lest your stubbornness take you into that British nest."

"We?" I demanded. "You and who else?"

"Hope," he answered quietly, and some of the bitterness fled away from me. "She and her father," he finished.

Months before, when I thought Hope cold, what Linn said would have been the end. I would then have supposed they did not wish me free. Now I realized their kindness and the love that had followed me so long. I bowed my head, and it was minutes before I spoke.

"I'll go to the Raritan, Linn. Mason belongs to me."

He tapped on the table. "You've missed something, Simon. Ogden says Norris went to Niagara."

As I realized the full implication of the news, I was appalled and looked at both men. Norris at Niagara could mean only one thing: a raid on the rivers, massacre, and pillage. The threat from the North would be a real thing.

"Linn," I cried. "Send a warning!"

His lips closed grimly. "No—the thing before us is the important one. You stop Mason, and I'll send you to the Susquehanna."

Half an hour later, I was mounted and ready, but Ogden remained indoors. Not too many people must be allowed to know him if he was to continue his usefulness. Linn came out and stood by my horse, giving final instructions. The spy password was to be "Princeton."

"Don't fool with the man; kill him. You can't get him to talk. Think of the folks at your home. Shoot the man as though he was a Seneca."

I knew where I had to go, even though my mind was a confusion of thoughts. Celine had eluded me; Norris was in Niagara. I thought of that long, green line of men marching down the Chemung with clouds of Indians on its flanks. Perhaps, as I rode along leading an extra horse, the war canoes were even now dropping down the river with their burdens of painted men. Once again, however, I had to push aside my own interests—this time to trap Mason.

Back roads were not good in this country, but they were the safest from observation. Though my route wound about a good deal, I reached the place where the river begins to widen into a bay, not long after first dark. When I found an old wharf, I tied my animals in a brushy thicket. This was the spot on the Raritan Bay Ogden had marked on the map.

He had said, "that night," but I had no way of knowing how many hours I would need to wait. He might be wrong; the spies might not come for days. But I was fortunate. Not long after midnight a dark bulk moved in from the sea. I loosened my coat drawn tight about me against the chill and went down to where I stood in the shadow but could watch the old wharf.

There was a vessel scarcely maintaining steerage way. I could hear the slap of little waves against her sides and the soft creaking of the blocks in her rigging. Two lights flashed a signal, then a boat splashed into the water and began to move toward the wharf. It was still a dark mass when it grated against the wharf posts and a man leaped ashore. I moved forward, my hand on the hilt of my broad knife.

"Is this the way to Princeton?" he asked.

It had been my fortune to be in many dangerous places, but never before had I felt the high tide of excitement moving in me as it did here this night beside the quiet river. The question came the second time before I could control my voice; then I remembered what Linn had said about a password.

"Yes, to Princeton. I have horses for the ride."

The animals had been tied a long time and were chilled and restless. Even in the gloom, my visitor managed to select the better of the two and calmly mounted. We moved out, but twice in the next hour we nearly encountered riders, and I asserted myself.

"No more chances. We'll wait for daylight; then we can tell who is coming."

The spy grumbled, but I found another good thicket, and there he insisted roughly that I build a fire regardless of any danger. By its light I would know certainly who the man was, though I was almost sure from his assurance that he was Mason. After all, being caught was not my risk.

The flames licked up, and as he held his fingers to the warmth, I saw this was the same good-looking face I had seen at Coleman's place.

"Kill him," Linn had said. "Don't take chances."

The man wrapped one of the blankets I had taken from the horses about his shoulders and sat down.

"I'm Mason," he announced. "Who are you?"

I was busy breaking sticks for the fire; then I took my own blanket from the horse I rode and stepped back to the fire.

"Who are you?" he said again.

I threw the blanket down and glared at him belligerently, angered at the arrogance in his tone. "Hell, man, do you suppose I risked my neck coming here to be snapped at? I'm one of Ogden's men, not a spit-and-polish lobster-back that has to whistle when somebody toots the fife."

To my surprise, he threw back his head and laughed, showing his white teeth. "I'm sorry and apologize, friend. It really doesn't matter who you are just so you get me through to Princeton and those rearing patriots down there."

Mollified, I tried a bold stroke. If the man was suspicious, I could shoot him.

"Name's Braide—Silas Braide, sir."

I thought he started, but I pulled the blanket about me, lighted my pipe, and started to smoke. He was lolling back against his saddle.

"Braide," he said thoughtfully. "Ever hear of the Loyalsock, a little river in Pennsylvania?"

Twisting his body about on the hard ground, he, for greater comfort, finally took off his belt and laid it and the weapons it carried beside him.

A tiny alarm signal was sounding in my brain as I remembered that Linn had told me to shoot this man on sight rather than to take chances with him. I tossed a twig toward the fire, trying to be casual. "Yes," I answered. "Folks of my name settled up there somewhere a long time ago. They tell me around here there are lots of Jersey people along the Susquehanna and the Loyalsock."

My reply must have been either convincing or disarming, for he seemed to be entirely relaxed and nodded at my remark. Linn had said this man would not talk, but the captain had not thought of a campfire in the brush with two men beside it who had nothing to do but kill time.

"Odd," he commented. "A woman in New York who passed under the name of Barry told me she had married a *Simon* Braide who took her to the Loyalsock."

Celine! My heart was pounding as if I were waiting for the word to fire at the opening of a duel. Mason was speaking easily and in a reflective tone as though thinking aloud.

"She helped our man Norris at Fort Pitt. She'd come from England hunting a young brother. Norris learned that Washington's General Knox, on an inspection trip, had commissioned a young fellow named Braide to draw maps. He set Celine watching this man; when she learned that Braide had money, she married him. Norris was wild, for he was mad about the woman. Well, he found the brother; then he followed this Celine and got in touch with her. She was tired of the woods and her husband. Norris staged a mock Indian raid and got the woman and the map away."

He leaned back chuckling, and it was quite plain he enjoyed telling the story of Norris' problems. "Braide," he said suddenly, "your tobacco smells good. Let me have a pipe."

I passed the sack over the flames, and while he filled and lighted a short laurel wood pipe, I put more fuel on the fire and resettled myself so that both my knife and pistol would be clear if I reached under my blanket. The man across the fire from me was about to die at his first hint of suspicion.

"The joke was Celine did not trust Norris or the brother. She gave the young man part of the map which he tried to peddle in Niagara, but that fool Brevecourt couldn't pay cash for it and, besides, did not think it valuable. Celine went to Philadelphia and stayed with Challis's family."

Mason was enjoying his own gossip, but he was so slow that I could not see how I would hold my self-control until he finished.

"Well, like I said, Niagara wouldn't buy and the brother got himself killed. Celine came to New York and made Norris's life a jealous hell as she had her fling with the officers. She was lovely—white shoulders, quick laughter."

He leaned forward abruptly, and his voice was bitter. "She cared for only a few things—the brother, brandy, and money."

There was that in the man's voice that made me feel for my knife and half draw it while I studied the stooping figure to see where I should strike. He shook his head slowly.

"She fooled me, too. When Norris left for Niagara, I had hopes. But—her husband came from England, and she sailed home with him a couple of weeks ago."

I fought back a gasp of sheer surprise and tried to cover with a cough; then I looked down at the fire lest he read my eyes.

He shifted his position; evidently he had finished his story, and he stretched out so the saddle was a pillow. His voice was muffled by his blanket which he drew up to his chin.

"Braide was lucky to lose her. She, of course, wasn't his wife. But—I think I loved her. Such women who can twist men so ought to be drowned when they are very young."

The last words trailed away. With the quickness of men trained in the field or the army, Mason was asleep.

So there in a thicket in the Jersey woods was the end of the long road. Freedom had come to me in such an incredible way that I could not fully savor its meaning. As Hope had shown me when we watched the nesting grouse, it had come when I did not expect it. No one would have dreamed that the answers would have come through a man like Mason.

Celine was gone, leaving behind her the evil she had wrought. Whatever she had touched, even this spy sleeping a few feet from me, she had harmed. All she had wanted was money, even when she and Norris ripped my work from the drawing board. Blanche had been right in hinting she was a woman like her, but Celine lacked Blanche's kindness. It was hard to think that anyone so small and seemingly frail could do what Celine had done.

For me, it was like coming out of the dark woods into the sunlight of a mountain meadow. Yet, even here, there were shadows. Before me, sleeping, was the man who would do his best to wreck the Pennsylvania Line and the patriot cause. Back in the north country was Norris, ready to release the war hatchets. I had until morning to think; then I must act.

* * *

Mason was gay as he ate the sketchy breakfast I was able to offer, and even more confidential than the night before over the campfire. He showed me two thin plates of lead between which was placed Clinton's letter. Probably that was a British device so the whole could be tossed into the water for destruction if exposure threatened.

"A month from now, Braide, this rebellion will be as dead as Rebel George swinging from a tree. It will be a great day for men like us. Why in the hell don't you smile?"

"Too damned cold," I muttered. "I'll do my smiling later."

Wrapped in my thinking, perhaps I did become careless. The man who rode a little to the back of me was shrewd, dangerous. We had ridden for perhaps an hour and had come to an open place when he spoke, not loud but distinctly.

"Braide—Simon Braide—you almost fooled me!" His pistol was up when I wheeled to face him, and I saw his heavy thumb flick back the hammer. My only chance was that I was riding one of the Indian horses Jed had trained a little. At the thrust of my knee, it swung about and into the shoulder of Mason's mount with a force that sent both of us asprawl on the ground. The cocked pistol roared, but the shot went wild. My own half-drawn weapon was hurled from my hand as I fell.

Mason was incredibly quick; he was upon me before I more than reached my knees, clutching at me with a wrestler's grip that showed me he was stronger than I was. His teeth were showing in a savage grimace. Desperately, I fought clear, stumbling, half erect. He did not strike at me with his hands, but his foot lashed up and caught me full on the chest in much the same way I had fought Pigeon in Butler's camp. I was thrown flat on my back a good six feet away.

The frightened horses had been milling about; they rushed between us, driving Mason back. My fumbling fingers found my own pistol, and I snapped it twice before I understood that the priming was gone from the pan.

We were in the clear now, not a dozen feet apart. He drew from its sheath the short sailor's sword he carried, and his leer changed to a savage grin as he stepped forward.

Strangely, I felt no fear. This man coming at me slowly, his bright blade ready, had unwittingly given me release from an evil which had troubled me for so long. It was as though I could not die until I had fully tasted my new freedom. I knew I would kill him.

Those of us who lived on the frontier learned some things well. At the distance which separated us, I could have split a shilling piece with a thrown tomahawk. I swept back the heavy pistol and hurled it, putting all the power of my arm into the throw. It struck Mason's temple, and he dropped like a pole-axed steer.

* * *

Long hours later, I rode into Linn's headquarters with Mason lashed like a sack to his own saddle. The captain came running out; the men gathered. I handed Linn the lead plates and Clinton's letter with its offer to the mutinous soldiers.

"Simon," Linn said, "the President of the Congress has met the mutineers. Likely the mutiny is settled."

I scarcely understood the purport of his words but pointed wearily to the horse I had led.

"That's Mason," I explained. "Take him down; he'll need a surgeon."

Linn stepped closer to the horse and examined my captive before he turned back to me. "For once you obeyed orders. The man is dead."

An hour later, having explained carefully all Mason had disclosed, I was again in the saddle. This time my face was set to the west where our rivers were. The threat from the North would be breaking upon the land, and I must hurry.

CHAPTER TWENTY-THREE

TIME AND distance threatened me all the lone homeward way. There was no exact word as to when Norris had gone to Niagara and no definite news that he would march on our valleys; yet I felt as sure of a raid as though I saw the vanguard of the enemy. And, from Mason, I understood some of Norris's seeming hatred for our locality; the thought made a raid by Indians and Rangers almost a personal responsibility. "He is to waste no time," Washington had sent to Boone. Surely the same thing applied to me now.

Yet, on my way and beside my meager campfires, I saw a brighter side. Celine was gone; I was free, and happiness could come when we had repelled whatever enemy had come down the river. That night in the gorge of the Tiadaghton, the barriers between Hope and me had broken down. Now, in spite of all my mistakes, I could go to her with free hands.

By the time I had come to the upper reaches of the Loyalsock Valley, I had developed a vast respect for the breeding of British cavalry horses. The one I rode had come from the Genessee, and he had probably saved my life in the fight with Mason. On his flank was the broad arrow brand of the British Army. While I had ridden carefully, I had pushed him hard over the ridges, across the valleys and streams. Not once did he fail me.

The farmyard of my own place was thronged when I crossed the ford, and I looked with a sinking heart. Here were women and children together with a sprinkling of old men. Pieces of household gear were piled up—the things one snatches when a home is threatened by fire or other awful danger. My fears were well grounded; Tories and Indians were in the Susquehanna Valley. No one seemed to know the strength of the raiders, but it was evidently a big force, at least of Indians. These people had fled to our valley, remembering that in the other raid this area had been by-passed.

"I'll get up to Wigtons," I told one old man who seemed to be a sort of leader. He looked at me wistfully and made no reply; yet I felt his eyes follow me when I rode on. He was too old for the battle lines.

The confusion was even worse at the Wigton home. Many of these refugees were strangers, but I did see Clarey Campbell's wife, and her home was a good ten miles above where the Bald Eagle Creek enters the Susquehanna. Here were the Brattons, the Caldwells, the Ewings, and dozens of other families. John Wigton, now an extremely sober man, moved about among these people, and his face lighted with relief when he saw me and gripped my hand.

"The patrol, John. What's happened?"

For once the big horseman cursed, a scathing stream of pure invective. "Holed up in the Nippenose Valley, caught flat-footed by a force of Indians in the Antes Gap. Those men wouldn't stay home once they had riding horses. About all I know is that the patrol went into the valley. John Short's got a whiskey still in there which may be the attraction. Anyway, they're fast, a good twenty men, and we've failed these people."

To my surprise, Jed was here and equally strange; he told his story briefly and to the point. He had gone after some of the big trout on the Tiadaghton, for late fishing appealed to him, and a band of Tories and Indians had come close to getting him. They had fired Tom King's place, killing one of his children and all his livestock. Jed had run for it, not having a horse with him.

The raiders were all over the big valley. The Clark family of six on Larry's Creek had been butchered. Tom King had a bullet hole in his arm but had brought in all his family except the little girl of ten. Again, no one seemed to have any idea how large a force we faced, but they had struck swiftly from as far west as Bald Eagle Creek and on the Lycoming, an area at least twenty miles long.

"This is it, John," I said. "Linn told me Norris went to Niagara a month ago. Where is Hope?"

"Gone to Colonel Kelly, Simon, but I warned her to go round the ridge, not to swim the river."

My heart sank a little, thinking of the ride the girl was making, but there was satisfaction in that, if the raid destroyed us, she might escape.

In all, Wigton had ninety men gathered along the Lycoming, strung out from the first sharp hills north of us to the creek's mouth. Jed Wigton and I, mounted, pushed westward to reconnoiter. We saw columns of smoke late in the afternoon and, a mile farther on, we had a brush with perhaps a half dozen Indians and a Ranger in his green coat.

Neither party suffered any casualties, though we did scatter them. We dropped back to the creek, which we intended to make our battle line, and before dark, they rushed us twice but we pushed them back with the loss of two of our men dead and one wounded. The worst was that we had felt the force of the raiders and knew they had strength enough so that a determined attack could finish us unless Kelly came with help.

* * *

After dark, I crossed the creek well up toward the hills and found the camp of the Rangers. From the vantage point where I hid, I saw that again I was right; there was no mistaking the tall figure in a green uniform that paced back and forth at a campfire. This was Norris, wearing the uniform of a Captain of Rangers. I counted two score of these green-coated troops, enough to stiffen whatever power the Indians might loose on us.

"John," I told Wigton on my return, "Norris is leading the pack. We'll have to get those men out of the Nippenose. Remember that deer path we found west of the point at Antes Gap? We could get the men and horses over it."

Wigton shook his shaggy head. "You must be daft, Simon. Half the horses would break their necks on the rocks. Maybe you forgot, too, that there's a river, a mountain pass, and a gang of scalp-hungry Senecas between us and the boys."

I laid a hand on his arm. "Listen, John. These folks trusted that patrol, and I'll bring it out—somehow. There are twenty troopers in the Nippenose. If we swung them against Norris's back in the morning, the Indians would break. Mount ten of your own men; when I get the patrol out. I'll have somebody sound that cow horn of Ben Forney's, then charge over the creek. They'll think it a trap, and it will be."

Wigton argued with me during the entire time it took to get ready; yet he knew well enough what I planned was the only thing that could save us, and I realized how deeply he felt his responsibility to these people whom he thought the patrol would protect.

With my face blacked with ashes and Wigton's pistol instead of my rifle, I slipped across the stream where tree branches cast shadows nearly the entire width. When I felt sure I was past the enemy lines, I swung into a jogging trot that would eat up the miles.

After two hours, I should be nearing the crossing at the Long Island. It was not a dark night and I must be cautious now, for somewhere ahead, perhaps over the river, certainly in Antes Gap, there were Indians, and I had to pass them somehow.

Moving carefully but following the main trail, I approached the river. Luck was with me for I saw a faint glow that would mean a fire down over the riverbank. But above and below, the stream was deep and too wide to swim; I had to pass it here at the ford.

Taking precious time, using minutes that would be costly before the night was over, I came to the bank and looked over. There, before a nearly burned-out fire, sat a single Indian, wrapped in a blanket with his musket propped against the bank.

Again, more lost minutes while I watched, A pistol shot would clear my way but might rouse the pack somewhere beyond the river. The Indian was not sleeping, for his arm appeared from his blanket as he added a stick to his fire. I picked up a stone, drew my heavy knife.

The Indian had settled himself when I threw the stone, and as his hand searched for his musket, I was upon him like a mountain cat, the big knife sweeping downward into his spine. He slumped under me.

Again I wasted time standing over the dead warrior, feeling a faint nausea at this killing. The firelight flickered, and I saw at the man's belt a bloody scalp. That was why this man watched—he had his trophy.

I took his horrible prize, wrapped it about a stone, and hurled it far out into the river. Then I dragged the body of the butcherer into a sitting position and propped him up with his musket so that he looked alive.

It was necessary to swim the first arm of the river, thereby wetting the charges in both the pistols I carried, but I could and did wade the other channel, coming out on the high bank and facing the dark mass of mountains with faint starshine upon them. My soaked buckskins made a soggy sound as I walked, so I slipped off my breeches and shivered in the sharp air that came down from the gap beyond me. Thoroughly chilled, I tried to wring out the garments, then tied them about my waist and trotted forward, gooseflesh rising on my bare knees and shanks.

The defile was as dark as any pocket and noisy with the chatter of the creek. I tried moving cautiously but found I lost too much time. When I turned the shoulder of the first mountain ahead, where I remembered there was a small meadow, I saw a huge fire that spread its glow from mountain to mountain in the narrow pass.

A little warmer now, I studied the situation. There would be Indians about that fire, some asleep, but there would be enough watchers to pull me down if I tried to run through. Then I saw my chance and took it without further thought.

Stepping into the creek, I eased my body down full length into water so cold it was almost paralyzing. But, foot by foot, I went forward. At the meadow where there was an undercut bank, I would have a foot of cover and the noise of the water would kill any small sounds I might make.

Abreast of the campfire, I moved inches at a time, feeling certain that, any moment, an Indian would see me, for I all but felt the warmth of the glow on my exposed back. The fan of light touched the hemlocks on my right, the rocky slope on the left. If they caught me now, those Indians would push my face down into the water while they butchered me, hacking with their axes at my back. Please God, if it happened, I hoped one axe might be sharp. I fought back the impulse to rise and make a break for it rather than inch past an ugly death.

The smell of fire was in my nostrils; my bare knees smarted from the rough gravel at the stream's bottom. I kept moving; then some blessed bushes close to my shoulder allowed me to lift my head. In a few yards I stood up, relief running through me like wine.

I was beyond the watchers, moving light and fast. The sky seemed a little brighter as I got closer to the valley, enough so that I saw a darting figure slip behind a big tree. Indians are not usually abroad in the dark, and I stepped back of the same tree and whistled softly.

My signal stopped short as I caught the odor of rancid bear fat. An Indian stood behind the tree, inches away. This was no time for dallying; I must run for it. I loosened the wet breeches so they would not impede my dash when an idea flashed on me. I swung the water-soaked buckskins back, then slapped them round the tree with a force that brought a startled gasp from the Indian. Next instant I was upon him, my big knife slashing. I felt its contact and heard a groan of pain; then I was running, holding the knife in one hand, the breeches in the other. I leaped a small stream, turned a shoulder of the hill, and ran into a knot of men standing about a half closed lanthorn.

"Lordy!" one man exclaimed. "Here's Simon Braide come to us with his pants in his hand!"

They led me to a campfire hidden in pines and plied me with hot whiskey and tea until I stopped shivering. My soaked clothing steamed in the fire's heat, and I felt better, enough so to demand why they had been trapped. One of the Forneys explained.

They had thought the small force that had come against them was the main one, and they had not believed it was worthwhile risking men and horses breaking through the narrow gap. None of them realized that there was a big raid in the valley, and they were aghast at the desperate situation of Wigton's force at the Lycoming.

"Hell, Simon," Abel Jones said, "you tell us what to do. We've got nigh forty horses and twenty men here in the valley."

There were six men here at the guard post, the others remaining back with the horses, but we were all together in less than a quarter of an hour. In the light of a fire, I sketched my map and explained my plan.

"A deer path climbs the west point above the gap. I'll take men and horses over it, over the river where I knifed the sentry a while ago, then hit Norris and his hellions in the back. We'll need Ben Forney's horn."

I looked round at the men who were listening intently. "Another thing, we'll take the whole string of horses. When they hear us, they'll think it a regular charge, not just a score of us."

Nobody offered any objection, but Forney, a naturally cautious man, was doubtful. "But that path only goes—"

"Get your horn, Ben," I interrupted. "John Wigton will be listening for that as we come up." I knew as well as Ben that the path did not go down the other side but along the ridge at the top.

Two of the men wanted to break through the gap, but I told them the sound of rifle fire up here would ruin our surprise.

"We cross the gap," I said, "work west along the slope to a dead chestnut, and up through scrub timber. That's the way the path goes."

"How about the other side?" Jones queried, and I laughed.

"Barring late rattlesnakes and a few bad rocks, a tough gang like this might get down there."

As I listened to the hum of their talking, I tried to remember the other side, for since the deer path turned on top of the ridge, the descent must be bad.

What was left of a thin moon rode high as eighteen of us, with a led horse apiece, filed westward across the gap. The other men remained behind to keep the Indians busy in case they attacked through the defile, and it had taken the casting of lots to find men to stay. The more difficult these tough men thought the job ahead, the more eager they were to try it.

When the slope lifted against us, the men crowded together, anxious to locate the dead chestnut landmark. Young Abner Carson found it and, after we had dismounted, led the way, climbing along the well-defined trail. The extra horses followed like trained dogs, trying to keep up to the others. Occasionally we pushed through laurel thickets, but the grade was not bad. These white-tailed deer are good engineers. The climb was like mounting a stairway toward the stars high and dim above us.

Presently, the men and horses were crowding the small, level space at the top. Leading, I started down the grade, not wishing to allow too much time for thought. I bore to my right and in a few minutes was among loose stones and boulders, some as big as small cabins. I wished for John Wigton or Jed or, above all, Yonido, but presently Ben Forney worked forward, and I yielded my place to him.

It is not likely that any of us who went down here that night will ever forget it or be unwilling to boast of having accomplished the impossible. None suggested turning back; each was eager to get through, for we had a tremendous stake on the Lycoming—the lives of relatives and friends.

The horses crowded close to their masters, blowing softly through their nostrils to express their uneasiness. The going was getting worse when I spoke to Earl Donalson, one of the older men,

"Should we use a torch, Earl?"

"No, their watchers might see us even at the Lycoming."

About halfway down, we had the first accident; one of the horses slipped and went over. When we heard it floundering and thrashing about below us, one man descended with a tomahawk and ended its misery. Minutes later, a second horse fell and saved the rest of us by its accident. We had been moving along the edge of a sheer drop without knowing it. We edged more to our right. Then we went down on hands and knees, feeling our way.

It seemed hours had passed while we worked downward, but Ben Forney's watch told us it had taken a scant forty-five minutes until we felt level ground under our feet and mounted again. Just as we were about to move, a crash in the brush stopped us, and I could hear the snicking of gun locks about me.

It turned out to be only the second horse that had fallen. Apparently unhurt, it wanted to be with the other animals. Turning sharply eastward, we rode hard for the ford, guiding ourselves by the notch of Antes Gap against the sky. At the river, two men waded to the island, and on their signal, we followed carefully, making as little sound of splashing as we could.

Donalson and I made a small raft of sticks on which we placed our pistols; then we swam over, finding nothing, not even the Indian I had killed. The absence of the dead man told us his friends had been near; perhaps they were watching now. We scouted carefully. This place could be a death trap to swimming men and horses. But there seemed to be nothing, and the horsemen came over.

Most of the firearms were dry, but we took no chances. Shielding it with a blanket, we built a small fire, and by its light, drew our charges and reloaded rifles and pistols.

An hour's reckless riding brought us to a high hill beyond the stream on which Larry Burt had his home. Here we stopped to wind our animals. A man near me had looked back, and I turned. From here one could look west and south. Beside the main river, a mixed column of smoke and flame lifted into the first lavender light of the morning, and about it circled a dark, shadowy mass outlined by the fire.

"Cabin," Earl Donalson muttered grimly.

I looked toward the east; the attack along the Lycoming would come soon.

I turned to Earl. "Will we make it in time?"

He turned from looking at the fire to the west. His lips were set in a gray line as he lifted his reins. "Just got to, and get back to them."

CHAPTER TWENTY-FOUR

EVERY MAN in our small, grim-faced cavalcade must have realized the situation. Ahead of us, Wigton held the thin line on the Lycoming Creek where a mass attack would center once it was full dawn. Norris would be there, leading and pressing home the attack with all his fanaticism. He would spare neither Rangers nor Indians; he would strike with all he had and not count the cost. Miles back of us was the other body of the enemy, capering about a burning house, having done their evil in the freshness of the morning. There was no guessing their strength.

Norris had been present when Butler's force set out for the Wyoming Valley. Doubtless he had studied that raid and would be profiting now from all the Rangers learned in those terrible days. Unlike Butler, this man would sweep the valley clean and give no thought to any suffering his native crew would visit on captives.

Men in buckskin, that was all we had, little military equipment, no disciplined troops, yet here along the Susquehanna into which our small rivers emptied, we would be holding in our hands the safety of the patriot cause as we leveled rifles. A break through us would open the way to Fort Augusta. Beyond that, there was little to prevent a descent on the lower counties now busy raising food and making equipment for our patriot armies.

So we rode grimly, each man with a led horse beside him. Tomahawks and knives were loose in belts, pistols primed, rifles and muskets double charged. I even saw one man with a big chopping axe across his pommel, reminding me of the night when I had ridden up the Loyalsock after those who had raided my home.

From the last hill we saw that we would be on time. The long line of Indian fires, which I had seen the night before, had burned down, only a few piles of red coals winking in the gray light. From our position at their back, we could see the enemy though they were screened by trees from Wigton's station beyond the stream. The main body was massed about a hundred yards below the regularly used ford of the Lycoming. My hope was that both Rangers and Indians would be too intent on their attack to note our approach until we were almost upon them.

Edging my horse close to Forney, I saw that he had the big cow horn in his hand. The ground now was reasonably good for riding. I waved my hand.

Forney's cheeks puffed until, even in this moment of stress, I marveled. Then the roaring bellow pealed into the face of the morning, sending echoes up and down the stream from the hills to the north.

We went forward as one man. Wigton and Jed had drilled this patrol force well, and it was out to redress itself for the danger it had permitted to come into our valleys. These riders would drive home or die in the saddle.

Our first volley of mixed bullets and buckshot crashed into the surprised mass of green-coated Rangers and painted Indians. Wigton's silver whistle shrilled from his side of the stream, and his mounted men splashed through the shallow water to catch our enemy between two fires.

Now we were among them, standing in our stirrups, emptying pistols, swinging clubbed muskets that could not be parried by Indian hatchets. Only the Rangers withstood us well, warding off the blows, sticking together, and moving along the water toward the hills. But the Indians broke like scattered game, running for the timber, throwing away muskets, dropping blankets, doing anything that would help them to make speed against the plunging horses.

There were riderless horses among us. I saw Forney reel back, his face a mass of blood from the Ranger's musket slug that killed him, and I caught the horn from his hand as I eased his fall to the ground.

The rush of our mounted men had scattered the force of the enemy, but it was by no means yet destroyed. Rangers were running about among the fleeing Indians, slapping them with their short swords until knots of the native men would turn and fire.

As my horse carried me forward, one of these green-coated soldiers not far from me leaped in front of three fleeing Indians, and I saw the hatchets flash as they cut him down. One of them stopped to snatch the scalp, but he was too slow, nor was he ready for my hatchet as I reached him and struck from the saddle.

The footmen who had held the ford were now across, moving forward at good pace. The country here was pretty open, just clumps of bushes and an occasional tree. To the north, however, were small rocky hills and beyond them, the timber. The riflemen went in couples; when they flushed an enemy, one fired; the other waited until the rifle was loaded before he, in turn, discharged his piece.

The Rangers were my main concern for they continued together, retreating slowly, firing and reloading mechanically. They were a well-drilled outfit. Presently, they gained their objective, a rocky hill where they piled up additional rocks to shelter them from our fire. Probably every man of them knew what would happen to white men who accompanied Indians on a frontier raid if they were captured. From their improvised fortress they beat back every rush we made and killed several horses besides wounding two troopers pretty badly.

I had a chance to talk with John Wigton when we had the hill surrounded and our riflemen were searching the place with bullets whenever they saw, or thought they saw, a target. He was shocked when I said that we had seen another force of invaders upriver.

"We'll have to attack them, Simon. The men here are scattered; another crowd of hostiles coming down will trap us against that gang of Tories on the hill."

He stood up suddenly and waved his cap to attract the attention of some of his men. At once it was jerked from his fingers by a rifle bullet. John dropped prone beside me. By and by, he looked at me with an apologetic grin.

"I'll get them, John; set enough of your fellows round this hill to hold those people."

I edged back carefully to the small clump of trees which sheltered the horses of those of us who had been firing at the Rangers. Up in the saddle, I sounded the big horn, and the men of the patrol and John Wigton's mounted fighters gathered at the signal. I explained briefly that we must get upriver and do it fast.

We rode close to the big river, and fortune was with us at first. Where the great Susquehanna, below Long Island, swings south against the mountain, we found a fleet of canoes and two boats that made me think of those which Boone's men had built—long double-ended craft. There were three Indian guards, and these went down under the hatchets of our men.

We were in possession of the provisions and stores of our attackers. Here was everything one might expect on a well-prepared expedition of this sort: parched corn, dried meats, powder, lead, extra clothing, besides the loot of settlers' houses, and a small puppy that seemed glad to see us.

Evidently the boats belonged to the Rangers, for we found bales of blankets and what convinced us that the attack down the river was even more than a raid on us—two swivel guns, about one-pounders, together with their mountings. The blanket bales covered round shot and powder packets for these pieces. We lost precious time looking over our find.

Suddenly we heard a yell from Jed who had not dismounted and sat his horse about a hundred yards back from the river. Almost immediately he wheeled his mount and galloped to us. "The whole damned Seneca nation's coming!" he cried.

Here again, as at Long Island, were fairly high banks with a beach along the stream where the boats were. A hundred yards below us, a fair-sized creek entered the river, and the ground to the west of us was low, covered with swamp brush, no place for cavalry work.

This I noted as we all scrambled up the bank. They were coming, a long line of painted warriors and an occasional green coat that meant a Ranger. My heart sank; there were twenty-five of us, more than a hundred of the attackers, and the presence of the Rangers would stiffen their allies.

With our first volley, the advancing line dropped prone; then smoke puffs lifted as they returned our fire. At my order, all the horses were taken down along the river and left there with Bob McNeal as guard.

It was the sort of fighting Indians liked, this crawling from bush to bush, then shooting. Near me, John Turner grunted and slumped, his rifle falling from his hand. The heavy slug had ripped across his shoulder breaking his spine. Minutes later, another of our men leaped to his feet, swinging his arms up above his head before he pitched down.

The men passed my word along; we crawled back, dropping over the riverbank and along the creek. I dragged Turner's body with me, but presently I missed Jed. The men I asked about him shook their heads. Cautiously, in back of where a bush stood, I crawled up the bank, then forward a little, and lay startled and helpless at what I saw.

The second man of our force to be killed lay in a small open space less than two yards square, and in back of a bush toward us, was Jed, motionless. At first, I thought he had been hit; then I saw that he held a pistol in one hand, his tomahawk in the other. I wanted to cry a warning; then I realized Jed was waiting for a warrior to come for the dead man's scalp. Probably he saw what I did—two painted warriors crawling forward.

I remembered the Genessee and a warrior who fell into the water, but certainly I had never guessed the prowess of this small horseman from the lower counties, nor his quickness. The two Indians entered the clearing, eased up on their knees; one reached for the dead patrolman's head.

Jed's pistol shot tore away the face of that man; he leaped and split the other's skull with his hatchet, then crouching low, started to drag in our dead comrade.

He had not come halfway to the bank until I saw a third warrior, not twenty yards from us, come to his knees and level his musket. My shot killed him; then I leaped forward and together Jed and I dragged the dead man over the bank. Jed grinned at me.

"Thanks, Simon. I didn't figure on a third one."

Abel Jones had come with the men from the Nippenose. He approached me, showing excitement which was unusual with him.

"Listen, Simon. Their main bunch's back there in a small hollow palavering. I just located them. If they rush us, we can't stop them."

I looked at him, perhaps a bit scornfully. Certainly if they did rush, we could not stop so many with scattered rifle fire. Enough of them would get through to finish us. He pointed.

The two swivel guns were complete with their mounts as I had noted.

"I can handle them things," Jones declared. "Help me."

In minutes, I knew that sometime this man Jones had fought in General Knox's favorite army branch, the artillery. With our help, he had the small gun out on the beach, powder crammed home and a heavy wad on top of that. Then he wrapped a double handful of rifle bullets in a cloth and crammed that down the muzzle with another wad following. While we loaded the second piece, Jed, rummaging, found a touch stick with its tow in the equipment.

The guns were heavy, but we boosted them up on the bank in a spot sheltered by tangled alders. Jones had the second piece set close to the first. He was grinning.

"First load goes down in that hollow, Simon. You watch for the second."

We were all watching. I was sure the Indians would see the small cannons. With tow aglow, Jones rose to his knees and brought his coal down on the touch hole.

The swivel gun emitted a tremendous roar; then we heard the screams of wounded and frightened men. Jones had judged well as we afterwards learned; his bag of bullets had struck right into a mass of attackers. Dozens of painted warriors leaped into the open, running. Jones was standing now, jerking round the second gun so it would bear on the runners. A second roar, and I saw warriors go down.

Our own men were up now, dashing forward, but there was none to oppose them. Among the dead, there in a sandy hollow, were two Rangers. There would be no further danger from this body. Indians never would face cannon.

* * *

We were back to the Lycoming a little after noon, and there was still some firing coming from the stony hill.

"Hour or so ago, a fellow in green stood and waved a flag," Wigton told me. "Then a white-haired man leaped up and knocked him down."

John was excited when I told him what happened, and he was delighted at the capture of stores, for we would need them to feed the men; but he had to go down to the boats directly when he heard about the swivel guns.

Abel Jones had come down with the boats. Now with plenty of willing hands to help, he set up one of his guns and pitched round shot into the Ranger's stronghold on the hill while admiring riflemen stood round and watched, cheering when dust flew up, marking where the balls struck.

When no reply had come from the entrenched Rangers for several hours in all, the men wanted to go forward, but John Wigton's caution would not allow that until young Fred Cady had climbed a tree and slid down so quickly that he must have scorched his legs.

"They're all down," he told us.

With rifles covering us, John Wigton and I walked slowly toward the hill and the improvised breastworks. John kept glancing at me as we walked, but I did not think these Rangers would shoot, having learned much about them on the march with Butler. Bitter, cruel, unscrupulous as they might be, theirs was, after all, a certain code.

Cady was right. When we looked into the small circle of rocks, they were all down but one man who rested on an elbow and stared at the ground. It was Norris. There was no mistaking the white hair, the long face, the bitter eyes he turned toward us. There was life in him, but he let himself drop back.

"Braide," he whispered, and I stepped up and knelt beside him.

"I would make my peace," he muttered.

We carried the desperately wounded man on a blanket from the rock fort to the shelter of some trees where we laid him with his head propped high against rolled coats and blankets. He had been hit twice and was going fast. John Wigton waved back the curious, and we two knelt, one on either side of the dying man.

"Braide—in the end—you live. I tried so hard to have you killed."

I thought of a man lying dead outside Niagara, a man with a gold piece in his pocket. The sinking captain moved his shoulders.

"I hated you because—Celine came to you. I had followed her to Pitt. She worked with us. Then you came—I wanted the map you were to make but—she knew you had money. It was her god. You thought you married her and took her away. I followed, met her on one of her rides—persuaded her to come with me again."

The dim eyes lighted a bit. "I had a pistol on you that morning of the raid when you left her but—I could hire killings done—I could not fire."

His breath was slower; he seemed to hold himself alive so he could finish.

"I forgot my cloth for her—lied, stole, schemed. I nearly wrecked Sullivan with false maps. Celine thought we could sell yours but trusted neither me nor her brother, giving us but a corner of the thing. Brevecourt laughed at us. Her brother was killed. From Philadelphia, where Challis sent her from your home, she came to New York. She played fast and loose, laughed at me when I begged. Now—she has gone back to England with her husband."

His eyes had glazed again; his voice was only a whisper. "She—I was told—she would have none of me. I denied my faith. I worshipped—only her."

His voice choked in a torrent of blood, and his body jerked upward until he all but sat erect. One hand partly raised as though he meant to salute.

"God save the King!" he whispered, and Norris, one time clergyman, then spy, now Captain of Rangers, was dead.

John Wigton closed the staring eyes when I eased the body down. The truth was all in my hands at last, all of it. We stood and a sharp little gust of wind swept against us, stirred the gray hair of the dead man lying there.

We found Norris's dispatch case in the little fort. It contained his orders which were to destroy us, then move down to Fort Augusta, at which point he would receive reinforcements. Tucked away in the case was a heavy piece of paper. John Wigton opened and spread it out.

There it was. Norris had not told the complete truth; this was my map with the one corner missing, the corner that had come so close to hanging me. True, this chart had long lost its value, but both of us looked at it dumbly.

"It goes to Knox," Wigton said, and I nodded my assent.

* * *

The aftermath of battle is not a pleasant thing even when one wins. We had utterly broken the raiders, killing more than ninety Indians and Rangers. But we had twelve of our own company dead and more wounded besides the settlers killed at their homes. Yet our people moved with an assurance, even at the task of burying those who had fallen. After all, we had stopped the raid; we had saved the river valleys, even Fort Augusta. Men in buckskin had turned back the tide of invasion.

"Top dogs we are, Simon," Jim Leidy told me. "Comes spring, me and my boys will move west of Fort Reed. Figger me and the boys can stop anything the Senecas has got after this."

* * *

Hope brought in Colonel Kelly and twenty-five men by mid-afternoon, and the big officer was sorry that he had been so slow.

"It's horses we need, John," he told Wigton. "By foot it is too slow. When the winter's past, you'll have to take us to the Genessee for more of that Indian stock."

Busy in getting the settlers back to their homes, helping with the cabins, dividing the Indian spoils, and a hundred other tasks, Hope, her father, and I had no time to talk or plan, but there did come an evening when we rode down to my house. There, as we sat by the table, with sparks flying up the chimney from a good fire, I at last had a chance to tell about Mason, how he had talked, what he had said. Now Norris had corroborated it.

From almost the first, Celine had been the evil genius in the picture to all who knew her. She committed bigamy for the money she could get from me and had wrecked the peace and plans of those who had worked with her, Norris most, then Mason. I felt a momentary touch of sorrow for the man buried back there on our battlefield until I remembered the scalps at the belts of his Indians.

Challis had sheltered the enemy; now he was gone, his bolt shot on the West Branch. Here on the big river, we had fought and won our battle. It would be hard to make us afraid again. And our victory had saved the country below.

When Wigton went out to get our horses, I had Hope close in my arms for a few minutes.

"I'm free, dear, free to ask—"

An odd look in her eyes stopped me. There was something there that frightened me.

"Hope," I demanded in alarm, "you will have me? Surely?"

Abruptly her face changed; she was smiling, and her arms slipped about my neck. She rumpled my hair with her fingers. "Simple Simon, my Simon. I would have come to you—"

There was something like starlight in the depths of her eyes. There was no need for her to finish. I had her now, and I would never let her go.

* * *

A week after our battle, when we were still getting things in order in our valley, soldiers, teams, and wagons arrived and began building the fort Knox had promised so long before. The big artilleryman had kept his word, and from the first high pickets the workmen set, one could look across and see the ruins of the chimney at burned Challis Hall.

A chaplain had come with these soldiers, and we could not miss the opportunity. He married Hope and me in the Wigton house.

To my surprise, John himself played the wedding march on the harpsichord. I did not realize he knew how to play. Our guests were the countryside people, and after the minister had finished, I happened to look across to Jed and was amazed to see tears in the little horseman's eyes. He raised his elbow promptly and wiped them away.

Next day, on two tall horses, Hope, bundled in a bright blanket coat, and I, wearing my best clothes, rode away bound for Philadelphia where we would buy some of the new things we wanted for our house. We took the short path and, from Gunner's Hill, looked back and down at the house by the river. Bright in the late fall sunshine, it stood, and we knew it would be truly home when we returned and could sit and listen to the chatter of the river.